FROM THE PAGES OF *ETHAN FROME AND SELECTED STORIES*

If you know Starkfield, Massachusetts, you know the post-office. If you know the post-office you must have seen Ethan Frome drive up to it, drop the reins on his hollow-backed bay and drag himself across the brick pavement to the white colonnade: and you must have asked who he was. (from *Ethan Frome,* page 8)

It was only when she drew toward her last illness, and his cousin Zenobia Pierce came over from the next valley to help him nurse her, that human speech was heard again in the house.
(from *Ethan Frome,* page 41)

Zeena came into the room with her dragging down-at-the-heel step, and quietly took her accustomed seat between them.
(from *Ethan Frome,* page 69)

The sled started with a bound, and they flew on through the dusk, gathering smoothness and speed as they went, with the hollow night opening out below them and the air singing by like an organ. Mattie sat perfectly still, but as they reached the bend at the foot of the hill, where the big elm thrust out a deadly elbow, he fancied that she shrank a little closer. (from *Ethan Frome,* page 89)

There was a last instant when the air shot past him like millions of fiery wires; and then the elm . . . (from *Ethan Frome,* page 93)

"The way they are now, I don't see's there's much difference between the Fromes up at the farm and the Fromes down in the graveyard."
page 99)

"I'm so bewildered by this new development—by his using you all this time as a pretext—that I really don't know where to turn for light on the mystery—" (from "The Pretext," page 130)

Across the level tracery of the gardens, it sent her, from open windows and hospitably smoking chimneys, the look of some warm human presence, of a mind slowly ripened on a sunny wall of experience. (from "Afterward," page 149)

"You won't know till long, long afterward." (from "Afterward," page 167)

Mrs. Ballinger is one of the ladies who pursue Culture in bands, as though it were dangerous to meet alone. (from "Xingu," page 203)

"Knowing how engrossing the subject is, you will understand how it happens that the club has let everything else go to the wall for the moment. Since we took up Xingu I might almost say—were it not for your books—that nothing else seems to us worth remembering." (from "Xingu," page 214)

"I fancy Osric Dane hardly expected to take a lesson in Xingu at Hillbridge!" (from "Xingu," page 220)

ETHAN FROME
AND SELECTED STORIES

EDITH WHARTON

With an Introduction and Notes
by Kent Ljungquist

George Stade
Consulting Editorial Director

BARNES & NOBLE CLASSICS
NEW YORK

Barnes & Noble Classics
New York

Published by Barnes & Noble Books
122 Fifth Avenue
New York, NY 10011

www.barnesandnoble.com/classics

"The Pretext" first appeared in *Scribner's Magazine* in August 1908; "Afterward," in *Century Magazine* in January 1910; and "The Legend," in *Scribner's* in March 1910. *Ethan Frome* was first published in 1911. Written in 1911, "Xingu" finally appeared in *Xingu and Other Stories* (1916), one of eleven collections of Wharton's short stories.

Published in 2004 by Barnes & Noble Classics with new Introduction, Notes, Biography, Chronology, Comments & Questions, and For Further Reading.

Ethan Frome and Selected Stories
ISBN-13: 978-1-59308-090-7
ISBN-10: 1-59308-090-5
LC Control Number 2003113226

Produced and published in conjunction with:
Fine Creative Media, Inc.
322 Eighth Avenue
New York, NY 10001

Michael J. Fine, President and Publisher

Printed in the United States of America

QM

13 15 17 19 20 18 16 14

EDITH WHARTON

Edith Newbold Jones was born January 24, 1862, into such wealth and privilege that her family inspired the phrase "keeping up with the Joneses." The youngest of three children, Edith spent her early years touring Europe with her parents and, upon the family's return to the United States, enjoyed a privileged childhood in New York and Newport, Rhode Island. Edith's creativity and talent soon became obvious: By the age of eighteen she had written a novella, *Fast and Loose* (as well as witty reviews of it), and published poetry in the *Atlantic Monthly*.

After a failed engagement, Edith married a wealthy sportsman, Edward Wharton. Despite similar backgrounds and a shared taste for travel, the marriage was not a success. Many of Wharton's novels chronicle unhappy marriages, in which the demands of love and vocation often conflict with the expectations of society. Wharton's first major novel, *The House of Mirth,* published in 1905, enjoyed considerable literary success. *Ethan Frome* appeared six years later, solidifying Wharton's reputation as an important novelist. Often in the company of her close friend Henry James, Wharton mingled with some of the most famous writers and artists of the day, including F. Scott Fitzgerald, André Gide, Sinclair Lewis, Jean Cocteau, and Jack London.

In 1913 Edith divorced Edward. She lived mostly in France for the remainder of her life. When World War I broke out, she organized hostels for refugees, worked as a fund-raiser, and wrote for American publications from battlefield frontlines. She was awarded the French Legion of Honor for her courage and distinguished work.

The Age of Innocence, a novel about New York in the 1870s, earned Wharton the Pulitzer Prize for fiction in 1921—the first time the award had been bestowed on a woman. Wharton traveled throughout

Europe to encourage young authors. She also continued to write, lying in her bed every morning, as she had always done, dropping each newly penned page on the floor to be collected and arranged when she was finished. Wharton suffered a stroke and died on August 11, 1937. She is buried in the American Cemetery in Versailles, France.

TABLE OF CONTENTS

THE WORLD OF EDITH WHARTON AND *ETHAN FROME*

1862 Edith Newbold Jones is born January 24 in New York City, the last of three children. Her parents are wealthy and socially well-connected.

1866 The Jones family leaves for Europe, where they will live for the next six years.

1870 In Germany, Edith falls ill with typhoid fever and for a time hovers between life and death. When she recovers, the family moves to Florence. Edith begins writing stories, which she recites to her family.

1872 The Joneses return to America, where they live in New York City and Newport, Rhode Island.

1877 Edith finishes a novella, *Fast and Loose*, which will be published a century later, in 1977. Henry James's novel *The American* appears.

1878 Edith's mother pays to publish a collection of Edith's poems, *Verses*.

1879 Edith is presented to society in New York City.

1880 A wealthy young man, Henry Leyden Stevens, proposes to Wharton. The *Atlantic Monthly* magazine publishes five of Wharton's poems.

1881 Henry James's novel *Portrait of a Lady* appears.

1882 Edith's father dies in the south of France. Edith and her mother return to the United States to find that Henry Stevens's mother disapproves of the engagement. It is broken off, and the Jones women return to France.

1883 While summering in Bar Harbor, Maine, Edith agrees to marry Edward Wharton, an independently wealthy sportsman from Massachusetts.

1885 Edith and Edward wed and over the next several years divide their time between Europe, New York, and Newport.

1889 Wharton's poems appear in *Scribner's Magazine* and the *Atlantic Monthly*.

1891 Wharton's first published story, "Mrs. Manstey's View," appears in *Scribner's Magazine*.

1897 *The Decoration of Houses* appears; it is a nonfiction work on interior design written by Wharton and architect Ogden Codman, Jr.

1898 Henry James's *The Turn of the Screw* is published.

1901 The Whartons begin to build The Mount, their summer home near Lenox, Massachusetts. Edith's mother dies in Paris.

1905 *The House of Mirth* is published. The novel quickly becomes one of the best-selling books of the year; its popularity solidifies Wharton's reputation as a major novelist. Wharton and Henry James develop a close friendship. George Bernard Shaw's play *Major Barbara* is performed in London.

1908 Wharton publishes *A Motor-Flight through France*, in which she recounts her travels with her husband, Edward, and Henry James. She meets Morton Fullerton, an American journalist living in London who is a friend of Henry James, and the two begin a passionate though short-lived love affair.

1911 Wharton's *Ethan Frome* is published; it was inspired by the New England life the author witnessed near her home in Lenox. After first meeting him in 1909, Wharton visits art historian Bernard Berenson in Italy.

1913 Edith and Edward divorce. Wharton moves to France, where she will spend most of the rest of her life. Willa Cather's *O Pioneers!* is published.

1914 Wharton travels to Tunisia and Algiers, then undertakes relief efforts during World War I. She finds homes for hundreds of Belgian orphans and raises money for refugees.

1916 Wharton receives the French Legion of Honor award for her war relief activities. Henry James dies.

1917 T. S. Eliot's book of poetry *Prufrock and Other Observations* appears.

1918 Willa Cather publishes *My Ántonia*.

1920 *The Age of Innocence,* a novel about New York society, is published to great success.

1921 Wharton becomes the first woman to be awarded the Pulitzer Prize for fiction, which she receives for *The Age of Innocence.* Eugene O'Neill's play *Anna Christie* opens in New York City.

1922 T. S. Eliot's *The Waste Land* is published.

1923 Yale University awards Wharton an honorary doctorate. Edna St. Vincent Millay receives the Pulitzer Prize for poetry.

1924 Wharton publishes a collection of novellas and short stories as *Old New York.*

1925 Sinclair Lewis publishes *Arrowsmith,* which he dedicates to Wharton. Fitzgerald's *The Great Gatsby* is published; the author sends Wharton an inscribed copy. Gertrude Stein publishes *The Making of Americans.* Virginia Woolf publishes *Mrs. Dalloway.*

1926 Ernest Hemingway publishes *The Sun Also Rises.*

1928 Edward Wharton dies. Poet Carl Sandburg's *Good Morning, America* is published.

1930 Wharton is elected to the American Academy of Arts and Letters. She continues to write, although her health is failing. Robert Frost's *Collected Poems* is published.

1933 Wharton publishes *Human Nature,* a collection of short stories.

1934 Wharton publishes "Roman Fever" in *Liberty* magazine for the then-astronomical sum of $3,000; one of her best-known short stories, it is based on her travels in Italy. She continues to write and publish stories and novels. *A Backward Glance,* an autobiography, is published.

1937 After a severe stroke, Edith Wharton dies on August 11. She is buried in Versailles, France.

INTRODUCTION

Known as a chronicler of the moneyed and propertied classes of New York City, Edith Wharton (1862–1937) was born during the Civil War and grew up in a traditional urban world of horse-drawn carriages and impressive brownstone residences. Her parents, Lucretia Rhinelander Jones and George Frederic Jones, came from socially prominent backgrounds. Edith thus represented a world of apparently sedate family life that extended back several generations. In her fiction she explored the manners, values, and codes of this complex social setting, and the conflicts her characters faced as the tides of change swept the United States in the late nineteenth and early twentieth centuries. In the years preceding her major works of long fiction, she established a solid reputation as an accomplished short story writer. Her interest in New York's upper-crust society eventually led to a series of successful novels, most notably *The House of Mirth* (1905), *The Custom of the Country* (1913), and *The Age of Innocence* (1920).

Respectful of the education, manners, and good breeding that an upbringing in an old New York family afforded, Wharton was also sensitive to the cultural attractions and social traditions of Europe. Like her friend and sometimes mentor Henry James (1843–1916), she traveled widely in Europe, making her first trip to the Continent between 1866 and 1872, soon after the Civil War. After her marriage to Bostonian Edward "Teddy" Wharton in 1885, she and her husband traveled to Europe annually, usually from late winter to early spring, when they returned to their cottage on the family estate at Newport, Rhode Island. She conceived some of her more significant works in Europe, and she wrote extensively about life in England and on the Continent. If this exposure to Europe refined the historical and cultural awareness that her polished New York upbringing ingrained in her, she was also aware of the price that could be paid for living in culturally and economically impoverished surroundings. Wharton was an analyst of the private relations between men and women in financially secure families and stable social networks, but she was also fascinated by the deprivations of fragile people in the remote villages of New England. Although New York would continue to be the dominant force in her creative work, she devoted considerable attention in stories and novels to rural New England settings and characters.

Wharton's New England was not a purely imaginative creation; she knew firsthand the coastal towns of the region, having spent extended periods during her childhood and adult years in Newport and in Bar Harbor, Maine. In her fairly late story "The Little Gentleman," first published in 1926 as "The Young Gentleman," she attempted to capture the atmosphere of the fictional seaport town of Harpledon, somewhere between Salem and Newburyport on the New England coast. As recounted by one of Harpledon's inhabitants, the primary characteristic of this coastal town was its resistance to change and progress: "How we resisted modern improvements, ridiculed fashionable 'summer resorts,' fought trolley-lines, overhead wires and telephones, wrote to the papers denouncing municipal vandalism and bought up (those that could afford it) one little heavy-roofed house after another, as the land-speculators threatened them." In this story as well as others, Wharton would penetrate the sometimes horrifying reality behind the quaint antiquity of local surroundings.

However charming the surfaces of the remote towns and villages, quaintness and rusticity were hardly the characteristics Wharton explored in other works about New England, the object of her intense if intermittent attention from the 1890s until the later years of her career. The sleepy town in Wharton's *Summer* (1917) is North Dormer, a "village of the hills, abandoned of men, left apart by railway, trolley, telegraph, and all the forces that link life to life in modern communities." Wharton's treatment of New England settings was varied, and her attitude toward the region complex. With regard to characters, she portrayed the working poor and rustic natives as well as proud aristocrats. As regards settings, she developed provincial seacoast locales, poverty-stricken farms, and the pseudo-sophisticated culture of university towns. Whatever the range of setting and characterization, the primary characteristics that seem to dominate *Ethan Frome* (1911) and *Summer* (the book she called her "hot Ethan") are isolation, remoteness, and barrenness. Reflecting an interest in New England that was developed over the course of nearly two decades, she came to a general conclusion about the region in a letter written to a friend: "This grim New England country, for all its beauty, gives nothing to compensate for the complete mental starvation."

In Newport she devoted considerable time to remodeling the cottage and grounds of her family estate, activities reflecting an interest in house design and landscape architecture developed in the early years of her marriage. Her keen visual sense led to her first book, *The Decoration of Houses* (1897), and she applied an appreciation of form, balance, and proportion to many of her literary and architectural creations. In 1899 she visited Lenox, Massachusetts, spent the summer and fall of 1900 there, and in 1901 finished negotiations for the purchase of a 113-acre plot of land that extended to the neighboring town of Lee. She modeled the property after an estate in England, and in 1902 she moved into the Mount, named after the home of a Revolutionary War ancestor. She returned there annually until 1908. As it was for Wharton, western Massachusetts had been a favorite vacation spot and summer retreat for artists, writers, and members of the intelligentsia since the early decades of the nineteenth century.

In her autobiography, Wharton referred to the estate as "my first real home," a place that offered an "escape to the real country" (Wharton, *A Backward Glance,* pp. 124–125; see "For Further Reading"). In its guise as a retreat it presented a relaxed setting for walks, gardening, and frequent automobile rides through the Berkshire countryside. She entertained visitors there, among them her close friend and confidant Walter Berry, who assisted her with revisions of *Ethan Frome*. James Edward Johnson, curator of the Metropolitan Museum of Art, also visited, and Sara and Charles Eliot Norton (1827–1908) came from their nearby home in Ashfield. When not entertaining companions or improving the house and grounds, Wharton pursued her serious literary projects. Since her time away from New York usually lasted from June to December, she wrote contentedly: "The country quiet stimulated my creative zeal" (*A Backward Glance*, p. 125). The Mount clearly occupied a special place in Wharton's personal and imaginative life. As she later noted: "only at the Mount . . . I was truly happy" (p. 149).

If Wharton developed a sensitivity to the quiet beauty of the New England landscape, she was even more intrigued by the region's historical evolution (or devolution) and its literary past. By 1900 New England's once flourishing maritime industry was past its prime, and many of its seaports presented images of economic and physical decay. Social and demographic changes had accelerated the movement of people westward and from the remote rural areas to the larger or mid-size New England cities and towns, leaving the smaller villages even further behind in relative prosperity. Changes in patterns of transportation did little but reinforce the varying chances for potential success and economic opportunity among inhabitants of these different localities. Proud New Yorkers would have accepted the claim that at the end of the century the city's cultural enhancements had matched its economic progress, and that New York had eclipsed Boston as the nation's literary center.

Wharton would have been aware that the first fateful meeting between Nathaniel Hawthorne (1804–1864) and Herman Melville (1819–1891) occurred in the Berkshires. Several of their charged encounters took place in "the little red house" in Lenox that the former occupied following his departure from Salem and after the publication of *The Scarlet Letter* (1850). She would have known that Hawthorne's stay in the Berkshires marked the period of composition for *The House of the Seven Gables* (1851), his romance about the cold and paralyzing hold that the dead hand of the past has on subsequent generations. In his preface to that work Hawthorne disclaimed a rigid adherence to rendering an actual New England locality, but in noting an author's faithfulness to his creation, maintained that he might "manage his atmospherical medium as to bring out or mellow the lights and deepen and enrich the shadows of the picture." In his volume *The Snow Image and Other Twice-Told Tales* (1851), Hawthorne included a tale with the title character Ethan Brand, a name with potential resonance for Wharton's own New England stories. (Ethan Frome is a character literally "branded" with a red gash across his forehead, one of the effects of the "smash-up," and one of Wharton's Starkfield stories, "Bewitched" [1925], contains characters named Brand.) If Wharton's tendency was to discount the influence on her work of American, and especially of New England, writers in favor of their European counterparts, several critics have nevertheless discerned Hawthornean echoes, not the least of which is her use in *Ethan Frome* of the name Zenobia, which Hawthorne used for a character in *The Blithedale Romance* (1852). The use of Puritan names (such as Ethan, Jotham, and Endurance), the impact of the past on the present, the tension between cold isolation and the warmth of community—a range of Wharton's themes and techniques seem to derive from Hawthorne. This is a general debt she seemed to acknowledge in her autobiography when she counseled "New Englanders who had for years sought reflection of local life" (*A Backward Glance,* p. 294) in the pages of other authors not to forget Hawthorne's signal contributions in that vein.

In the introduction to a student's edition of *Ethan Frome,* published eleven years after the novel's first appearance, Wharton claimed that her knowledge of New England village life derived from firsthand observation and experience. She was referring to her initial visits to the region, her establishment of a home there, and her fairly frequent sojourns across the countryside of western Massachusetts. As noted in the reminiscence of a friend who visited her during her days in Lenox:

> One windy afternoon we were driving in the country near Lenox, and on the top of a hill on the left of the road stood a battered two-story house, unpainted, with a neglected door-yard tenanted by hens and chickens, and a few bedraggled children sitting on the stone steps before the open door. "It is about a place like that," said Mrs. Wharton, "that I mean to write a story. Only last week I went to the village meeting-house in Lenox and sat there for an hour alone, trying to think what such lives must be, and some day I shall write a story about it" (quoted in Lubbock, *Portrait of Edith Wharton,* pp. 22–23).

If this image of a neglected, decaying farmhouse provided some initial inspiration for her story, Wharton later claimed that previous literary renderings of the region had presented only a partial picture that failed to capture the harsh effects of its forbidding landscape. Previous writers may have accurately documented the region's botanical and dialectal traits—that is, its plants and trees, and the vernacular speech of its inhabitants—but Wharton sensed that what she called the "outcropping granite" had been overlooked. (Extending her figure of stone emerging from native soil, she wittily commented on the taciturn demeanor of New Englanders, scarcely more articulate than the cold, hard outcroppings under their feet.) While not mentioning the names of these writers in her introduction, Wharton clearly had in mind representatives of the New England local-color genre, who had made the region and its customs a primary focus in their fiction. According to literary historians, the local-color movement was a vigorous force in American letters from roughly 1870 to 1910; but it was sometimes pigeonholed by its critics as a "woman's genre," exclusively tied to private domestic matters. Although its primary practitioners—Sarah Orne Jewett (1849–1909), Mary Wilkins Freeman (1852–1930), and Rose Terry Cooke (1827–1892)—often wrote pungently and critically about their region and its inhabitants, critics, when not questioning the movement's sentimental tendencies, sometimes reduced the genre to an ornamental or descriptive mode of writing.

Sensitive to the criticism that she was attempting to portray a region from an outsider's perspective (and thus a less expert one than a native's), Wharton later took pains to underscore the accuracy of her rendering. As she noted in her autobiography, "'Ethan Frome' was written after I spent ten years in the hill-region of New England where the scene is laid, during which years I had come to know well the aspect, the dialect, and mental and moral attitude of the hill-people" (*A Backward Glance,* p. 296). Casting a backward glance on a local-color movement that had perhaps run its course, she aimed to capture a more austere atmosphere than had been presented in the works of some of her predecessors. "For years I had wanted to draw life as it really was in the derelict mountain villages of New England, a life even in my time and a thousandfold more a generation earlier, utterly unlike that seen through the rose-coloured spectacles of my predecessors, Mary Wilkins and Sarah Orne Jewett" (p. 293). Wharton clearly wanted to leave her readers with the impression that her portrayal of New England life was based on patient observation and careful study. Several years before *Ethan Frome,* in fact, she published *The Fruit of the Tree* (1907), a long novel of marital and class tensions in a New England mill town. In order to assure accuracy in that novel, she visited the mills in North Adams in western Massachusetts.

Wharton tended to measure her literary achievements against those of male writers; in her introduction, she further distinguished her efforts from previous treatments of New England by discounting her role as a mere recorder of the more superficial or external features of her setting. She thus emphasized the steps in the construction of *Ethan Frome*—that is, her role as a conscious literary craftsman. She noted that her initial conception derived from an academic exercise intended to polish her proficiency in the French language. Developed in Paris in 1907, the French sketch of "Ethan Frome" contained three characters (the male was named Hart) and achieved a length that encompassed two scenes, or vignettes, that survived in the published version. The fragment contained a triangular relationship among a husband, his sick wife, and the wife's niece, to whom the "Ethan-character" is attracted; but it lacked the structure that would give focus as well as depth to the narrative. Wharton eventually hit upon the device of a storyteller, but she did not choose one steeped in the lore and history of New England. Rather than a character like the herbalist and healer Mrs. Todd in Jewett's *The Country of the Pointed Firs* (1896), a native authority on the region's legends and values, Wharton chose someone from outside New England to narrate the story—a looker-on, an observer.

In her desire for "roundness"—Wharton seemed to resort recurrently to the terminology of the "plastic arts" or visual media—she would supplement the narrator's perspective with those of her minor characters. The fresh, acute perspective derived from the narrator's growing insight and awareness would compensate for what he lacked in inside background knowledge of the Frome household. While the device of an observer might lend "an air of artificiality" to a tale of sophisticated characters, Wharton noted, this defect might be mitigated if the narrator brought a sophisticated perspective to a tale of simple people. Her narrator would thus serve as a kind of intermediary between the reticent and reserved villagers and

Wharton's readers, giving "voice" to characters nearly inarticulate or resigned to silence.

Wharton's use of an observer eases the reader's entry into Ethan's story. In the opening of the novel the narrator recaptures his first arresting glimpse of Wharton's central character, when he had been struck by Frome's physiognomy and bearing. Harmon Gow, who had driven the stage between Starkfield and other towns in the region's pre-trolley days, provides further background on Frome. From Gow the narrator learns of Ethan's age and of his reluctance to escape Starkfield because of obligations to care for his failing parents. The narrator also hears not only Gow's chilling comment on Ethan's endurance—"Ethan'll likely touch a hundred"—but also his opinion that Ethan's stay in Starkfield constituted a kind of imprisonment: "Guess he's been in Starkfield too many winters. Most of the smart ones get away" (p. 9). The narrator's interview of Gow develops the tale only "as far as his [Gow's] mental and moral reach permitted" (p. 10), and he hopes that the more educated, sophisticated Mrs. Ned Hale, with whom he is staying, will provide greater insight. He cannot cut through her reserve and reticence, however, even though she has more firsthand knowledge of the aftermath of the accident that scarred Frome's forehead. Implying a suffering too great for words, her only comment is: "It was awful" (p. 12).

The narrator infers that he must piece together Ethan's story from different sources, and that consequently each retelling will be a little bit different. The meaning of the story, he infers, will be found even in gaps or silences after he has accumulated a succession of hints, suggestions, and clues that surround Frome. For all the narrator's curiosity about the Frome household, this technique gives his telling an elliptical effect, a sense that much has been left unsaid or not fully articulated. When the winter snows prevent the narrator's return to Starkfield after Frome volunteers to drive him to his business appointment, he is granted a night's shelter at the farm. Enveloped by the severe storm, the narrator experiences a "soft universal diffusion more confusing than the gusts and eddies of the morning." In the "formless night" his disorientation temporarily intensifies, and "even [Ethan's] sense of direction, and the bay's homing instinct, finally ceased to serve" (p. 17). The narrator's perplexity and bewilderment imply a need to reorient himself, to jolt himself, so to speak, into a perspective that demands clearer sight and more acute insight. It is at this point that Wharton effects the transition back to the period of Ethan's youth. Although some critics have quarreled with the subjective nature of her narrator's perceptions, there seems little doubt that Wharton intended his narrative to be more than one version of events among others. Accordingly, it is a "vision"; in her 1922 introduction she noted: "Only the narrator has scope to see it all, to resolve it back into simplicity, and to put it in its rightful place among his larger categories."

In structural terms, the opening of the door to Frome's farmhouse marks the end of the novel's introductory frame. The narrator has literally brought the reader to the threshold of Frome's private world. This narrative threshold, marked by an ellipsis, signals the transition from one crucial piece of the story to another, a rather imprecise line that separates Frome's outer and inner worlds. What occupies the space between the opening and closing frames is the narrator's imaginative vision, his attempt to offer a way out of his temporary disorientation and a way to picture the essential elements of the tragic story.

If this narrative device solved Wharton's structural challenge by introducing a nearly perfect symmetry to the tale, it also offered temporal perspective on events that happened a generation earlier. The narrator notes something in Ethan's "past history" or his "present way of living" (p. 15) that has driven him more deeply into himself. The narrator arrives in Starkfield in "the degenerate day of trolley, bicycle and rural delivery, when communication was easy between the scattered mountain villages, and the bigger towns in the valleys, such as Bettsbridge and Shadd's Falls, had libraries, theatres and Y. M. C. A. halls to which the youth of the hills could descend for recreation" (p. 10); but he is offered a glimpse into a life that had been shut down in Ethan's young manhood. This contrast between past and present reinforces the reader's understanding that the plot of Ethan's story hinges on a temporal outline in which the climax (or anticlimax) occurred a generation later than the initial acts of the tragedy.

The opening frame of the novel, essentially a prolonged transit up to the door of the farmhouse, offers an entrée (both literal and figurative) into Frome's private world. If the term "frame" connotes a structural principle, the introductory and closing sections, as already suggested, highlight the central narrative by putting frames around a picture of Frome that the storyteller develops. In an appendix to her autobiography Wharton acknowledged, "I always saw the visible universe as a series of pictures" (Wharton, "Life and I"). Even during her youth and adolescence she possessed a "visual sensibility" that was "intense." In her author's introduction, more specifically, she stresses the "natural" and "picture-making" merit of the narrative device she employs. In like terms she notes the need for fidelity to the "essential elements of my picture." As outlined in her introduction, her art of composition (what Edgar Allan Poe called his "Philosophy of Composition") is as much a process of drawing pictures of her deeply rooted, reticent characters as of rendering their speech and conduct.

In this regard it is worth noting that in 1936 Owen and Donald Davis dramatized *Ethan Frome* in New York, in a production successful enough to evolve into a national theatrical tour. The producers obviously sensed latent potential for the stage in adapting Wharton's narrative, despite its small cast, its compression, and its clipped dialogue. The author herself had explicitly used dramatic terms to trace the arc of Frome's career: climax, anticlimax, the acts of the tragedy. Early in the narrative, moreover, Ethan glides on the snow "like a stage-apparition behind thickening veils of gauze" (p. 15). If occasionally light penetrates through the "screen of snow" (p. 18), the wintry landscape offers a series of layering or veiling effects, similar to the varied uses of theatrical screens or curtains. In a narrative in which the spoken word may receive less emphasis than gesture and expression, characters become "silhouettes" in a "shadowy pantomime" (p. 28). Wharton even alludes in her introduction to the casual novelist's temptation to resort to "added ornament, or a trick of drapery or lighting."

It is interesting to note that in a foreword to the dramatization Wharton praised the stage version for avoiding the "grimacing enlargement of gesture and language" sometimes deemed necessary to carry a work of fiction across the footlights. What she hoped would stay with her audience were the "strained starved faces" of her characters. Starting in the novel with her figure of granite outcroppings half-emerged from the soil, Wharton moves from images of stasis and inactivity—the idle wheel at Frome's saw-mill and the sagging sheds burdened by the weight of snows—to ones of stifled energy. The narrator notes "an orchard of starved apple-trees writhing over a hillside among outcroppings of slate that nuzzled up through the snow like animals pushing out their noses to breathe" (p. 16). Such images are part of an elaborate "mise-en-scène" in which Wharton derives varied effects from the narrator's precise observation of the local setting.

Wharton's technique is scenographic, and her nine brief chapters following the opening frame constitute a succession of local pictures. Precise details contribute incrementally to a series of intimate pictorial scenes, the point of view framed by a perspective that derives from an observer who comes from a world outside Starkfield, and this focus is eventually constrained by attention to the inner workings of the Frome household. In chapter IV, for example, Ethan imagines the kitchen and its "homelike look," the consequence of Zeena's absence and the potential for a night alone with Mattie, and he tries to downplay anything that might ruin "the sweetness of the picture" (p. 40). Similarly, in chapter VI, after his night with Mattie, he expresses relief that he had "done nothing to trouble the sweetness of the picture" (p. 56). Each of these "picture-like" scenes occurs within the enclosed setting of Starkfield; most of the chapter-length close-scenes occur inside the Frome farmhouse, and even the arrangement of each room in the house is composed like a simple set within a small theater. Each scene achieves its own effect, each derives its subtle coloration from the winter weather, and scenes and faces are affected by light (analogous to a theatrical spotlight). In each scene Wharton makes use of basic props, the most notorious of which is the broken pickle dish that shatters a happy evening and that ominously prefigures the broken lives of Ethan and Mattie.

In chapter V, the basic inventory of props includes a stove, a lamp, a chair, a clock, a pipe, and a bit of sewing. Rather than stressing light, this central chapter is touched by darkness under a muffled sky, an atmosphere as "dark as Egypt" (p. 52). Assuming that the broken dish will be easily repaired the next morning, Ethan naively envisions a "scene" that was "just as he dreamed of" earlier in the day. Within the context of Wharton's complex, multiple ironies,

Ethan has conjured up a dream of "complete well being," a "sense of being in another world, where all was warmth and harmony and time could bring no change" (p. 51). This dreamlike atmosphere is undercut by Zeena's absence, represented by her empty rocking chair. Rather than a clichéd pretty picture, this scene leads to momentary disorientation in the guise of Ethan's vision of Zeena's countenance, usually "framed" (p. 51) by the patch-work cushion, but now obscuring and then obliterating the gaze that he had fixed on Mattie's pretty face. The scene takes place in a room with all "its ancient implications of conformity and order" (p. 53), and Ethan's "return to reality" is punctuated by the "spectral rocking" of Zeena's empty chair and by his recognition that this was the "only evening" (p. 54) that he and Mattie would ever spend alone together.

In the subsequent chapter, despite Ethan's best efforts to recover "the same scene of shining comfort as on the previous evening" (p. 60), once again his naive hopes are undermined, this time by Zeena's return from the Flats. She has returned resolute in her desire to replace Mattie with a hired girl, and the ensuing exchange in chapter VII is marked by recriminations about past events and their straitened circumstances. Ethan is so shocked by the "horror of the scene" (p. 63) that he seeks escape in his "cold dark 'study'" (p. 72), hoping to avoid any "sequel to the scene in the kitchen" (p. 72). He eventually confronts the reality that Zeena would never "cease to be part of the scene" (p. 75).

Art and cultural historian John Conron notes, in *American Picturesque* (Pennsylvania State University Press, 2000), that in local art and literature the lines between setting and character are "elastic" and "breachable." Via her scenographic method, Wharton has painstakingly developed a narrative in which Starkfield and its surrounding landscape, and her central and minor characters, the domestic space of their homes, their individual histories, and their family histories are all intertwined. For example, Mrs. Ned Hale's wan refinement is "not out of keeping" (a term derived from landscape aesthetics and house design) with her "pale old-fashioned house" (p. 11). An even more striking example is offered by the Frome farmhouse, clearly part of the scenery but hardly described in such a way to suggest quaintness or refined taste. It is one of "those lonely New England farm-houses that make the landscape lonelier," and Ethan's clipped identification—"That's my place"—only intensifies the "distress and oppression of the scene," a flash of sunlight exposing "its plaintive ugliness" (p. 16). The identification of house, human figure, and setting could not be more direct or explicit than in the narrator's characterization of Ethan as "part of the mute melancholy landscape, an incarnation of its frozen woe, with all that was warm and sentient in him fast bound below the surface" (p. 13). The identification of man and landscape takes on symbolic resonance when the narrator notices that the traditional "L" of this New England farmhouse, usually representing workrooms and storerooms at a right angle to the living quarters, has been removed. The house has a "forlorn and stunted look," and the narrator, linking the lame Frome and other inhabitants of the harsh New England climate with their surroundings, observes "in the diminished dwelling the image of his [Frome's] own shrunken body" (p. 17).

If initially Ethan appeared to an observer to be "the most striking figure in Starkfield," possessed of a "careless powerful look" (p. 8), this figure in motion arouses curiosity not only about the cause of his lameness but about a "depth of moral isolation too remote for casual access" (p. 13). Wharton's visual education, developed through years of self-study in the painting, art, architecture, and the textured culture of Europe, is here adapted to penetrating the austere, granite-like surfaces of her local setting in *Ethan Frome*. During the years of refining her acute visual sensibility, she found in John Ruskin (1819–1900), the author of *Modern Painters* (5 volumes, 1843–1860), an "interpreter of visual impressions" who did her "incomparable service." Like her model Ruskin, she explored all the varied ramifications of "expression, character, types of countenance, color" implicit in her deceptively simple characters' lives.

From such a perspective, Wharton moves logically to a study of facial expressiveness, of the "strained starved faces" of her characters. As already noted, features of the landscape offer a means of reading human character; but Wharton extends her interpretation of Frome's physical bearing, including "his brown seamed profile" (p. 13), to reflect hidden energies and concealed emotions. Although critics have suggested that Wharton overdoes her descriptions of inscrutable New England faces, this pictorializing of physical features is essential to the unfolding of her dramatic story, especially with regard to her female characters. Thus Mattie's face, when lifted in Ethan's direction, "looked like a window that has caught the sunset" (p. 23). The morning after the dance, her face is "part of the sun's red and of the pure glitter on the snow" (p. 36). In contrast, a pale light from a lamp "drew out of the darkness" Zeena's "puckered throat . . . and deepened fantastically the hollows and prominences of her high-boned face" (p. 33). Similarly, light makes Zeena's "face look more than usually drawn and bloodless, sharpened the three parallel creases between ear and cheek, and drew querulous lines from her thin nose to the corners of her mouth" (p. 39). Just as Zeena had raised a lamp against the black background of the kitchen, Mattie's light brings out her distinguishing features: her "slim young throat," "a lustrous fleck on her lips," "her eyes with velvet shade," and a "milky whiteness above the black curve of her brows" (p. 47).

Upon her return from the Flats, Zeena, the hypochondriac and wasting wife, has a new "mien of wan authority" (p. 61). Her voice, moreover, has a new tone, neither whining nor reproachful but resolute. Zeena's high-boned face, thin figure, and gray hair have caused several critics to see her as a witchlike character. As the narrative progresses toward its closing chapters, this figure of apparently wasting energy assumes greater power over Ethan: "She was no longer the listless creature who had lived at his side in a state of sullen self-absorption, but a mysterious alien presence, an evil energy secreted from the long years of silent brooding. It was the sense of his helplessness that sharpened his antipathy" (p. 66). In the early chapters of *Ethan Frome,* Wharton uses faces as images in which to read the history of past suffering and disappointment. As she moves to the closing frame, facial expressions and gestures signify the long years of endurance that await the inhabitants of the Frome household after the smash-up. Zeena acts like "one singled out for a great fate" (p. 61), and Ethan envisions Mattie's future as fulfilling the fate of so many working girls he had seen during his days in Worcester: "There came back to him miserable tales he had heard at Worcester, and the faces of girls whose lives had begun as hopefully as Mattie's" (p. 68).

The female protagonist of *Summer,* Charity Royall, comments on the lack of development in her isolated village: "Things don't change at North Dormer: people just get used to them." If the break between the opening frame in *Ethan Frome* and the storyteller's narrative offers an abrupt shift from the present time to the period of Ethan's youth, the effect of the temporal change in the closing frame is exactly the opposite. The series of "scenes" and "pictures" that the narrator has rendered give a clear impression of the extended effects of the smash-up on the lives of his three characters. Clearly Wharton's local art has taken the reader beyond what Ruskin would have called the "surface picturesque," eliciting perhaps a vague melancholy in the face of the inevitable erosion of time. In chapter V, Ethan undergoes a "momentary shock" when he imagines that the absent Zeena's presence is so palpable that she nearly erases that of Mattie: "It was almost as if the other face [that is, Zeena's], the face of the superseded woman, had obliterated that of the intruder" (p. 51). This image anticipates the shocking vision of Zeena's face that comes into Ethan's consciousness just as the sled, in its fatal descent, bears down on the elm: "But suddenly his wife's face, with twisted, monstrous lineaments, thrust itself between him and his goal" (p. 93). Suggesting a more complicated and expressive set of feelings than that offered by surface pictures, the faces of Wharton's characters eventually reflect a suffering that has been long endured, as if in a changeless environment marked by hopeless routine. In the closing frame, Zeena has "pale opaque eyes which revealed nothing and reflected nothing, and her narrow lips were of the same sallow colour as her face" (p. 99). If physiognomy is a means of reading personal history, it is Mattie's once bright and vital face that has come to resemble Zeena's: "Her hair was as grey as her companion's, her face as bloodless and shrivelled, but amber-tinted, with swarthy shadows sharpening the nose and hollowing the temples. Under her shapeless dress her body kept its limp immobility, and her dark eyes had the bright witch-like stare that disease of the spine sometimes gives" (p. 95). The faces of the two women, sometimes confused in Ethan's consciousness, have come to resemble each other. Mattie and Zeena, in effect, have reversed roles, the latter assuming the role of caregiver, thus repeating the "doctoring" activities she performed in years past for Ethan's sickly mother.

The contrast to the opening frame, in which the narrator's queries had elicited almost no reply from Mrs. Ned Hale, seems obvious. In a reversal of the rhythm of the exchange in the opening, the narrator is now content to let his reserve work on the taciturn townspeople. They are now curious as to what insights he has gained after being the first visitor to have spent a night in the Frome household in many years. Mrs. Hale had assumed that our unnamed visitor had been lost or "buried under a snow-drift" (p. 96), but when he emerges, part of his enhanced "vision" includes the now more expressive words of the townspeople who had previously been so reluctant to speak. (In Wharton's 1910 story "The Legend," a famous figure drops out of sight, only to emerge "frozen stiff" [p. 184] from the snow, with a new name. That name, significantly, is "Winterman.") The outsider has indeed come to learn, via his penetration of the household and by his attention to the hints and comments offered by the townspeople, how much the wintry landscape has influenced the inner and outer lives of its inhabitants. Here, as in much of Wharton's New England fiction, the lines between life and death are blurred. A representative of Starkfield offers the last word on the range of pain and suffering experienced by members of the Frome household. Mrs. Hale notes: "I don't see's there's much difference between the Fromes up at the farm and the Fromes down in the graveyard; 'cept that down there they're all quiet, and the women have got to hold their tongues" (p. 95).

Like Wharton's other New England stories, "The Pretext" (1908), written several years before *Ethan Frome,* has been criticized for its bleakness. If Ethan Frome yearns for escape with the youthful Mattie, Mrs. Margaret Ransom has found a fleeting alternative to the routine of her existence that is as "flat as the pattern of the wall-paper" (p. 104). Her escape comes in the guise of a young Englishman, Guy Dawnish, who, like Ethan, aspires to be an engineer. Rather than a rustic setting, this story takes place in the staid New England university town of Wentworth. Wharton's meticulous attention to the expressive features of her characters' faces is once again evident throughout the story, and Dawnish's visits to the aging Mrs. Ransom occur in a wintry light. During the second winter of the young man's visits, Mrs. Ransom comes to question the "relentless domesticity" (p. 106) of her relations to her husband. More significantly, she reproaches herself as she confronts "her rigid New England ancestry" (p. 104).

Like *Ethan Frome,* this story is about "frozen lives" (p. 104) and the legacy of the Puritan past; it also shares with the novel an interest in meaningful and accurate observation—that is, vision. The story is literally framed by two brief scenes in which Mrs. Ransom is engaged in self-evaluation while gazing in a mirror. Is Margaret Ransom's vision in the closing scene acute in that she has realized that Guy has used her as a "pretext," as a visit from his English relative seems to suggest? According to this interpretation, Guy's affection for Mrs. Ransom has been insincere, and he has used Mrs. Ransom's name to protect the identity of his real lover. The relative's repeated "I don't see," however, calls into serious question the accuracy of her insight into the situation, and the ultimate illusion may be Mrs. Ransom's. Her all-too-quiet resignation to "an aching vision of the length of the years that stretched before her" (p. 131)—much like the long years of endurance in the Frome household—may be based on the questionable assumption that a young man easily grows weary of a flirtation with a middle-aged, ordinary-looking woman. As in *Ethan Frome,* the reader of "The Pretext" is invited to explore multiple perspectives.

Whatever the case, at the time she wrote "The Pretext," Wharton had embarked on a relationship with the young journalist Morton Fullerton, which began as a friendship in 1907 and eventually deepened into intimacy in 1908. The affair continued until 1910, the year she was writing *Ethan Frome,* and several critics have detected autobiographical echoes of her liaison with Fullerton and of her unhappy marriage to the sickly Teddy Wharton in several of her works.

Most of Wharton's fictional works follow the principles of realism, but in *The Writing of Fiction* (1925) and in her preface to *Ghosts* (1937) she expresses a fondness for the supernatural tale. "Afterward" (1910), a ghost story set in England, shares with *Ethan Frome* an interest in the "back-waters of existence," a setting that can breed "strange acuities of emotion" (p. 138). The Boynes, the couple in the story, come to England to escape the pace of life in the United States. Mary's husband is a successful engineer eager to find time to work on a book-length project. As in *Ethan Frome,* the past literally comes back to haunt the couple in the guise of a figure who had committed suicide—a victim, unbeknownst to Mary, of her husband's cheating in business dealings. The recognition that this figure is a ghost comes "afterward"; but the real horror of the story does not derive from stock Gothic machinery so much as from the wife's belated realization of her husband's ruthless nature. As in *Ethan Frome*, a husband and wife have fallen into silence, and Mary learns about parts of his life he had kept from her. Once again Wharton penetrates the superficial veneer of a couple's relationship to reveal the secret tensions in an apparently stable marriage.

In the Higher Thought Club of "The Pretext," the Uplift Club of "The Legend" (1910), and the Lunch Club of "Xingu" (1916), Wharton makes fun of the cultural pretensions of her day. In "The Legend," the devotees of "Pellerinism" fail to recognize the great figure who is the founder of the philosophy they study and follow. "Xingu" takes place in Hillbridge, Wharton's version of a New England university town and the setting of several of her other stories, including "The Recovery" (1901). In the Lunch Club, the assembled ladies are mistresses of derivative knowledge and pseudo-sophisticated erudition. Their conversation turns to what they think to be mystical and occult philosophy, but only gradually do they realize that Xingu is a river in Brazil. Into their midst they welcome the celebrated novelist Osric Dane, author of the newly published *The Wings of Death*. As several Wharton critics have noted, Dane may be a satiric portrayal of her mentor Henry James, author of *The Wings of the Dove* (1902). Wharton may be having some gentle fun at the expense of James's obscure writing style, especially in his lengthy and involved later novels. As one of Wharton's "culture band" notes of the ending of *The Wings of Death:* "The beautiful part of it . . . is surely just this—that no one can tell *how* 'The Wings of Death' ends. Osric Dane, overcome by the awful significance of her own meaning, has mercifully veiled it—perhaps even from herself" (p. 206). Critic Barbara White suggests there may also be a little of Edith Wharton herself in Dane; Wharton may be poking gentle fun at herself, particularly at the charges of pessimism and bleakness that critics applied to several of her works. One club member wonders aloud if the "pessimistic tendency" of Dane's book expresses her "own convictions." Perhaps alluding to Wharton's settings, the same speaker alludes to the "sombre background" that throws her characters into "vivid relief" (p. 212). If Wharton gave subtle shadings to her scenic contrasts in *Ethan Frome* and other works, this artistry is reduced in Dane's hands to "the dark hopelessness of it all—the wonderful tone-scheme of black on black" (p. 207).

Kent Ljungquist has been Professor of English at Worcester Polytechnic Institute (the technological college in Worcester, Massachusetts, mentioned in *Ethan Frome*) since 1987. At WPI he teaches courses in American Realism, regional writing, and supernatural fiction. He has done both critical and editorial work on a range of nineteenth-century authors: Edgar Allan Poe, James Fenimore Cooper, James Russell Lowell, Henry Wadsworth Longfellow, Henry David Thoreau, Ralph Waldo Emerson, Walt Whitman, Herman Melville, Thomas Wentworth Higginson, Mary Hallock Foote, Elizabeth Oakes Smith, and Frederic S. Cozzens. He is the author of *The Grand and the Fair: Poe's Landscape Aesthetics and Pictorial Techniques* (1984), coeditor of Cooper's *The Deerslayer* (1987), and editor of several reference works: *The Facts on File Bibliography of American Fiction to 1865* (1994), *Nineteenth-Century American Fiction Writers* (1998), *Antebellum Writers in the South* (2000), and *Antebellum Writers in New York* (2000). He serves on the editorial boards of both *Poe Studies/Dark Romanticism* and the *Edgar Allan Poe Review*.

ETHAN FROME AND SELECTED STORIES

ETHAN FROME

INTRODUCTION
BY EDITH WHARTON

I HAD KNOWN SOMETHING of New England village life long before I made my home in the same county as my imaginary Starkfield; though, during the years spent there, certain of its aspects became much more familiar to me.

Even before that final initiation, however, I had had an uneasy sense that the New England of fiction bore little–except a vague botanical and dialectical—resemblance to the harsh and beautiful land as I had seen it. Even the abundant enumeration of sweet-fern, asters and mountain-laurel, and the conscientious reproduction of the vernacular, left me with the feeling that the outcropping granite had in both cases been overlooked. I give the impression merely as a personal one; it accounts for "Ethan Frome," and may, to some readers, in a measure justify it.

So much for the origin of the story; there is nothing else of interest to say of it, except as concerns its construction.

The problem before me, as I saw in the first flash, was this: I had to deal with a subject of which the dramatic climax, or rather the anticlimax, occurs a generation later than the first acts of the tragedy. This enforced lapse of time would seem to anyone persuaded—as I have always been—that every subject (in the novelist's sense of the term) implicitly *contains its own form and dimensions,* to mark Ethan Frome as the subject for a novel. But I never thought this for a moment, for I had felt, at the same time, that the theme of my tale was not one on which many variations could be played. It must be treated as starkly and summarily as life had always presented itself to my protagonists; any attempt to elaborate and complicate their sentiments would necessarily have falsified the whole. They were, in truth, these figures, my *granite outcroppings;* but half-emerged from the soil, and scarcely more articulate.

This incompatibility between subject and plan would perhaps have seemed to suggest that my "situation" was after all one to be rejected. Every novelist has been visited by the insinuating wraiths of false "good situations," siren-subjects luring his cockle-shell to the rocks; their voice is oftenest heard, and their mirage-sea beheld, as he traverses the waterless desert which awaits him half-way through whatever work is actually in hand. I knew well enough what song those sirens sang, and had often tied myself to my dull job until they were out of hearing—perhaps carrying a lost masterpiece in their rainbow veils. But I had no such fear of them in the case of Ethan Frome. It was the first subject I had ever approached with full confidence in its value, for my own purpose, and a relative faith in my power to render at least a part of what I saw in it.

Every novelist, again, who "intends upon" his art, has lit upon such subjects, and been fascinated by the difficulty of presenting them in the fullest relief, yet without an added ornament, or a trick of drapery or lighting. This was my task, if I were to tell the story of Ethan Frome; and my scheme of construction—which met with the immediate and unqualified disapproval of the few friends to whom I tentatively outlined it—I still think justified in the given case. It appears to me, indeed, that, while an air of artificiality is lent to a tale of complex and sophisticated people which the novelist causes to be guessed at and interpreted by any mere looker-on, there need be no such drawback if the looker-on is sophisticated, and the people he interprets are simple. If he is capable of seeing all around them, no violence is done to probability in allowing him to exercise this faculty; it is natural enough that he should act as the sympathizing intermediary between his rudimentary characters and the more complicated minds to whom he is trying to present them. But this is all self-evident, and needs explaining only to those who have never thought of fiction as an art of composition.

The real merit of my construction seems to me to lie in a minor detail. I had to find means to bring my tragedy, in a way at once natural and picture-making, to the knowledge of its narrator. I might have sat him down before a village gossip who would have poured out the whole affair to him in a breath, but in doing this I should have been false to two essential elements of my picture: first, the deep-rooted reticence and inarticulateness of the people I was trying to draw, and secondly the effect of "roundness" (in the plastic sense) produced by letting their case be seen through eyes as different as those of Harmon Gow and Mrs. Ned Hale. Each of my chroniclers contributes to the narrative *just so much as he or she is capable of understanding* of what, to them, is a complicated and mysterious case; and only the narrator of the tale has scope enough to see it all, to resolve it back into simplicity, and to put it in its rightful place among his larger categories.

I make no claim for originality in following a method of which "La Grande Bretêche" and "The Ring and the Book" had set me the magnificent example; my one merit is, perhaps, to have guessed that the proceeding there employed was also applicable to my small tale.

I have written this brief analysis—the first I have ever published of any of my books—because, as an author's introduction to his work, I can imagine nothing of any value to his readers except a statement as to why he decided to attempt the work in question, and why he selected one form rather than another for its embodiment. These primary aims, the only ones that can be explicitly stated, must, by the artist, be almost instinctively felt and acted upon before there can pass into his creation that imponderable something more which causes life to circulate in it, and preserves it for a little from decay.

EDITH WHARTON.

ETHAN FROME[1]

I HAD THE STORY, bit by bit, from various people, and, as generally happens in such cases, each time it was a different story.

If you know Starkfield, Massachusetts,[2] you know the post-office. If you know the post-office you must have seen Ethan Frome drive up to it, drop the reins on his hollow-backed bay and drag himself across the brick pavement to the white colonnade: and you must have asked who he was.

It was there that, several years ago, I saw him for the first time; and the sight pulled me up sharp. Even then he was the most striking figure in Starkfield, though he was but the ruin of a man. It was not so much his great height that marked him, for the "natives" were easily singled out by their lank longitude from the stockier foreign breed: it was the careless powerful look he had, in spite of a lameness checking each step like the jerk of a chain. There was something bleak and unapproachable in his face, and he was so stiffened and grizzled that I took him for an old man and was surprised to hear that he was not more than fifty-two. I had this from Harmon Gow, who had driven the stage from Bettsbridge to Starkfield in pre-trolley days and knew the chronicle of all the families on his line.

"He's looked that way ever since he had his smash-up; and that's twenty-four years ago come next February," Harmon threw out between reminiscent pauses.

The "smash-up" it was—I gathered from the same informant—which, besides drawing the red gash across Ethan Frome's forehead, had so shortened and warped his right side that it cost him a visible effort to take the few steps from his buggy to the post-office window. He used to drive in from his farm every day at about noon, and as that was my own hour for fetching my mail I often passed him in the porch or stood beside him while we waited on the motions of the distributing hand behind the grating. I noticed that, though he came so punctually, he seldom received anything but a copy of the *Bettsbridge Eagle,* which he put without a glance into his sagging pocket. At intervals, however, the post-master would hand him an envelope addressed to Mrs. Zenobia—or Mrs. Zeena—Frome,[3] and usually bearing conspicuously in the upper left-hand corner the address of some manufacturer of patent medicine and the name of his specific. These documents my neighbour would also pocket without a glance, as if too much used to them to wonder at their number and variety, and would then turn away with a silent nod to the post-master.

Every one in Starkfield knew him and gave him a greeting tempered to his own grave mien; but his taciturnity was respected and it was only on rare occasions that one of the older men of the place detained him for a word. When this happened he would listen quietly, his blue eyes on the speaker's face, and answer in so low a tone that his words never reached me; then he would climb stiffly into his buggy, gather up the reins in his left hand and drive slowly away in the direction of his farm.

"It was a pretty bad smash-up?" I questioned Harmon, looking after Frome's retreating figure, and thinking how gallantly his lean brown head, with its shock of light hair, must have sat on his strong shoulders before they were bent out of shape.

"Wust kind," my informant assented. "More'n enough to kill most men. But the Fromes are tough. Ethan'll likely touch a hundred."

"Good God!" I exclaimed. At the moment Ethan Frome, after climbing to his seat, had leaned over to assure himself of the security of a wooden box—also with a druggist's label on it—which he had placed in the back of the buggy, and I saw his face as it probably looked when he thought himself alone. "*That* man touch a hundred? He looks as if he was dead and in hell now!"

Harmon drew a slab of tobacco from his pocket, cut off a wedge and pressed it into the leather pouch of his cheek. "Guess he's been in Starkfield too many winters. Most of the smart ones get away."

"Why didn't *he?*"

"Somebody had to stay and care for the folks. There warn't ever anybody but Ethan. Fust his father—then his mother—then his wife."

"And then the smash-up?"

Harmon chuckled sardonically. "That's so. He *had* to stay then."

"I see. And since then they've had to care for him?"

Harmon thoughtfully passed his tobacco to the other cheek. "Oh, as to that: I guess it's always Ethan done the caring."

Though Harmon Gow developed the tale as far as his mental and moral reach permitted there were perceptible gaps between his facts, and I had the sense that the deeper meaning of the story was in the gaps. But one phrase stuck in my memory and served as the nucleus about which I grouped my subsequent inferences: "Guess he's been in Starkfield too many winters."

Before my own time there was up I had learned to know what that meant. Yet I had come in the degenerate day of trolley, bicycle and rural delivery, when communication was easy between the scattered mountain villages, and the bigger towns in the valleys, such as Bettsbridge and Shadd's Falls, had libraries, theatres and Y. M. C. A. halls to which the youth of the hills could descend for recreation. But when winter shut down on Starkfield, and the village lay under a sheet of snow perpetually renewed from the pale skies, I began to see what life there—or rather its negation—must have been in Ethan Frome's young manhood.

I had been sent up by my employers on a job connected with the big power-house at Corbury Junction, and a long-drawn carpenters' strike had so delayed the work that I found myself anchored at Starkfield—the nearest habitable spot—for the best part of the winter. I chafed at first, and then, under the hypnotising effect of routine, gradually began to find a grim satisfaction in the life. During the early part of my stay I had been struck by the contrast between the vitality of the climate and the deadness of the community. Day by day, after the December snows were over, a blazing blue sky poured down torrents of light and air on the white landscape, which gave them back in an intenser glitter. One would have supposed that such an atmosphere must quicken the emotions as well as the blood; but it seemed to produce no change except that of retarding still more the sluggish pulse of Starkfield. When I had been there a little longer, and had seen this phase of crystal clearness followed by long stretches of sunless cold; when the storms of February had pitched their white tents about the devoted village and the wild cavalry of March winds had charged down to their support;

I began to understand why Starkfield emerged from its six months' siege like a starved garrison capitulating without quarter. Twenty years earlier the means of resistance must have been far fewer, and the enemy in command of almost all the lines of access between the beleaguered villages; and, considering these things, I felt the sinister force of Harmon's phrase: "Most of the smart ones get away." But if that were the case, how could any combination of obstacles have hindered the flight of a man like Ethan Frome?

During my stay at Starkfield I lodged with a middle-aged widow colloquially known as Mrs. Ned Hale. Mrs. Hale's father had been the village lawyer of the previous generation, and "lawyer Varnum's house," where my landlady still lived with her mother, was the most considerable mansion in the village. It stood at one end of the main street, its classic portico and small-paned windows looking down a flagged path between Norway spruces to the slim white steeple of the Congregational church. It was clear that the Varnum fortunes were at the ebb, but the two women did what they could to preserve a decent dignity; and Mrs. Hale, in particular, had a certain wan refinement not out of keeping with her pale old-fashioned house.

In the "best parlour," with its black horse-hair and mahogany weakly illuminated by a gurgling Carcel lamp,* I listened every evening to another and more delicately shaded version of the Starkfield chronicle. It was not that Mrs. Ned Hale felt, or affected, any social superiority to the people about her; it was only that the accident of a finer sensibility and a little more education had put just enough distance between herself and her neighbours to enable her to judge them with detachment. She was not unwilling to exercise this faculty, and I had great hopes of getting from her the missing facts of Ethan Frome's story, or rather such a key to his character as should co-ordinate the facts I knew. Her mind was a store-house of innocuous anecdote and any question about her acquaintances brought forth a volume of detail; but on the subject of Ethan Frome I found her unexpectedly reticent. There was no hint of disapproval in her reserve; I merely felt in her an insurmountable reluctance to

---

*Lamp in which oil is pumped through the wick tube by clockwork; named after French inventor Bertrand Carcel (1750–1812).

speak of him or his affairs, a low "Yes, I knew them both . . . it was awful . . ." seeming to be the utmost concession that her distress could make to my curiosity.

So marked was the change in her manner, such depths of sad initiation did it imply, that, with some doubts as to my delicacy, I put the case anew to my village oracle, Harmon Gow; but got for my pains only an uncomprehending grunt.

"Ruth Varnum was always as nervous as a rat; and, come to think of it, she was the first one to see 'em after they was picked up. It happened right below lawyer Varnum's, down at the bend of the Corbury road, just round about the time that Ruth got engaged to Ned Hale. The young folks was all friends, and I guess she just can't bear to talk about it. She's had troubles enough of her own."

All the dwellers in Starkfield, as in more notable communities, had had troubles enough of their own to make them comparatively indifferent to those of their neighbours; and though all conceded that Ethan Frome's had been beyond the common measure, no one gave me an explanation of the look in his face which, as I persisted in thinking, neither poverty nor physical suffering could have put there. Nevertheless, I might have contented myself with the story pieced together from these hints had it not been for the provocation of Mrs. Hale's silence, and—a little later—for the accident of personal contact with the man.

On my arrival at Starkfield, Denis Eady, the rich Irish grocer, who was the proprietor of Starkfield's nearest approach to a livery stable, had entered into an agreement to send me over daily to Corbury Flats, where I had to pick up my train for the Junction. But about the middle of the winter Eady's horses fell ill of a local epidemic. The illness spread to the other Starkfield stables and for a day or two I was put to it to find a means of transport. Then Harmon Gow suggested that Ethan Frome's bay was still on his legs and that his owner might be glad to drive me over.

I stared at the suggestion. "Ethan Frome? But I've never even spoken to him. Why on earth should he put himself out for me?"

Harmon's answer surprised me still more. "I don't know as he would; but I know he wouldn't be sorry to earn a dollar."

I had been told that Frome was poor, and that the saw-mill and the arid acres of his farm yielded scarcely enough to keep his household through the winter; but I had not supposed him to be in such want as Harmon's words implied, and I expressed my wonder.

"Well, matters ain't gone any too well with him," Harmon said. "When a man's been setting round like a hulk for twenty years or more, seeing things that want doing, it eats inter him, and he loses his grit. That Frome farm was always 'bout as bare's a milkpan when the cat's been round; and you know what one of them old watermills is wuth nowadays. When Ethan could sweat over 'em both from sunup to dark he kinder choked a living out of 'em; but his folks ate up most everything, even then, and I don't see how he makes out now. Fust his father got a kick, out haying, and went soft in the brain, and gave away money like Bible texts afore he died. Then his mother got queer and dragged along for years as weak as a baby; and his wife Zeena, she's always been the greatest hand at doctoring in the county. Sickness and trouble: that's what Ethan's had his plate full up with, ever since the very first helping."

The next morning, when I looked out, I saw the hollow-backed bay between the Varnum spruces, and Ethan Frome, throwing back his worn bearskin, made room for me in the sleigh at his side. After that, for a week, he drove me over every morning to Corbury Flats, and on my return in the afternoon met me again and carried me back through the icy night to Starkfield. The distance each way was barely three miles, but the old bay's pace was slow, and even with firm snow under the runners we were nearly an hour on the way. Ethan Frome drove in silence, the reins loosely held in his left hand, his brown seamed profile, under the helmet-like peak of the cap, relieved against the banks of snow like the bronze image of a hero. He never turned his face to mine, or answered, except in monosyllables, the questions I put, or such slight pleasantries as I ventured. He seemed a part of the mute melancholy landscape, an incarnation of its frozen woe, with all that was warm and sentient in him fast bound below the surface; but there was nothing unfriendly in his silence. I simply felt that he lived in a depth of moral isolation too remote for casual access, and I had the sense that his loneliness was not merely the result of his personal plight, tragic as I guessed that to be, but had in it, as Harmon Gow had hinted, the profound accumulated cold of many Starkfield winters.

Only once or twice was the distance between us bridged for a moment; and the glimpses thus gained confirmed my desire to know more. Once I happened to speak of an engineering job I had been on the previous year in Florida, and of the contrast between the winter landscape about us and that in which I had found myself the year before; and to my surprise Frome said suddenly: "Yes: I was down there once, and for a good while afterward I could call up the sight of it in winter. But now it's all snowed under."

He said no more, and I had to guess the rest from the inflection of his voice and his sharp relapse into silence.

Another day, on getting into my train at the Flats, I missed a volume of popular science—I think it was on some recent discoveries in bio-chemistry—which I had carried with me to read on the way. I thought no more about it till I got into the sleigh again that evening, and saw the book in Frome's hand.

"I found it after you were gone," he said.

I put the volume into my pocket and we dropped back into our usual silence; but as we began to crawl up the long hill from Corbury Flats to the Starkfield ridge I became aware in the dusk that he had turned his face to mine.

"There are things in that book that I didn't know the first word about," he said.

I wondered less at his words than at the queer note of resentment in his voice. He was evidently surprised and slightly aggrieved at his own ignorance.

"Does that sort of thing interest you?" I asked.

"It used to."

"There are one or two rather new things in the book: there have been some big strides lately in that particular line of research." I waited a moment for an answer that did not come; then I said: "If you'd like to look the book through I'd be glad to leave it with you."

He hesitated, and I had the impression that he felt himself about to yield to a stealing tide of inertia; then, "Thank you—I'll take it," he answered shortly.

I hoped that this incident might set up some more direct communication between us. Frome was so simple and straightforward that I was sure his curiosity about the book was based on a genuine interest in its subject. Such tastes and acquirements in a man of his condition made the contrast more poignant between his outer situation and his inner needs, and I hoped that the chance of giving expression to the latter might at least unseal his lips. But something in his past history, or in his present way of living, had apparently driven him too deeply into himself for any casual impulse to draw him back to his kind. At our next meeting he made no allusion to the book, and our intercourse seemed fated to remain as negative and one-sided as if there had been no break in his reserve.

Frome had been driving me over to the Flats for about a week when one morning I looked out of my window into a thick snowfall. The height of the white waves massed against the garden-fence and along the wall of the church showed that the storm must have been going on all night, and that the drifts were likely to be heavy in the open. I thought it probable that my train would be delayed; but I had to be at the power-house for an hour or two that afternoon, and I decided, if Frome turned up, to push through to the Flats and wait there till my train came in. I don't know why I put it in the conditional, however, for I never doubted that Frome would appear. He was not the kind of man to be turned from his business by any commotion of the elements; and at the appointed hour his sleigh glided up through the snow like a stage-apparition behind thickening veils of gauze.

I was getting to know him too well to express either wonder or gratitude at his keeping his appointment; but I exclaimed in surprise as I saw him turn his horse in a direction opposite to that of the Corbury road.

"The railroad's blocked by a freight-train that got stuck in a drift below the Flats," he explained, as we jogged off into the stinging whiteness.

"But look here—where are you taking me, then?"

"Straight to the Junction, by the shortest way," he answered, pointing up School House Hill with his whip.

"To the Junction—in this storm? Why, it's a good ten miles!"

"The bay'll do it if you give him time. You said you had some business there this afternoon. I'll see you get there."

He said it so quietly that I could only answer: "You're doing me the biggest kind of a favour."

"That's all right," he rejoined.

Abreast of the schoolhouse the road forked, and we dipped down a lane to the left, between hemlock boughs bent inward to their trunks by the weight of the snow. I had often walked that way on Sundays, and knew that the solitary roof showing through bare branches near the bottom of the hill was that of Frome's saw-mill. It looked exanimate enough, with its idle wheel looming above the black stream dashed with yellow-white spume, and its cluster of sheds sagging under their white load. Frome did not even turn his head as we drove by, and still in silence we began to mount the next slope. About a mile farther, on a road I had never travelled, we came to an orchard of starved apple-trees writhing over a hillside among outcroppings of slate that nuzzled up through the snow like animals pushing out their noses to breathe. Beyond the orchard lay a field or two, their boundaries lost under drifts; and above the fields, huddled against the white immensities of land and sky, one of those lonely New England farm-houses that make the landscape lonelier.

"That's my place," said Frome, with a sideway jerk of his lame elbow; and in the distress and oppression of the scene I did not know what to answer. The snow had ceased, and a flash of watery sunlight exposed the house on the slope above us in all its plaintive ugliness. The black wraith of a deciduous creeper flapped from the porch, and the thin wooden walls, under their worn coat of paint, seemed to shiver in the wind that had risen with the ceasing of the snow.

"The house was bigger in my father's time: I had to take down the 'L,' a while back," Frome continued, checking with a twitch of the left rein the bay's evident intention of turning in through the broken-down gate.

I saw then that the unusually forlorn and stunted look of the house was partly due to the loss of what is known in New England as the "L": that long deep-roofed adjunct usually built at right angles to the main house, and connecting it, by way of store-rooms and tool-house, with the wood-shed and cow-barn. Whether because of its symbolic sense, the image it presents of a life linked with the soil, and enclosing in itself the chief sources of warmth and nourishment, or whether merely because of the consolatory thought that it enables the dwellers in that harsh climate to get to their morning's work without facing the weather, it is certain that the "L" rather than the house itself seems to be the centre, the actual hearth-stone of the New England farm. Perhaps this connection of ideas, which had often occurred to me in my rambles about Starkfield, caused me to hear a wistful note in Frome's words, and to see in the diminished dwelling the image of his own shrunken body.

"We're kinder side-tracked here now," he added, "but there was considerable passing before the railroad was carried through to the Flats." He roused the lagging bay with another twitch; then, as if the mere sight of the house had let me too deeply into his confidence for any farther pretence of reserve, he went on slowly: "I've always set down the worst of mother's trouble to that. When she got the rheumatism so bad she couldn't move around she used to sit up there and watch the road by the hour; and one year, when they was six months mending the Bettsbridge pike after the floods, and Harmon Gow had to bring his stage round this way, she picked up so that she used to get down to the gate most days to see him. But after the trains begun running nobody ever come by here to speak of, and mother never could get it through her head what had happened, and it preyed on her right along till she died."

As we turned into the Corbury road the snow began to fall again, cutting off our last glimpse of the house; and Frome's silence fell with it, letting down between us the old veil of reticence. This time the wind did not cease with the return of the snow. Instead, it sprang up to a gale which now and then, from a tattered sky, flung pale sweeps of sunlight over a landscape chaotically tossed. But the bay was as good as Frome's word, and we pushed on to the Junction through the wild white scene.

In the afternoon the storm held off, and the clearness in the west seemed to my inexperienced eye the pledge of a fair evening. I finished my business as quickly as possible, and we set out for Starkfield with a good chance of getting there for supper. But at sunset the clouds gathered again, bringing an earlier night, and the snow began to fall straight and steadily from a sky without wind, in a soft universal diffusion more confusing than the gusts and eddies of the morning. It seemed to be a part of the thickening darkness, to be the winter night itself descending on us layer by layer.

The small ray of Frome's lantern was soon lost in this smothering medium, in which even his sense of direction, and the bay's homing instinct, finally ceased to serve us. Two or three times some ghostly landmark sprang up to warn us that we were astray, and then was sucked back into the mist; and when we finally regained our road the old horse began to show signs of exhaustion. I felt myself to blame for having accepted Frome's offer, and after a short discussion I persuaded him to let me get out of the sleigh and walk along through the snow at the bay's side. In this way we struggled on for another mile or two, and at last reached a point where Frome, peering into what seemed to me formless night, said: "That's my gate down yonder."

The last stretch had been the hardest part of the way. The bitter cold and the heavy going had nearly knocked the wind out of me, and I could feel the horse's side ticking like a clock under my hand.

"Look here, Frome," I began, "there's no earthly use in your going any farther—" but he interrupted me: "Nor you neither. There's been about enough of this for anybody."

I understood that he was offering me a night's shelter at the farm, and without answering I turned into the gate at his side, and followed him to the barn, where I helped him to unharness and bed down the tired horse. When this was done he unhooked the lantern from the sleigh, stepped out again into the night, and called to me over his shoulder: "This way."

Far off above us a square of light trembled through the screen of snow. Staggering along in Frome's wake I floundered toward it, and in the darkness almost fell into one of the deep drifts against the front of the house. Frome scrambled up the slippery steps of the porch, digging a way through the snow with his heavily booted foot. Then he lifted his lantern, found the latch, and led the way into the house. I went after him into a low unlit passage, at the back of which a ladder-like staircase rose into obscurity. On our right a line of light marked the door of the room which had sent its ray across the night; and behind the door I heard a woman's voice droning querulously.

Frome stamped on the worn oil-cloth to shake the snow from his boots, and set down his lantern on a kitchen chair which was the only piece of furniture in the hall. Then he opened the door.

"Come in," he said; and as he spoke the droning voice grew still . . .

It was that night that I found the clue to Ethan Frome, and began to put together this vision of his story. . . . .

. . . .

. . . .

CHAPTER ONE

THE VILLAGE LAY UNDER two feet of snow, with drifts at the windy corners. In a sky of iron the points of the Dipper hung like icicles and Orion flashed his cold fires. The moon had set, but the night was so transparent that the white house-fronts between the elms looked gray against the snow, clumps of bushes made black stains on it, and the basement windows of the church sent shafts of yellow light far across the endless undulations.

Young Ethan Frome walked at a quick pace along the deserted street, past the bank and Michael Eady's new brick store and Lawyer Varnum's house with the two black Norway spruces at the gate. Opposite the Varnum gate, where the road fell away toward the Corbury valley, the church reared its slim white steeple and narrow peristyle.* As the young man walked toward it the upper windows drew a black arcade along the side wall of the building, but from the lower openings, on the side where the ground sloped steeply down to the Corbury road, the light shot its long bars, illuminating many fresh furrows in the track leading to the basement door, and showing, under an adjoining shed, a line of sleighs with heavily blanketed horses.

The night was perfectly still, and the air so dry and pure that it gave little sensation of cold. The effect produced on Frome was rather of a complete absence of atmosphere, as though nothing less tenuous than ether intervened between the white earth under his feet and the metallic dome overhead. "It's like being in an exhausted receiver,"[4] he thought. Four or five years earlier he had taken a year's course at a technological college at Worcester,[5] and dabbled in the laboratory with a friendly professor of physics; and the images supplied by that

*Set of columns surrounding a building or enclosing a court.

experience still cropped up, at unexpected moments, through the totally different associations of thought in which he had since been living. His father's death, and the misfortunes following it, had put a premature end to Ethan's studies; but though they had not gone far enough to be of much practical use they had fed his fancy and made him aware of huge cloudy meanings behind the daily face of things.

As he strode along through the snow the sense of such meanings glowed in his brain and mingled with the bodily flush produced by his sharp tramp. At the end of the village he paused before the darkened front of the church. He stood there a moment, breathing quickly, and looking up and down the street, in which not another figure moved. The pitch of the Corbury road, below lawyer Varnum's spruces, was the favourite coasting-ground of Starkfield, and on clear evenings the church corner rang till late with the shouts of the coasters; but to-night not a sled darkened the whiteness of the long declivity. The hush of midnight lay on the village, and all its waking life was gathered behind the church windows, from which strains of dance-music flowed with the broad bands of yellow light.

The young man, skirting the side of the building, went down the slope toward the basement door. To keep out of range of the revealing rays from within he made a circuit through the untrodden snow and gradually approached the farther angle of the basement wall. Thence, still hugging the shadow, he edged his way cautiously forward to the nearest window, holding back his straight spare body and craning his neck till he got a glimpse of the room.

Seen thus, from the pure and frosty darkness in which he stood, it seemed to be seething in a mist of heat. The metal reflectors of the gas-jets sent crude waves of light against the whitewashed walls, and the iron flanks of the stove at the end of the hall looked as though they were heaving with volcanic fires. The floor was thronged with girls and young men. Down the side wall facing the window stood a row of kitchen chairs from which the older women had just risen. By this time the music had stopped, and the musicians—a fiddler, and the young lady who played the harmonium on Sundays—were hastily refreshing themselves at one corner of the supper-table which aligned its devastated pie-dishes and ice-cream saucers on the platform at the end of the hall. The guests were preparing to leave, and the tide had already set toward the passage where coats and wraps were hung, when a young man with a sprightly foot and a shock of black hair shot into the middle of the floor and clapped his hands. The signal took instant effect. The musicians hurried to their instruments, the dancers—some already half-muffled for departure—fell into line[6] down each side of the room, the older spectators slipped back to their chairs, and the lively young man, after diving about here and there in the throng, drew forth a girl who had already wound a cherry-coloured "fascinator"* about her head, and, leading her up to the end of the floor, whirled her down its length to the bounding tune of a Virginia reel.†

Frome's heart was beating fast. He had been straining for a glimpse of the dark head under the cherry-coloured scarf and it vexed him that another eye should have been quicker than his. The leader of the reel, who looked as if he had Irish blood in his veins, danced well, and his partner caught his fire. As she passed down the line, her light figure swinging from hand to hand in circles of increasing swiftness, the scarf flew off her head and stood out behind her shoulders, and Frome, at each turn, caught sight of her laughing panting lips, the cloud of dark hair about her forehead, and the dark eyes which seemed the only fixed points in a maze of flying lines.

The dancers were going faster and faster, and the musicians, to keep up with them, belaboured their instruments like jockeys lashing their mounts on the home-stretch; yet it seemed to the young man at the window that the reel would never end. Now and then he turned his eyes from the girl's face to that of her partner, which, in the exhilaration of the dance, had taken on a look of almost impudent ownership. Denis Eady was the son of Michael Eady, the ambitious Irish grocer, whose suppleness and effrontery had given Starkfield its first notion of "smart" business methods, and whose new brick store testified to the success of the attempt. His son seemed likely to follow in his steps, and was meanwhile applying the same arts to the conquest of the Starkfield maidenhood. Hitherto Ethan Frome had been content to think him a mean fellow; but now he positively invited a horse-whipping. It was strange that the

---

*Woman's head scarf, made of lace or crochet.

†American country dance in which partners face each other in parallel lines.

girl did not seem aware of it: that she could lift her rapt face to her dancer's, and drop her hands into his, without appearing to feel the offence of his look and touch.

Frome was in the habit of walking into Starkfield to fetch home his wife's cousin, Mattie Silver, on the rare evenings when some chance of amusement drew her to the village. It was his wife who had suggested, when the girl came to live with them, that such opportunities should be put in her way. Mattie Silver came from Stamford,* and when she entered the Fromes' household to act as her cousin Zeena's aid it was thought best, as she came without pay, not to let her feel too sharp a contrast between the life she had left and the isolation of a Starkfield farm. But for this—as Frome sardonically reflected—it would hardly have occurred to Zeena to take any thought for the girl's amusement.

When his wife first proposed that they should give Mattie an occasional evening out he had inwardly demurred at having to do the extra two miles to the village and back after his hard day on the farm; but not long afterward he had reached the point of wishing that Starkfield might give all its nights to revelry.

Mattie Silver had lived under his roof for a year, and from early morning till they met at supper he had frequent chances of seeing her; but no moments in her company were comparable to those when, her arm in his, and her light step flying to keep time with his long stride, they walked back through the night to the farm. He had taken to the girl from the first day, when he had driven over to the Flats to meet her, and she had smiled and waved to him from the train, crying out, "You must be Ethan!" as she jumped down with her bundles, while he reflected, looking over her slight person: "She don't look much on housework, but she ain't a fretter, anyhow." But it was not only that the coming to his house of a bit of hopeful young life was like the lighting of a fire on a cold hearth. The girl was more than the bright serviceable creature he had thought her. She had an eye to see and an ear to hear: he could show her things and tell her things, and taste the bliss of feeling that all he imparted left long reverberations and echoes he could wake at will.

---

*Town in southwestern Connecticut with a population of about 11,000 in the 1880s.

It was during their night walks back to the farm that he felt most intensely the sweetness of this communion. He had always been more sensitive than the people about him to the appeal of natural beauty. His unfinished studies had given form to this sensibility and even in his unhappiest moments field and sky spoke to him with a deep and powerful persuasion. But hitherto the emotion had remained in him as a silent ache, veiling with sadness the beauty that evoked it. He did not even know whether any one else in the world felt as he did, or whether he was the sole victim of this mournful privilege. Then he learned that one other spirit had trembled with the same touch of wonder: that at his side, living under his roof and eating his bread, was a creature to whom he could say: "That's Orion down yonder; the big fellow to the right is Aldebaran, and the bunch of little ones—like bees swarming—they're the Pleiades* . . ." or whom he could hold entranced before a ledge of granite thrusting up through the fern while he unrolled the huge panorama of the ice age, and the long dim stretches of succeeding time. The fact that admiration for his learning mingled with Mattie's wonder at what he taught was not the least part of his pleasure. And there were other sensations, less definable but more exquisite, which drew them together with a shock of silent joy: the cold red of sunset behind winter hills, the flight of cloud-flocks over slopes of golden stubble, or the intensely blue shadows of hemlocks on sunlit snow. When she said to him once: "It looks just as if it was painted!" it seemed to Ethan that the art of definition could go no farther, and that words had at last been found to utter his secret soul. . . .

As he stood in the darkness outside the church these memories came back with the poignancy of vanished things. Watching Mattie whirl down the floor from hand to hand he wondered how he could ever have thought that his dull talk interested her. To him, who was never gay but in her presence, her gaiety seemed plain proof of indifference. The face she lifted to her dancers was the same which, when she saw him, always looked like a window that has caught the sunset. He even noticed two or three gestures which, in his fatuity, he had thought she kept for him: a way of throwing her head back

---

*Orion: constellation of stars east of the constellation Taurus on the equator; Aldebaran: red star of the first magnitude in Taurus; the Pleiades: cluster of stars in Taurus.

when she was amused, as if to taste her laugh before she let it out, and a trick of sinking her lids slowly when anything charmed or moved her.

The sight made him unhappy, and his unhappiness roused his latent fears. His wife had never shown any jealousy of Mattie, but of late she had grumbled increasingly over the house-work and found oblique ways of attracting attention to the girl's inefficiency. Zeena had always been what Starkfield called "sickly," and Frome had to admit that, if she were as ailing as she believed, she needed the help of a stronger arm than the one which lay so lightly in his during the night walks to the farm. Mattie had no natural turn for house-keeping, and her training had done nothing to remedy the defect. She was quick to learn, but forgetful and dreamy, and not disposed to take the matter seriously. Ethan had an idea that if she were to marry a man she was fond of the dormant instinct would wake, and her pies and biscuits become the pride of the county; but domesticity in the abstract did not interest her. At first she was so awkward that he could not help laughing at her; but she laughed with him and that made them better friends. He did his best to supplement her unskilled efforts, getting up earlier than usual to light the kitchen fire, carrying in the wood overnight, and neglecting the mill for the farm that he might help her about the house during the day. He even crept down on Saturday nights to scrub the kitchen floor after the women had gone to bed; and Zeena, one day, had surprised him at the churn and had turned away silently, with one of her queer looks.

Of late there had been other signs of her disfavour, as intangible but more disquieting. One cold winter morning, as he dressed in the dark, his candle flickering in the draught of the ill-fitting window, he had heard her speak from the bed behind him.

"The doctor don't want I should be left without anybody to do for me," she said in her flat whine.

He had supposed her to be asleep, and the sound of her voice had startled him, though she was given to abrupt explosions of speech after long intervals of secretive silence.

He turned and looked at her where she lay indistinctly outlined under the dark calico quilt, her high-boned face taking a grayish tinge from the whiteness of the pillow.

"Nobody to do for you?" he repeated.

"If you say you can't afford a hired girl when Mattie goes."

Frome turned away again, and taking up his razor stooped to catch the reflection of his stretched cheek in the blotched looking-glass above the wash-stand.

"Why on earth should Mattie go?"

"Well, when she gets married, I mean," his wife's drawl came from behind him.

"Oh, she'd never leave us as long as you needed her," he returned, scraping hard at his chin.

"I wouldn't ever have it said that I stood in the way of a poor girl like Mattie marrying a smart fellow like Denis Eady," Zeena answered in a tone of plaintive self-effacement.

Ethan, glaring at his face in the glass, threw his head back to draw the razor from ear to chin. His hand was steady, but the attitude was an excuse for not making an immediate reply.

"And the doctor don't want I should be left without anybody," Zeena continued. "He wanted I should speak to you about a girl he's heard about, that might come——"

Ethan laid down the razor and straightened himself with a laugh.

"Denis Eady! If that's all, I guess there's no such hurry to look round for a girl."

"Well, I'd like to talk to you about it," said Zeena obstinately.

He was getting into his clothes in fumbling haste. "All right. But I haven't got the time now; I'm late as it is," he returned, holding his old silver turnip-watch to the candle.

Zeena, apparently accepting this as final, lay watching him in silence while he pulled his suspenders over his shoulders and jerked his arms into his coat; but as he went toward the door she said, suddenly and incisively: "I guess you're always late, now you shave every morning."

That thrust had frightened him more than any vague insinuations about Denis Eady. It was a fact that since Mattie Silver's coming he had taken to shaving every day; but his wife always seemed to be asleep when he left her side in the winter darkness, and he had stupidly assumed that she would not notice any change in his appearance. Once or twice in the past he had been faintly disquieted by Zenobia's way of letting things happen without seeming to remark them, and then, weeks afterward, in a casual phrase, revealing that she had all along taken her notes and drawn her inferences. Of late, however, there had been no room in his thoughts for such vague apprehensions. Zeena herself, from an oppressive reality, had faded into an insubstantial shade. All his life was lived in the sight and sound of Mattie Silver, and he could no longer conceive of its being otherwise. But now, as he stood outside the church, and saw Mattie spinning down the floor with Denis Eady, a throng of disregarded hints and menaces wove their cloud about his brain. . . .

CHAPTER TWO

As the dancers poured out of the hall Frome, drawing back behind the projecting storm-door, watched the segregation of the grotesquely muffled groups, in which a moving lantern ray now and then lit up a face flushed with food and dancing. The villagers, being afoot, were the first to climb the slope to the main street, while the country neighbours packed themselves more slowly into the sleighs under the shed.

"Ain't you riding, Mattie?" a woman's voice called back from the throng about the shed, and Ethan's heart gave a jump. From where he stood he could not see the persons coming out of the hall till they had advanced a few steps beyond the wooden sides of the storm-door; but through its cracks he heard a clear voice answer: "Mercy no! Not on such a night."

She was there, then, close to him, only a thin board between. In another moment she would step forth into the night, and his eyes, accustomed to the obscurity, would discern her as clearly as though she stood in daylight. A wave of shyness pulled him back into the dark angle of the wall, and he stood there in silence instead of making his presence known to her. It had been one of the wonders of their intercourse that from the first, she, the quicker, finer, more expressive, instead of crushing him by the contrast, had given him something of her own ease and freedom; but now he felt as heavy and loutish as in his student days, when he had tried to "jolly" the Worcester girls at a picnic.

He hung back, and she came out alone and paused within a few yards of him. She was almost the last to leave the hall, and she stood looking uncertainly about her as if wondering why he did not show himself. Then a man's figure approached, coming so close to her that under their formless wrappings they seemed merged in one dim outline.

"Gentleman friend gone back on you? Say, Matt, that's tough! No, I wouldn't be mean enough to tell the other girls. I ain't as low-down as that." (How Frome hated his cheap banter!) "But look a here, ain't it lucky I got the old man's cutter* down there waiting for us?"

Frome heard the girl's voice, gaily incredulous: "What on earth's your father's cutter doin' down there?"

"Why, waiting for me to take a ride. I got the roan colt too. I kinder knew I'd want to take a ride to-night," Eady, in his triumph, tried to put a sentimental note into his bragging voice.

The girl seemed to waver, and Frome saw her twirl the end of her scarf irresolutely about her fingers. Not for the world would he have made a sign to her, though it seemed to him that his life hung on her next gesture.

"Hold on a minute while I unhitch the colt," Denis called to her, springing toward the shed.

She stood perfectly still, looking after him, in an attitude of tranquil expectancy torturing to the hidden watcher. Frome noticed that she no longer turned her head from side to side, as though peering through the night for another figure. She let Denis Eady lead out the horse, climb into the cutter and fling back the bearskin to make room for her at his side; then, with a swift motion of flight, she turned about and darted up the slope toward the front of the church.

"Good-bye! Hope you'll have a lovely ride!" she called back to him over her shoulder.

Denis laughed, and gave the horse a cut that brought him quickly abreast of her retreating figure.

"Come along! Get in quick! It's as slippery as thunder on this turn," he cried, leaning over to reach out a hand to her.

She laughed back at him: "Good-night! I'm not getting in."

By this time they had passed beyond Frome's earshot and he could only follow the shadowy pantomime of their silhouettes as they continued to move along the crest of the slope above him. He saw Eady, after a moment, jump from the cutter and go toward the girl with the reins over one arm. The other he tried to slip through

*Small, one-horse sleigh.

hers; but she eluded him nimbly, and Frome's heart, which had swung out over a black void, trembled back to safety. A moment later he heard the jingle of departing sleigh bells and discerned a figure advancing alone toward the empty expanse of snow before the church.

In the black shade of the Varnum spruces he caught up with her and she turned with a quick "Oh!"

"Think I'd forgotten you, Matt?" he asked with sheepish glee.

She answered seriously: "I thought maybe you couldn't come back for me."

"Couldn't? What on earth could stop me?"

"I knew Zeena wasn't feeling any too good to-day."

"Oh, she's in bed long ago." He paused, a question struggling in him. "Then you meant to walk home all alone?"

"Oh, I ain't afraid!" she laughed.

They stood together in the gloom of the spruces, an empty world glimmering about them wide and grey under the stars. He brought his question out.

"If you thought I hadn't come, why didn't you ride back with Denis Eady?"

"Why, where *were* you? How did you know? I never saw you!"

Her wonder and his laughter ran together like spring rills in a thaw. Ethan had the sense of having done something arch and ingenious. To prolong the effect he groped for a dazzling phrase, and brought out, in a growl of rapture: "Come along."

He slipped an arm through hers, as Eady had done, and fancied it was faintly pressed against her side; but neither of them moved. It was so dark under the spruces that he could barely see the shape of her head beside his shoulder. He longed to stoop his cheek and rub it against her scarf. He would have liked to stand there with her all night in the blackness. She moved forward a step or two and then paused again above the dip of the Corbury road. Its icy slope, scored by innumerable runners, looked like a mirror scratched by travellers at an inn.

"There was a whole lot of them coasting before the moon set," she said.

"Would you like to come in and coast with them some night?" he asked.

"Oh, *would* you, Ethan? It would be lovely!"

"We'll come to-morrow if there's a moon."

She lingered, pressing closer to his side. "Ned Hale and Ruth Varnum came just as *near* running into the big elm at the bottom. We were all sure they were killed." Her shiver ran down his arm. "Wouldn't it have been too awful? They're so happy!"

"Oh, Ned ain't much at steering. I guess I can take you down all right!" he said disdainfully.

He was aware that he was "talking big," like Denis Eady; but his reaction of joy had unsteadied him, and the inflection with which she had said of the engaged couple "They're so happy!" made the words sound as if she had been thinking of herself and him.

"The elm *is* dangerous, though. It ought to be cut down," she insisted.

"Would you be afraid of it, with me?"

"I told you I ain't the kind to be afraid," she tossed back, almost indifferently; and suddenly she began to walk on with a rapid step.

These alterations of mood were the despair and joy of Ethan Frome. The motions of her mind were as incalculable as the flit of a bird in the branches. The fact that he had no right to show his feelings, and thus provoke the expression of hers, made him attach a fantastic importance to every change in her look and tone. Now he thought she understood him, and feared; now he was sure she did not, and despaired. To-night the pressure of accumulated misgivings sent the scale drooping toward despair, and her indifference was the more chilling after the flush of joy into which she had plunged him by dismissing Denis Eady. He mounted School House Hill at her side and walked on in silence till they reached the lane leading to the saw-mill; then the need of some definite assurance grew too strong for him.

"You'd have found me right off if you hadn't gone back to have that last reel with Denis," he brought out awkwardly. He could not pronounce the name without a stiffening of the muscles of his throat.

"Why, Ethan, how could I tell you were there?"

"I suppose what folks say is true," he jerked out at her, instead of answering.

She stopped short, and he felt, in the darkness, that her face was lifted quickly to his. "Why, what do folks say?"

"It's natural enough you should be leaving us," he floundered on, following his thought.

"Is that what they say?" she mocked back at him; then, with a sudden drop of her sweet treble: "You mean that Zeena—ain't suited with me any more?" she faltered.

Their arms had slipped apart and they stood motionless, each seeking to distinguish the other's face.

"I know I ain't anything like as smart as I ought to be," she went on, while he vainly struggled for expression. "There's lots of things a hired girl could do that come awkward to me still—and I haven't got much strength in my arms. But if she'd only tell me I'd try. You know she hardly ever says anything, and sometimes I can see she ain't suited, and yet I don't know why." She turned on him with a sudden flash of indignation. "You'd ought to tell me, Ethan Frome—you'd ought to! Unless *you* want me to go too——"

Unless he wanted her to go too! The cry was balm to his raw wound. The iron heavens seemed to melt and rain down sweetness. Again he struggled for the all-expressive word, and again, his arm in hers, found only a deep "Come along."

They walked on in silence through the blackness of the hemlock-shaded lane, where Ethan's saw-mill gloomed through the night, and out again into the comparative clearness of the fields. On the farther side of the hemlock belt the open country rolled away before them grey and lonely under the stars. Sometimes their way led them under the shade of an overhanging bank or through the thin obscurity of a clump of leafless trees. Here and there a farm-house stood far back among the fields, mute and cold as a grave-stone. The night was so still that they heard the frozen snow crackle under their feet. The crash of a loaded branch falling far off in the woods reverberated like a musket-shot, and once a fox barked, and Mattie shrank closer to Ethan, and quickened her steps.

At length they sighted the group of larches at Ethan's gate, and as they drew near it the sense that the walk was over brought back his words.

"Then you don't want to leave us, Matt?"

He had to stoop his head to catch her stifled whisper: "Where'd I go, if I did?"

The answer sent a pang through him but the tone suffused him with joy. He forgot what else he had meant to say and pressed her against him so closely that he seemed to feel her warmth in his veins.

"You ain't crying are you, Matt?"

"No, of course I'm not," she quavered.

They turned in at the gate and passed under the shaded knoll where, enclosed in a low fence, the Frome grave-stones slanted at crazy angles through the snow. Ethan looked at them curiously. For years that quiet company had mocked his restlessness, his desire for change and freedom. "We never got away—how should you?" seemed to be written on every headstone; and whenever he went in or out of his gate he thought with a shiver: "I shall just go on living here till I join them." But now all desire for change had vanished, and the sight of the little enclosure gave him a warm sense of continuance and stability.

"I guess we'll never let you go, Matt," he whispered, as though even the dead, lovers once, must conspire with him to keep her; and brushing by the graves, he thought: "We'll always go on living here together, and some day she'll lie there beside me."

He let the vision possess him as they climbed the hill to the house. He was never so happy with her as when he abandoned himself to these dreams. Half-way up the slope Mattie stumbled against some unseen obstruction and clutched his sleeve to steady herself. The wave of warmth that went through him was like the prolongation of his vision. For the first time he stole his arm about her, and she did not resist. They walked on as if they were floating on a summer stream.

Zeena always went to bed as soon as she had had her supper, and the shutterless windows of the house were dark. A dead cucumber-vine dangled from the porch like the crape streamer tied to the door for a death, and the thought flashed through Ethan's brain: "If it was there for Zeena—" Then he had a distinct sight of his wife lying in their bedroom asleep, her mouth slightly open, her false teeth in a tumbler by the bed . . .

They walked around to the back of the house, between the rigid gooseberry bushes. It was Zeena's habit, when they came back late from the village, to leave the key of the kitchen door under the mat. Ethan stood before the door, his head heavy with dreams, his arm still about Mattie. "Matt—" he began, not knowing what he meant to say.

She slipped out of his hold without speaking, and he stooped down and felt for the key.

"It's not there!" he said, straightening himself with a start.

They strained their eyes at each other through the icy darkness. Such a thing had never happened before.

"Maybe she's forgotten it," Mattie said in a tremulous whisper; but both of them knew that it was not like Zeena to forget.

"It might have fallen off into the snow," Mattie continued, after a pause during which they had stood intently listening.

"It must have been pushed off, then," he rejoined in the same tone. Another wild thought tore through him. What if tramps had been there—what if . . .

Again he listened, fancying he heard a distant sound in the house; then he felt in his pocket for a match, and kneeling down, passed its light slowly over the rough edges of snow about the doorstep.

He was still kneeling when his eyes, on a level with the lower panel of the door, caught a faint ray beneath it. Who could be stirring in that silent house? He heard a step on the stairs, and again for an instant the thought of tramps tore through him. Then the door opened and he saw his wife.

Against the dark background of the kitchen she stood up tall and angular, one hand drawing a quilted counterpane to her flat breast, while the other held a lamp. The light, on a level with her chin, drew out of the darkness her puckered throat and the projecting wrist of the hand that clutched the quilt, and deepened fantastically the hollows and prominences of her high-boned face under its ring of crimping-pins. To Ethan, still in the rosy haze of his hour with Mattie, the sight came with the intense precision of the last dream before waking. He felt as if he had never before known what his wife looked like.

She drew aside without speaking, and Mattie and Ethan passed into the kitchen, which had the deadly chill of a vault after the dry cold of the night.

"Guess you forgot about us, Zeena," Ethan joked, stamping the snow from his boots.

"No. I just felt so mean I couldn't sleep."

Mattie came forward, unwinding her wraps, the colour of the

cherry scarf in her fresh lips and cheeks. "I'm so sorry, Zeena! Isn't there anything I can do?"

"No; there's nothing." Zeena turned away from her. "You might 'a' shook off that snow outside," she said to her husband.

She walked out of the kitchen ahead of them and pausing in the hall raised the lamp at arm's-length, as if to light them up the stairs.

Ethan paused also, affecting to fumble for the peg on which he hung his coat and cap. The doors of the two bedrooms faced each other across the narrow upper landing, and to-night it was peculiarly repugnant to him that Mattie should see him follow Zeena.

"I guess I won't come up yet awhile," he said, turning as if to go back to the kitchen.

Zeena stopped short and looked at him. "For the land's sake—what you going to do down here?"

"I've got the mill accounts to go over."

She continued to stare at him, the flame of the unshaded lamp bringing out with microscopic cruelty the fretful lines of her face.

"At this time o' night? You'll ketch your death. The fire's out long ago."

Without answering he moved away toward the kitchen. As he did so his glance crossed Mattie's and he fancied that a fugitive warning gleamed through her lashes. The next moment they sank to her flushed cheeks and she began to mount the stairs ahead of Zeena.

"That's so. It *is* powerful cold down here," Ethan assented; and with lowered head he went up in his wife's wake, and followed her across the threshold of their room.

CHAPTER THREE

THERE WAS SOME HAULING to be done at the lower end of the wood-lot, and Ethan was out early the next day.

The winter morning was as clear as crystal. The sunrise burned red in a pure sky, the shadows on the rim of the wood-lot were darkly blue, and beyond the white and scintillating fields patches of far-off forest hung like smoke.

It was in the early morning stillness, when his muscles were swinging to their familiar task and his lungs expanding with long draughts of mountain air, that Ethan did his clearest thinking. He and Zeena had not exchanged a word after the door of their room had closed on them. She had measured out some drops from a medicine-bottle on a chair by the bed and, after swallowing them, and wrapping her head in a piece of yellow flannel, had lain down with her face turned away. Ethan undressed hurriedly and blew out the light so that he should not see her when he took his place at her side. As he lay there he could hear Mattie moving about in her room, and her candle, sending its small ray across the landing, drew a scarcely perceptible line of light under his door. He kept his eyes fixed on the light till it vanished. Then the room grew perfectly black, and not a sound was audible but Zeena's asthmatic breathing. Ethan felt confusedly that there were many things he ought to think about, but through his tingling veins and tired brain only one sensation throbbed: the warmth of Mattie's shoulder against his. Why had he not kissed her when he held her there? A few hours earlier he would not have asked himself the question. Even a few minutes earlier, when they had stood alone outside the house, he would not have dared to think of kissing her. But since he had seen her lips in the lamplight he felt that they were his.

Now, in the bright morning air, her face was still before him.

It was part of the sun's red and of the pure glitter on the snow. How the girl had changed since she had come to Starkfield! He remembered what a colourless slip of a thing she had looked the day he had met her at the station. And all the first winter, how she had shivered with cold when the northerly gales shook the thin clapboards and the snow beat like hail against the loose-hung windows!

He had been afraid that she would hate the hard life, the cold and loneliness; but not a sign of discontent escaped her. Zeena took the view that Mattie was bound to make the best of Starkfield since she hadn't any other place to go to; but this did not strike Ethan as conclusive. Zeena, at any rate, did not apply the principle in her own case.

He felt all the more sorry for the girl because misfortune had, in a sense, indentured her to them. Mattie Silver was the daughter of a cousin of Zenobia Frome's, who had inflamed his clan with mingled sentiments of envy and admiration by descending from the hills to Connecticut, where he had married a Stamford girl and succeeded to her father's thriving "drug" business. Unhappily Orin Silver, a man of far-reaching aims, had died too soon to prove that the end justifies the means. His accounts revealed merely what the means had been; and these were such that it was fortunate for his wife and daughter that his books were examined only after his impressive funeral. His wife died of the disclosure, and Mattie, at twenty, was left alone to make her way on the fifty dollars obtained from the sale of her piano. For this purpose her equipment, though varied, was inadequate. She could trim a hat, make molasses candy, recite "Curfew shall not ring to-night," and play "The Lost Chord"[7] and a pot-pourri from "Carmen." When she tried to extend the field of her activities in the direction of stenography and book-keeping her health broke down, and six months on her feet behind the counter of a department store did not tend to restore it. Her nearest relations had been induced to place their savings in her father's hands, and though, after his death, they ungrudgingly acquitted themselves of the Christian duty of returning good for evil by giving his daughter all the advice at their disposal, they could hardly be expected to supplement it by material aid. But when Zenobia's doctor recommended her looking about for some one to help her with the house-work the clan instantly saw the chance of exacting a compensation from

Mattie. Zenobia, though doubtful of the girl's efficiency, was tempted by the freedom to find fault without much risk of losing her; and so Mattie came to Starkfield.

Zenobia's fault-finding was of the silent kind, but not the less penetrating for that. During the first months Ethan alternately burned with the desire to see Mattie defy her and trembled with fear of the result. Then the situation grew less strained. The pure air, and the long summer hours in the open, gave back life and elasticity to Mattie, and Zeena, with more leisure to devote to her complex ailments, grew less watchful of the girl's omissions; so that Ethan, struggling on under the burden of his barren farm and failing saw-mill, could at least imagine that peace reigned in his house.

There was really, even now, no tangible evidence to the contrary; but since the previous night a vague dread had hung on his sky-line. It was formed of Zeena's obstinate silence, of Mattie's sudden look of warning, of the memory of just such fleeting imperceptible signs as those which told him, on certain stainless mornings, that before night there would be rain.

His dread was so strong that, man-like, he sought to postpone certainty. The hauling was not over till mid-day, and as the lumber was to be delivered to Andrew Hale, the Starkfield builder, it was really easier for Ethan to send Jotham Powell,[8] the hired man, back to the farm on foot, and drive the load down to the village himself. He had scrambled up on the logs,[9] and was sitting astride of them, close over his shaggy grays, when, coming between him and their streaming necks, he had a vision of the warning look that Mattie had given him the night before.

"If there's going to be any trouble I want to be there," was his vague reflection, as he threw to Jotham the unexpected order to unhitch the team and lead them back to the barn.

It was a slow trudge home through the heavy fields, and when the two men entered the kitchen Mattie was lifting the coffee from the stove and Zeena was already at the table. Her husband stopped short at sight of her. Instead of her usual calico wrapper and knitted shawl she wore her best dress of brown merino, and above her thin strands of hair, which still preserved the tight undulations of the crimping-pins, rose a hard perpendicular bonnet, as to which Ethan's clearest notion was that he had to pay five dollars for it at the Bettsbridge

Emporium. On the floor beside her stood his old valise and a bandbox wrapped in newspapers.

"Why, where are you going, Zeena?" he exclaimed.

"I've got my shooting pains so bad that I'm going over to Bettsbridge to spend the night with Aunt Martha Pierce and see that new doctor," she answered in a matter-of-fact tone, as if she had said she was going into the store-room to take a look at the preserves, or up to the attic to go over the blankets.

In spite of her sedentary habits such abrupt decisions were not without precedent in Zeena's history. Twice or thrice before she had suddenly packed Ethan's valise and started off to Bettsbridge, or even Springfield, to seek the advice of some new doctor, and her husband had grown to dread these expeditions because of their cost. Zeena always came back laden with expensive remedies, and her last visit to Springfield* had been commemorated by her paying twenty dollars for an electric battery of which she had never been able to learn the use. But for the moment his sense of relief was so great as to preclude all other feelings. He had now no doubt that Zeena had spoken the truth in saying, the night before, that she had sat up because she felt "too mean" to sleep: her abrupt resolve to seek medical advice showed that, as usual, she was wholly absorbed in her health.

As if expecting a protest, she continued plaintively; "If you're too busy with the hauling I presume you can let Jotham Powell drive me over with the sorrel in time to ketch the train at the Flats."

Her husband hardly heard what she was saying. During the winter months there was no stage between Starkfield and Bettsbridge, and the trains which stopped at Corbury Flats were slow and infrequent. A rapid calculation showed Ethan that Zeena could not be back at the farm before the following evening. . . .

"If I'd supposed you'd 'a' made any objection to Jotham Powell's driving me over—" she began again, as though his silence had implied refusal. On the brink of departure she was always seized with a flux of words. "All I know is," she continued, "I can't go on the way I am much longer. The pains are clear away down to my ankles now, or I'd 'a' walked in to Starkfield on my own feet, sooner'n put

---

*City in western Massachusetts, located in the Connecticut River Valley at the hub of regional routes between New York and Boston.

you out, and asked Michael Eady to let me ride over on his wagon to the Flats, when he sends to meet the train that brings his groceries. I'd 'a' had two hours to wait in the station, but I'd sooner 'a' done it, even with this cold, than to have you say——"

"Of course Jotham'll drive you over," Ethan roused himself to answer. He became suddenly conscious that he was looking at Mattie while Zeena talked to him, and with an effort he turned his eyes to his wife. She sat opposite the window, and the pale light reflected from the banks of snow made her face look more than usually drawn and bloodless, sharpened the three parallel creases between ear and cheek, and drew querulous lines from her thin nose to the corners of her mouth. Though she was but seven years her husband's senior, and he was only twenty-eight, she was already an old woman.

Ethan tried to say something befitting the occasion, but there was only one thought in his mind: the fact that, for the first time since Mattie had come to live with them, Zeena was to be away for a night. He wondered if the girl were thinking of it too. . . .

He knew that Zeena must be wondering why he did not offer to drive her to the Flats and let Jotham Powell take the lumber to Starkfield, and at first he could not think of a pretext for not doing so; then he said: "I'd take you over myself, only I've got to collect the cash for the lumber."

As soon as the words were spoken he regretted them, not only because they were untrue—there being no prospect of his receiving cash payment from Hale—but also because he knew from experience the imprudence of letting Zeena think he was in funds on the eve of one of her therapeutic excursions. At the moment, however, his one desire was to avoid the long drive with her behind the ancient sorrel who never went out of a walk.

Zeena made no reply: she did not seem to hear what he had said. She had already pushed her plate aside, and was measuring out a draught from a large bottle at her elbow.

"It ain't done me a speck of good, but I guess I might as well use it up," she remarked; adding, as she pushed the empty bottle toward Mattie: "If you can get the taste out it'll do for pickles."

CHAPTER FOUR

As soon as his wife had driven off Ethan took his coat and cap from the peg. Mattie was washing up the dishes, humming one of the dance tunes of the night before. He said "So long, Matt," and she answered gaily "So long, Ethan"; and that was all.

It was warm and bright in the kitchen. The sun slanted through the south window on the girl's moving figure, on the cat dozing in a chair, and on the geraniums brought in from the door-way, where Ethan had planted them in the summer to "make a garden" for Mattie. He would have liked to linger on, watching her tidy up and then settle down to her sewing; but he wanted still more to get the hauling done and be back at the farm before night.

All the way down to the village he continued to think of his return to Mattie. The kitchen was a poor place, not "spruce" and shining as his mother had kept it in his boyhood; but it was surprising what a homelike look the mere fact of Zeena's absence gave it. And he pictured what it would be like that evening, when he and Mattie were there after supper. For the first time they would be alone together indoors, and they would sit there, one on each side of the stove, like a married couple, he in his stocking feet and smoking his pipe, she laughing and talking in that funny way she had, which was always as new to him as if he had never heard her before.

The sweetness of the picture, and the relief of knowing that his fears of "trouble" with Zeena were unfounded, sent up his spirits with a rush, and he, who was usually so silent, whistled and sang aloud as he drove through the snowy fields. There was in him a slumbering spark of sociability which the long Starkfield winters had not yet extinguished. By nature grave and inarticulate, he admired recklessness and gaiety in others and was warmed to the marrow by friendly human intercourse. At Worcester, though he had the name of keeping to himself and not being much of a hand at a good time, he had secretly gloried in being clapped on the back and hailed as "Old Ethe" or "Old Stiff"; and the cessation of such familiarities had increased the chill of his return to Starkfield.

There the silence had deepened about him year by year. Left alone, after his father's accident, to carry the burden of farm and mill, he had had no time for convivial loiterings in the village; and when his mother fell ill the loneliness of the house grew more oppressive than that of the fields. His mother had been a talker in her day, but after her "trouble" the sound of her voice was seldom heard, though she had not lost the power of speech. Sometimes, in the long winter evenings, when in desperation her son asked her why she didn't "say something," she would lift a finger and answer: "Because I'm listening"; and on stormy nights, when the loud wind was about the house, she would complain, if he spoke to her: "They're talking so out there that I can't hear you."

It was only when she drew toward her last illness, and his cousin Zenobia Pierce came over from the next valley to help him nurse her, that human speech was heard again in the house. After the mortal silence of his long imprisonment Zeena's volubility was music in his ears. He felt that he might have "gone like his mother" if the sound of a new voice had not come to steady him. Zeena seemed to understand his case at a glance. She laughed at him for not knowing the simplest sick-bed duties and told him to "go right along out" and leave her to see to things. The mere fact of obeying her orders, of feeling free to go about his business again and talk with other men, restored his shaken balance and magnified his sense of what he owed her. Her efficiency shamed and dazzled him. She seemed to possess by instinct all the household wisdom that his long apprenticeship had not instilled in him. When the end came it was she who had to tell him to hitch up and go for the undertaker, and she thought it "funny" that he had not settled beforehand who was to have his mother's clothes and the sewing-machine. After the funeral, when he saw her preparing to go away, he was seized with an unreasoning dread of being left alone on the farm; and before he knew what he was doing he had asked her to stay there with him. He had often thought since that it would not have happened if his mother had died in spring instead of winter . . .

When they married it was agreed that, as soon as he could

straighten out the difficulties resulting from Mrs. Frome's long illness, they would sell the farm and saw-mill and try their luck in a large town. Ethan's love of nature did not take the form of a taste for agriculture. He had always wanted to be an engineer, and to live in towns, where there were lectures and big libraries and "fellows doing things." A slight engineering job in Florida, put in his way during his period of study at Worcester,[10] increased his faith in his ability as well as his eagerness to see the world; and he felt sure that, with a "smart" wife like Zeena, it would not be long before he had made himself a place in it.

Zeena's native village was slightly larger and nearer to the railway than Starkfield, and she had let her husband see from the first that life on an isolated farm was not what she had expected when she married. But purchasers were slow in coming, and while he waited for them Ethan learned the impossibility of transplanting her. She chose to look down on Starkfield, but she could not have lived in a place which looked down on her. Even Bettsbridge or Shadd's Falls would not have been sufficiently aware of her, and in the greater cities which attracted Ethan she would have suffered a complete loss of identity. And within a year of their marriage she developed the "sickliness" which had since made her notable even in a community rich in pathological instances. When she came to take care of his mother she had seemed to Ethan like the very genius of health, but he soon saw that her skill as a nurse had been acquired by the absorbed observation of her own symptoms.

Then she too fell silent. Perhaps it was the inevitable effect of life on the farm, or perhaps, as she sometimes said, it was because Ethan "never listened." The charge was not wholly unfounded. When she spoke it was only to complain, and to complain of things not in his power to remedy; and to check a tendency to impatient retort he had first formed the habit of not answering her, and finally of thinking of other things while she talked. Of late, however, since he had had reasons for observing her more closely, her silence had begun to trouble him. He recalled his mother's growing taciturnity, and wondered if Zeena were also turning "queer." Women did, he knew. Zeena, who had at her fingers' ends the pathological chart of the whole region, had cited many cases of the kind while she was nursing his mother; and he himself knew of certain lonely farm-houses in the neighbourhood where stricken creatures pined, and of others where sudden tragedy had come of their presence. At times, looking at Zeena's shut face, he felt the chill of such forebodings. At other times her silence seemed deliberately assumed to conceal far-reaching intentions, mysterious conclusions drawn from suspicions and resentments impossible to guess. That supposition was even more disturbing than the other; and it was the one which had come to him the night before, when he had seen her standing in the kitchen door.

Now her departure for Bettsbridge had once more eased his mind, and all his thoughts were on the prospect of his evening with Mattie. Only one thing weighed on him, and that was his having told Zeena that he was to receive cash for the lumber. He foresaw so clearly the consequences of this imprudence that with considerable reluctance he decided to ask Andrew Hale for a small advance on his load.

When Ethan drove into Hale's yard the builder was just getting out of his sleigh.

"Hello, Ethe!" he said. "This comes handy."

Andrew Hale was a ruddy man with a big grey moustache and a stubbly double-chin unconstrained by a collar; but his scrupulously clean shirt was always fastened by a small diamond stud. This display of opulence was misleading, for though he did a fairly good business it was known that his easygoing habits and the demands of his large family frequently kept him what Starkfield called "behind." He was an old friend of Ethan's family, and his house one of the few to which Zeena occasionally went, drawn there by the fact that Mrs. Hale, in her youth, had done more "doctoring" than any other woman in Starkfield, and was still a recognised authority on symptoms and treatment.

Hale went up to the greys and patted their sweating flanks.

"Well, sir," he said, "you keep them two as if they was pets."

Ethan set about unloading the logs and when he had finished his job he pushed open the glazed door of the shed which the builder used as his office. Hale sat with his feet up on the stove, his back propped against a battered desk strewn with papers: the place, like the man, was warm, genial and untidy.

"Sit right down and thaw out," he greeted Ethan.

The latter did not know how to begin, but at length he managed to bring out his request for an advance of fifty dollars. The blood rushed to his thin skin under the sting of Hale's astonishment. It was the builder's custom to pay at the end of three months, and there was no precedent between the two men for a cash settlement.

Ethan felt that if he had pleaded an urgent need Hale might have made shift to pay him; but pride, and an instinctive prudence, kept him from resorting to this argument. After his father's death it had taken time to get his head above water, and he did not want Andrew Hale, or any one else in Starkfield, to think he was going under again. Besides, he hated lying; if he wanted the money he wanted it, and it was nobody's business to ask why. He therefore made his demand with the awkwardness of a proud man who will not admit to himself that he is stooping; and he was not much surprised at Hale's refusal.

The builder refused genially, as he did everything else: he treated the matter as something in the nature of a practical joke, and wanted to know if Ethan meditated buying a grand piano or adding a "cupolo" to his house; offering, in the latter case, to give his services free of cost.

Ethan's arts were soon exhausted, and after an embarrassed pause he wished Hale good day and opened the door of the office. As he passed out the builder suddenly called after him: "See here—you ain't in a tight place, are you?"

"Not a bit," Ethan's pride retorted before his reason had time to intervene.

"Well, that's good! Because I *am,* a shade. Fact is, I was going to ask you to give me a little extra time on that payment. Business is pretty slack, to begin with, and then I'm fixing up a little house for Ned and Ruth when they're married. I'm glad to do it for 'em, but it costs." His look appealed to Ethan for sympathy. "The young people like things nice. You know how it is yourself: it's not so long ago since you fixed up your own place for Zeena."

Ethan left the greys in Hale's stable and went about some other business in the village. As he walked away the builder's last phrase lingered in his ears, and he reflected grimly that his seven years with Zeena seemed to Starkfield "not so long."

The afternoon was drawing to an end, and here and there a lighted pane spangled the cold grey dusk and made the snow look whiter. The bitter weather had driven every one indoors and Ethan had the long rural street to himself. Suddenly he heard the brisk play of sleigh-bells and a cutter passed him, drawn by a free-going horse. Ethan recognised Michael Eady's roan colt, and young Denis Eady, in a handsome new fur cap, leaned forward and waved a greeting. "Hello, Ethe!" he shouted and spun on.

The cutter was going in the direction of the Frome farm, and Ethan's heart contracted as he listened to the dwindling bells. What more likely than that Denis Eady had heard of Zeena's departure for Bettsbridge, and was profiting by the opportunity to spend an hour with Mattie? Ethan was ashamed of the storm of jealousy in his breast. It seemed unworthy of the girl that his thoughts of her should be so violent.

He walked on to the church corner and entered the shade of the Varnum spruces, where he had stood with her the night before. As he passed into their gloom he saw an indistinct outline just ahead of him. At his approach it melted for an instant into two separate shapes and then conjoined again, and he heard a kiss, and a half-laughing "Oh!" provoked by the discovery of his presence. Again the outline hastily disunited and the Varnum gate slammed on one half while the other hurried on ahead of him. Ethan smiled at the discomfiture he had caused. What did it matter to Ned Hale and Ruth Varnum if they were caught kissing each other? Everybody in Starkfield knew they were engaged. It pleased Ethan to have surprised a pair of lovers on the spot where he and Mattie had stood with such a thirst for each other in their hearts; but he felt a pang at the thought that these two need not hide their happiness.

He fetched the grays from Hale's stable and started on his long climb back to the farm. The cold was less sharp than earlier in the day and a thick fleecy sky threatened snow for the morrow. Here and there a star pricked through, showing behind it a deep well of blue. In an hour or two the moon would push over the ridge behind the farm, burn a gold-edged rent in the clouds, and then be swallowed by them. A mournful peace hung on the fields, as though they felt the relaxing grasp of the cold and stretched themselves in their long winter sleep.

Ethan's ears were alert for the jingle of sleigh-bells, but not a sound broke the silence of the lonely road. As he drew near the farm he saw, through the thin screen of larches at the gate, a light twinkling in the house above him. "She's up in her room," he said to himself, "fixing herself up for supper"; and he remembered Zeena's sarcastic stare when Mattie, on the evening of her arrival, had come down to supper with smoothed hair and a ribbon at her neck.

He passed by the graves on the knoll and turned his head to glance at one of the older headstones, which had interested him deeply as a boy because it bore his name.

SACRED TO THE MEMORY OF
ETHAN FROME AND ENDURANCE HIS WIFE,[11]
WHO DWELLED TOGETHER IN PEACE
FOR FIFTY YEARS.

He used to think that fifty years sounded like a long time to live together, but now it seemed to him that they might pass in a flash. Then, with a sudden dart of irony, he wondered if, when their turn came, the same epitaph would be written over him and Zeena.

He opened the barn-door and craned his head into the obscurity, half-fearing to discover Denis Eady's roan colt in the stall beside the sorrel. But the old horse was there alone, mumbling his crib with toothless jaws, and Ethan whistled cheerfully while he bedded down the greys and shook an extra measure of oats into their mangers. His was not a tuneful throat, but harsh melodies burst from it as he locked the barn and sprang up the hill to the house. He reached the kitchen-porch and turned the door-handle; but the door did not yield to his touch.

Startled at finding it locked he rattled the handle violently; then he reflected that Mattie was alone and that it was natural she should barricade herself at nightfall. He stood in the darkness expecting to hear her step. It did not come, and after vainly straining his ears he called out in a voice that shook with joy: "Hello, Matt!"

Silence answered; but in a minute or two he caught a sound on the stairs and saw a line of light about the door-frame, as he had seen it the night before. So strange was the precision with which the incidents of the previous evening were repeating themselves that he half expected, when he heard the key turn, to see his wife before him on the threshold; but the door opened, and Mattie faced him.

She stood just as Zeena had stood, a lifted lamp in her hand, against the black background of the kitchen. She held the light at the same level, and it drew out with the same distinctness her slim young throat and the brown wrist no bigger than a child's. Then, striking upward, it threw a lustrous fleck on her lips, edged her eyes with velvet shade, and laid a milky whiteness above the black curve of her brows.

She wore her usual dress of darkish stuff, and there was no bow at her neck; but through her hair she had run a streak of crimson ribbon. This tribute to the unusual transformed and glorified her. She seemed to Ethan taller, fuller, more womanly in shape and motion. She stood aside, smiling silently, while he entered, and then moved away from him with something soft and flowing in her gait. She set the lamp on the table, and he saw that it was carefully laid for supper, with fresh dough-nuts, stewed blueberries and his favourite pickles in a dish of gay red glass. A bright fire glowed in the stove and the cat lay stretched before it, watching the table with a drowsy eye.

Ethan was suffocated with the sense of well-being. He went out into the passage to hang up his coat and pull off his wet boots. When he came back Mattie had set the teapot on the table and the cat was rubbing itself persuasively against her ankles.

"Why, Puss! I nearly tripped over you," she cried, the laughter sparkling through her lashes.

Again Ethan felt a sudden twinge of jealousy. Could it be his coming that gave her such a kindled face?

"Well, Matt, any visitors?" he threw off, stooping down carelessly to examine the fastening of the stove.

She nodded and laughed "Yes, one," and he felt a blackness settling on his brows.

"Who was that?" he questioned, raising himself up to slant a glance at her beneath his scowl.

Her eyes danced with malice. "Why, Jotham Powell. He came in after he got back, and asked for a drop of coffee before he went down home."

The blackness lifted and light flooded Ethan's brain. "That all? Well, I hope you made out to let him have it." And after a pause he felt it right to add: "I suppose he got Zeena over to the Flats all right?"

"Oh, yes; in plenty of time."

The name threw a chill between them, and they stood a moment looking sideways at each other before Mattie said with a shy laugh. "I guess it's about time for supper."

They drew their seats up to the table, and the cat, unbidden, jumped between them into Zeena's empty chair. "Oh, Puss!" said Mattie, and they laughed again.

Ethan, a moment earlier, had felt himself on the brink of eloquence; but the mention of Zeena had paralysed him. Mattie seemed to feel the contagion of his embarrassment, and sat with downcast lids, sipping her tea, while he feigned an insatiable appetite for dough-nuts and sweet pickles. At last, after casting about for an effective opening, he took a long gulp of tea, cleared his throat, and said: "Looks as if there'd be more snow."

She feigned great interest. "Is that so? Do you suppose it'll interfere with Zeena's getting back?" She flushed red as the question escaped her, and hastily set down the cup she was lifting.

Ethan reached over for another helping of pickles. "You never can tell, this time of year, it drifts so bad on the Flats." The name had benumbed him again, and once more he felt as if Zeena were in the room between them.

"Oh, Puss, you're too greedy! " Mattie cried.

The cat, unnoticed, had crept up on muffled paws from Zeena's seat to the table, and was stealthily elongating its body in the direction of the milk-jug, which stood between Ethan and Mattie. The two leaned forward at the same moment and their hands met on the handle of the jug. Mattie's hand was underneath, and Ethan kept his clasped on it a moment longer than was necessary. The cat, profiting by this unusual demonstration, tried to effect an unnoticed retreat, and in doing so backed into the pickle-dish, which fell to the floor with a crash.

Mattie, in an instant, had sprung from her chair and was down on her knees by the fragments.

"Oh, Ethan, Ethan—it's all to pieces! What will Zeena say?"

But this time his courage was up. "Well, she'll have to say it to the cat, any way!" he rejoined with a laugh, kneeling down at Mattie's side to scrape up the swimming pickles.

She lifted stricken eyes to him. “Yes, but, yo meant it should be used, not even when there wa had to get up on the step-ladder to reach it down of the china-closet, where she keeps it with all her best thi of course she'll want to know why I did it——”

The case was so serious that it called forth all of Ethan's latent resolution.

“She needn't know anything about it if you keep quiet. I'll get another just like it to-morrow. Where did it come from? I'll go to Shadd's Falls for it if I have to!”

“Oh, you'll never get another even there! It was a wedding present—don't you remember? It came all the way from Philadelphia, from Zeena's aunt that married the minister. That's why she wouldn't ever use it. Oh, Ethan, Ethan, what in the world shall I do?”

She began to cry, and he felt as if every one of her tears were pouring over him like burning lead. “Don't, Matt, don't—oh, *don't!*” he implored her.

She struggled to her feet, and he rose and followed her helplessly while she spread out the pieces of glass on the kitchen dresser. It seemed to him as if the shattered fragments of their evening lay there.

“Here, give them to me,” he said in a voice of sudden authority.

She drew aside, instinctively obeying his tone. “Oh, Ethan, what are you going to do?”

Without replying he gathered the pieces of glass into his broad palm and walked out of the kitchen to the passage. There he lit a candle-end, opened the china-closet, and, reaching his long arm up to the highest shelf, laid the pieces together with such accuracy of touch that a close inspection convinced him of the impossibility of detecting from below that the dish was broken. If he glued it together the next morning months might elapse before his wife noticed what had happened, and meanwhile he might after all be able to match the dish at Shadd's Falls or Bettsbridge. Having satisfied himself that there was no risk of immediate discovery he went back to the kitchen with a lighter step, and found Mattie disconsolately removing the last scraps of pickle from the floor.

“It's all right, Matt. Come back and finish supper,” he commanded her.

Completely reassured, she shone on him through tear-hung lashes, and his soul swelled with pride as he saw how his tone subdued her. She did not even ask what he had done. Except when he was steering a big log down the mountain to his mill he had never known such a thrilling sense of mastery.

CHAPTER FIVE

THEY FINISHED SUPPER, AND while Mattie cleared the table Ethan went to look at the cows and then took a last turn about the house. The earth lay dark under a muffled sky and the air was so still that now and then he heard a lump of snow come thumping down from a tree far off on the edge of the wood-lot.

When he returned to the kitchen Mattie had pushed up his chair to the stove and seated herself near the lamp with a bit of sewing. The scene was just as he had dreamed of it that morning. He sat down, drew his pipe from his pocket and stretched his feet to the glow. His hard day's work in the keen air made him feel at once lazy and light of mood, and he had a confused sense of being in another world, where all was warmth and harmony and time could bring no change. The only drawback to his complete well-being was the fact that he could not see Mattie from where he sat; but he was too indolent to move and after a moment he said: "Come over here and sit by the stove."

Zeena's empty rocking-chair stood facing him. Mattie rose obediently, and seated herself in it. As her young brown head detached itself against the patch-work cushion that habitually framed his wife's gaunt countenance, Ethan had a momentary shock. It was almost as if the other face, the face of the superseded woman, had obliterated that of the intruder. After a moment Mattie seemed to be affected by the same sense of constraint. She changed her position, leaning forward to bend her head above her work, so that he saw only the foreshortened tip of her nose and the streak of red in her hair; then she slipped to her feet, saying "I can't see to sew," and went back to her chair by the lamp.

Ethan made a pretext of getting up to replenish the stove, and when he returned to his seat he pushed it sideways that he might get a view of her profile and of the lamplight falling on her hands.

The cat, who had been a puzzled observer of these unusual movements, jumped up into Zeena's chair, rolled itself into a ball, and lay watching them with narrowed eyes.

Deep quiet sank on the room. The clock ticked above the dresser, a piece of charred wood fell now and then in the stove, and the faint sharp scent of the geraniums mingled with the odour of Ethan's smoke, which began to throw a blue haze about the lamp and to hang its greyish cobwebs in the shadowy corners of the room.

All constraint had vanished between the two, and they began to talk easily and simply. They spoke of every-day things, of the prospect of snow, of the next church sociable, of the loves and quarrels of Starkfield. The commonplace nature of what they said produced in Ethan an illusion of long-established intimacy which no outburst of emotion could have given, and he set his imagination adrift on the fiction that they had always spent their evenings thus and would always go on doing so . . .

"This is the night we were to have gone coasting, Matt," he said at length, with the rich sense, as he spoke, that they could go on any other night they chose, since they had all time before them.

She smiled back at him. "I guess you forgot!"

"No, I didn't forget; but it's as dark as Egypt outdoors. We might go to-morrow if there's a moon."

She laughed with pleasure, her head tilted back, the lamplight sparkling on her lips and teeth. "That would be lovely, Ethan!"

He kept his eyes fixed on her, marvelling at the way her face changed with each turn of their talk, like a wheat-field under a summer breeze. It was intoxicating to find such magic in his clumsy words, and he longed to try new ways of using it.

"Would you be scared to go down the Corbury road with me on a night like this?" he asked.

Her cheeks burned redder. "I ain't any more scared than you are!"

"Well, *I'd* be scared, then; I wouldn't do it. That's an ugly corner down by the big elm. If a fellow didn't keep his eyes open he'd go plumb into it." He luxuriated in the sense of protection and authority which his words conveyed. To prolong and intensify the feeling he added: "I guess we're well enough here."

She let her lids sink slowly, in the way he loved. "Yes, we're well enough here," she sighed.

Her tone was so sweet that he took the pipe from his mouth and drew his chair up to the table. Leaning forward, he touched the farther end of the strip of brown stuff that she was hemming. "Say, Matt," he began with a smile, "what do you think I saw under the Varnum spruces, coming along home just now? I saw a friend of yours getting kissed."

The words had been on his tongue all the evening, but now that he had spoken them they struck him as inexpressibly vulgar and out of place.

Mattie blushed to the roots of her hair and pulled her needle rapidly twice or thrice through her work, insensibly drawing the end of it away from him. "I suppose it was Ruth and Ned," she said in a low voice, as though he had suddenly touched on something grave.

Ethan had imagined that his allusion might open the way to the accepted pleasantries, and these perhaps in turn to a harmless caress, if only a mere touch on her hand. But now he felt as if her blush had set a flaming guard about her. He supposed it was his natural awkwardness that made him feel so. He knew that most young men made nothing at all of giving a pretty girl a kiss, and he remembered that the night before, when he had put his arm about Mattie, she had not resisted. But that had been out-of-doors, under the open irresponsible night. Now, in the warm lamplit room, with all its ancient implications of conformity and order, she seemed infinitely farther away from him and more unapproachable.

To ease his constraint he said: "I suppose they'll be setting a date before long."

"Yes. I shouldn't wonder if they got married some time along in the summer." She pronounced the word *married* as if her voice caressed it. It seemed a rustling covert leading to enchanted glades. A pang shot through Ethan, and he said, twisting away from her in his chair: "It'll be your turn next, I wouldn't wonder."

She laughed a little uncertainly. "Why do you keep on saying that?"

He echoed her laugh. "I guess I do it to get used to the idea."

He drew up to the table again and she sewed on in silence, with dropped lashes, while he sat in fascinated contemplation of the way in which her hands went up and down above the strip of stuff, just as he had seen a pair of birds make short perpendicular flights over a nest they were building. At length, without turning her head or lifting her lids, she said in a low tone: "It's not because you think Zeena's got anything against me, is it?"

His former dread started up full-armed at the suggestion. "Why, what do you mean?" he stammered.

She raised distressed eyes to his, her work dropping on the table between them. "I don't know. I thought last night she seemed to have."

"I'd like to know what," he growled.

"Nobody can tell with Zeena." It was the first time they had ever spoken so openly of her attitude toward Mattie, and the repetition of the name seemed to carry it to the farther corners of the room and send it back to them in long repercussions of sound. Mattie waited, as if to give the echo time to drop, and then went on: "She hasn't said anything to *you*?"

He shook his head. "No, not a word."

She tossed the hair back from her forehead with a laugh. "I guess I'm just nervous, then. I'm not going to think about it any more."

"Oh, no—don't let's think about it, Matt!"

The sudden heat of his tone made her colour mount again, not with a rush, but gradually, delicately, like the reflection of a thought stealing slowly across her heart. She sat silent, her hands clasped on her work, and it seemed to him that a warm current flowed toward him along the strip of stuff that still lay unrolled between them. Cautiously he slid his hand palm-downward along the table till his finger-tips touched the end of the stuff. A faint vibration of her lashes seemed to show that she was aware of his gesture, and that it had sent a counter-current back to her; and she let her hands lie motionless on the other end of the strip.

As they sat thus he heard a sound behind him and turned his head. The cat had jumped from Zeena's chair to dart at a mouse in the wainscot, and as a result of the sudden movement the empty chair had set up a spectral rocking.

"She'll be rocking in it herself this time to-morrow," Ethan thought. "I've been in a dream, and this is the only evening we'll ever have together." The return to reality was as painful as the return to consciousness after taking an anæsthetic. His body and brain ached with indescribable weariness, and he could think of nothing to say or to do that should arrest the mad flight of the moments.

His alteration of mood seemed to have communicated itself to Mattie. She looked up at him languidly, as though her lids were weighted with sleep and it cost her an effort to raise them. Her glance fell on his hand, which now completely covered the end of her work and grasped it as if it were a part of herself. He saw a scarcely perceptible tremor cross her face, and without knowing what he did he stooped his head and kissed the bit of stuff in his hold. As his lips rested on it he felt it glide slowly from beneath them, and saw that Mattie had risen and was silently rolling up her work. She fastened it with a pin, and then, finding her thimble and scissors, put them with the roll of stuff into the box covered with fancy paper which he had once brought to her from Bettsbridge.

He stood up also, looking vaguely about the room. The clock above the dresser struck eleven.

"Is the fire all right?" she asked in a low voice.

He opened the door of the stove and poked aimlessly at the embers. When he raised himself again he saw that she was dragging toward the stove the old soap-box lined with carpet in which the cat made its bed. Then she recrossed the floor and lifted two of the geranium pots in her arms, moving them away from the cold window. He followed her and brought the other geraniums, the hyacinth bulbs in a cracked custard bowl and the German ivy trained over an old croquet hoop.

When these nightly duties were performed there was nothing left to do but to bring in the tin candlestick from the passage, light the candle and blow out the lamp. Ethan put the candlestick in Mattie's hand and she went out of the kitchen ahead of him, the light that she carried before her making her dark hair look like a drift of mist on the moon.

"Good night, Matt," he said as she put her foot on the first step of the stairs.

She turned and looked at him a moment. "Good night, Ethan," she answered, and went up.

When the door of her room had closed on her he remembered that he had not even touched her hand.

CHAPTER SIX

THE NEXT MORNING AT breakfast Jotham Powell was between them, and Ethan tried to hide his joy under an air of exaggerated indifference, lounging back in his chair to throw scraps to the cat, growling at the weather, and not so much as offering to help Mattie when she rose to clear away the dishes.

He did not know why he was so irrationally happy, for nothing was changed in his life or hers. He had not even touched the tip of her fingers or looked her full in the eyes. But their evening together had given him a vision of what life at her side might be, and he was glad now that he had done nothing to trouble the sweetness of the picture. He had a fancy that she knew what had restrained him . . .

There was a last load of lumber to be hauled to the village, and Jotham Powell—who did not work regularly for Ethan in winter—had "come round" to help with the job. But a wet snow, melting to sleet, had fallen in the night and turned the roads to glass. There was more wet in the air and it seemed likely to both men that the weather would "milden" toward afternoon and make the going safer. Ethan therefore proposed to his assistant that they should load the sledge at the wood-lot, as they had done on the previous morning, and put off the "teaming" to Starkfield till later in the day. This plan had the advantage of enabling him to send Jotham to the Flats after dinner to meet Zenobia, while he himself took the lumber down to the village.

He told Jotham to go out and harness up the greys, and for a moment he and Mattie had the kitchen to themselves. She had plunged the breakfast dishes into a tin dish-pan and was bending above it with her slim arms bared to the elbow, the steam from the hot water beading her forehead and tightening her rough hair into little brown rings like the tendrils on the traveller's joy.*

Ethan stood looking at her, his heart in his throat. He wanted to say: "We shall never be alone again like this." Instead, he reached down his tobacco-pouch from a shelf of the dresser, put it into his pocket and said: "I guess I can make out to be home for dinner."

She answered "All right, Ethan," and he heard her singing over the dishes as he went.

As soon as the sledge was loaded he meant to send Jotham back to the farm and hurry on foot into the village to buy the glue for the pickle-dish. With ordinary luck he should have had time to carry out this plan; but everything went wrong from the start. On the way over to the wood-lot one of the greys slipped on a glare of ice and cut his knee; and when they got him up again Jotham had to go back to the barn for a strip of rag to bind the cut. Then, when the loading finally began, a sleety rain was coming down once more, and the tree trunks were so slippery that it took twice as long as usual to lift them and get them in place on the sledge. It was what Jotham called a sour morning for work, and the horses, shivering and stamping under their wet blankets, seemed to like it as little as the men. It was long past the dinner-hour when the job was done, and Ethan had to give up going to the village because he wanted to lead the injured horse home and wash the cut himself.

He thought that by starting out again with the lumber as soon as he had finished his dinner he might get back to the farm with the glue before Jotham and the old sorrel had had time to fetch Zenobia from the Flats; but he knew the chance was a slight one. It turned on the state of the roads and on the possible lateness of the Bettsbridge train. He remembered afterward, with a grim flash of self-derision, what importance he had attached to the weighing of these probabilities . . .

As soon as dinner was over he set out again for the wood-lot, not daring to linger till Jotham Powell left. The hired man was still drying his wet feet at the stove, and Ethan could only give Mattie a quick look as he said beneath his breath: "I'll be back early."

---

*Deciduous, thick-stemmed climbing plant *(Clematis vitalba)* that often grows on hedges, fences, and trellises.

He fancied that she nodded her comprehension; and with that scant solace he had to trudge off through the rain.

He had driven his load half-way to the village when Jotham Powell overtook him, urging the reluctant sorrel toward the Flats. "I'll have to hurry up to do it," Ethan mused, as the sleigh dropped down ahead of him over the dip of the school-house hill. He worked like ten at the unloading, and when it was over hastened on to Michael Eady's for the glue. Eady and his assistant were both "down street," and young Denis, who seldom deigned to take their place, was lounging by the stove with a knot of the golden youth of Starkfield. They hailed Ethan with ironic compliment and offers of conviviality; but no one knew where to find the glue. Ethan, consumed with the longing for a last moment alone with Mattie, hung about impatiently while Denis made an ineffectual search in the obscurer corners of the store.

"Looks as if we were all sold out. But if you'll wait around till the old man comes along maybe he can put his hand on it."

"I'm obliged to you, but I'll try if I can get it down at Mrs. Homan's," Ethan answered, burning to be gone.

Denis's commercial instinct compelled him to aver on oath that what Eady's store could not produce would never be found at the widow Homan's; but Ethan, heedless of this boast, had already climbed to the sledge and was driving on to the rival establishment. Here, after considerable search, and sympathetic questions as to what he wanted it for, and whether ordinary flour paste wouldn't do as well if she couldn't find it, the widow Homan finally hunted down her solitary bottle of glue to its hiding-place in a medley of cough-lozenges and corset-laces.

"I hope Zeena ain't broken anything she sets store by," she called after him as he turned the greys toward home.

The fitful bursts of sleet had changed into a steady rain and the horses had heavy work even without a load behind them. Once or twice, hearing sleigh-bells, Ethan turned his head, fancying that Zeena and Jotham might overtake him; but the old sorrel was not in sight, and he set his face against the rain and urged on his ponderous pair.

The barn was empty when the horses turned into it and, after giving them the most perfunctory ministrations they had ever received from him, he strode up to the house and pushed open the kitchen door.

Mattie was there alone, as he had pictured her. She was bending over a pan on the stove; but at the sound of his step she turned with a start and sprang to him.

"See, here, Matt, I've got some stuff to mend the dish with! Let me get at it quick," he cried, waving the bottle in one hand while he put her lightly aside; but she did not seem to hear him.

"Oh, Ethan—Zeena's come," she said in a whisper, clutching his sleeve.

They stood and stared at each other, pale as culprits.

"But the sorrel's not in the barn!" Ethan stammered.

"Jotham Powell brought some goods over from the Flats for his wife, and he drove right on home with them," she explained.

He gazed blankly about the kitchen, which looked cold and squalid in the rainy winter twilight.

"How is she?" he asked, dropping his voice to Mattie's whisper.

She looked away from him uncertainly. "I don't know. She went right up to her room."

"She didn't say anything?"

"No."

Ethan let out his doubts in a low whistle and thrust the bottle back into his pocket. "Don't fret; I'll come down and mend it in the night," he said. He pulled on his wet coat again and went back to the barn to feed the greys.

While he was there Jotham Powell drove up with the sleigh, and when the horses had been attended to Ethan said to him: "You might as well come back up for a bite." He was not sorry to assure himself of Jotham's neutralising presence at the supper table, for Zeena was always "nervous" after a journey. But the hired man, though seldom loth to accept a meal not included in his wages, opened his stiff jaws to answer slowly: "I'm obliged to you, but I guess I'll go along back."

Ethan looked at him in surprise. "Better come up and dry off. Looks as if there'd be something hot for supper."

Jotham's facial muscles were unmoved by this appeal and, his vocabulary being limited, he merely repeated: "I guess I'll go along back."

To Ethan there was something vaguely ominous in this stolid rejection of free food and warmth, and he wondered what had happened on the drive to nerve Jotham to such stoicism. Perhaps Zeena had failed to see the new doctor or had not liked his counsels: Ethan knew that in such cases the first person she met was likely to be held responsible for her grievance.

When he re-entered the kitchen the lamp lit up the same scene of shining comfort as on the previous evening. The table had been as carefully laid, a clear fire glowed in the stove, the cat dozed in its warmth, and Mattie came forward carrying a plate of dough-nuts.

She and Ethan looked at each other in silence; then she said, as she had said the night before: "I guess it's about time for supper."

CHAPTER SEVEN

ETHAN WENT OUT INTO the passage to hang up his wet garments. He listened for Zeena's step and, not hearing it, called her name up the stairs. She did not answer, and after a moment's hesitation he went up and opened her door. The room was almost dark, but in the obscurity he saw her sitting by the window, bolt upright, and knew by the rigidity of the outline projected against the pane that she had not taken off her travelling dress.

"Well, Zeena," he ventured from the threshold.

She did not move, and he continued: "Supper's about ready. Ain't you coming?"

She replied: "I don't feel as if I could touch a morsel."

It was the consecrated formula, and he expected it to be followed, as usual, by her rising and going down to supper. But she remained seated, and he could think of nothing more felicitous than: "I presume you're tired after the long ride."

Turning her head at this, she answered solemnly: "I'm a great deal sicker than you think."

Her words fell on his ear with a strange shock of wonder. He had often heard her pronounce them before—what if at last they were true?

He advanced a step or two into the dim room. "I hope that's not so, Zeena," he said.

She continued to gaze at him through the twilight with a mien of wan authority, as of one consciously singled out for a great fate. "I've got complications," she said.

Ethan knew the word for one of exceptional import. Almost everybody in the neighbourhood had "troubles," frankly localized and specified; but only the chosen had "complications." To have them was in itself a distinction, though it was also, in most cases, a death-warrant. People struggled on for years with "troubles," but they almost always succumbed to "complications."

Ethan's heart was jerking to and fro between two extremities of feeling, but for the moment compassion prevailed. His wife looked so hard and lonely, sitting there in the darkness with such thoughts.

"Is that what the new doctor told you?" he asked, instinctively lowering his voice.

"Yes. He says any regular doctor would want me to have an operation."

Ethan was aware that, in regard to the important question of surgical intervention, the female opinion of the neighbourhood was divided, some glorying in the prestige conferred by operations while others shunned them as indelicate. Ethan, from motives of economy, had always been glad that Zeena was of the latter faction.

In the agitation caused by the gravity of her announcement he sought a consolatory short cut. "What do you know about this doctor anyway? Nobody ever told you that before."

He saw his blunder before she could take it up: she wanted sympathy, not consolation.

"I didn't need to have anybody tell me I was losing ground every day. Everybody but you could see it. And everybody in Bettsbridge knows about Dr. Buck. He has his office in Worcester, and comes over once a fortnight to Shadd's Falls and Bettsbridge for consultations. Eliza Spears was wasting away with kidney trouble before she went to him, and now she's up and around, and singing in the choir."

"Well, I'm glad of that. You must do just what he tells you," Ethan answered sympathetically.

She was still looking at him. "I mean to," she said. He was struck by a new note in her voice. It was neither whining nor reproachful, but drily resolute.

"What does he want you should do?" he asked, with a mounting vision of fresh expenses.

"He wants I should have a hired girl. He says I oughtn't to have to do a single thing around the house."

"A hired girl?" Ethan stood transfixed.

"Yes. And Aunt Martha found me one right off. Everybody said I was lucky to get a girl to come away out here, and I agreed to give her a dollar extry to make sure. She'll be over to-morrow afternoon."

Wrath and dismay contended in Ethan. He had foreseen an immediate demand for money, but not a permanent drain on his scant resources. He no longer believed what Zeena had told him of the supposed seriousness of her state: he saw in her expedition to Bettsbridge only a plot hatched between herself and her Pierce relations to foist on him the cost of a servant; and for the moment wrath predominated.

"If you meant to engage a girl you ought to have told me before you started," he said.

"How could I tell you before I started? How did I know what Dr. Buck would say?"

"Oh, Dr. Buck—" Ethan's incredulity escaped in a short laugh. "Did Dr. Buck tell you how I was to pay her wages?"

Her voice rose furiously with his. "No, he didn't. For I'd 'a' been ashamed to tell *him* that you grudged me the money to get back my health, when I lost it nursing your own mother!"

"*You* lost your health nursing mother?"

"Yes; and my folks all told me at the time you couldn't do no less than marry me after——"

"Zeena!"

Through the obscurity which hid their faces their thoughts seemed to dart at each other like serpents shooting venom. Ethan was seized with horror of the scene and shame at his own share in it. It was as senseless and savage as a physical fight between two enemies in the darkness.

He turned to the shelf above the chimney, groped for matches and lit the one candle in the room. At first its weak flame made no impression on the shadows; then Zeena's face stood grimly out against the uncurtained pane, which had turned from grey to black.

It was the first scene of open anger between the couple in their sad seven years together, and Ethan felt as if he had lost an irretrievable advantage in descending to the level of recrimination. But the practical problem was there and had to be dealt with.

"You know I haven't got the money to pay for a girl, Zeena. You'll have to send her back: I can't do it."

"The doctor says it'll be my death if I go on slaving the way I've had to. He doesn't understand how I've stood it as long as I have."

"Slaving!—" He checked himself again, "You sha'n't lift a hand, if he says so. I'll do everything round the house myself——"

She broke in: "You're neglecting the farm enough already," and this being true, he found no answer, and left her time to add ironically: "Better send me over to the almshouse and done with it . . . I guess there's been Fromes there afore now."

The taunt burned into him, but he let it pass. "I haven't got the money. That settles it."

There was a moment's pause in the struggle, as though the combatants were testing their weapons. Then Zeena said in a level voice: "I thought you were to get fifty dollars from Andrew Hale for that lumber."

"Andrew Hale never pays under three months." He had hardly spoken when he remembered the excuse he had made for not accompanying his wife to the station the day before; and the blood rose to his frowning brows.

"Why, you told me yesterday you'd fixed it up with him to pay cash down. You said that was why you couldn't drive me over to the Flats."

Ethan had no suppleness in deceiving. He had never before been convicted of a lie, and all the resources of evasion failed him. "I guess that was a misunderstanding," he stammered.

"You ain't got the money?"

"No."

"And you ain't going to get it?"

"No."

"Well, I couldn't know that when I engaged the girl, could I?"

"No." He paused to control his voice. "But you know it now. I'm sorry, but it can't be helped. You're a poor man's wife, Zeena; but I'll do the best I can for you."

For a while she sat motionless, as if reflecting, her arms stretched along the arms of her chair, her eyes fixed on vacancy. "Oh, I guess we'll make out," she said mildly.

The change in her tone reassured him. "Of course we will! There's a whole lot more I can do for you, and Mattie——"

Zeena, while he spoke, seemed to be following out some elaborate mental calculation. She emerged from it to say: "There'll be Mattie's board less, anyhow——"

Ethan, supposing the discussion to be over, had turned to go down to supper. He stopped short, not grasping what he heard. "Mattie's board less—?" he began.

Zeena laughed. It was an odd unfamiliar sound—he did not remember ever having heard her laugh before. "You didn't suppose I was going to keep two girls, did you? No wonder you were scared at the expense!"

He still had but a confused sense of what she was saying. From the beginning of the discussion he had instinctively avoided the mention of Mattie's name, fearing he hardly knew what: criticism, complaints, or vague allusions to the imminent probability of her marrying. But the thought of a definite rupture had never come to him, and even now could not lodge itself in his mind.

"I don't know what you mean," he said. "Mattie Silver's not a hired girl. She's your relation."

"She's a pauper that's hung onto us all after her father'd done his best to ruin us. I've kep' her here a whole year: it's somebody else's turn now."

As the shrill words shot out Ethan heard a tap on the door, which he had drawn shut when he turned back from the threshold.

"Ethan—Zeena!" Mattie's voice sounded gaily from the landing, "do you know what time it is? Supper's been ready half an hour."

Inside the room there was a moment's silence; then Zeena called out from her seat: "I'm not coming down to supper."

"Oh, I'm sorry! Aren't you well? Sha'n't I bring you up a bite of something?"

Ethan roused himself with an effort and opened the door. "Go along down, Matt. Zeena's just a little tired. I'm coming."

He heard her "All right!" and her quick step on the stairs; then he shut the door and turned back into the room. His wife's attitude was unchanged, her face inexorable, and he was seized with the despairing sense of his helplessness.

"You ain't going to do it, Zeena?"

"Do what?" she emitted between flattened lips.

"Send Mattie away—like this?"

"I never bargained to take her for life!"

He continued with rising vehemence: "You can't put her out of the house like a thief—a poor girl without friends or money. She's done her best for you and she's got no place to go to. You may forget she's your kin but everybody else'll remember it. If you do a thing like that what do you suppose folks'll say of you?"

Zeena waited a moment, as if giving him time to feel the full force of the contrast between his own excitement and her composure. Then she replied in the same smooth voice: "I know well enough what they say of my having kep' her here as long as I have."

Ethan's hand dropped from the door-knob, which he had held clenched since he had drawn the door shut on Mattie. His wife's retort was like a knife-cut across the sinews and he felt suddenly weak and powerless. He had meant to humble himself, to argue that Mattie's keep didn't cost much, after all, that he could make out to buy a stove and fix up a place in the attic for the hired girl—but Zeena's words revealed the peril of such pleadings.

"You mean to tell her she's got to go—at once?" he faltered out, in terror of letting his wife complete her sentence.

As if trying to make him see reason she replied impartially: "The girl will be over from Bettsbridge to-morrow, and I presume she's got to have somewheres to sleep."

Ethan looked at her with loathing. She was no longer the listless creature who had lived at his side in a state of sullen self-absorption, but a mysterious alien presence, an evil energy secreted from the long years of silent brooding. It was the sense of his helplessness that sharpened his antipathy. There had never been anything in her that one could appeal to; but as long as he could ignore and command he had remained indifferent. Now she had mastered him and he abhorred her. Mattie was her relation, not his: there were no means by which he could compel her to keep the girl under her roof. All the long misery of his baffled past, of his youth of failure, hardship and vain effort, rose up in his soul in bitterness and seemed to take shape before him in the woman who at every turn had barred his way. She had taken everything else from him; and now she meant to take the one thing that made up for all the others. For a moment such a flame of hate rose in him that it ran down his arm and clenched his fist against her. He took a wild step forward and then stopped.

"You're—you're not coming down?" he said in a bewildered voice.

"No. I guess I'll lay down on the bed a little while," she answered mildly; and he turned and walked out of the room.

In the kitchen Mattie was sitting by the stove, the cat curled up on her knees. She sprang to her feet as Ethan entered and carried the covered dish of meat-pie to the table.

"I hope Zeena isn't sick?" she asked.

"No."

She shone at him across the table. "Well, sit right down then. You must be starving." She uncovered the pie and pushed it over to him. So they were to have one more evening together, her happy eyes seemed to say!

He helped himself mechanically and began to eat; then disgust took him by the throat and he laid down his fork.

Mattie's tender gaze was on him and she marked the gesture.

"Why, Ethan, what's the matter? Don't it taste right?"

"Yes—it's first-rate. Only I—" He pushed his plate away, rose from his chair, and walked around the table to her side. She started up with frightened eyes.

"Ethan, there's something wrong! I *knew* there was!"

She seemed to melt against him in her terror, and he caught her in his arms, held her fast there, felt her lashes beat his cheek like netted butterflies.

"What is it—what is it?" she stammered; but he had found her lips at last and was drinking unconsciousness of everything but the joy they gave him.

She lingered a moment, caught in the same strong current; then she slipped from him and drew back a step or two, pale and troubled. Her look smote him with compunction, and he cried out, as if he saw her drowning in a dream: "You can't go, Matt! I'll never let you!"

"Go—go?" she stammered. "Must I go?"

The words went on sounding between them as though a torch of warning flew from hand to hand through a black landscape.

Ethan was overcome with shame at his lack of self-control in flinging the news at her so brutally. His head reeled and he had to support himself against the table. All the while he felt as if he were still kissing her, and yet dying of thirst for her lips.

"Ethan, what has happened? Is Zeena mad with me?"

Her cry steadied him, though it deepened his wrath and pity. "No, no," he assured her, "it's not that. But this new doctor has scared her about herself. You know she believes all they say the first time she sees them. And this one's told her she won't get well unless she lays up and don't do a thing about the house—not for months——"

He paused, his eyes wandering from her miserably. She stood silent a moment, drooping before him like a broken branch. She was so small and weak-looking that it wrung his heart; but suddenly she lifted her head and looked straight at him. "And she wants somebody handier in my place? Is that it?"

"That's what she says to-night."

"If she says it to-night she'll say it to-morrow."

Both bowed to the inexorable truth: they knew that Zeena never changed her mind, and that in her case a resolve once taken was equivalent to an act performed.

There was a long silence between them; then Mattie said in a low voice: "Don't be too sorry, Ethan."

"Oh, God—oh, God," he groaned. The glow of passion he had felt for her had melted to an aching tenderness. He saw her quick lids beating back the tears, and longed to take her in his arms and soothe her.

"You're letting your supper get cold," she admonished him with a pale gleam of gaiety.

"Oh, Matt—Matt—where'll you go to?"

Her lids sank and a tremor crossed her face. He saw that for the first time the thought of the future came to her distinctly. "I might get something to do over at Stamford," she faltered, as if knowing that he knew she had no hope.

He dropped back into his seat and hid his face in his hands. Despair seized him at the thought of her setting out alone to renew the weary quest for work. In the only place where she was known she was surrounded by indifference or animosity; and what chance had she, inexperienced and untrained, among the million bread-seekers of the cities? There came back to him miserable tales he had heard at Worcester, and the faces of girls whose lives had begun as hopefully as Mattie's. . . . It was not possible to think of such things without a revolt of his whole being. He sprang up suddenly.

"You can't go, Matt! I won't let you! She's always had her way, but I mean to have mine now——"

Mattie lifted her hand with a quick gesture, and he heard his wife's step behind him.

Zeena came into the room with her dragging down-at-the-heel step, and quietly took her accustomed seat between them.

"I felt a little mite better, and Dr. Buck says I ought to eat all I can to keep my strength up, even if I ain't got any appetite," she said in her flat whine, reaching across Mattie for the teapot. Her "good" dress had been replaced by the black calico and brown knitted shawl which formed her daily wear, and with them she had put on her usual face and manner. She poured out her tea, added a great deal of milk to it, helped herself largely to pie and pickles, and made the familiar gesture of adjusting her false teeth before she began to eat. The cat rubbed itself ingratiatingly against her, and she said "Good Pussy," stooped to stroke it and gave it a scrap of meat from her plate.

Ethan sat speechless, not pretending to eat, but Mattie nibbled valiantly at her food and asked Zeena one or two questions about her visit to Bettsbridge. Zeena answered in her every-day tone and, warming to the theme, regaled them with several vivid descriptions of intestinal disturbances among her friends and relatives. She looked straight at Mattie as she spoke, a faint smile deepening the vertical lines between her nose and chin.

When supper was over she rose from her seat and pressed her hand to the flat surface over the region of her heart. "That pie of yours always sets a mite heavy, Matt," she said, not ill-naturedly. She seldom abbreviated the girl's name, and when she did so it was always a sign of affability.

"I've a good mind to go and hunt up those stomach powders I got last year over in Springfield," she continued. "I ain't tried them for quite a while, and maybe they'll help the heartburn."

Mattie lifted her eyes. "Can't I get them for you, Zeena?" she ventured.

"No. They're in a place you don't know about," Zeena answered darkly, with one of her secret looks.

She went out of the kitchen and Mattie, rising, began to clear the dishes from the table. As she passed Ethan's chair their eyes met and clung together desolately. The warm still kitchen looked as peaceful as the night before. The cat had sprung to Zeena's rocking-chair, and the heat of the fire was beginning to draw out the faint sharp scent of the geraniums. Ethan dragged himself wearily to his feet.

"I'll go out and take a look around," he said, going toward the passage to get his lantern.

As he reached the door he met Zeena coming back into the room, her lips twitching with anger, a flush of excitement on her sallow face. The shawl had slipped from her shoulders and was dragging at her down-trodden heels, and in her hands she carried the fragments of the red glass pickle-dish.

"I'd like to know who done this," she said, looking sternly from Ethan to Mattie.

There was no answer, and she continued in a trembling voice: "I went to get those powders I'd put away in father's old spectacle-case, top of the china-closet, where I keep the things I set store by, so's folks sha'n't meddle with them—" Her voice broke, and two small tears hung on her lashless lids and ran slowly down her cheeks. "It takes the stepladder to get at the top shelf, and I put Aunt Philura Maple's pickle-dish up there o' purpose when we was married, and it's never been down since, 'cept for the spring cleaning, and then I always lifted it with my own hands, so's 't shouldn't get broke." She laid the fragments reverently on the table. "I want to know who done this," she quavered.

At the challenge Ethan turned back into the room and faced her. "I can tell you, then. The cat done it."

"The *cat?*"

"That's what I said."

She looked at him hard, and then turned her eyes to Mattie, who was carrying the dish-pan to the table.

"I'd like to know how the cat got into my china-closet," she said.

"Chasin' mice, I guess," Ethan rejoined. There was a mouse round the kitchen all last evening."

Zeena continued to look from one to the other; then she emitted her small strange laugh. "I knew the cat was a smart cat," she said in a high voice, "but I didn't know he was smart enough to pick up the pieces of my pickle-dish and lay 'em edge to edge on the very shelf he knocked 'em off of."

Mattie suddenly drew her arms out of the steaming water. "It wasn't Ethan's fault, Zeena! The cat *did* break the dish; but I got it down from the china-closet, and I'm the one to blame for its getting broken."

Zeena stood beside the ruin of her treasure, stiffening into a stony image of resentment, "*You* got down my pickle-dish—what for?"

A bright flush flew to Mattie's cheeks. "I wanted to make the supper-table pretty," she said.

"You wanted to make the supper-table pretty; and you waited till my back was turned, and took the thing I set most store by of anything I've got, and wouldn't never use it, not even when the minister come to dinner, or Aunt Martha Pierce come over from Bettsbridge—" Zeena paused with a gasp, as if terrified by her own evocation of the sacrilege. "You're a bad girl, Mattie Silver, and I always known it. It's the way your father begun, and I was warned of it when I took you, and I tried to keep my things where you couldn't get at 'em—and now you've took from me the one I cared for most of all—" She broke off in a short spasm of sobs that passed and left her more than ever like a shape of stone.

"If I'd 'a' listened to folks, you'd 'a' gone before now, and this wouldn't 'a' happened," she said; and gathering up the bits of broken glass she went out of the room as if she carried a dead body . . .

CHAPTER EIGHT

When Ethan was called back to the farm by his father's illness his mother gave him, for his own use, a small room behind the untenanted "best parlour." Here he had nailed up shelves for his books, built himself a box-sofa out of boards and a mattress, laid out his papers on a kitchen-table, hung on the rough plaster wall an engraving of Abraham Lincoln and a calendar with "Thoughts from the Poets," and tried, with these meagre properties, to produce some likeness to the study of a "minister" who had been kind to him and lent him books when he was at Worcester. He still took refuge there in summer, but when Mattie came to live at the farm he had had to give her his stove, and consequently the room was uninhabitable for several months of the year.

To this retreat he descended as soon as the house was quiet, and Zeena's steady breathing from the bed had assured him that there was to be no sequel to the scene in the kitchen. After Zeena's departure he and Mattie had stood speechless, neither seeking to approach the other. Then the girl had returned to her task of clearing up the kitchen for the night and he had taken his lantern and gone on his usual round outside the house. The kitchen was empty when he came back to it; but his tobacco-pouch and pipe had been laid on the table, and under them was a scrap of paper torn from the back of a seedsman's catalogue, on which three words were written: "Don't trouble, Ethan."

Going into his cold dark "study" he placed the lantern on the table and, stooping to its light, read the message again and again. It was the first time that Mattie had ever written to him, and the possession of the paper gave him a strange new sense of her nearness; yet it deepened his anguish by reminding him that henceforth they would have no other way of communicating with each other. For the life of her smile, the warmth of her voice, only cold paper and dead words!

Confused motions of rebellion stormed in him. He was too young, too strong, too full of the sap of living, to submit so easily to the destruction of his hopes. Must he wear out all his years at the side of a bitter querulous woman? Other possibilities had been in him, possibilities sacrificed, one by one, to Zeena's narrow-mindedness and ignorance. And what good had come of it? She was a hundred times bitterer and more discontented than when he had married her: the one pleasure left her was to inflict pain on him. All the healthy instincts of self-defence rose up in him against such waste . . .

He bundled himself into his old coon-skin coat and lay down on the box-sofa to think. Under his cheek he felt a hard object with strange protuberances. It was a cushion which Zeena had made for him when they were engaged—the only piece of needlework he had ever seen her do. He flung it across the floor and propped his head against the wall . . .

He knew a case of a man over the mountain—a young fellow of about his own age—who had escaped from just such a life of misery by going West with the girl he cared for. His wife had divorced him, and he had married the girl and prospered. Ethan had seen the couple the summer before at Shadd's Falls, where they had come to visit relatives. They had a little girl with fair curls, who wore a gold locket and was dressed like a princess. The deserted wife had not done badly either. Her husband had given her the farm and she had managed to sell it, and with that and the alimony she had started a lunch-room at Bettsbridge and bloomed into activity and importance. Ethan was fired by the thought. Why should he not leave with Mattie the next day, instead of letting her go alone? He would hide his valise under the seat of the sleigh, and Zeena would suspect nothing till she went upstairs for her afternoon nap and found a letter on the bed . . .

His impulses were still near the surface, and he sprang up, re-lit the lantern, and sat down at the table. He rummaged in the drawer for a sheet of paper, found one, and began to write.

"Zeena, I've done all I could for you, and I don't see as it's been any use. I don't blame you, nor I don't blame myself. Maybe both of us will do better separate. I'm going to try my luck West, and you can sell the farm and mill, and keep the money——"

His pen paused on the word, which brought home to him the relentless conditions of his lot. If he gave the farm and mill to Zeena what would be left him to start his own life with? Once in the West he was sure of picking up work—he would not have feared to try his chance alone. But with Mattie depending on him the case was different. And what of Zeena's fate? Farm and mill were mortgaged to the limit of their value, and even if she found a purchaser—in itself an unlikely chance—it was doubtful if she could clear a thousand dollars on the sale. Meanwhile, how could she keep the farm going? It was only by incessant labour and personal supervision that Ethan drew a meagre living from his land, and his wife, even if she were in better health than she imagined, could never carry such a burden alone.

Well, she could go back to her people, then, and see what they would do for her. It was the fate she was forcing on Mattie—why not let her try it herself? By the time she had discovered his whereabouts, and brought suit for divorce, he would probably—wherever he was—be earning enough to pay her a sufficient alimony. And the alternative was to let Mattie go forth alone, with far less hope of ultimate provision . . .

He had scattered the contents of the table-drawer in his search for a sheet of paper, and as he took up his pen his eye fell on an old copy of the *Bettsbridge Eagle.* The advertising sheet was folded uppermost, and he read the seductive words: "Trips to the West: Reduced Rates."

He drew the lantern nearer and eagerly scanned the fares; then the paper fell from his hand and he pushed aside his unfinished letter. A moment ago he had wondered what he and Mattie were to live on when they reached the West; now he saw that he had not even the money to take her there. Borrowing was out of the question: six months before he had given his only security to raise funds for necessary repairs to the mill, and he knew that without security no one at Starkfield would lend him ten dollars. The inexorable facts closed in on him like prison-warders handcuffing a convict. There was no way out—none. He was a prisoner for life, and now his one ray of light was to be extinguished.

He crept back heavily to the sofa, stretching himself out with limbs so leaden that he felt as if they would never move again. Tears rose in his throat and slowly burned their way to his lids.

As he lay there, the window-pane that faced him, growing gradually lighter, inlaid upon the darkness a square of moon-suffused sky. A crooked tree-branch crossed it, a branch of the apple-tree under which, on summer evenings, he had sometimes found Mattie sitting when he came up from the mill. Slowly the rim of the rainy vapours caught fire and burnt away, and a pure moon swung into the blue. Ethan, rising on his elbow, watched the landscape whiten and shape itself under the sculpture of the moon. This was the night on which he was to have taken Mattie coasting, and there hung the lamp to light them! He looked out at the slopes bathed in lustre, the silver-edged darkness of the woods, the spectral purple of the hills against the sky, and it seemed as though all the beauty of the night had been poured out to mock his wretchedness . . .

He fell asleep, and when he woke the chill of the winter dawn was in the room. He felt cold and stiff and hungry, and ashamed of being hungry. He rubbed his eyes and went to the window. A red sun stood over the grey rim of the fields, behind trees that looked black and brittle. He said to himself: "This is Matt's last day," and tried to think what the place would be without her.

As he stood there he heard a step behind him and she entered.

"Oh, Ethan—were you here all night?"

She looked so small and pinched, in her poor dress, with the red scarf wound about her, and the cold light turning her paleness sallow, that Ethan stood before her without speaking.

"You must be frozen," she went on, fixing lustreless eyes on him.

He drew a step nearer. "How did you know I was here?"

"Because I heard you go down stairs again after I went to bed, and I listened all night, and you didn't come up."

All his tenderness rushed to his lips. He looked at her and said: "I'll come right along and make up the kitchen fire."

They went back to the kitchen, and he fetched the coal and kindlings and cleared out the stove for her, while she brought in the milk and the cold remains of the meat-pie. When warmth began to radiate from the stove, and the first ray of sunlight lay on the kitchen floor, Ethan's dark thoughts melted in the mellower air. The sight of Mattie going about her work as he had seen her on so many mornings made it seem impossible that she should ever cease to be a part of the scene. He said to himself that he had doubtless exaggerated the significance of Zeena's threats, and that she too, with the return of daylight, would come to a saner mood.

He went up to Mattie as she bent above the stove, and laid his hand on her arm. "I don't want you should trouble either," he said, looking down into her eyes with a smile.

She flushed up warmly and whispered back: "No, Ethan, I ain't going to trouble."

"I guess things'll straighten out," he added.

There was no answer but a quick throb of her lids, and he went on: "She ain't said anything this morning?"

"No. I haven't seen her yet."

"Don't you take any notice when you do."

With this injunction he left her and went out to the cow-barn. He saw Jotham Powell walking up the hill through the morning mist, and the familiar sight added to his growing conviction of security.

As the two men were clearing out the stalls Jotham rested on his pitch-fork to say: "Dan'l Byrne's goin' over to the Flats to-day noon, an' he c'd take Mattie's trunk along, and make it easier ridin' when I take her over in the sleigh."

Ethan looked at him blankly, and he continued: "Mis' Frome said the new girl'd be at the Flats at five, and I was to take Mattie then, so's 't she could ketch the six o'clock train for Stamford."

Ethan felt the blood drumming in his temples. He had to wait a moment before he could find voice to say: "Oh, it ain't so sure about Mattie's going——"

"That so?" said Jotham indifferently; and they went on with their work.

When they returned to the kitchen the two women were already at breakfast. Zeena had an air of unusual alertness and activity. She drank two cups of coffee and fed the cat with the scraps left in the pie-dish; then she rose from her seat and, walking over to the window, snipped two or three yellow leaves from the geraniums. "Aunt Martha's ain't got a faded leaf on 'em; but they pine away when they ain't cared for," she said reflectively. Then she turned to Jotham and asked: "What time'd you say Dan'l Byrne'd be along?"

The hired man threw a hesitating glance at Ethan. "Round about noon," he said.

Zeena turned to Mattie. "That trunk of yours is too heavy for the sleigh, and Dan'l Byrne'll be round to take it over to the Flats," she said.

"I'm much obliged to you, Zeena," said Mattie.

"I'd like to go over things with you first," Zeena continued in an unperturbed voice. "I know there's a huckabuck towel missing; and I can't take out what you done with that match-safe 't used to stand behind the stuffed owl in the parlour."

She went out, followed by Mattie, and when the men were alone Jotham said to his employer: "I guess I better let Dan'l come round, then."

Ethan finished his usual morning tasks about the house and barn; then he said to Jotham: "I'm going down to Starkfield. Tell them not to wait dinner."

The passion of rebellion had broken out in him again. That which had seemed incredible in the sober light of day had really come to pass, and he was to assist as a helpless spectator at Mattie's banishment. His manhood was humbled by the part he was compelled to play and by the thought of what Mattie must think of him. Confused impulses struggled in him as he strode along to the village. He had made up his mind to do something, but he did not know what it would be.

The early mist had vanished and the fields lay like a silver shield under the sun. It was one of the days when the glitter of winter shines through a pale haze of spring. Every yard of the road was alive with Mattie's presence, and there was hardly a branch against the sky or a tangle of brambles on the bank in which some bright shred of memory was not caught. Once, in the stillness, the call of a bird in a mountain ash was so like her laughter that his heart tightened and then grew large; and all these things made him see that something must be done at once.

Suddenly it occurred to him that Andrew Hale, who was a kind-hearted man, might be induced to reconsider his refusal and advance a small sum on the lumber if he were told that Zeena's ill-health made it necessary to hire a servant. Hale, after all, knew enough of Ethan's situation to make it possible for the latter to renew his appeal without too much loss of pride; and, moreover, how much did pride count in the ebullition of passions in his breast?

The more he considered his plan the more hopeful it seemed. If he could get Mrs. Hale's ear he felt certain of success, and with fifty dollars in his pocket nothing could keep him from Mattie . . .

His first object was to reach Starkfield before Hale had started for his work; he knew the carpenter had a job down the Corbury road and was likely to leave his house early. Ethan's long strides grew more rapid with the accelerated beat of his thoughts, and as he reached the foot of School House Hill he caught sight of Hale's sleigh in the distance. He hurried forward to meet it, but as it drew nearer he saw that it was driven by the carpenter's youngest boy and that the figure at his side, looking like a large upright cocoon in spectacles, was that of Mrs. Hale. Ethan signed to them to stop, and Mrs. Hale leaned forward, her pink wrinkles twinkling with benevolence.

"Mr. Hale? Why, yes, you'll find him down home now. He ain't going to his work this forenoon. He woke up with a touch o' lumbago, and I just made him put on one of old Dr. Kidder's plasters and set right up into the fire."

Beaming maternally on Ethan, she bent over to add: "I on'y just heard from Mr. Hale 'bout Zeena's going over to Bettsbridge to see that new doctor. I'm real sorry she's feeling so bad again! I hope he thinks he can do something for her. I don't know anybody round here's had more sickness than Zeena. I always tell Mr. Hale I don't know what she'd 'a' done if she hadn't 'a' had you to look after her; and I used to say the same thing 'bout your mother. You've had an awful mean time, Ethan Frome."

She gave him a last nod of sympathy while her son chirped to the horse; and Ethan, as she drove off, stood in the middle of the road and stared after the retreating sleigh.

It was a long time since any one had spoken to him as kindly as Mrs. Hale. Most people were either indifferent to his troubles, or disposed to think it natural that a young fellow of his age should have carried without repining the burden of three crippled lives. But Mrs. Hale had said, "You've had an awful mean time, Ethan Frome," and he felt less alone with his misery. If the Hales were sorry for him they would surely respond to his appeal . . .

He started down the road toward their house, but at the end of a few yards he pulled up sharply, the blood in his face. For the first time, in the light of the words he had just heard, he saw what he was about to do. He was planning to take advantage of the Hales' sympathy to obtain money from them on false pretences. That was a plain statement of the cloudy purpose which had driven him in headlong to Starkfield.

With the sudden perception of the point to which his madness had carried him, the madness fell and he saw his life before him as it was. He was a poor man, the husband of a sickly woman, whom his desertion would leave alone and destitute; and even if he had had the heart to desert her he could have done so only by deceiving two kindly people who had pitied him.

He turned and walked slowly back to the farm.

CHAPTER NINE

AT THE KITCHEN DOOR Daniel Byrne sat in his sleigh behind a big-boned grey who pawed the snow and swung his long head restlessly from side to side.

Ethan went into the kitchen and found his wife by the stove. Her head was wrapped in her shawl, and she was reading a book called "Kidney Troubles and Their Cure" on which he had had to pay extra postage only a few days before.

Zeena did not move or look up when he entered, and after a moment he asked: "Where's Mattie?"

Without lifting her eyes from the page she replied: "I presume she's getting down her trunk."

The blood rushed to his face. "Getting down her trunk—alone?"

"Jotham Powell's down in the wood-lot, and Dan'l Byrne says he darsn't leave that horse," she returned.

Her husband, without stopping to hear the end of the phrase, had left the kitchen and sprung up the stairs. The door of Mattie's room was shut, and he wavered a moment on the landing. "Matt," he said in a low voice; but there was no answer, and he put his hand on the door-knob.

He had never been in her room except once, in the early summer, when he had gone there to plaster up a leak in the eaves, but he remembered exactly how everything had looked: the red-and-white quilt on her narrow bed, the pretty pin-cushion on the chest of drawers, and over it the enlarged photograph of her mother, in an oxydized frame, with a bunch of dyed grasses at the back. Now these and all other tokens of her presence had vanished and the room looked as bare and comfortless as when Zeena had shown her into it on the day of her arrival. In the middle of the floor stood her trunk, and on the trunk she sat in her Sunday dress, her back turned to the door and her face in her hands. She had not heard Ethan's call because she was sobbing and she did not hear his step till he stood close behind her and laid his hands on her shoulders.

"Matt—oh, don't—oh, *Matt!*"

She started up, lifting her wet face to his. "Ethan—I thought I wasn't ever going to see you again!"

He took her in his arms, pressing her close, and with a trembling hand smoothed away the hair from her forehead.

"Not see me again? What do you mean?"

She sobbed out: "Jotham said you told him we wasn't to wait dinner for you, and I thought——"

"You thought I meant to cut it?" he finished for her grimly.

She clung to him without answering, and he laid his lips on her hair, which was soft yet springy, like certain mosses on warm slopes, and had the faint woody fragrance of fresh sawdust in the sun.

Through the door they heard Zeena's voice calling out from below: "Dan'l Byrne says you better hurry up if you want him to take that trunk."

They drew apart with stricken faces. Words of resistance rushed to Ethan's lips and died there. Mattie found her handkerchief and dried her eyes; then, bending down, she took hold of a handle of the trunk.

Ethan put her aside. "You let go, Matt," he ordered her.

She answered: "It takes two to coax it round the corner"; and submitting to this argument he grasped the other handle, and together they manœuvred the heavy trunk out to the landing.

"Now let go," he repeated; then he shouldered the trunk and carried it down the stairs and across the passage to the kitchen. Zeena, who had gone back to her seat by the stove, did not lift her head from her book as he passed. Mattie followed him out of the door and helped him to lift the trunk into the back of the sleigh. When it was in place they stood side by side on the door-step, watching Daniel Byrne plunge off behind his fidgety horse.

It seemed to Ethan that his heart was bound with cords which an unseen hand was tightening with every tick of the clock. Twice he opened his lips to speak to Mattie and found no breath. At length, as she turned to re-enter the house, he laid a detaining hand on her.

"I'm going to drive you over, Matt," he whispered.

She murmured back: "I think Zeena wants I should go with Jotham."

"I'm going to drive you over," he repeated; and she went into the kitchen without answering.

At dinner Ethan could not eat. If he lifted his eyes they rested on Zeena's pinched face, and the corners of her straight lips seemed to quiver away into a smile. She ate well, declaring that the mild weather made her feel better, and pressed a second helping of beans on Jotham Powell, whose wants she generally ignored.

Mattie, when the meal was over, went about her usual task of clearing the table and washing up the dishes. Zeena, after feeding the cat, had returned to her rocking-chair by the stove, and Jotham Powell, who always lingered last, reluctantly pushed back his chair and moved toward the door.

On the threshold he turned back to say to Ethan: "What time'll I come round for Mattie?"

Ethan was standing near the window, mechanically filling his pipe while he watched Mattie move to and fro. He answered: "You needn't come round; I'm going to drive her over myself."

He saw the rise of the colour in Mattie's averted cheek, and the quick lifting of Zeena's head.

"I want you should stay here this afternoon, Ethan," his wife said. "Jotham can drive Mattie over."

Mattie flung an imploring glance at him, but he repeated curtly: "I'm going to drive her over myself."

Zeena continued in the same even tone: "I wanted you should stay and fix up that stove in Mattie's room afore the girl gets here. It ain't been drawing right for nigh on a month now."

Ethan's voice rose indignantly. "If it was good enough for Mattie I guess it's good enough for a hired girl."

"That girl that's coming told me she was used to a house where they had a furnace," Zeena persisted with the same monotonous mildness.

"She'd better ha' stayed there then," he flung back at her; and turning to Mattie he added in a hard voice: "You be ready by three, Matt; I've got business at Corbury."

Jotham Powell had started for the barn, and Ethan strode down after him aflame with anger. The pulses in his temples throbbed and a fog was in his eyes. He went about his task without knowing what force directed him, or whose hands and feet were fulfilling its orders.

It was not till he led out the sorrel and backed him between the shafts of the sleigh that he once more became conscious of what he was doing. As he passed the bridle over the horse's head, and wound the traces around the shafts, he remembered the day when he had made the same preparations in order to drive over and meet his wife's cousin at the Flats. It was little more than a year ago, on just such a soft afternoon, with a "feel" of spring in the air. The sorrel, turning the same big ringed eye on him, nuzzled the palm of his hand in the same way; and one by one all the days between rose up and stood before him . . .

He flung the bearskin into the sleigh, climbed to the seat, and drove up to the house. When he entered the kitchen it was empty, but Mattie's bag and shawl lay ready by the door. He went to the foot of the stairs and listened. No sound reached him from above, but presently he thought he heard some one moving about in his deserted study, and pushing open the door he saw Mattie, in her hat and jacket, standing with her back to him near the table.

She started at his approach and turning quickly, said: "Is it time?"

"What are you doing here, Matt?" he asked her.

She looked at him timidly. "I was just taking a look round—that's all," she answered, with a wavering smile.

They went back into the kitchen without speaking, and Ethan picked up her bag and shawl.

"Where's Zeena?" he asked.

"She went upstairs right after dinner. She said she had those shooting pains again, and didn't want to be disturbed."

"Didn't she say good-bye to you?"

"No. That was all she said."

Ethan, looking slowly about the kitchen, said to himself with a shudder that in a few hours he would be returning to it alone. Then the sense of unreality overcame him once more, and he could not bring himself to believe that Mattie stood there for the last time before him.

"Come on," he said almost gaily, opening the door and putting her bag into the sleigh. He sprang to his seat and bent over to tuck the rug about her as she slipped into the place at his side. "Now then, go 'long," he said, with a shake of the reins that sent the sorrel placidly jogging down the hill.

"We got lots of time for a good ride, Matt!" he cried, seeking her hand beneath the fur and pressing it in his. His face tingled and he felt dizzy, as if he had stopped in at the Starkfield saloon on a zero day for a drink.

At the gate, instead of making for Starkfield, he turned the sorrel to the right, up the Bettsbridge road. Mattie sat silent, giving no sign of surprise; but after a moment she said: "Are you going round by Shadow Pond?"

He laughed and answered: "I knew you'd know!"

She drew closer under the bearskin, so that, looking sideways around his coat-sleeve, he could just catch the tip of her nose and a blown brown wave of hair. They drove slowly up the road between fields glistening under the pale sun, and then bent to the right down a lane edged with spruce and larch. Ahead of them, a long way off, a range of hills stained by mottlings of black forest flowed away in round white curves against the sky. The lane passed into a pine-wood with boles reddening in the afternoon sun and delicate blue shadows on the snow. As they entered it the breeze fell and a warm stillness seemed to drop from the branches with the dropping needles. Here the snow was so pure that the tiny tracks of wood-animals had left on it intricate lace-like patterns, and the bluish cones caught in its surface stood out like ornaments of bronze.

Ethan drove on in silence till they reached a part of the wood where the pines were more widely spaced, then he drew up and helped Mattie to get out of the sleigh. They passed between the aromatic trunks, the snow breaking crisply under their feet, till they came to a small sheet of water with steep wooded sides. Across its frozen surface, from the farther bank, a single hill rising against the western sun threw the long conical shadow which gave the lake its name. It was a shy secret spot, full of the same dumb melancholy that Ethan felt in his heart.

He looked up and down the little pebbly beach till his eye lit on a fallen tree-trunk half submerged in snow.

"There's where we sat at the picnic," he reminded her.

The entertainment of which he spoke was one of the few that they had taken part in together: a "church picnic" which, on a long afternoon of the preceding summer, had filled the retired place with merry-making. Mattie had begged him to go with her but he had refused. Then, toward sunset, coming down from the mountain where he had been felling timber, he had been caught by some strayed revellers and drawn into the group by the lake, where Mattie, encircled by facetious youths, and bright as a blackberry under her spreading hat, was brewing coffee over a gipsy fire. He remembered the shyness he had felt at approaching her in his uncouth clothes, and then the lighting up of her face, and the way she had broken through the group to come to him with a cup in her hand. They had sat for a few minutes on the fallen log by the pond, and she had missed her gold locket, and set the young men searching for it; and it was Ethan who had spied it in the moss. . . . That was all; but all their intercourse had been made up of just such inarticulate flashes, when they seemed to come suddenly upon happiness as if they had surprised a butterfly in the winter woods . . .

"It was right there I found your locket," he said, pushing his foot into a dense tuft of blueberry bushes.

"I never saw anybody with such sharp eyes!" she answered.

She sat down on the tree-trunk in the sun and he sat down beside her.

"You were as pretty as a picture in that pink hat," he said.

She laughed with pleasure. "Oh, I guess it was the hat!" she rejoined.

They had never before avowed their inclination so openly, and Ethan, for a moment, had the illusion that he was a free man, wooing the girl he meant to marry. He looked at her hair and longed to touch it again, and to tell her that it smelt of the woods; but he had never learned to say such things.

Suddenly she rose to her feet and said: "We mustn't stay here any longer."

He continued to gaze at her vaguely, only half-roused from his dream. "There's plenty of time," he answered.

They stood looking at each other as if the eyes of each were straining to absorb and hold fast the other's image. There were things he had to say to her before they parted, but he could not say them in that place of summer memories, and he turned and followed her in silence to the sleigh. As they drove away the sun sank behind the hill and the pine-boles turned from red to grey.

By a devious track between the fields they wound back to the

Starkfield road. Under the open sky the light was still clear, with a reflection of cold red on the eastern hills. The clumps of trees in the snow seemed to draw together in ruffled lumps, like birds with their heads under their wings; and the sky, as it paled, rose higher, leaving the earth more alone.

As they turned into the Starkfield road Ethan said: "Matt, what do you mean to do?"

She did not answer at once, but at length she said: "I'll try to get a place in a store."

"You know you can't do it. The bad air and the standing all day nearly killed you before."

"I'm a lot stronger than I was before I came to Starkfield."

"And now you're going to throw away all the good it's done you!"

There seemed to be no answer to this, and again they drove on for a while without speaking. With every yard of the way some spot where they had stood, and laughed together or been silent, clutched at Ethan and dragged him back.

"Isn't there any of your father's folks could help you?"

"There isn't any of 'em I'd ask."

He lowered his voice to say: "You know there's nothing I wouldn't do for you if I could."

"I know there isn't."

"But I can't——"

She was silent, but he felt a slight tremor in the shoulder against his.

"Oh, Matt," he broke out, "if I could ha' gone with you now I'd ha' done it——"

She turned to him, pulling a scrap of paper from her breast. "Ethan—I found this," she stammered. Even in the failing light he saw it was the letter to his wife that he had begun the night before and forgotten to destroy. Through his astonishment there ran a fierce thrill of joy. "Matt—" he cried; "if I could ha' done it, would you?"

"Oh, Ethan, Ethan—what's the use?" With a sudden movement she tore the letter in shreds and sent them fluttering off into the snow.

"Tell me, Matt! Tell me!" he adjured her.

She was silent for a moment; then she said, in such a low tone that he had to stoop his head to hear her: "I used to think of it sometimes, summer nights, when the moon was so bright I couldn't sleep."

His heart reeled with the sweetness of it. "As long ago as that?"

She answered, as if the date had long been fixed for her: "The first time was at Shadow Pond."

"Was that why you gave me my coffee before the others?"

"I don't know. Did I? I was dreadfully put out when you wouldn't go to the picnic with me; and then, when I saw you coming down the road, I thought maybe you'd gone home that way o' purpose; and that made me glad."

They were silent again. They had reached the point where the road dipped to the hollow by Ethan's mill and as they descended the darkness descended with them, dropping down like a black veil from the heavy hemlock boughs.

"I'm tied hand and foot, Matt. There isn't a thing I can do," he began again.

"You must write to me sometimes, Ethan."

"Oh, what good'll writing do? I want to put my hand out and touch you. I want to do for you and care for you. I want to be there when you're sick and when you're lonesome."

"You mustn't think but what I'll do all right."

"You won't need me, you mean? I suppose you'll marry!"

"Oh, Ethan!" she cried.

"I don't know how it is you make me feel, Matt. I'd a'most rather have you dead than that!"

"Oh, I wish I was, I wish I was!" she sobbed.

The sound of her weeping shook him out of his dark anger, and he felt ashamed.

"Don't let's talk that way," he whispered.

"Why shouldn't we, when it's true? I've been wishing it every minute of the day."

"Matt! You be quiet! Don't you say it."

"There's never anybody been good to me but you."

"Don't say that either, when I can't lift a hand for you!"

"Yes; but it's true just the same."

They had reached the top of School House Hill and Starkfield lay below them in the twilight. A cutter, mounting the road from the village, passed them by in a joyous flutter of bells, and they straightened themselves and looked ahead with rigid faces. Along the main street lights had begun to shine from the house-fronts and stray figures were turning in here and there at the gates. Ethan, with a touch of his whip, roused the sorrel to a languid trot.

As they drew near the end of the village the cries of children reached them, and they saw a knot of boys, with sleds behind them, scattering across the open space before the church.

"I guess this'll be their last coast for a day or two," Ethan said, looking up at the mild sky.

Mattie was silent, and he added: "We were to have gone down last night."

Still she did not speak and, prompted by an obscure desire to help himself and her through their miserable last hour, he went on discursively: "Ain't it funny we haven't been down together but just that once last winter?"

She answered: "It wasn't often I got down to the village."

"That's so," he said.

They had reached the crest of the Corbury road, and between the indistinct white glimmer of the church and the black curtain of the Varnum spruces the slope stretched away below them without a sled on its length. Some erratic impulse prompted Ethan to say: "How'd you like me to take you down now?"

She forced a laugh. "Why, there isn't time!"

"There's all the time we want. Come along!" His one desire now was to postpone the moment of turning the sorrel toward the Flats.

"But the girl," she faltered. "The girl'll be waiting at the station."

"Well, let her wait. You'd have to if she didn't. Come!"

The note of authority in his voice seemed to subdue her, and when he had jumped from the sleigh she let him help her out, saying only, with a vague feint of reluctance: "But there isn't a sled round anywheres."

"Yes, there is! Right over there under the spruces."

He threw the bearskin over the sorrel, who stood passively by the roadside, hanging a meditative head. Then he caught Mattie's hand and drew her after him toward the sled.

She seated herself obediently and he took his place behind her, so close that her hair brushed his face. "All right, Matt?" he called out, as if the width of the road had been between them.

She turned her head to say: "It's dreadfully dark. Are you sure you can see?"

He laughed contemptuously: "I could go down this coast with my eyes tied!" and she laughed with him, as if she liked his audacity. Nevertheless he sat still a moment, straining his eyes down the long hill, for it was the most confusing hour of the evening, the hour when the last clearness from the upper sky is merged with the rising night in a blur that disguises landmarks and falsifies distances.

"Now!" he cried.

The sled started with a bound, and they flew on through the dusk, gathering smoothness and speed as they went, with the hollow night opening out below them and the air singing by like an organ. Mattie sat perfectly still, but as they reached the bend at the foot of the hill, where the big elm thrust out a deadly elbow, he fancied that she shrank a little closer.

"Don't be scared, Matt!" he cried exultantly, as they spun safely past it and flew down the second slope; and when they reached the level ground beyond, and the speed of the sled began to slacken, he heard her give a little laugh of glee.

They sprang off and started to walk back up the hill. Ethan dragged the sled with one hand and passed the other through Mattie's arm.

"Were you scared I'd run you into the elm?" he asked with a boyish laugh.

"I told you I was never scared with you," she answered.

The strange exaltation of his mood had brought on one of his rare fits of boastfulness. "It *is* a tricky place, though. The least swerve, and we'd never ha' come up again. But I can measure distances to a hair's-breadth—always could."

She murmured: "I always say you've got the surest eye . . ."

Deep silence had fallen with the starless dusk, and they leaned on each other without speaking; but at every step of their climb Ethan said to himself: "It's the last time we'll ever walk together."

They mounted slowly to the top of the hill. When they were abreast of the church he stooped his head to her to ask: "Are you tired?" and she answered, breathing quickly: "It was splendid!"

With a pressure of his arm he guided her toward the Norway spruces. "I guess this sled must be Ned Hale's. Anyhow I'll leave it where I found it." He drew the sled up to the Varnum gate and rested it against the fence. As he raised himself he suddenly felt Mattie close to him among the shadows.

"Is this where Ned and Ruth kissed each other?" she whispered breathlessly, and flung her arms about him. Her lips, groping for his, swept over his face, and he held her fast in a rapture of surprise.

"Good-bye—good-bye," she stammered, and kissed him again.

"Oh, Matt, I can't let you go!" broke from him in the same old cry.

She freed herself from his hold and he heard her sobbing. "Oh, I can't go either!" she wailed.

"Matt! What'll we do? What'll we do?"

They clung to each other's hands like children, and her body shook with desperate sobs.

Through the stillness they heard the church clock striking five.

"Oh, Ethan, it's time!" she cried.

He drew her back to him. "Time for what? You don't suppose I'm going to leave you now?"

"If I missed my train where'd I go?"

"Where are you going if you catch it?"

She stood silent, her hands lying cold and relaxed in his.

"What's the good of either of us going anywheres without the other one now?" he said.

She remained motionless, as if she had not heard him. Then she snatched her hands from his, threw her arms about his neck, and pressed a sudden drenched cheek against his face. "Ethan! Ethan! I want you to take me down again!"

"Down where?"

"The coast. Right off," she panted. "So 't we'll never come up any more."

"Matt! What on earth do you mean?"

She put her lips close against his ear to say: "Right into the big elm. You said you could. So 't we'd never have to leave each other any more."

"Why, what are you talking of? You're crazy!"

"I'm not crazy; but I will be if I leave you."

"Oh, Matt, Matt—" he groaned.

She tightened her fierce hold about his neck. Her face lay close to his face.

"Ethan, where'll I go if I leave you? I don't know how to get along alone. You said so yourself just now. Nobody but you was ever good to me. And there'll be that strange girl in the house . . . and she'll sleep in my bed, where I used to lay nights and listen to hear you come up the stairs . . ."

The words were like fragments torn from his heart. With them came the hated vision of the house he was going back to—of the stairs he would have to go up every night, of the woman who would wait for him there. And the sweetness of Mattie's avowal, the wild wonder of knowing at last that all that had happened to him had happened to her too, made the other vision more abhorrent, the other life more intolerable to return to . . .

Her pleadings still came to him between short sobs, but he no longer heard what she was saying. Her hat had slipped back and he was stroking her hair. He wanted to get the feeling of it into his hand, so that it would sleep there like a seed in winter. Once he found her mouth again, and they seemed to be by the pond together in the burning August sun. But his cheek touched hers, and it was cold and full of weeping, and he saw the road to the Flats under the night and heard the whistle of the train up the line.

The spruces swathed them in blackness and silence. They might have been in their coffins underground. He said to himself: "Perhaps it'll feel like this . . ." and then again: "After this I sha'n't feel anything . . ."

Suddenly he heard the old sorrel whinny across the road, and thought: "He's wondering why he doesn't get his supper . . ."

"Come," Mattie whispered, tugging at his hand.

Her sombre violence constrained him: she seemed the embodied instrument of fate. He pulled the sled out, blinking like a night-bird as he passed from the shade of the spruces into the transparent dusk of the open. The slope below them was deserted. All Starkfield was at supper, and not a figure crossed the open space before the church. The sky, swollen with the clouds that announce a thaw, hung as low as before a summer storm. He strained his eyes through the dimness, and they seemed less keen, less capable than usual.

He took his seat on the sled and Mattie instantly placed herself in front of him. Her hat had fallen into the snow and his lips were in her hair. He stretched out his legs, drove his heels into the road to keep the sled from slipping forward, and bent her head back between his hands. Then suddenly he sprang up again.

"Get up," he ordered her.

It was the tone she always heeded, but she cowered down in her seat, repeating vehemently: "No, no, no!"

"Get up!"

"Why?"

"I want to sit in front."

"No, no! How can you steer in front?"

"I don't have to. We'll follow the track."

They spoke in smothered whispers, as though the night were listening.

"Get up! Get up!" he urged her; but she kept on repeating: "Why do you want to sit in front?

"Because I—because I want to feel you holding me," he stammered, and dragged her to her feet.

The answer seemed to satisfy her, or else she yielded to the power of his voice. He bent down, feeling in the obscurity for the glassy slide worn by preceding coasters, and placed the runners carefully between its edges. She waited while he seated himself with crossed legs in the front of the sled; then she crouched quickly down at his back and clasped her arms about him. Her breath in his neck set him shuddering again, and he almost sprang from his seat. But in a flash he remembered the alternative. She was right: this was better than parting. He leaned back and drew her mouth to his.

Just as they started he heard the sorrel's whinny again, and the familiar wistful call, and all the confused images it brought with it, went with him down the first reach of the road. Half-way down there was a sudden drop, then a rise, and after that another long delirious descent. As they took wing for this it seemed to him that they were flying indeed, flying far up into the cloudy night, with Starkfield immeasurably below them, falling away like a speck in space . . . Then the big elm shot up ahead, lying in wait for them at the bend of the road, and he said between his teeth: "We can fetch it;* I know we can fetch it——"

As they flew toward the tree Mattie pressed her arms tighter, and her blood seemed to be in his veins. Once or twice the sled swerved a little under them. He slanted his body to keep it headed for the elm, repeating to himself again and again: "I know we can fetch it"; and little phrases she had spoken ran through his head and danced before him on the air. The big tree loomed bigger and closer, and as they bore down on it he thought: "It's waiting for us: it seems to know." But suddenly his wife's face, with twisted monstrous lineaments, thrust itself between him and his goal, and he made an instinctive movement to brush it aside. The sled swerved in response, but he righted it again, kept it straight, and drove down on the black projecting mass. There was a last instant when the air shot past him like millions of fiery wires; and then the elm . . .[12]

The sky was still thick, but looking straight up he saw a single star, and tried vaguely to reckon whether it were Sirius,† or—or— The effort tired him too much, and he closed his heavy lids and thought that he would sleep . . . The stillness was so profound that he heard a little animal twittering somewhere near by under the snow. It made a small frightened *cheep* like a field mouse, and he wondered languidly if it were hurt. Then he understood that it must be in pain: pain so excruciating that he seemed, mysteriously, to feel it shooting through his own body. He tried in vain to roll over in the direction of the sound, and stretched his left arm out across the snow. And now it was as though he felt rather than heard the twittering; it seemed to be under his palm, which rested on something soft and springy. The thought of the animal's suffering was intolerable to him and he struggled to raise himself, and could not because a rock, or some huge mass, seemed to be lying on him. But he continued to finger about cautiously with his left hand, thinking he might get hold of the little creature and help it; and all at once he knew that the soft thing he had touched was Mattie's hair and that his hand was on her face.

---

*Bring about an action.

†Star of the constellation Canis Major, also called the Dog Star; the brightest star in the sky.

He dragged himself to his knees, the monstrous load on him moving with him as he moved, and his hand went over and over her face, and he felt that the twittering came from her lips . . .

He got his face down close to hers, with his ear to her mouth, and in the darkness he saw her eyes open and heard her say his name.

"Oh, Matt, I thought we'd fetched it," he moaned; and far off, up the hill, he heard the sorrel whinny, and thought: "I ought to be getting him his feed . . ."

. . . .

. . . .

. . . .

THE QUERULOUS DRONE CEASED as I entered Frome's kitchen, and of the two women sitting there I could not tell which had been the speaker.

One of them, on my appearing, raised her tall bony figure from her seat, not as if to welcome me—for she threw me no more than a brief glance of surprise—but simply to set about preparing the meal which Frome's absence had delayed. A slatternly calico wrapper hung from her shoulders and the wisps of her thin grey hair were drawn away from a high forehead and fastened at the back by a broken comb. She had pale opaque eyes which revealed nothing and reflected nothing, and her narrow lips were of the same sallow colour as her face.

The other woman was much smaller and slighter. She sat huddled in an arm-chair near the stove, and when I came in she turned her head quickly toward me, without the least corresponding movement of her body. Her hair was as grey as her companion's, her face as bloodless and shrivelled, but amber-tinted, with swarthy shadows sharpening the nose and hollowing the temples. Under her shapeless dress her body kept its limp immobility, and her dark eyes had the bright witch-like stare that disease of the spine sometimes gives.

Even for that part of the country the kitchen was a poor-looking place. With the exception of the dark-eyed woman's chair, which looked like a soiled relic of luxury bought at a country auction, the furniture was of the roughest kind. Three coarse china plates and a broken-nosed milk-jug had been set on a greasy table scored with knife-cuts, and a couple of straw-bottomed chairs and a kitchen dresser of unpainted pine stood meagrely against the plaster walls.

"My, it's cold here! The fire must be 'most out," Frome said, glancing about him apologetically as he followed me in.

The tall woman, who had moved away from us toward the dresser, took no notice; but the other, from her cushioned niche, answered complainingly, in a high thin voice. "It's on'y just been made up this very minute. Zeena fell asleep and slep' ever so long, and I thought I'd be frozen stiff before I could wake her up and get her to 'tend to it."

I knew then that it was she who had been speaking when we entered.

Her companion, who was just coming back to the table with the remains of a cold mince-pie in a battered pie-dish, set down her unappetising burden without appearing to hear the accusation brought against her.

Frome stood hesitatingly before her as she advanced; then he looked at me and said: "This is my wife, Mis' Frome." After another interval he added, turning toward the figure in the arm-chair: "And this is Miss Mattie Silver . . ."

* * * * * * * * * * *

Mrs. Hale, tender soul, had pictured me as lost in the Flats and buried under a snow-drift; and so lively was her satisfaction on seeing me safely restored to her the next morning that I felt my peril had caused me to advance several degrees in her favour.

Great was her amazement, and that of old Mrs. Varnum, on learning that Ethan Frome's old horse had carried me to and from Corbury Junction through the worst blizzard of the winter; greater still their surprise when they heard that his master had taken me in for the night.

Beneath their wondering exclamations I felt a secret curiosity to know what impressions I had received from my night in the Frome household, and divined that the best way of breaking down their reserve was to let them try to penetrate mine. I therefore confined myself to saying, in a matter-of-fact tone, that I had been received with great kindness, and that Frome had made a bed for me in a room on the ground-floor which seemed in happier days to have been fitted up as a kind of writing-room or study.

"Well," Mrs. Hale mused, "in such a storm I suppose he felt he couldn't do less than take you in—but I guess it went hard with Ethan. I don't believe but what you're the only stranger has set foot in that house for over twenty years. He's that proud he don't even like his oldest friends to go there; and I don't know as any do, any more, except myself and the doctor . . ."

"You still go there, Mrs. Hale?" I ventured.

"I used to go a good deal after the accident, when I was first married; but after awhile I got to think it made 'em feel worse to see us. And then one thing and another came, and my own troubles . . . But I generally make out to drive over there round about New Year's, and once in the summer. Only I always try to pick a day when Ethan's off somewheres. It's bad enough to see the two women sitting there—but *his* face, when he looks round that bare place, just kills me . . . You see, I can look back and call it up in his mother's day, before their troubles."

Old Mrs. Varnum, by this time, had gone up to bed, and her daughter and I were sitting alone, after supper, in the austere seclusion of the horse-hair parlour. Mrs. Hale glanced at me tentatively, as though trying to see how much footing my conjectures gave her; and I guessed that if she had kept silence till now it was because she had been waiting, through all the years, for some one who should see what she alone had seen.

I waited to let her trust in me gather strength before I said: "Yes, it's pretty bad, seeing all three of them there together."

She drew her mild brows into a frown of pain. "It was just awful from the beginning. I was here in the house when they were carried up—they laid Mattie Silver in the room you're in. She and I were great friends, and she was to have been my bridesmaid in the spring . . . When she came to I went up to her and stayed all night. They gave her things to quiet her, and she didn't know much till to'rd morning, and then all of a sudden she woke up just like herself, and looked straight at me out of her big eyes, and said . . . Oh, I don't know why I'm telling you all this," Mrs. Hale broke off, crying.

She took off her spectacles, wiped the moisture from them, and put them on again with an unsteady hand. "It got about the next day," she went on, "that Zeena Frome had sent Mattie off in a hurry because she had a hired girl coming, and the folks here could never rightly tell what she and Ethan were doing that night coasting, when they'd ought to have been on their way to the Flats to ketch the train . . . I never knew myself what Zeena thought—I don't to this day. Nobody knows Zeena's thoughts. Anyhow, when she heard o' the accident she came right in and stayed with Ethan over to the minister's, where they'd carried him. And as soon as the doctors said that Mattie could be moved, Zeena sent for her and took her back to the farm."

"And there she's been ever since?"

Mrs. Hale answered simply: "There was nowhere else for her to go;" and my heart tightened at the thought of the hard compulsions of the poor.

"Yes, there she's been," Mrs. Hale continued, "and Zeena's done for her, and done for Ethan, as good as she could. It was a miracle, considering how sick she was—but she seemed to be raised right up just when the call came to her. Not as she's ever given up doctoring, and she's had sick spells right along; but she's had the strength given her to care for those two for over twenty years, and before the accident came she thought she couldn't even care for herself."

Mrs. Hale paused a moment, and I remained silent, plunged in the vision of what her words evoked. "It's horrible for them all," I murmured.

"Yes: it's pretty bad. And they ain't any of 'em easy people either. Mattie *was,* before the accident; I never knew a sweeter nature. But she's suffered too much—that's what I always say when folks tell me how she's soured. And Zeena, she was always cranky. Not but what she bears with Mattie wonderful—I've seen that myself. But sometimes the two of them get going at each other, and then Ethan's face'd break your heart . . . When I see that, I think it's *him* that suffers most . . . anyhow it ain't Zeena, because she ain't got the time . . . It's a pity, though," Mrs. Hale ended, sighing, "that they're all shut up there'n that one kitchen. In the summertime, on pleasant days, they move Mattie into the parlour, or out in the door-yard, and that makes it easier . . . but winters there's the fires to be thought of; and there ain't a dime to spare up at the Fromes'."

Mrs. Hale drew a deep breath, as though her memory were eased of its long burden, and she had no more to say; but suddenly an impulse of complete avowal seized her.

She took off her spectacles again, leaned toward me across the bead-work table-cover, and went on with lowered voice: "There was one day, about a week after the accident, when they all thought Mattie couldn't live. Well, I say it's a pity she *did.* I said it right out to our minister once, and he was shocked at me. Only he wasn't with me that morning when she first came to . . . And I say, if she'd ha' died, Ethan might ha' lived; and the way they are now, I don't see's there's much difference between the Fromes up at the farm and the Fromes down in the graveyard; 'cept that down there they're all quiet, and the women have got to hold their tongues."

THE PRETEXT[1]

I.

Mrs. Ransom, when the front door had closed on her visitor, passed with a spring from the drawing-room to the narrow hall, and thence up the narrow stairs to her bedroom.

Though slender, and still light of foot, she did not always move so quickly: hitherto, in her life, there had not been much to hurry for, save the recurring domestic tasks that compel haste without fostering elasticity; but some impetus of youth revived, communicated to her by her talk with Guy Dawnish, now found expression in her girlish flight upstairs, her girlish impatience to bolt herself into her room with her throbs and her blushes.

Her blushes? Was she really blushing?

She approached the cramped eagle-topped mirror above her plain prim dressing-table: just such a meagre concession to the weakness of the flesh as every old-fashioned house in Wentworth[2] counted among its relics. The face reflected in this unflattering surface—for even the mirrors of Wentworth erred on the side of depreciation—did not seem, at first sight, a suitable theatre for the display of the tenderer emotions, and its owner blushed more deeply as the fact was forced upon her.

Her fair hair had grown too thin—it no longer quite hid the blue veins in the candid forehead that one seemed to see turned toward professorial desks, in large bare halls where a snowy winter light fell uncompromisingly on rows of "thoughtful women." Her mouth was thin, too, and a little strained; her lips were too pale; and there were lines in the corners of her eyes. It was a face which had grown middle-aged while it waited for the joys of youth.

Well—but if she could still blush? Instinctively she drew back a little, so that her scrutiny became less microscopic, and the pretty lingering pink threw a veil over her pallour, the hollows in her temples, the faint wrinkles of inexperience about her lips and eyes.

How a little colour helped! It made her eyes so deep and shining. She saw now why bad women rouged. . . . her redness deepened at the thought.

But suddenly she noticed for the first time that the collar of her dress was too low. It showed the shrunken lines of the throat. She rummaged feverishly in a tidy scentless drawer, and snatching out a bit of black velvet, bound it about her neck. Yes—that was better. It gave her the relief she needed. Relief—contrast—that was it! She had never had any, either in her appearance or in her setting. She was as flat as the pattern of the wall-paper—and so was her life. And all the people about her had the same look. Wentworth was the kind of place where husbands and wives gradually grew to resemble each other—one or two of her friends, she remembered, had told her lately that she and Ransom were beginning to look alike. . . .

But why had she always, so tamely, allowed her aspect to conform to her situation? Perhaps a gayer exterior would have provoked a brighter fate. Even now—she turned back to the glass, loosened her tight strands of hair, ran the fine end of the comb under them with a frizzing motion, and then disposed them, more lightly and amply, above her eager face. Yes—it was really better; it made a difference. She smiled at herself with a timid coquetry, and her lips seemed rosier as she smiled. Then she laid down the comb and the smile faded. It made a difference, certainly—but was it right to try to make one's hair look thicker and wavier than it really was? Between that and rouging the ethical line seemed almost imperceptible, and the spectre of her rigid New England ancestry rose reprovingly before her. She was sure that none of her grandmothers had ever simulated a curl or encouraged a blush. A blush, indeed! What had any of them ever had to blush for in all their frozen lives? And what, in Heaven's name, had she? She sat down in the stiff mahogany rocking-chair beside her work-table and tried to collect herself. From childhood she had been taught to "collect herself"—but never before had her small sensations and aspirations been so widely scattered, diffused over so vague and uncharted an expanse. Hitherto they had lain in neatly sorted and easily accessible bundles on the high shelves of a perfectly ordered moral consciousness. And now—now that for the first time they *needed* collecting—now that the little winged and scattered bits of self were dancing madly down the vagrant winds of fancy, she knew no spell to call them to the fold again. The best way, no doubt—if only her bewilderment permitted—was to go back to the beginning—the beginning, at least, of to-day's visit—to recapitulate, word for word and look for look. . . .

She clasped her hands on the arms of the chair, checked its swaying with a thrust of her foot, and fixed her eyes on the inward vision. . . .

To begin with, what had made to-day's visit so different from the others? It became suddenly vivid to her that there had been many, almost daily, others, since Guy Dawnish's coming to Wentworth. Even the previous winter—the winter of his arrival from England—his visits had been numerous enough to make Wentworth aware that—very naturally—Mrs. Ransom was "looking after" the stray young Englishman committed to her husband's care by an eminent Q. C.* whom the Ransoms had known on one of their London visits, and with whom Ransom had since maintained professional relations. All this was in the natural order of things, as sanctioned by the social code of Wentworth. Every one was kind to Guy Dawnish—some rather importunately so, as Margaret Ransom had smiled to observe—but it was recognised as fitting that she should be kindest, since he was in a sense her property, since his people in England, by profusely acknowledging her kindness, had given it the domestic sanction without which, to Wentworth, any social relation between the sexes remained unhallowed and to be viewed askance. Yes! And even this second winter, when the visits had become so much more frequent, so admitted a part of the day's routine, there had not been, from any one, a hint of surprise or of conjecture.

Mrs. Ransom smiled with a faint bitterness. She was protected by her age, no doubt—her age and her past, and the image her mirror gave back to her. . . .

Her door-handle turned suddenly, and the bolt's resistance was met by an impatient knock.

"Margaret!"

She started up, her brightness fading, and unbolted the door to admit her husband.

---

*Queen's Counsel; barrister (attorney) who serves as counsel to the queen.

"Why are you locked in? Why, you're not dressed yet!" he exclaimed.

It was possible for Ransom to reach his dressing-room by a slight circuit through the passage; but it was characteristic of the relentless domesticity of their relation that he chose, as a matter of course, the directer way through his wife's bedroom. She had never before been disturbed by this practice, which she accepted as inevitable, but had merely adapted her own habits to it, delaying her hasty toilet till he was safe in his room, or completing it before she heard his step on the stair; since a scrupulous traditional prudery had miraculously survived this massacre of all the privacies.

"Oh, I shan't dress this evening—I shall just have some tea in the library after you've gone," she answered absently. "Your things are laid out," she added, rousing herself.

He looked surprised. "The dinner's at seven. I suppose the speeches will begin at nine. I thought you were coming to hear them."

She wavered. "I don't know. I think not. Mrs. Sperry's ill, and I've no one else to go with."

He glanced at his watch. "Why not get hold of Dawnish? Wasn't he here just now? Why didn't you ask him?"

She turned toward her dressing-table and straightened the comb and brush with a nervous hand. Her husband had given her, that morning, two tickets for the ladies' gallery in Hamblin Hall, where the great public dinner of the evening was to take place—a banquet offered by the faculty of Wentworth to visitors of academic eminence—and she had meant to ask Dawnish to go with her: it had seemed the most natural thing to do, till the end of his visit came, and then, after all, she had not spoken. . . .

"It's too late now," she murmured, bending over her pincushion.

"Too late? Not if you telephone him."

Her husband came toward her, and she turned quickly to face him, lest he should suspect her of trying to avoid his eye. To what duplicity was she already committed!

Ransom laid a friendly hand on her arm: "Come along, Margaret. You know I speak for the bar." She was aware, in his voice, of a little note of surprise at his having to remind her of this.

"Oh, yes. I meant to go, of course—"

"Well, then—" He opened his dressing-room door, and caught a glimpse of the retreating house-maid's skirt. "Here's Maria now. Maria! Call up Mr. Dawnish—at Mrs. Creswell's, you know. Tell him Mrs. Ransom wants him to go with her to hear the speeches this evening—the *speeches,* you understand?—and he's to call for her at a quarter before nine."

Margaret heard the Irish "Yessir" on the stairs, and stood motionless while her husband added loudly: "And bring me some towels when you come up." Then he turned back into his wife's room.

"Why, it would be a thousand pities for Guy to miss this. He's so interested in the way we do things over here—and I don't know that he's ever heard me speak in public." Again the slight note of fatuity! Was it possible that Ransom was fatuous?

He paused in front of her, his short-sighted unobservant glance turned unexpectedly on her face.

"You're not going like that, are you?" he asked, with glaring eyeglasses.

"Like what?" she faltered, lifting a conscious hand to the velvet at her throat.

"With your hair in such a fearful mess. Have you been shampooing it? You look like the Brant girl at the end of a tennis-match."

The Brant girl was their horror—the horror of all right-thinking Wentworth; a laced, whale-boned, frizzle-headed, high-heeled daughter of iniquity, who came—from New York, of course—on long disturbing tumultuous visits to a Wentworth aunt, working havoc among the freshmen, and leaving, when she departed, an angry wake of criticism that ruffled the social waters for weeks. *She,* too, had tried her hand at Guy—with ludicrous unsuccess. And now, to be compared to her—to be accused of looking "New Yorky!"[3] Ah, there are times when husbands are obtuse; and Ransom, as he stood there, thick and yet juiceless, in his dry legal middle age, with his wiry dust-coloured beard and his perpetual *pince-nez,** seemed to his wife a sudden embodiment of this traditional attribute. Not that she had ever fancied herself, poor soul, a *"femme incomprise."*† She had, on the contrary, prided herself on

---

*Eyeglasses clipped to the nose by a spring.
†Misunderstood wife (French).

being understood by her husband almost as much as on her own complete comprehension of him. Wentworth laid a good deal of stress on "motives"; and Margaret Ransom and her husband had dwelt in complete community of motive. It had been the proudest day of her life when, without consulting her, he had refused an offer of partnership in an eminent New York firm because he preferred the distinction of practising in Wentworth, of being known as the legal representative of the University. Wentworth, in fact, had always been the bond between the two; they were united in their veneration for that estimable seat of learning, and in their modest yet vivid consciousness of possessing its tone. The Wentworth "tone" is unmistakable: it permeates every part of the social economy, from the *coiffure** of the ladies to the preparation of the food. It has its sumptuary laws† as well as its curriculum of learning. It sits in judgment not only on its own townsmen but on the rest of the world—enlightening, criticising, ostracising a heedless universe—and non-conformity to Wentworth standards involves obliteration from Wentworth's consciousness.

In a world without traditions, without reverence, without stability, such little expiring centres of prejudice and precedent make an irresistible appeal to those instincts for which a democracy has neglected to provide.[4] Wentworth, with its "tone," its backward references, its inflexible aversions and condemnations, its hard moral outline preserved intact against a whirling background of experiment, had been all the poetry and history of Margaret Ransom's life. Yes, what she had really esteemed in her husband was the fact of his being so intense an embodiment of Wentworth; so long and closely identified, for instance, with its legal affairs, that he was almost a part of its university existence, that of course, at a college banquet, he would inevitably speak for the bar!

It was wonderful of how much consequence all this had seemed till now. . . .

---

*Hairstyle (French).

†Codes regulating standards of dress.

II.

When, punctually at ten minutes to seven, her husband had emerged from the house, Margaret Ransom remained seated in her bedroom, addressing herself anew to the difficult process of self-collection. As an aid to this endeavour, she bent forward and looked out of the window, following Ransom's figure as it receded down the elm-shaded street. He moved almost alone between the prim flowerless grass-plots, the white porches, the protrusion of irrelevant shingled gables, which stamped the empty street as part of an American college town. She had always been proud of living in Hill Street, where the university people congregated, proud to associate her husband's retreating back, as he walked daily to his office, with backs literary and pedagogic, backs of which it was whispered, for the edification of duly-impressed visitors: "Wait till that old boy turns—that's so-and-so."

This had been her world, a world destitute of personal experience, but filled with a rich sense of privilege and distinction, of being not as those millions were who, denied the inestimable advantage of living at Wentworth, pursued elsewhere careers foredoomed to futility.

And now—!

She rose and turned to her work-table, where she had dropped, on entering, the handful of photographs that Guy Dawnish had left with her. While he sat so close, pointing out and explaining, she had hardly taken in the details; but now, on the full tones of his low young voice, they came back with redoubled distinctness. This was Guise Abbey, his uncle's place in Wiltshire,* where, under his grandfather's rule, Guy's own boyhood had been spent: a long gabled

---

*Area of southern England; home to such historic sites as Stonehenge and Salisbury Cathedral.

Jacobean* façade, many-chimneyed, ivy-draped, overhung (she felt sure) by the boughs of a venerable rookery. And in this other picture—the walled garden at Guise—that was his uncle, Lord Askern, a hale gouty-looking figure, planted robustly on the terrace, a gun on his shoulder and a couple of setters at his feet. And here was the river below the park, with Guy "punting"† a girl in a flapping hat—how Margaret hated the flap that hid the girl's face! And here was the tennis-court, with Guy among a jolly cross-legged group of youths in flannels, and pretty girls about the tea-table under the big lime: in the centre the curate handing bread and butter, and in the middle distance a footman approaching with more cups.

Margaret raised this picture closer to her eyes, puzzling, in the diminished light, over the face of the girl nearest to Guy Dawnish—bent above him in profile, while he laughingly lifted his head. No hat hid this profile, which stood out clearly against the foliage behind it.

"And who is that handsome girl?" Margaret had said, detaining the photograph as he pushed it aside, and struck by the fact that, of the whole group, he had left only this member unnamed.

"Oh, only Gwendolen Matcher—I've always known her—. Look at this: the almshouses at Guise. Aren't they jolly?"

And then—without her having had the courage to ask if the girl in the punt were also Gwendolen Matcher—they passed on to photographs of his rooms at Oxford, of a cousin's studio in London—one of Lord Askern's grandsons was "artistic"—of the rose-hung cottage in Wales to which, on the old Earl's death, his daughter-in-law, Guy's mother, had retired.

Every one of the photographs opened a window on the life Margaret had been trying to picture since she had known him—a life so rich, so romantic, so packed—in the mere casual vocabulary of daily life—with historic reference and poetic allusion, that she felt almost oppressed by this distant whiff of its air. The very words he used fascinated and bewildered her. He seemed to have been born into all sorts of connections, political, historical, official, that made the Ransom situation at Wentworth as featureless as the top-shelf of a

---

*In a style associated with the reign of King James I, who ruled Great Britain from 1603 to 1625.

†Moving a square, flat-bottomed boat, called a punt, with a long pole.

dark closet. Some one in the family had "asked for the Chiltern Hundreds"[5]—one uncle was an Elder Brother of the Trinity House[6]—some one else was the Master of a College—some one was in command at Devonport[7]—the Army, the Navy, the House of Commons, the House of Lords, the most venerable seats of learning, were all woven into the dense background of this young man's light unconscious talk. For the unconsciousness was unmistakable. Margaret was not without experience of the transatlantic visitor who sounds loud names and evokes reverberating connections. The poetry of Guy Dawnish's situation lay in the fact that it was so completely a part of early associations and accepted facts. Life was like that in England—in Wentworth, of course (where he had been sent, through his uncle's influence, for two years' training in the neighbouring electrical works at Smedden)—in Wentworth, though "immensely jolly," it was different. The fact that he was qualifying to be an electrical engineer—with the hope of a secretaryship at the London end of the great Smedden Company—that, at best, he was returning home to a life of industrial "grind," this fact, though avowedly a bore, did not disconnect him from that brilliant pinnacled past, that many-faceted existence in which the brightest episodes of the whole body of English fiction seemed collectively reflected. Of course he would have to work—younger sons' sons almost always had to—but his uncle Askern (like Wentworth) was "immensely jolly," and Guise always open to him, and his other uncle, the Master, a capital old boy too—and in town he could always put up with his clever aunt, Lady Caroline Duckett, who had made a "beastly marriage" and was horribly poor, but who knew everybody jolly and amusing, and had always been particularly kind to him.

It was not—and Margaret had not, even in her own thoughts, to defend herself from the imputation—it was not what Wentworth would have called the "material side" of her friend's situation that captivated her. She was austerely proof against such appeals: her enthusiasms were all of the imaginative order. What subjugated her was the unexampled prodigality with which he poured for her the same draught of tradition of which Wentworth held out its little teacupful. He besieged her with a million Wentworths in one—saying, as it were: "All these are mine for the asking—and I choose you instead!"

For this, she told herself somewhat dizzily, was what it came to—the summing-up toward which her conscientious efforts at self-collection had been gradually pushing her: with all this in reach, Guy Dawnish was leaving Wentworth reluctantly.

"I *was* a bit lonely here at first—but *now!*" And again: "It will be jolly, of course, to see them all again—but there are some things one doesn't easily give up. . . ."

If he had known only Wentworth, it would have been wonderful enough that he should have chosen her out of all Wentworth—but to have known that other life, and to set her in the balance against it—poor Margaret Ransom, in whom, at the moment, nothing seemed of weight but her years! Ah, it might well produce, in nerves, and brain, and poor unpractised pulses, a flushed tumult of sensation, the rush of a great wave of life, under which memory struggled in vain to reassert itself, to particularise again just what his last words—the very last—had been. . . .

When consciousness emerged, quivering, from this retrospective assault, it pushed Margaret Ransom—feeling herself a mere leaf in the blast—toward the writing-table from which her innocent and voluminous correspondence habitually flowed. She had a letter to write now—much shorter but more difficult than any she had ever been called on to indite.

"Dear Mr. Dawnish," she began, "since telephoning you just now I have decided not—"

Maria's voice, at the door, announced that tea was in the library: "And I s'pose it's the brown silk you'll wear to the speaking?"

In the usual order of the Ransom existence, its mistress's toilet was performed unassisted; and the mere enquiry—at once friendly and deferential—projected, for Margaret, a strong light on the importance of the occasion. That she should answer "But I am not going," when the going was so manifestly part of a household solemnity about which the thoughts below stairs fluttered in proud participation; that in face of such participation she should utter a word implying indifference or hesitation—nay, revealing herself the transposed uprooted thing she had been on the verge of becoming; to do this was—well! infinitely harder than to perform the alternative act of tearing up the sheet of note-paper under her reluctant pen.

Yes, she said, she would wear the brown silk. . . .

III.

All the heat and glare from the long illuminated table, about which the fumes of many courses still hung in a savoury fog, seemed to surge up to the ladies' gallery, and concentrate themselves in the burning cheeks of a slender figure withdrawn behind the projection of a pillar.

It never occurred to Margaret Ransom that she was sitting in the shade. She supposed that the full light of the chandeliers was beating on her face—and there were moments when it seemed as though all the heads about the great horse-shoe below, bald, shaggy, sleek, close-thatched, or thinly latticed, were equipped with an additional pair of eyes, set at an angle which enabled them to rake her face as relentlessly as the electric burners.

In the lull after a speech, the gallery was fluttering with the rustle of programmes consulted, and Mrs. Sheff (the Brant girl's aunt) leaned forward to say enthusiastically: "And now we're to hear Mr. Ransom!"

A louder buzz rose from the table, and the heads (without relaxing their upward vigilance) seemed to merge and flow together, like an attentive flood, toward the upper end of the horse-shoe, where all the threads of Margaret Ransom's consciousness were suddenly drawn into what seemed a small speck, no more—a black speck that rose, hung in air, dissolved into gyrating gestures, became distended, enormous, preponderant—became her husband "speaking."

"It's the heat—" Margaret gasped, pressing her handkerchief to her whitening lips, and finding just strength enough left to push back farther into the shadow.

She felt a touch on her arm. "It *is* horrible—shall we go?" a voice suggested; and, "Yes, yes, let us go," she whispered, feeling, with a great throb of relief, *that* to be the only possible, the only conceivable, solution. To sit and listen to her husband *now*—how could she ever have thought she could survive it? Luckily, under the lingering hubbub from below, his opening words were inaudible, and she had only to run the gauntlet of sympathetic feminine glances, shot after her between waving fans and programmes, as, guided by Guy Dawnish, she managed to reach the door. It was really so hot that even Mrs. Sheff was not much surprised—till long afterward. . . .

The winding staircase was empty, half dark and blessedly silent. In a committee room below Dawnish found the inevitable water jug, and filled a glass for her, while she leaned back, confronted only by a frowning college President in an emblazoned frame. The academic frown descended on her like an anathema when she rose and followed her companion out of the building.

Hamblin Hall stands at the end of the long green "Campus" with its sextuple line of elms—the boast and singularity of Wentworth. A pale spring moon, rising above the dome of the University Library, at the opposite end of the elm-walk, diffused a pearly mildness in the sky, melted to thin haze the shadows of the trees, and turned to golden yellow the lights of the college windows. Against this soft suffusion of light the Library cupola assumed a Bramantesque grace,[8] the white steeple of the congregational church became a campanile* topped by a winged spirit, and the scant porticoes of the older halls the colonnades of classic temples.

"This is better—" Dawnish said, as they passed down the steps and under the shadow of the elms.

They moved on a little way in silence before he began again: "You're too tired to walk. Let us sit down a few minutes."

Her feet, in truth, were leaden, and not far off a group of park benches, encircling the pedestal of a patriot in bronze, invited them to rest. But Dawnish was guiding her toward a lateral path which bent, through shrubberies, toward a strip of turf between two buildings.

"It will be cooler by the river," he said, moving on without waiting for a possible protest. None came: it seemed easier, for the moment, to let herself be led without any conventional feint of resistance. And besides, there was nothing wrong about *this*—the

*Bell tower, usually freestanding, near a church.

wrong would have been in sitting up there in the glare, pretending to listen to her husband, a dutiful wife among her kind. . . .

The path descended, as both knew, to the chosen, the inimitable spot of Wentworth: that fugitive curve of the river, where, before hurrying on to glut the brutal industries of South Wentworth and Smedden, it simulated for a few hundred yards the leisurely pace of an ancient university stream, with willows on its banks and a stretch of turf extending from the grounds of Hamblin Hall to the boat houses at the farther bend. Here, too, were benches beneath the willows, and so close to the river that the voice of its gliding softened and filled out the reverberating silence between Margaret and her companion, and made her feel that she knew why he had brought her there.

"Do you feel better?" he asked gently as he sat down beside her.

"Oh, yes. I only needed a little air."

"I'm so glad you did. Of course the speeches were tremendously interesting—but I prefer this. What a good night!"

"Yes."

There was a pause, which now, after all, the soothing accompaniment of the river seemed hardly sufficient to fill.

"I wonder what time it is. I ought to be going home," Margaret began at length.

"Oh, it's not late. They'll be at it for hours in there—yet."

She made a faint inarticulate sound. She wanted to say: "No—Robert's speech was to be the last—" but she could not bring herself to pronounce Ransom's name, and at the moment no other way of refuting her companion's statement occurred to her.

The young man leaned back luxuriously, reassured by her silence. "You see it's my last chance—and I want to make the most of it."

"Your last chance?" How stupid of her to repeat his words on that cooing note of interrogation! It was just such a lead as the Brant girl might have given him.

"To be with you—like this. I haven't had so many. And there's less than a week left."

She attempted to laugh. "Perhaps it will sound longer if you call it five days."

The flatness of that, again! And she knew there were people who called her intelligent. Fortunately he did not seem to notice it; but her laugh continued to sound in her own ears—the coquettish chirp of middle age! She decided that if he spoke again—if he *said anything*—she would make no farther effort at evasion: she would take it directly, seriously, frankly—she would not be doubly disloyal.

"Besides," he continued, throwing his arm along the back of the bench, and turning toward her so that his face was like a dusky bas-relief with a silver rim—"besides, there's something I've been wanting to tell you."

The sound of the river seemed to cease altogether: the whole world became silent.

Margaret had trusted her inspiration farther than it appeared likely to carry her. Again she could think of nothing happier than to repeat, on the same witless note of interrogation: "To tell me?"

"You only."

The constraint, the difficulty, seemed to be on his side now: she divined it by the renewed shifting of his attitude—he was capable, usually, of such fine intervals of immobility—and by a confusion in his utterance that set her own voice throbbing in her throat.

"You've been so perfect to me," he began again. "It's not my fault if you've made me feel that you would understand everything—make allowances for everything—see just how a man may have held out, and fought against a thing—as long as he had the strength. . . . This may be my only chance; and I can't go away without telling you."

He had turned from her now, and was staring at the river, so that his profile was projected against the moonlight in all its beautiful young dejection.

There was a slight pause, as though he waited for her to speak; then she leaned forward and laid her hand on his.

"If I have really been—if I have done for you even the least part of what you say . . . what you imagine . . . will you do for me, now, just one thing in return?"

He sat motionless, as if fearing to frighten away the shy touch on his hand, and she left it there, conscious of her gesture only as part of the high ritual of their farewell.

"What do you want me to do?" he asked in a low tone.

"*Not* to tell me!" she breathed on a deep note of entreaty.

"*Not* to tell you—?"

"Anything—*anything*—just to leave our . . . our friendship . . . as it has been—as—as a painter, if a friend asked him, might leave a picture—not quite finished, perhaps, . . . but all the more exquisite. . . ."

She felt the hand under hers slip away, recover itself, and seek her own, which had flashed out of reach in the same instant—felt the start that swept him round on her as if he had been caught and turned about by the shoulders.

"You—*you*—?" he stammered, in a strange voice full of fear and tenderness; but she held fast, so centred in her inexorable resolve that she was hardly conscious of the effect her words might be producing.

"Don't you see," she hurried on, "don't you *feel* how much safer it is—yes, I'm willing to put it so!—how much safer to leave everything undisturbed . . . just as . . . as it has grown of itself . . . without trying to say: 'It's this or that' . . . ? It's what we each choose to call it to ourselves, after all, isn't it? Don't let us try to find a name that . . . that we should both agree upon . . . we probably shouldn't succeed." She laughed abruptly. "And ghosts vanish when one names them!" she ended with a break in her voice.

When she ceased her heart was beating so violently that there was a rush in her ears like the noise of the river after rain, and she did not immediately make out what he was answering. But as she recovered her lucidity she said to herself that, whatever he was saying, she must not hear it; and she began to speak again, half playfully, half appealingly, with an eloquence of entreaty, an ingenuity in argument, of which she had never dreamed herself capable. And then, suddenly, strangling hands seemed to reach up from her heart to her throat, and she had to stop.

Her companion remained motionless. He had not tried to regain her hand, and his eyes were away from her, on the river. But his nearness had become something formidable and exquisite—something she had never before imagined. A flush of guilt swept over her—vague reminiscences of French novels and of opera plots. This was what such women felt, then . . . this was "shame." . . . Phrases of the newspaper and the pulpit danced before her. . . . She dared not speak, and his silence began to frighten her. Had ever a heart beat so wildly before in Wentworth?

He turned at last, and taking her two hands, quite simply, kissed them one after the other.

"I shall never forget—" he said in a confused voice, unlike his own.

A return of strength enabled her to rise, and even to let her eyes meet his for a moment.

"Thank you," she said, simply also.

She turned away from the bench, regaining the path that led back to the college buildings, and he walked beside her in silence. When they reached the elm walk it was dotted with dispersing groups. The "speaking" was at an end, and Hamblin Hall had poured its audience out into the moonlight. Margaret felt a rush of relief, followed by a receding wave of regret. She had the distinct sensation that her hour—her one hour—was over.

One of the groups just ahead broke up as they approached, and projected Ransom's solid bulk against the moonlight.

"My husband," she said, hastening forward; and she never afterward forgot the look of his back—heavy, round-shouldered, yet a little pompous—in a badly fitting overcoat that stood out at the neck and hid his collar. She had never before noticed how he dressed.

IV.

They met again, inevitably, before Dawnish left; but the thing she feared did not happen—he did not try to see her alone.

It even became clear to her, in looking back, that he had deliberately avoided doing so; and this seemed merely an added proof of his "understanding," of that deep undefinable communion that set them alone in an empty world, as if on a peak above the clouds.

The five days passed in a flash; and when the last one came, it brought to Margaret Ransom an hour of weakness, of profound disorganisation, when old barriers fell, old convictions faded—when to be alone with him for a moment became, after all, the one craving of her heart. She knew he was coming that afternoon to say "good-bye"—and she knew also that Ransom was to be away at South Wentworth. She waited alone in her pale little drawing-room, with its scant kakemonos,* its one or two chilly reproductions from the antique, its slippery Chippendale† chairs. At length the bell rang, and her world became a rosy cloud—through which she presently discerned the austere form of Mrs. Sperry, wife of the Professor of palæontology, who had come to talk over with her the next winter's programme for the Higher Thought Club. They debated the question for an hour, and when Mrs. Sperry departed Margaret had a confused impression that the course was to deal with the influence of the First Crusade on the development of European architecture—but the sentient part of her knew only that Dawnish had not come.

He "bobbed in," as he would have put it, after dinner—having, it

*Japanese hangings or scrolls made of silk or paper.
†Rococo style of furniture named after English cabinetmaker Thomas Chippendale (1718–1779).

appeared, run across Ransom early in the day, and learned that the latter would be absent till evening. Margaret was in the study with her husband when the door opened and Dawnish stood there. Ransom—who had not had time to dress—was seated at his desk, a pile of shabby law books at his elbow, the light from a hanging lamp falling on his grayish stubble of hair, his sallow forehead and spectacled eyes. Dawnish, towering higher than usual against the shadows of the room, and refined by his unusual pallour, hung a moment on the threshold, then came in, explaining himself profusely—laughing, accepting a cigar, letting Ransom push an arm-chair forward—a Dawnish she had never seen, ill at ease, ejaculatory, yet somehow more mature, more obscurely in command of himself.

Margaret drew back, seating herself in the shade, in such a way that she saw her husband's head first, and beyond it their visitor's, relieved against the dusk of the book shelves. Her heart was still—she felt no throbbing in her throat or temples: all her life seemed concentrated in the hand that lay on her knee, the hand he would touch when they said good-bye.

Afterward her heart rang all the changes, and there was a mood in which she reproached herself for cowardice—for having deliberately missed her one moment with him, the moment in which she might have sounded the depths of life, for joy or anguish. But that mood was fleeting and infrequent. In quieter hours she blushed for it—she even trembled to think that he might have guessed such a regret in her. It seemed to convict her of a lack of fineness that he should have had, in his youth and his power, a tenderer, surer sense of the peril of a rash touch—should have handled the case so much more delicately.

At first her days were fire and the nights long solemn vigils. Her thoughts were no longer vulgarised and defaced by any notion of "guilt." She was ashamed now of her shame. What had happened was as much outside the sphere of her marriage as some transaction in a star. It had simply given her a secret life of incommunicable joys, as if all the wasted springs of her youth had been stored in some hidden pool, and she could return there now to bathe in them.

After that there came a phase of loneliness, through which the life about her loomed phantasmal and remote. She thought the dead must feel thus, repeating the vain gestures of the living beside some

Stygian* shore. She wondered if any other woman had lived to whom *nothing had ever happened?* And then his first letter came. . . .

It was a charming letter—a perfect letter. The little touch of awkwardness and constraint under its boyish spontaneity told her more than whole pages of eloquence. He spoke of their friendship—of their good days together . . . Ransom, chancing to come in while she read, noticed the foreign stamps; and she was able to hand him the letter, saying gaily: "There's a message for you," and knowing all the while that *her* message was safe in her heart.

On the days when the letters came the outlines of things grew indistinct, and she could never afterward remember what she had done or how the business of life had been carried on. It was always a surprise when she found dinner on the table as usual, and Ransom seated opposite to her, running over the evening paper.

But though Dawnish continued to write, with all the English loyalty to the outward observances of friendship, his communications came only at intervals of several weeks, and between them she had time to repossess herself, to regain some sort of normal contact with life. And the customary, the recurring, gradually reclaimed her, the net of habit tightened again—her daily life became real, and her one momentary escape from it an exquisite illusion. Not that she ceased to believe in the miracle that had befallen her; she still treasured the reality of her one moment beside the river. What reason was there for doubting it? She could hear the ring of truth in young Dawnish's voice: "It's not my fault if you've made me feel that you would understand everything. . . ." No! she believed in her miracle, and the belief sweetened and illumined her life; but she came to see that what was for her the transformation of her whole being might well have been, for her companion, a mere passing explosion of gratitude, of boyish good-fellowship touched with the pang of leave-taking. She even reached the point of telling herself that it was "better so": this view of the episode so defended it from the alternating extremes of self-reproach and derision, so enshrined it in a pale immortality to which she could make her secret pilgrimages without reproach.

---

*Relating to the river Styx, principal river of the underworld in classical mythology.

For a long time she had not been able to pass by the bench under the willows—she even avoided the elm walk till autumn had stripped its branches. But every day, now, she noted a step toward recovery; and at last a day came when, walking along the river, she said to herself, as she approached the bench: "I used not to be able to pass here without thinking of him; *and now I am not thinking of him at all!*"

This seemed such convincing proof of her recovery that she began, as spring returned, to permit herself, now and then, a quiet session on the bench—a dedicated hour from which she went back fortified to her task.

She had not heard from her friend for six weeks or more—the intervals between his letters were growing longer. But that was "best" too, and she was not anxious, for she knew he had obtained the post he had been preparing for, and that his active life in London had begun. The thought reminded her, one mild March day, that in leaving the house she had thrust in her reticule a letter from a Wentworth friend who was abroad on a holiday. The envelope bore the London post mark, a fact showing that the lady's face was turned toward home. Margaret seated herself on her bench, and began to read the letter.

The London described was that of shops and museums—as remote as possible from the setting of Guy Dawnish's existence. But suddenly Margaret's eye fell on his name, and the page began to tremble in her hands.

"I heard such a funny thing yesterday about your friend Mr. Dawnish. We went to a tea at Professor Bunce's (I do wish you knew the Bunces—their atmosphere is so *uplifting*), and there I met that Miss Bruce-Pringle who came out last year to take a course in histology at the Annex. Of course she asked about you and Mr. Ransom, and then she told me she had just seen Mr. Dawnish's aunt—the clever one he was always talking about, Lady Caroline something—and that they were all in a dreadful state about him. I wonder if you knew he was engaged when he went to America? He never mentioned it to *us*. She said it was not a positive engagement, but an understanding with a girl he has always been devoted to, who lives near their place in Wiltshire; and both families expected the marriage to take place as soon as he got back. It seems the girl is an heiress (you know *how low* the English ideals are compared with ours), and Miss Bruce-Pringle said his relations were perfectly delighted at his 'being provided for,' as she called it. Well, when he got back he asked the girl to release him; and she and her family were furious, and so were his people; but he holds out, and won't marry her, and won't give a reason, except that he has 'formed an unfortunate attachment.' Did you ever hear anything so peculiar? His aunt, who is quite wild about it, says it must have happened at Wentworth, because he didn't go anywhere else in America. Do you suppose it *could* have been the Brant girl? But why 'unfortunate' when everybody knows she would have jumped at him?"

Margaret folded the letter and looked out across the river. It was not the same river, but a mystic current shot with moonlight. The bare willows wove a leafy veil above her head, and beside her she felt the nearness of youth and tempestuous tenderness. It had all happened just here, on this very seat by the river—it had come to her, and passed her by, and she had not held out a hand to detain it. . . .

Well! Was it not, by that very abstention, made more deeply and ineffaceably hers? She could argue thus while she had thought the episode, on his side, a mere transient effect of propinquity; but now that she knew it had altered the whole course of his life, now that it took on substance and reality, asserted a separate existence outside of her own troubled consciousness—now it seemed almost cowardly to have missed her share in it.

She walked home in a dream. Now and then, when she passed an acquaintance, she wondered if the pain and glory were written on her face. But Mrs. Sperry, who stopped her at the corner of Maverick Street to say a word about the next meeting of the Higher Thought Club, seemed to remark no change in her.

When she reached home Ransom had not yet returned from the office, and she went straight to the library to tidy his writing-table. It was part of her daily duty to bring order out of the chaos of his papers, and of late she had fastened on such small recurring tasks as some one falling over a precipice might snatch at the weak bushes in its clefts.

When she had sorted the letters she took up some pamphlets and newspapers, glancing over them to see if they were to be kept. Among the papers was a page torn from a London *Times* of the previous month. Her eye ran down its columns and suddenly a paragraph flamed out.

"We are requested to state that the marriage arranged between Mr. Guy Dawnish, son of the late Colonel the Hon. Roderick Dawnish, of Malby, Wilts, and Gwendolen, daughter of Samuel Matcher, Esq., of Armingham Towers, Wilts, will not take place."

Margaret dropped the paper and sat down, hiding her face against the stained baize of the desk. She remembered the photograph of the tennis-court at Guise—she remembered the handsome girl at whom Guy Dawnish looked up, laughing. A gust of tears shook her, loosening the dry surface of conventional feeling, welling up from unsuspected depths. She was sorry—very sorry, yet so glad—so ineffably, impenitently glad.

V.

There came a reaction in which she decided to write to him. She even sketched out a letter of sisterly, almost motherly, remonstrance, in which she reminded him that he "still had all his life before him." But she reflected that so, after all, had she; and that seemed to weaken the argument.

In the end she decided not to send the letter. He had never spoken to her of his engagement to Gwendolen Matcher, and his letters had contained no allusion to any sentimental disturbance in his life. She had only his few broken words, that night by the river, on which to build her theory of the case. But illuminated by the phrase "an unfortunate attachment" the theory towered up, distinct and immovable, like some high landmark by which travellers shape their course. She had been loved—extraordinarily loved. But he had chosen that she should know of it by his silence rather than by his speech. He had understood that only on those terms could their transcendant communion continue—that he must lose her to keep her. To break that silence would be like spilling a cup of water in a waste of sand. There would be nothing left for her thirst.

Her life, thenceforward, was bathed in a tranquil beauty. The days flowed by like a river beneath the moon—each ripple caught the brightness and passed it on. She began to take a renewed interest in her familiar round of duties. The tasks which had once seemed colourless and irksome had now a kind of sacrificial sweetness, a symbolic meaning into which she alone was initiated. She had been restless—had longed to travel; now she felt that she should never again care to leave Wentworth. But if her desire to wander had ceased she travelled in spirit, performing invisible pilgrimages in the footsteps of her friend. She regretted that her one short visit to England had taken her so little out of London—that her acquaintance with the landscape had been formed chiefly through the windows of a railway carriage. She threw herself into the architectural studies of the Higher Thought Club, and distinguished herself, at the spring meetings, by her fluency, her competence, her inexhaustible curiosity on the subject of the growth of English Gothic. She ransacked the shelves of the college library, she borrowed photographs of the cathedrals, she pored over the folio pages of "The Seats of Noblemen and Gentlemen." She was like some banished princess who learns that she has inherited a domain in her own country, who knows that she will never see it, yet feels, wherever she walks, its soil beneath her feet.

May was half over, and the Higher Thought Club was to hold its last meeting, previous to the college festivities which, in early June, agreeably disorganised the social routine of Wentworth. The meeting was to take place in Margaret Ransom's drawing-room, and on the day before she sat upstairs preparing for her dual duties as hostess and orator—for she had been invited to read the final paper of the course.

In order to sum up with precision her conclusions on the subject of English Gothic, she had been re-reading an analysis of the structural features of the principal English cathedrals; and she was murmuring over to herself the phrase: "The longitudinal arches of Lincoln have an approximately elliptical form"[9] when there came a knock on the door, and Maria's voice announced: "There's a lady down in the parlour."

Margaret's soul dropped from the heights of the shadowy vaulting to the dead level of an afternoon call at Wentworth.

"A lady? Did she give no name?"

Maria became confused. "She only said she was a lady—" and in reply to her mistress's look of mild surprise: "Well, ma'am, she told me so three or four times over."

Margaret laid her book down, leaving it open at the description of Lincoln, and slowly descended the stairs. As she did so, she repeated to herself: "The longitudinal arches are elliptical."

On the threshold below, she had the odd impression that her bare inanimate drawing-room was brimming with life and noise—an impression produced, as she presently perceived, by the resolute forward dash—it was almost a pounce—of the one small figure restlessly measuring its length.

The dash checked itself within a yard of Margaret, and the

lady—a stranger—held back long enough to stamp on her hostess a sharp impression of sallowness, leanness, keenness, before she said, in a voice that might have been addressing an unruly committee meeting: "I am Lady Caroline Duckett—a fact I found it impossible to make clear to the young woman who let me in."

A warm wave rushed up from Margaret's heart to her face. She held out both hands impulsively. "Oh, I'm so glad—I'd no idea—"

Her voice sank under her visitor's impartial scrutiny.

"I don't wonder," said the latter dryly. "I suppose she didn't mention either that my object in calling here was to see Mrs. Ransom?"

"Oh, yes—won't you sit down?" Margaret pushed a chair forward. She seated herself at a little distance, brain and heart humming with a confused interchange of signals. This dark sharp woman was his aunt—the "clever aunt" who had had such a hard life, but had always managed to keep her head above water. Margaret remembered that Guy had spoken of her kindness—perhaps she would seem kinder when they had talked together a little. Meanwhile the first impression she produced was of an amplitude out of all proportion to her somewhat scant exterior. With her small flat figure, her shabby heterogeneous dress, she was as dowdy as any Professor's wife at Wentworth; but her dowdiness (Margaret borrowed a literary analogy to define it), her dowdiness was somehow "of the centre." Like the insignificant emissary of a great power, she was to be judged rather by her passports than her person.

While Margaret was receiving these impressions, Lady Caroline, with quick bird-like twists of her head, was gathering others from the pale void spaces of the drawing-room. Her eyes, divided by a sharp nose like a bill, seemed to be set far enough apart to see at separate angles; but suddenly she bent both of them on Margaret.

"This *is* Mrs. Ransom's house?" she asked, with an emphasis on the verb that gave a distinct hint of unfulfilled expectations.

Margaret assented.

"Because your American houses, especially in the provincial towns, all look so remarkably alike, that I thought I might have been mistaken; and as my time is extremely limited—in fact I'm sailing on Wednesday—"

She paused long enough to let Margaret say: "I had no idea you were in America."

Lady Caroline made no attempt to take this up.—"and so much of it," she carried on her sentence, "has been wasted in talking to people I really hadn't the slightest desire to see, that you must excuse me if I go straight to the point."

Margaret felt a sudden tension of the heart. "Of course," she said, while a voice within her cried: "He's dead—he has left me a message."

There was another pause; then Lady Caroline went on with increasing asperity: "So that—in short—if I *could* see Mrs. Ransom at once—"

Margaret looked up in surprise. "I am Mrs. Ransom," she said.

The other stared a moment, with much the same look of cautious incredulity that had marked her inspection of the drawing-room. Then light came to her.

"Oh, I beg your pardon. I should have said that I wished to see Mrs. *Robert* Ransom, not Mrs. Ransom. But I understood that in the States you don't make those distinctions." She paused a moment, and then went on, before Margaret could answer: "Perhaps, after all, it's as well that I should see you instead, since you're evidently one of the household—your son and his wife live with you, I suppose? Yes, on the whole, then, it's better—I shall be able to talk so much more frankly." She spoke as if, as a rule, circumstances prevented her giving rein to this prosperity. "And frankness, of course, is the only way out of this—this extremely tiresome complication. You know, I suppose, that my nephew thinks he's in love with your daughter-in-law?"

Margaret made a slight movement, but her visitor pressed on without heeding it. "Oh, don't fancy, please, that I'm pretending to take a high moral ground—though his mother does, poor dear! I can perfectly imagine that in a place like this—I've just been walking about it for two hours—a young man of Guy's age would *have* to provide himself with some sort of distraction; and he's not the kind to go in for anything objectionable. Oh, we quite allow for that—we should allow for the whole affair, if it hadn't so preposterously ended in his throwing over the girl he was engaged to, and upsetting an arrangement that affected a number of people besides himself. I understand that in the States it's different—the young people have only themselves to consider. In England—in our class, I mean—a great deal may depend on a young man's making a good match; and in Guy's case I may say that his mother and sisters (I won't include myself, though I might) have been simply stranded—thrown overboard—by his freak. You can understand how serious it is when I tell you that it's that and nothing else that has brought me all the way to America. And my first idea was to go straight to your daughter-in-law, since her influence is the only thing we can count on now, and put it to her fairly, as I'm putting it to you. But, on the whole, I dare say it's better to see you first—you might give me an idea of the line to take with her. I'm prepared to throw myself on her mercy!"

Margaret rose from her chair, outwardly rigid in proportion to her inward tremor.

"You don't understand—" she began.

Lady Caroline brushed the interruption aside. "Oh, but I do—completely! I cast no reflection on your daughter-in-law. Guy has made it quite clear to us that his attachment is—has, in short, not been rewarded. But don't you see that that's the worst part of it? There'd be much more hope of his recovering if Mrs. Robert Ransom had—had—"

Margaret's voice broke from her in a cry. "I am Mrs. Robert Ransom," she said.

If Lady Caroline Duckett had hitherto given her hostess the impression of a person not easily silenced, this fact added sensibly to the effect produced by the intense stillness which now fell on her.

She sat quite motionless, her large bangled hands clasped about the meagre fur boa she had unwound from her neck on entering, her rusty black veil pushed up to the edge of a "fringe" of doubtful authenticity, her thin lips parted on a gasp that seemed to sharpen itself on the edges of her teeth. So overwhelming and helpless was her silence that Margaret began to feel a motion of pity beneath her indignation—a desire at least to facilitate the excuses which must terminate their disastrous colloquy. But when Lady Caroline found voice she did not use it to excuse herself.

"You *can't* be," she said, quite simply.

"Can't be?" Margaret stammered, with a flushing cheek.

"I mean, it's some mistake. Are there *two* Mrs. Robert Ransoms in the same town? Your family arrangements are so extremely puzzling." She had a farther rush of enlightenment. "Oh, I *see!* I ought of course to have asked for Mrs. Robert Ransom *Junior!*"

The idea sent her to her feet with a haste which showed her impatience to make up for lost time.

"There is no other Mrs. Robert Ransom at Wentworth," said Margaret.

"No other—no 'Junior'? Are you *sure?*" Lady Caroline fell back into her seat again. "Then I simply don't see," she murmured.

Margaret's blush had fixed itself on her throbbing forehead. She remained standing, while her strange visitor continued to gaze at her with a perturbation in which the consciousness of indiscretion had evidently as yet no part.

"I simply don't see," she repeated.

Suddenly she sprang up, and advancing to Margaret, laid an inspired hand on her arm. "But, my dear woman, you can help us out all the same; you can help us to find out *who it is*—and you will, won't you? Because, as it's not you, you can't in the least mind what I've been saying—"

Margaret, freeing her arm from her visitor's hold, drew back a step; but Lady Caroline instantly rejoined her.

"Of course, I can see that if it *had* been, you might have been annoyed: I dare say I put the case stupidly—but I'm so bewildered by this new development—by his using you all this time as a pretext—that I really don't know where to turn for light on the mystery—"

She had Margaret in her imperious grasp again, but the latter broke from her with a more resolute gesture.

"I'm afraid I have no light to give you," she began; but once more Lady Caroline caught her up.

"Oh, but do please understand me! I condemn Guy most strongly for using your name—when we all know you'd been so amazingly kind to him! I haven't a word to say in his defence—but of course the important thing now is: *who is the woman, since you're not?*"

The question rang out loudly, as if all the pale puritan corners of the room flung it back with a shudder at the speaker. In the silence that ensued Margaret felt the blood ebbing back to her heart; then she said, in a distinct and level voice: "I know nothing of the history of Mr. Dawnish."

Lady Caroline gave a stare and a gasp. Her distracted hand groped for her boa, and she began to wind it mechanically about her long neck.

"It would really be an enormous help to us—and to poor Gwendolen Matcher," she persisted pleadingly. "And you'd be doing Guy himself a good turn."

Margaret remained silent and motionless while her visitor drew on one of the worn gloves she had pulled off to adjust her veil. Lady Caroline gave the veil a final twitch.

"I've come a tremendously long way," she said, "and, since it isn't you, I can't think why you won't help me. . . ."

When the door had closed on her visitor Margaret Ransom went slowly up the stairs to her room. As she dragged her feet from one step to another, she remembered how she had sprung up the same steep flight after that visit of Guy Dawnish's when she had looked in the glass and seen on her face the blush of youth.

When she reached her room she bolted the door as she had done that day, and again looked at herself in the narrow mirror above her dressing-table. It was just a year since then—the elms were budding again, the willows hanging their green veil above the bench by the river. But there was no trace of youth left in her face—she saw it now as others had doubtless always seen it. If it seemed as it did to Lady Caroline Duckett, what look must it have worn to the fresh gaze of young Guy Dawnish?

A pretext—she had been a pretext. He had used her name to screen some one else—or perhaps merely to escape from a situation of which he was weary. She did not care to conjecture what his motive had been—everything connected with him had grown so remote and alien. She felt no anger—only an unspeakable sadness, a sadness which she knew would never be appeased.

She looked at herself long and steadily: she wished to clear her eyes of all illusions. Then she turned away and took her usual seat beside her work-table. From where she sat she could look down the empty elm-shaded street, up which, at this hour every day, she was sure to see her husband's figure advancing. She would see it presently—she would see it for many years to come. She had an aching vision of the length of the years that stretched before her. Strange that one who was not young should still, in all likelihood, have so long to live!

Nothing was changed in the setting of her life, perhaps nothing would ever change in it. She would certainly live and die in Wentworth. And meanwhile the days would go on as usual, bringing the usual obligations. As the word flitted through her brain she remembered that she had still to put the finishing touches to the paper she was to read the next afternoon at the meeting of the Higher Thought Club.

The book she had been reading lay face downward beside her, where she had left it an hour ago. She took it up, and slowly and painfully, like a child labouriously spelling out the syllables, she went on with the rest of the sentence:

—"and they spring from a level not much above that of the springing of the transverse and diagonal ribs, which are so arranged as to give a convex curve to the surface of the vaulting conoid."*[10]

*Cone-like shape.

AFTERWARD[1]

I.

"Oh, there *is* one, of course, but you'll never know it."

The assertion, laughingly flung out six months earlier in a bright June garden, came back to Mary Boyne with a new perception of its significance as she stood, in the December dusk, waiting for the lamps to be brought into the library.

The words had been spoken by their friend Alida Stair, as they sat at tea on her lawn at Pangbourne, in reference to the very house of which the library in question was the central, the pivotal "feature." Mary Boyne and her husband, in quest of a country place in one of the southern or southwestern counties, had, on their arrival in England, carried their problem straight to Alida Stair, who had successfully solved it in her own case; but it was not until they had rejected, almost capriciously, several practical and judicious suggestions that she threw out: "Well, there's Lyng, in Dorsetshire.[2] It belongs to Hugo's cousins, and you can get it for a song."

The reason she gave for its being obtainable on these terms—its remoteness from a station, its lack of electric light, hot-water pipes, and other vulgar necessities—were exactly those pleading in its favour with two romantic Americans perversely in search of the economic drawbacks which were associated, in their tradition, with unusual architectural felicities.

"I should never believe I was living in an old house unless I was thoroughly uncomfortable," Ned Boyne, the more extravagant of the two, had jocosely insisted; "the least hint of 'convenience' would make me think it had been bought out of an exhibition, with the pieces numbered, and set up again." And they had proceeded to enumerate, with humorous precision, their various doubts and demands, refusing to believe that the house their cousin recommended was *really* Tudor* till they learned it had no heating system, or that the village church was literally in the grounds till she assured them of the deplorable uncertainty of the water-supply.

"It's too uncomfortable to be true!" Edward Boyne had continued to exult as the avowal of each disadvantage was successively wrung from her; but he had cut short his rhapsody to ask, with a relapse to distrust: "And the ghost? You've been concealing from us the fact that there is no ghost!"

Mary, at the moment, had laughed with him, yet almost with her laugh, being possessed of several sets of independent perceptions, had been struck by a note of flatness in Alida's answering hilarity.

"Oh, Dorsetshire's full of ghosts, you know."

"Yes, yes; but that won't do. I don't want to have to drive ten miles to see somebody else's ghost. I want one of my own on the premises. *Is* there a ghost at Lyng?"

His rejoinder had made Alida laugh again, and it was then that she had flung back tantalisingly: "Oh, there *is* one, of course, but you'll never know it."

"Never know it?" Boyne pulled her up. "But what in the world constitutes a ghost except the fact of its being known for one?"

"I can't say. But that's the story."

"That there's a ghost, but that nobody knows it's a ghost?"

"Well—not till afterward, at any rate."

"Till afterward?"

"Not till long long afterward."

"But if it's once been identified as an unearthly visitant, why hasn't its *signalement*† been handed down in the family? How has it managed to preserve its incognito?"

Alida could only shake her head. "Don't ask me. But it has."

"And then suddenly—" Mary spoke up as if from cavernous depths of divination—"suddenly, long afterward, one says to one's self *'That was it?'* "

She was startled at the sepulchral sound with which her question fell on the banter of the other two, and she saw the shadow of the

---

*Style of architecture that prevailed in England during the reign of the royal house of Tudor (1485–1603).

†Description (French).

same surprise flit across Alida's pupils. "I suppose so. One just has to wait."

"Oh, hang waiting!" Ned broke in. "Life's too short for a ghost who can only be enjoyed in retrospect. Can't we do better than that, Mary?"

But it turned out that in the event they were not destined to, for within three months of their conversation with Mrs. Stair they were settled at Lyng, and the life they had yearned for, to the point of planning it in advance in all its daily details, had actually begun for them.

It was to sit, in the thick December dusk, by just such a wide-hooded fireplace, under just such black oak rafters, with the sense that beyond the mullioned panes* the downs† were darkened to a deeper solitude: it was for the ultimate indulgence of such sensations that Mary Boyne, abruptly exiled from New York by her husband's business, had endured for nearly fourteen years the soul-deadening ugliness of a Middle Western town,[3] and that Boyne had ground on doggedly at his engineering till, with a suddenness that still made her blink, the prodigious windfall of the Blue Star Mine had put them at a stroke in possession of life and the leisure to taste it. They had never for a moment meant their new state to be one of idleness; but they meant to give themselves only to harmonious activities. She had her vision of painting and gardening (against a background of grey walls), he dreamed of the production of his long-planned book on the "Economic Basis of Culture"; and with such absorbing work ahead no existence could be too sequestered: they could not get far enough from the world, or plunge deep enough into the past.

Dorsetshire had attracted them from the first by an air of remoteness out of all proportion to its geographical position. But to the Boynes it was one of the ever-recurring wonders of the whole incredibly compressed island—a nest of counties, as they put it—that for the production of its effects so little of a given quality went so far: that so few miles made a distance, and so short a distance a difference.

"It's that," Ned had once enthusiastically explained, "that gives

---

*Windows divided by vertical bars.

†Hilly, treeless uplands.

such depth to their effects, such relief to their contrasts. They've been able to lay the butter so thick on every delicious mouthful."

The butter had certainly been laid on thick at Lyng: the old house hidden under a shoulder of the downs had almost all the finer marks of commerce with a protracted past. The mere fact that it was neither large nor exceptional made it, to the Boynes, abound the more completely in its special charm—the charm of having been for centuries a deep dim reservoir of life. The life had probably not been of the most vivid order: for long periods, no doubt, it had fallen as noiselessly into the past as the quiet drizzle of autumn fell, hour after hour, into the fish-pond between the yews; but these back-waters of existence sometimes breed, in their sluggish depths, strange acuities of emotion, and Mary Boyne had felt from the first the mysterious stir of intenser memories.

The feeling had never been stronger than on this particular after-noon when, waiting in the library for the lamps to come, she rose from her seat and stood among the shadows of the hearth.[4] Her husband had gone off, after luncheon, for one of his long tramps on the downs. She had noticed of late that he preferred to go alone; and, in the tried security of their personal relations, had been driven to conclude that his book was bothering him, and that he needed the afternoons to turn over in solitude the problems left from the morning's work. Certainly the book was not going as smoothly as she had thought it would, and there were lines of perplexity between his eyes such as had never been there in his engineering days. He had often, then, looked fagged to the verge of illness, but the native demon of "worry" had never branded his brow. Yet the few pages he had so far read to her—the introduction, and a sum-mary of the opening chapter—showed a firm hold on his subject, and an increasing confidence in his powers.

The fact threw her into deeper perplexity, since, now that he had done with "business" and its disturbing contingencies, the one other possible source of anxiety was eliminated. Unless it were his health, then? But physically he had gained since they had come to Dorset-shire, grown robuster, ruddier and fresher-eyed. It was only within the last week that she had felt in him the undefinable change which made her restless in his absence, and as tongue-tied in his presence as though it were *she* who had a secret to keep from him!

The thought that there *was* a secret somewhere between them struck her with a sudden rap of wonder, and she looked about her down the long room.

"Can it be the house?" she mused.

The room itself might have been full of secrets. They seemed to be piling themselves up, as evening fell, like the layers and layers of velvet shadow dropping from the low ceiling, the rows of books, the smoke-blurred sculpture of the hearth.

"Why, of course—the house is haunted!" she reflected.

The ghost—Alida's imperceptible ghost—after figuring largely in the banter of their first month or two at Lyng, had been gradually left aside as too ineffectual for imaginative use. Mary had, indeed, as became the tenant of a haunted house, made the customary inquiries among her rural neighbours, but, beyond a vague "They dü say so, Ma'am," the villagers had nothing to impart. The elusive spectre had apparently never had sufficient identity for a legend to crystallise about it, and after a time the Boynes had set the matter down to their profit-and-loss account, agreeing that Lyng was one of the few houses good enough in itself to dispense with supernatural enhancements.

"And I suppose, poor ineffectual demon, that's why it beats its beautiful wings in vain in the void," Mary had laughingly concluded.

"Or, rather," Ned answered in the same strain, "why, amid so much that's ghostly, it can never affirm its separate existence as *the* ghost." And thereupon their invisible housemate had finally dropped out of their references, which were numerous enough to make them soon unaware of the loss.

Now, as she stood on the hearth, the subject of their earlier curiosity revived in her with a new sense of its meaning—a sense gradually acquired through daily contact with the scene of the lurking mystery. It was the house itself, of course, that possessed the ghost-seeing faculty, that communed visually but secretly with its own past; if one could only get into close enough communion with the house, one might surprise its secret, and acquire the ghost-sight on one's own account. Perhaps, in his long hours in this very room, where she never trespassed till the afternoon, her husband *had* acquired it already, and was silently carrying about the weight of whatever it had revealed to him. Mary was too well versed in the code of the spectral world not to know that one could not talk about the ghosts one saw: to do so was almost as great a breach of taste as to name a lady in a club. But this explanation did not really satisfy her. "What, after all, except for the fun of the shudder," she reflected, "would he really care for any of their old ghosts?" And thence she was thrown back once more on the fundamental dilemma: the fact that one's greater or less susceptibility to spectral influences had no particular bearing on the case, since, when one *did* see a ghost at Lyng, one did not know it.

"Not till long afterward," Alida Stair had said. Well, supposing Ned *had* seen one when they first came, and had known only within the last week what had happened to him? More and more under the spell of the hour, she threw back her thoughts to the early days of their tenancy, but at first only to recall a lively confusion of unpacking, settling, arranging of books, and calling to each other from remote corners of the house as, treasure after treasure, it revealed itself to them. It was in this particular connection that she presently recalled a certain soft afternoon of the previous October, when, passing from the first rapturous flurry of exploration to a detailed inspection of the old house, she had pressed (like a novel heroine) a panel that opened on a flight of corkscrew stairs leading to a flat ledge of the roof—the roof which, from below, seemed to slope away on all sides too abruptly for any but practised feet to scale.

The view from this hidden coign* was enchanting, and she had flown down to snatch Ned from his papers and give him the freedom of her discovery. She remembered still how, standing at her side, he had passed his arm about her while their gaze flew to the long tossed horizon-line of the downs, and then dropped contentedly back to trace the arabesque of yew hedges about the fish-pond, and the shadow of the cedar on the lawn.

"And now the other way," he had said, turning her about within his arm; and closely pressed to him, she had absorbed, like some long satisfying draught, the picture of the grey-walled court, the squat lions on the gates, and the lime-avenue reaching up to the highroad under the downs.

---

*Vantage point.

It was just then, while they gazed and held each other, that she had felt his arm relax, and heard a sharp "Hullo!" that made her turn to glance at him.

Distinctly, yes, she now recalled that she had seen, as she glanced, a shadow of anxiety, of perplexity, rather, fall across his face; and, following his eyes, had beheld the figure of a man—a man in loose greyish clothes, as it appeared to her—who was sauntering down the lime-avenue to the court with the doubtful gait of a stranger who seeks his way. Her short-sighted eyes had given her but a blurred impression of slightness and greyishness, with something foreign, or at least unlocal, in the cut of the figure or its dress; but her husband had apparently seen more—seen enough to make him push past her with a hasty "Wait!" and dash down the stairs without pausing to give her a hand.

A slight tendency to dizziness obliged her, after a provisional clutch at the chimney against which they had been leaning, to follow him first more cautiously; and when she had reached the landing she paused again, for a less definite reason, leaning over the banister to strain her eyes through the silence of the brown sun-flecked depths. She lingered there till, somewhere in those depths, she heard the closing of a door; then, mechanically impelled, she went down the shallow flights of steps till she reached the lower hall.

The front door stood open on the sunlight of the court, and hall and court were empty. The library door was open, too, and after listening in vain for any sound of voices within, she crossed the threshold, and found her husband alone, vaguely fingering the papers on his desk.

He looked up, as if surprised at her entrance, but the shadow of anxiety had passed from his face, leaving it even, as she fancied, a little brighter and clearer than usual.

"What was it? Who was it?" she asked.

"Who?" he repeated, with the surprise still all on his side.

"The man we saw coming toward the house."

He seemed to reflect. "The man? Why, I thought I saw Peters; I dashed after him to say a word about the stable drains, but he had disappeared before I could get down."

"Disappeared? But he seemed to be walking so slowly when we saw him."

Boyne shrugged his shoulders. "So I thought; but he must have got up steam in the interval. What do you say to our trying a scramble up Meldon Steep before sunset?"

That was all. At the time the occurrence had been less than nothing, had, indeed, been immediately obliterated by the magic of their first vision from Meldon Steep, a height which they had dreamed of climbing ever since they had first seen its bare spine rising above the roof of Lyng. Doubtless it was the mere fact of the other incident's having occurred on the very day of their ascent to Meldon that had kept it stored away in the fold of memory from which it now emerged; for in itself it had no mark of the portentous. At the moment there could have been nothing more natural than that Ned should dash himself from the roof in the pursuit of dilatory tradesmen. It was the period when they were always on the watch for one or the other of the specialists employed about the place; always lying in wait for them, and rushing out at them with questions, reproaches or reminders. And certainly in the distance the grey figure had looked like Peters.

Yet now, as she reviewed the scene, she felt her husband's explanation of it to have been invalidated by the look of anxiety on his face. Why had the familiar appearance of Peters made him anxious? Why, above all, if it was of such prime necessity to confer with him on the subject of the stable drains, had the failure to find him produced such a look of relief? Mary could not say that any one of these questions had occurred to her at the time, yet, from the promptness with which they now marshalled themselves at her summons, she had a sense that they must all along have been there, waiting their hour.

II.

Weary with her thoughts, she moved to the window. The library was now quite dark, and she was surprised to see how much faint light the outer world still held.

As she peered out into it across the court, a figure shaped itself far down the perspective of bare limes: it looked a mere blot of deeper grey in the greyness, and for an instant, as it moved toward her, her heart thumped to the thought "It's the ghost!"

She had time, in that long instant, to feel suddenly that the man of whom, two months earlier, she had had a distant vision from the roof, was now, at his predestined hour, about to reveal himself as *not* having been Peters; and her spirit sank under the impending fear of the disclosure. But almost with the next tick of the clock the figure, gaining substance and character, showed itself even to her weak sight as her husband's; and she turned to meet him, as he entered, with the confession of her folly.

"It's really too absurd," she laughed out, "but I never *can* remember!"

"Remember what?" Boyne questioned as they drew together.

"That when one sees the Lyng ghost one never knows it."

Her hand was on his sleeve, and he kept it there, but with no response in his gesture or in the lines of his preoccupied face.

"Did you think you'd seen it?" he asked, after an appreciable interval.

"Why, I actually took *you* for it, my dear, in my mad determination to spot it!"

"Me—just now?" His arm dropped away, and he turned from her with a faint echo of her laugh. "Really, dearest, you'd better give it up, if that's the best you can do."

"Oh, yes, I give it up. Have *you?*" she asked, turning round on him abruptly.

The parlour-maid had entered with letters and a lamp, and the light struck up into Boyne's face as he bent above the tray she presented.

"Have *you?*" Mary perversely insisted, when the servant had disappeared on her errand of illumination.

"Have I what?" he rejoined absently, the light bringing out the sharp stamp of worry between his brows as he turned over the letters.

"Given up trying to see the ghost." Her heart beat a little at the experiment she was making.

Her husband, laying his letters aside, moved away into the shadow of the hearth.

"I never tried," he said, tearing open the wrapper of a newspaper.

"Well, of course," Mary persisted, "the exasperating thing is that there's no use trying, since one can't be sure till so long afterward."

He was unfolding the paper as if he had hardly heard her; but after a pause, during which the sheets rustled spasmodically between his hands, he looked up to ask, "Have you any idea *how long?*"

Mary had sunk into a low chair beside the fireplace. From her seat she glanced over, startled, at her husband's profile, which was projected against the circle of lamplight.

"No; none. Have *you?*" she retorted, repeating her former phrase with an added stress of intention.

Boyne crumpled the paper into a bunch, and then, inconsequently, turned back with it toward the lamp.

"Lord, no! I only meant," he explained, with a faint tinge of impatience, "is there any legend, any tradition, as to that?"

"Not that I know of," she answered; but the impulse to add "What makes you ask?" was checked by the reappearance of the parlour-maid, with tea and a second lamp.

With the dispersal of shadows, and the repetition of the daily domestic office, Mary Boyne felt herself less oppressed by that sense of something mutely imminent which had darkened her afternoon. For a few moments she gave herself to the details of her task, and when she looked up from it she was struck to the point of bewilderment by the change in her husband's face. He had seated himself near the farther lamp, and was absorbed in the perusal of his letters; but was it something he had found in them, or merely the shifting of her own point of view, that had restored his features to their normal aspect? The longer she looked the more definitely the change affirmed itself. The lines of tension had vanished, and such traces of fatigue as lingered were of the kind easily attributable to steady mental effort. He glanced up, as if drawn by her gaze, and met her eyes with a smile.

"I'm dying for my tea, you know; and here's a letter for you," he said.

She took the letter he held out in exchange for the cup she proffered him, and, returning to her seat, broke the seal with the languid gesture of the reader whose interests are all enclosed in the circle of one cherished presence.

Her next conscious motion was that of starting to her feet, the letter falling to them as she rose, while she held out to her husband a newspaper clipping.

"Ned! What's this? What does it mean?"

He had risen at the same instant, almost as if hearing her cry before she uttered it; and for a perceptible space of time he and she studied each other, like adversaries watching for an advantage, across the space between her chair and his desk.

"What's what? You fairly made me jump!" Boyne said at length, moving toward her with a sudden half-exasperated laugh. The shadow of apprehension was on his face again, not now a look of fixed foreboding, but a shifting vigilance of lips and eyes that gave her the sense of his feeling himself invisibly surrounded.

Her hand shook so that she could hardly give him the clipping.

"This article—from the *Waukesha Sentinel*—that a man named Elwell has brought suit against you—that there was something wrong about the Blue Star Mine. I can't understand more than half."

They continued to face each other as she spoke, and to her astonishment she saw that her words had the almost immediate effect of dissipating the strained watchfulness of his look.

"Oh, *that!*" He glanced down the printed slip, and then folded it with the gesture of one who handles something harmless and familiar. "What's the matter with you this afternoon, Mary? I thought you'd got bad news."

She stood before him with her undefinable terror subsiding slowly under the reassurance of his tone.

"You knew about this, then—it's all right?"

"Certainly I knew about it; and it's all right."

"But what *is* it? I don't understand. What does this man accuse you of?"

"Pretty nearly every crime in the calendar." Boyne had tossed the clipping down, and thrown himself into an arm-chair near the fire. "Do you want to hear the story? It's not particularly interesting—just a squabble over interests in the Blue Star."

"But who is this Elwell? I don't know the name."

"Oh, he's a fellow I put into it—gave him a hand up. I told you all about him at the time."

"I daresay. I must have forgotten." Vainly she strained back among her memories. "But if you helped him, why does he make this return?"

"Probably some shyster lawyer got hold of him and talked him over. It's all rather technical and complicated. I thought that kind of thing bored you."

His wife felt a sting of compunction. Theoretically, she deprecated the American wife's detachment from her husband's professional interests, but in practice she had always found it difficult to fix her attention on Boyne's report of the transactions in which his varied interests involved him. Besides, she had felt during their years of exile, that, in a community where the amenities of living could be obtained only at the cost of efforts as arduous as her husband's professional labours, such brief leisure as he and she could command should be used as an escape from immediate preoccupations, a flight to the life they always dreamed of living. Once or twice, now that this new life had actually drawn its magic circle about them, she had asked herself if she had done right; but hitherto such conjectures had been no more than the retrospective excursions of an active fancy. Now, for the first time, it startled her a little to find how little she knew of the material foundation on which her happiness was built.

She glanced at her husband, and was again reassured by the composure of his face; yet she felt the need of more definite grounds for her reassurance.

"But doesn't this suit worry you? Why have you never spoken to me about it?"

He answered both questions at once. "I didn't speak of it at first because it *did* worry me—annoyed me, rather. But it's all ancient history now. Your correspondent must have got hold of a back number of the *Sentinel*."

She felt a quick thrill of relief. "You mean it's over? He's lost his case?"

There was a just perceptible delay in Boyne's reply. "The suit's been withdrawn—that's all."

But she persisted, as if to exonerate herself from the inward charge of being too easily put off. "Withdrawn it because he saw he had no chance?"

"Oh, he had no chance," Boyne answered.

She was still struggling with a dimly felt perplexity at the back of her thoughts.

"How long ago was it withdrawn?"

He paused, as if with a slight return of his former uncertainty. "I've just had the news now; but I've been expecting it."

"Just now—in one of your letters?"

"Yes; in one of my letters."

She made no answer, and was aware only, after a short interval of waiting, that he had risen, and, strolling across the room, had placed himself on the sofa at her side. She felt him, as he did so, pass an arm about her, she felt his hand seek hers and clasp it, and turning slowly, drawn by the warmth of his cheek, she met his smiling eyes.

"It's all right—it's all right?" she questioned, through the flood of her dissolving doubts; and "I give you my word it was never righter!" he laughed back at her, holding her close.

III.

One of the strangest things she was afterward to recall out of all the next day's strangeness was the sudden and complete recovery of her sense of security.

It was in the air when she woke in her low-ceiled, dusky room; it went with her down-stairs to the breakfast-table, flashed out at her from the fire, and reduplicated itself from the flanks of the urn and the sturdy flutings of the Georgian* teapot. It was as if, in some roundabout way, all her diffused fears of the previous day, with their moment of sharp concentration about the newspaper article—as if this dim questioning of the future, and startled return upon the past, had between them liquidated the arrears of some haunting moral obligation. If she had indeed been careless of her husband's affairs, it was, her new state seemed to prove, because her faith in him instinctively justified such carelessness; and his right to her faith had now affirmed itself in the very face of menace and suspicion. She had never seen him more untroubled, more naturally and unconsciously himself, than after the cross-examination to which she had subjected him: it was almost as if he had been aware of her doubts, and had wanted the air cleared as much as she did.

It was as clear, thank Heaven! as the bright outer light that surprised her almost with a touch of summer when she issued from the house for her daily round of the gardens. She had left Boyne at his desk, indulging herself, as she passed the library door, by a last peep at his quiet face, where he bent, pipe in mouth, above his papers; and now she had her own morning's task to perform. The task involved, on such charmed winter days, almost as much happy

*Relating to a style characteristic of the reigns of Kings George I, II, III, and IV of England (1714–1830).

loitering about the different quarters of her demesne as if spring were already at work there. There were such endless possibilities still before her, such opportunities to bring out the latent graces of the old place, without a single irreverent touch of alteration, that the winter was all too short to plan what spring and autumn executed. And her recovered sense of safety gave, on this particular morning, a peculiar zest to her progress through the sweet still place. She went first to the kitchen-garden, where the espaliered* pear-trees drew complicated patterns on the walls, and pigeons were fluttering and preening about the silvery-slated roof of their cot.† There was something wrong about the piping of the hot-house, and she was expecting an authority from Dorchester,‡ who was to drive out between trains and make a diagnosis of the boiler. But when she dipped into the damp heat of the green-houses, among the spiced scents and waxy pinks and reds of old-fashioned exotics—even the flora of Lyng was in the note!—she learned that the great man had not arrived, and, the day being too rare to waste in an artificial atmosphere, she came out again and paced along the springy turf of the bowling-green to the gardens behind the house. At their farther end rose a grass terrace, looking across the fish-pond and yew hedges to the long house-front with its twisted chimney-stacks and blue roof angles all drenched in the pale gold moisture of the air.

Seen thus, across the level tracery of the gardens, it sent her, from open windows and hospitably smoking chimneys, the look of some warm human presence, of a mind slowly ripened on a sunny wall of experience. She had never before had such a sense of her intimacy with it, such a conviction that its secrets were all beneficent, kept, as they said to children, "for one's good," such a trust in its power to gather up her life and Ned's into the harmonious pattern of the long long story it sat there weaving in the sun.

She heard steps behind her, and turned, expecting to see the gardener accompanied by the engineer from Dorchester. But only one figure was in sight, that of a youngish slightly built man, who, for reasons she could not on the spot have given, did not remotely

---

*Trained to grow flat against a wall or trellis.

†Small house or cottage.

‡Town in southern England.

resemble her notion of an authority on hot-house boilers. The newcomer, on seeing her, lifted his hat, and paused with the air of a gentleman—perhaps a traveller—who wishes to make it known that his intrusion is involuntary. Lyng occasionally attracted the more cultivated traveller, and Mary half-expected to see the stranger dissemble a camera, or justify his presence by producing it. But he made no gesture of any sort, and after a moment she asked, in a tone responding to the courteous hesitation of his attitude: "Is there any one you wish to see?"

"I came to see Mr. Boyne," he answered. His intonation, rather than his accent, was faintly American, and Mary, at the note, looked at him more closely. The brim of his soft felt hat cast a shade on his face, which, thus obscured, wore to her short-sighted gaze a look of seriousness, as of a person arriving "on business," and civilly but firmly aware of his rights.

Past experience had made her equally sensible to such claims; but she was jealous of her husband's morning hours, and doubtful of his having given any one the right to intrude on them.

"Have you an appointment with my husband?" she asked.

The visitor hesitated, as if unprepared for the question.

"I think he expects me," he replied.

It was Mary's turn to hesitate. "You see this is his time for work: he never sees any one in the morning."

He looked at her a moment without answering; then, as if accepting her decision, he began to move away. As he turned, Mary saw him pause and glance up at the peaceful house-front. Something in his air suggested weariness and disappointment, the dejection of the traveller who has come from far off and whose hours are limited by the time-table. It occurred to her that if this were the case her refusal might have made his errand vain, and a sense of compunction caused her to hasten after him.

"May I ask if you have come a long way?"

He gave her the same grave look. "Yes—I have come a long way."

"Then, if you'll go to the house, no doubt my husband will see you now. You'll find him in the library."

She did not know why she had added the last phrase, except from a vague impulse to atone for her previous inhospitality. The visitor seemed about to express his thanks, but her attention was distracted by the approach of the gardener with a companion who bore all the marks of being the expert from Dorchester.

"This way," she said, waving the stranger to the house; and an instant later she had forgotten him in the absorption of her meeting with the boiler-maker.

The encounter led to such far-reaching results that the engineer ended by finding it expedient to ignore his train, and Mary was beguiled into spending the remainder of the morning in absorbed confabulation among the flower-pots. When the colloquy ended, she was surprised to find that it was nearly luncheon-time, and she half expected, as she hurried back to the house, to see her husband coming out to meet her. But she found no one in the court but an under-gardener raking the gravel, and the hall, when she entered it, was so silent that she guessed Boyne to be still at work.

Not wishing to disturb him, she turned into the drawing-room, and there, at her writing-table, lost herself in renewed calculations of the outlay to which the morning's conference had pledged her. The fact that she could permit herself such follies had not yet lost its novelty; and somehow, in contrast to the vague fears of the previous days, it now seemed an element of her recovered security, of the sense that, as Ned had said, things in general had never been "righter."

She was still luxuriating in a lavish play of figures when the parlour-maid, from the threshold, roused her with an enquiry as to the expediency of serving luncheon. It was one of their jokes that Trimmle announced luncheon as if she were divulging a state secret, and Mary, intent upon her papers, merely murmured an absent-minded assent.

She felt Trimmle wavering doubtfully on the threshold, as if in rebuke of such unconsidered assent; then her retreating steps sounded down the passage, and Mary, pushing away her papers, crossed the hall and went to the library door. It was still closed, and she wavered in her turn, disliking to disturb her husband, yet anxious that he should not exceed his usual measure of work. As she stood there, balancing her impulses, Trimmle returned with the announcement of luncheon, and Mary, thus impelled, opened the library door.

Boyne was not at his desk, and she peered about her, expecting to discover him before the book-shelves, somewhere down the length of the room; but her call brought no response, and gradually it became clear to her that he was not there.

She turned back to the parlour-maid.

"Mr. Boyne must be up-stairs. Please tell him that luncheon is ready."

Trimmle appeared to hesitate between the obvious duty of obedience and an equally obvious conviction of the foolishness of the injunction laid on her. The struggle resulted in her saying: "If you please, Madam, Mr. Boyne's not up-stairs."

"Not in his room? Are you sure?"

"I'm sure, Madam."

Mary consulted the clock. "Where is he, then?"

"He's gone out," Trimmle announced, with the superior air of one who has respectfully waited for the question that a well-ordered mind would have put first.

Mary's conjecture had been right, then. Boyne must have gone to the gardens to meet her, and since she had missed him, it was clear that he had taken the shorter way by the south door, instead of going round to the court. She crossed the hall to the French window opening directly on the yew garden, but the parlour-maid, after another moment of inner conflict, decided to bring out: "Please, Madam, Mr. Boyne didn't go that way."

Mary turned back. "Where *did* he go? And when?"

"He went out of the front door, up the drive, Madam." It was a matter of principle with Trimmle never to answer more than one question at a time.

"Up the drive? At this hour?" Mary went to the door herself, and glanced across the court through the tunnel of bare limes. But its perspective was as empty as when she had scanned it on entering.

"Did Mr. Boyne leave no message?"

Trimmle seemed to surrender herself to a last struggle with the forces of chaos.

"No, Madam. He just went out with the gentleman."

"The gentleman? What gentleman?" Mary wheeled about, as if to front this new factor.

"The gentleman who called, Madam," said Trimmle resignedly.

"When did a gentleman call? Do explain yourself, Trimmle!"

Only the fact that Mary was very hungry, and that she wanted to consult her husband about the green-houses, would have caused her to lay so unusual an injunction on her attendant; and even now she was detached enough to note in Trimmle's eye the dawning defiance of the respectful subordinate who has been pressed too hard.

"I couldn't exactly say the hour, Madam, because I didn't let the gentleman in," she replied, with an air of discreetly ignoring the irregularity of her mistress's course.

"You didn't let him in?"

"No, Madam. When the bell rang I was dressing, and Agnes——"

"Go and ask Agnes, then," said Mary.

Trimmle still wore her look of patient magnanimity. "Agnes would not know, Madam, for she had unfortunately burnt her hand in trimming the wick of the new lamp from town"—Trimmle, as Mary was aware, had always been opposed to the new lamp—"and so Mrs. Dockett sent the kitchen-maid instead."

Mary looked again at the clock. "It's after two! Go and ask the kitchen-maid if Mr. Boyne left any word."

She went into luncheon without waiting, and Trimmle presently brought her there the kitchen-maid's statement that the gentleman had called about eleven o'clock, and that Mr. Boyne had gone out with him without leaving any message. The kitchen-maid did not even know the caller's name, for he had written it on a slip of paper, which he had folded and handed to her, with the injunction to deliver it at once to Mr. Boyne.

Mary finished her luncheon, still wondering, and when it was over, and Trimmle had brought the coffee to the drawing-room, her wonder had deepened to a first faint tinge of disquietude. It was unlike Boyne to absent himself without explanation at so unwonted an hour, and the difficulty of identifying the visitor whose summons he had apparently obeyed made his disappearance the more unaccountable. Mary Boyne's experience as the wife of a busy engineer, subject to sudden calls and compelled to keep irregular hours, had trained her to the philosophic acceptance of surprises; but since Boyne's withdrawal from business he had adopted a Benedictine*

---

*Monastic; relating to the order of Saint Benedict, founded c.530.

regularity of life. As if to make up for the dispersed and agitated years, with their "stand-up" lunches, and dinners rattled down to the joltings of the dining-cars, he cultivated the last refinements of punctuality and monotony, discouraging his wife's fancy for the unexpected, and declaring that to a delicate taste there were infinite gradations of pleasure in the recurrences of habit.

Still, since no life can completely defend itself from the unforeseen, it was evident that all Boyne's precautions would sooner or later prove unavailable, and Mary concluded that he had cut short a tiresome visit by walking with his caller to the station, or at least accompanying him for part of the way.

This conclusion relieved her from farther preoccupation, and she went out herself to take up her conference with the gardener. Thence she walked to the village post-office, a mile or so away; and when she turned toward home the early twilight was setting in.

She had taken a foot-path across the downs, and as Boyne, meanwhile, had probably returned from the station by the highroad, there was little likelihood of their meeting. She felt sure, however, of his having reached the house before her; so sure that, when she entered it herself, without even pausing to inquire of Trimmle, she made directly for the library. But the library was still empty, and with an unwonted exactness of visual memory she observed that the papers on her husband's desk lay precisely as they had lain when she had gone in to call him to luncheon.

Then of a sudden she was seized by a vague dread of the unknown. She had closed the door behind her on entering, and as she stood alone in the long silent room, her dread seemed to take shape and sound, to be there breathing and lurking among the shadows. Her short-sighted eyes strained through them, half-discerning an actual presence, something aloof, that watched and knew; and in the recoil from that intangible presence she threw herself on the bell-rope and gave it a sharp pull.

The sharp summons brought Trimmle in precipitately with a lamp, and Mary breathed again at this sobering reappearance of the usual.

"You may bring tea if Mr. Boyne is in," she said, to justify her ring.

"Very well, Madam. But Mr. Boyne is not in," said Trimmle, putting down the lamp.

"Not in? You mean he's come back and gone out again?"

"No, Madam. He's never been back."

The dread stirred again, and Mary knew that now it had her fast.

"Not since he went out with—the gentleman?"

"Not since he went out with the gentleman."

"But who *was* the gentleman?" Mary insisted, with the shrill note of some one trying to be heard through a confusion of noises.

"That I couldn't say, Madam." Trimmle, standing there by the lamp, seemed suddenly to grow less round and rosy, as though eclipsed by the same creeping shade of apprehension.

"But the kitchen-maid knows—wasn't it the kitchen-maid who let him in?"

"She doesn't know either, Madam, for he wrote his name on a folded paper."

Mary, through her agitation, was aware that they were both designating the unknown visitor by a vague pronoun, instead of the conventional formula which, till then, had kept their allusions within the bounds of conformity. And at the same moment her mind caught at the suggestion of the folded paper.

"But he must have a name! Where's the paper?"

She moved to the desk, and began to turn over the documents that littered it. The first that caught her eye was an unfinished letter in her husband's hand, with his pen lying across it, as though dropped there at a sudden summons.

"My dear Parvis"—who was Parvis?—"I have just received your letter announcing Elwell's death, and while I suppose there is now no farther risk of trouble, it might be safer——"

She tossed the sheet aside, and continued her search; but no folded paper was discoverable among the letters and pages of manuscript which had been swept together in a heap, as if by a hurried or a startled gesture.

"But the kitchen-maid *saw* him. Send her here," she commanded, wondering at her dulness in not thinking sooner of so simple a solution.

Trimmle vanished in a flash, as if thankful to be out of the room, and when she reappeared, conducting the agitated underling, Mary had regained her self-possession, and had her questions ready.

The gentleman was a stranger, yes—that she understood. But

what had he said? And, above all, what had he looked like? The first question was easily enough answered, for the disconcerting reason that he had said so little—had merely asked for Mr. Boyne, and, scribbling something on a bit of paper, had requested that it should at once be carried in to him.

"Then you don't know what he wrote? You're not sure it *was* his name?"

The kitchen-maid was not sure, but supposed it was, since he had written it in answer to her inquiry as to whom she should announce.

"And when you carried the paper in to Mr. Boyne, what did he say?"

The kitchen-maid did not think that Mr. Boyne had said anything, but she could not be sure, for just as she had handed him the paper and he was opening it, she had become aware that the visitor had followed her into the library, and she had slipped out, leaving the two gentlemen together.

"But then, if you left them in the library, how do you know that they went out of the house?"

This question plunged the witness into a momentary inarticulateness, from which she was rescued by Trimmle, who, by means of ingenious circumlocutions, elicited the statement that before she could cross the hall to the back passage she had heard the two gentlemen behind her, and had seen them go out of the front door together.

"Then, if you saw the strange gentleman twice, you must be able to tell me what he looked like."

But with this final challenge to her powers of expression it became clear that the limit of the kitchen-maid's endurance had been reached. The obligation of going to the front door to "show in" a visitor was in itself so subversive of the fundamental order of things that it had thrown her faculties into hopeless disarray, and she could only stammer out, after various panting efforts: "His hat, mum, was different-like, as you might say——"

"Different? How different?" Mary flashed out, her own mind, in the same instant, leaping back to an image left on it that morning, and then lost under layers of subsequent impressions.

"His hat had a wide brim, you mean? and his face was pale—a youngish face?" Mary pressed her, with a white-lipped intensity of interrogation. But if the kitchen-maid found any adequate answer to this challenge, it was swept away for her listener down the rushing current of her own convictions. The stranger—the stranger in the garden! Why had Mary not thought of him before? She needed no one now to tell her that it was he who had called for her husband and gone away with him. But who was he, and why had Boyne obeyed him?

IV.

It leaped out at her suddenly, like a grin out of the dark, that they had often called England so little—"such a confoundedly hard place to get lost in."

A confoundedly hard place to get lost in! That had been her husband's phrase. And now, with the whole machinery of official investigation sweeping its flashlights from shore to shore, and across the dividing straits; now, with Boyne's name blazing from the walls of every town and village, his portrait (how that wrung her!) hawked up and down the country like the image of a hunted criminal; now the little compact populous island, so policed, surveyed and administered, revealed itself as a Sphinx-like guardian of abysmal mysteries, staring back into his wife's anguished eyes as if with the wicked joy of knowing something they would never know!

In the fortnight since Boyne's disappearance there had been no word of him, no trace of his movements. Even the usual misleading reports that raise expectancy in tortured bosoms had been few and fleeting. No one but the kitchen-maid had seen Boyne leave the house, and no one else had seen "the gentleman" who accompanied him. All enquiries in the neighbourhood failed to elicit the memory of a stranger's presence that day in the neighbourhood of Lyng. And no one had met Edward Boyne, either alone or in company, in any of the neighbouring villages, or on the road across the downs, or at either of the local railway-stations. The sunny English noon had swallowed him as completely as if he had gone out into Cimmerian* night.

Mary, while every official means of investigation was working at its highest pressure, had ransacked her husband's papers for any

*Very dark or gloomy; the Cimmerians, described by the ancient Greek poet Homer, were a legendary people living in a land of perpetual darkness.

trace of antecedent complications, of entanglements or obligations unknown to her, that might throw a ray into the darkness. But if any such had existed in the background of Boyne's life, they had vanished like the slip of paper on which the visitor had written his name. There remained no possible thread of guidance except—if it were indeed an exception—the letter which Boyne had apparently been in the act of writing when he received his mysterious summons. That letter, read and reread by his wife, and submitted by her to the police, yielded little enough to feed conjecture.

"I have just heard of Elwell's death, and while I suppose there is now no farther risk of trouble, it might be safer——" That was all. The "risk of trouble" was easily explained by the newspaper clipping which had apprised Mary of the suit brought against her husband by one of his associates in the Blue Star enterprise. The only new information conveyed by the letter was the fact of its showing Boyne, when he wrote it, to be still apprehensive of the results of the suit, though he had told his wife that it had been withdrawn, and though the letter itself proved that the plaintiff was dead. It took several days of cabling to fix the identity of the "Parvis" to whom the fragment was addressed, but even after these enquiries had shown him to be a Waukesha lawyer, no new facts concerning the Elwell suit were elicited. He appeared to have had no direct concern in it, but to have been conversant with the facts merely as an acquaintance, and possible intermediary; and he declared himself unable to guess with what object Boyne intended to seek his assistance.

This negative information, sole fruit of the first fortnight's search, was not increased by a jot during the slow weeks that followed. Mary knew that the investigations were still being carried on, but she had a vague sense of their gradually slackening, as the actual march of time seemed to slacken. It was as though the days, flying horror-struck from the shrouded image of the one inscrutable day, gained assurance as the distance lengthened, till at last they fell back into their normal gait. And so with the human imaginations at work on the dark event. No doubt it occupied them still, but week by week and hour by hour it grew less absorbing, took up less space, was slowly but inevitably crowded out of the foreground of consciousness by the new problems perpetually bubbling up from the cloudy caldron of human experience.

Even Mary Boyne's consciousness gradually felt the same lowering of velocity. It still swayed with the incessant oscillations of conjecture; but they were slower, more rhythmical in their beat. There were even moments of weariness when, like the victim of some poison which leaves the brain clear, but holds the body motionless, she saw herself domesticated with the Horror, accepting its perpetual presence as one of the fixed conditions of life.

These moments lengthened into hours and days, till she passed into a phase of stolid acquiescence. She watched the routine of daily life with the incurious eye of a savage on whom the meaningless processes of civilisation make but the faintest impression. She had come to regard herself as part of the routine, a spoke of the wheel, revolving with its motion; she felt almost like the furniture of the room in which she sat, an insensate object to be dusted and pushed about with the chairs and tables. And this deepening apathy held her fast at Lyng, in spite of the entreaties of friends and the usual medical recommendation of "change." Her friends supposed that her refusal to move was inspired by the belief that her husband would one day return to the spot from which he had vanished, and a beautiful legend grew up about this imaginary state of waiting. But in reality she had no such belief: the depths of anguish enclosing her were no longer lighted by flashes of hope. She was sure that Boyne would never come back, that he had gone out of her sight as completely as if Death itself had waited that day on the threshold. She had even renounced, one by one, the various theories as to his disappearance which had been advanced by the press, the police, and her own agonised imagination. In sheer lassitude her mind turned from these alternatives of horror, and sank back into the blank fact that he was gone.

No, she would never know what had become of him—no one would ever know. But the house *knew;* the library in which she spent her long lonely evenings knew. For it was here that the last scene had been enacted, here that the stranger had come, and spoken the word which had caused Boyne to rise and follow him. The floor she trod had felt his tread; the books on the shelves had seen his face; and there were moments when the intense consciousness of the old dusky walls seemed about to break out into some audible revelation of their secret. But the revelation never came, and she knew it would never come. Lyng was not one of the garrulous old houses that betray the secrets entrusted to them. Its very legend proved that it had always been the mute accomplice, the incorruptible custodian, of the mysteries it had surprised. And Mary Boyne, sitting face to face with its silence, felt the futility of seeking to break it by any human means.

V.

"I DON'T SAY IT *wasn't* straight, and yet I don't say it *was* straight. It was business."

Mary, at the words, lifted her head with a start, and looked intently at the speaker.

When, half an hour before, a card with "Mr. Parvis" on it had been brought up to her, she had been immediately aware that the name had been a part of her consciousness ever since she had read it at the head of Boyne's unfinished letter. In the library she had found awaiting her a small sallow man with a bald head and gold eyeglasses, and it sent a tremor through her to know that this was the person to whom her husband's last known thought had been directed.

Parvis, civilly, but without vain preamble—in the manner of a man who has his watch in his hand—had set forth the object of his visit. He had "run over" to England on business, and finding himself in the neighbourhood of Dorchester, had not wished to leave it without paying his respects to Mrs. Boyne; and without asking her, if the occasion offered, what she meant to do about Bob Elwell's family.

The words touched the spring of some obscure dread in Mary's bosom. Did her visitor, after all, know what Boyne had meant by his unfinished phrase? She asked for an elucidation of his question, and noticed at once that he seemed surprised at her continued ignorance of the subject. Was it possible that she really knew as little as she said?

"I know nothing—you must tell me," she faltered out; and her visitor thereupon proceeded to unfold his story. It threw, even to her confused perceptions, and imperfectly initiated vision, a lurid glare on the whole hazy episode of the Blue Star Mine. Her husband had made his money in that brilliant speculation at the cost of "getting ahead" of some one less alert to seize the chance; and the victim of his ingenuity was young Robert Elwell, who had "put him on" to the Blue Star scheme.

Parvis, at Mary's first cry, had thrown her a sobering glance through his impartial glasses.

"Bob Elwell wasn't smart enough, that's all; if he had been, he might have turned round and served Boyne the same way. It's the kind of thing that happens every day in business. I guess it's what the scientists call the survival of the fittest[5]—see?" said Mr. Parvis, evidently pleased with the aptness of his analogy.

Mary felt a physical shrinking from the next question she tried to frame: it was as though the words on her lips had a taste that nauseated her.

"But then—you accuse my husband of doing something dishonourable?"

Mr. Parvis surveyed the question dispassionately. "Oh, no, I don't. I don't even say it wasn't straight." He glanced up and down the long lines of books, as if one of them might have supplied him with the definition he sought. "I don't say it *wasn't* straight, and yet I don't say it *was* straight. It was business." After all, no definition in his category could be more comprehensive than that.

Mary sat staring at him with a look of terror. He seemed to her like the indifferent emissary of some evil power.

"But Mr. Elwell's lawyers apparently did not take your view, since I suppose the suit was withdrawn by their advice."

"Oh, yes; they knew he hadn't a leg to stand on, technically. It was when they advised him to withdraw the suit that he got desperate. You see, he'd borrowed most of the money he lost in the Blue Star, and he was up a tree. That's why he shot himself when they told him he had no show."

The horror was sweeping over Mary in great deafening waves.

"He shot himself? He killed himself because of *that?*"

"Well, he didn't kill himself, exactly. He dragged on two months before he died." Parvis emitted the statement as unemotionally as a gramophone grinding out its "record."

"You mean that he tried to kill himself, and failed? And tried again?"

"Oh, he didn't have to *try* again," said Parvis grimly.

They sat opposite each other in silence, he swinging his eye-glasses thoughtfully about his finger, she, motionless, her arms stretched along her knees in an attitude of rigid tension.

"But if you knew all this," she began at length, hardly able to force her voice above a whisper, "how is it that when I wrote you at the time of my husband's disappearance you said you didn't understand his letter?"

Parvis received this without perceptible embarrassment: "Why, I didn't understand it—strictly speaking. And it wasn't the time to talk about it, if I had. The Elwell business was settled when the suit was withdrawn. Nothing I could have told you would have helped you to find your husband."

Mary continued to scrutinise him. "Then why are you telling me now?"

Still Parvis did not hesitate. "Well, to begin with, I supposed you knew more than you appear to—I mean about the circumstances of Elwell's death. And then people are talking of it now; the whole matter's been raked up again. And I thought if you didn't know you ought to."

She remained silent, and he continued: "You see, it's only come out lately what a bad state Elwell's affairs were in. His wife's a proud woman, and she fought on as long as she could, going out to work, and taking sewing at home when she got too sick—something with the heart, I believe. But she had his mother to look after, and the children, and she broke down under it, and finally had to ask for help. That called attention to the case, and the papers took it up, and a subscription was started. Everybody out there liked Bob Elwell, and most of the prominent names in the place are down on the list, and people began to wonder why——"

Parvis broke off to fumble in an inner pocket. "Here," he continued, "here's an account of the whole thing from the *Sentinel*—a little sensational, of course. But I guess you'd better look it over."

He held out a newspaper to Mary, who unfolded it slowly, remembering, as she did so, the evening when, in that same room, the perusal of a clipping from the *Sentinel* had first shaken the depths of her security.

As she opened the paper, her eyes, shrinking from the glaring headlines, "Widow of Boyne's Victim Forced to Appeal for Aid," ran down the column of text to two portraits inserted in it. The first was her husband's, taken from a photograph made the year they had come to England. It was the picture of him that she liked best, the one that stood on the writing-table up-stairs in her bedroom. As the eyes in the photograph met hers, she felt it would be impossible to read what was said of him, and closed her lids with the sharpness of the pain.

"I thought if you felt disposed to put your name down——" she heard Parvis continue.

She opened her eyes with an effort, and they fell on the other portrait. It was that of a youngish man, slightly built, with features somewhat blurred by the shadow of a projecting hat-brim. Where had she seen that outline before? She stared at it confusedly, her heart hammering in her ears. Then she gave a cry.

"This is the man—the man who came for my husband!"

She heard Parvis start to his feet, and was dimly aware that she had slipped backward into the corner of the sofa, and that he was bending above her in alarm. She straightened herself, and reached out for the paper, which she had dropped.

"It's the man! I should know him anywhere!" she persisted in a voice that sounded to her own ears like a scream.

Parvis's answer seemed to come to her from far off, down endless fog-muffled windings.

"Mrs. Boyne, you're not very well. Shall I call somebody? Shall I get a glass of water?"

"No, no, no!" She threw herself toward him, her hand frantically clutching the newspaper. "I tell you, it's the man! I *know* him! He spoke to me in the garden!"

Parvis took the journal from her, directing his glasses to the portrait. "It can't be, Mrs. Boyne. It's Robert Elwell."

"Robert Elwell?" Her white stare seemed to travel into space. "Then it was Robert Elwell who came for him."

"Came for Boyne? The day he went away from here?" Parvis's voice dropped as hers rose. He bent over, laying a fraternal hand on her, as if to coax her gently back into her seat. "Why, Elwell was dead! Don't you remember?"

Mary sat with her eyes fixed on the picture, unconscious of what he was saying.

"Don't you remember Boyne's unfinished letter to me—the one you found on his desk that day? It was written just after he'd heard of Elwell's death." She noticed an odd shake in Parvis's unemotional voice. "Surely you remember!" he urged her.

Yes, she remembered: that was the profoundest horror of it. Elwell had died the day before her husband's disappearance; and this was Elwell's portrait; and it was the portrait of the man who had spoken to her in the garden. She lifted her head and looked slowly about the library. The library could have borne witness that it was also the portrait of the man who had come in that day to call Boyne from his unfinished letter. Through the misty surgings of her brain she heard the faint boom of half-forgotten words—words spoken by Alida Stair on the lawn at Pangbourne before Boyne and his wife had ever seen the house at Lyng, or had imagined that they might one day live there.

"This was the man who spoke to me," she repeated.

She looked again at Parvis. He was trying to conceal his disturbance under what he probably imagined to be an expression of indulgent commiseration; but the edges of his lips were blue. "He thinks me mad; but I'm not mad," she reflected; and suddenly there flashed upon her a way of justifying her strange affirmation.

She sat quiet, controlling the quiver of her lips, and waiting till she could trust her voice; then she said, looking straight at Parvis: "Will you answer me one question, please? When was it that Robert Elwell tried to kill himself?"

"When—when?" Parvis stammered.

"Yes; the date. Please try to remember."

She saw that he was growing still more afraid of her. "I have a reason," she insisted.

"Yes, yes. Only I can't remember. About two months before, I should say."

"I want the date," she repeated.

Parvis picked up the newspaper. "We might see here," he said, still humouring her. He ran his eyes down the page. "Here it is. Last October—the——"

She caught the words from him. "The 20th, wasn't it?" With a sharp look at her, he verified. "Yes, the 20th. Then you *did* know?"

"I know now." Her gaze continued to travel past him. "Sunday, the 20th—that was the day he came first."

Parvis's voice was almost inaudible. "Came *here* first?"

"Yes."

"You saw him twice, then?"

"Yes, twice." She just breathed it at him. "He came first on the 20th of October. I remember the date because it was the day we went up Meldon Steep for the first time." She felt a faint gasp of inward laughter at the thought that but for that she might have forgotten.

Parvis continued to scrutinise her, as if trying to intercept her gaze.

"We saw him from the roof," she went on. "He came down the lime-avenue toward the house. He was dressed just as he is in that picture. My husband saw him first. He was frightened, and ran down ahead of me; but there was no one there. He had vanished."

"Elwell had vanished?" Parvis faltered.

"Yes." Their two whispers seemed to grope for each other. "I couldn't think what had happened. I see now. He *tried* to come then; but he wasn't dead enough—he couldn't reach us. He had to wait for two months to die; and then he came back again—and Ned went with him."

She nodded at Parvis with the look of triumph of a child who has worked out a difficult puzzle. But suddenly she lifted her hands with a desperate gesture, pressing them to her temples.

"Oh, my God! I sent him to Ned—I told him where to go! I sent him to this room!" she screamed.

She felt the walls of books rush toward her, like inward falling ruins; and she heard Parvis, a long way off, through the ruins, crying to her, and struggling to get at her. But she was numb to his touch, she did not know what he was saying. Through the tumult she heard but one clear note, the voice of Alida Stair, speaking on the lawn at Pangbourne.

"You won't know till afterward," it said. "You won't know till long, long afterward."

THE LEGEND[1]

I.

The incident had begun by Bernald's running across Doctor Robert Wade one hot summer night at the University Club, and by Wade's saying, in the tone of unprofessional laxity which the shadowy stillness of the place invited: "I got hold of a queer fish at St. Martin's the other day—case of heat-prostration picked up in Central Park. When we'd patched him up I found he had nowhere to go, and not a dollar in his pocket, and I sent him down to our place at Portchester to rebuild."

The opening roused his hearer's attention. Bob Wade had an instinctive sense of values that Bernald had learned to trust.

"What sort of chap? Young or old?"

"Oh, every age—full of years, and yet with a lot left. He called himself sixty on the books."

"Sixty's a good age for some kinds of living. And age is purely subjective. How has he used his sixty years?"

"Well—part of them in educating himself, apparently. He's a scholar—humanities, languages, and so forth."

"Oh—decayed gentleman," Bernald murmured, disappointed.

"Decayed? Not much!" cried the doctor with his accustomed literalness. "I only mentioned that side of Winterman—his name's Winterman—because it was the side my mother noticed first. I suppose women generally do. But it's only a part—a small part. The man's the big thing."

"Really big?"

"Well—there again . . . When I took him down to the country, looking rather like a tramp from a 'Shelter,' with an untrimmed beard, and a suit of reach-me-downs he'd slept round the Park in for a week, I felt sure my mother'd carry the silver up to her room, and send for the gardener's dog to sleep in the hall. But she didn't."

"I see. 'Women and children love him.' Oh, Wade!" Bernald groaned.

"Not a bit of it! You're out again. We don't love him, either of us. But we *feel* him—the air's charged with him. You'll see."

And Bernald agreed that he *would* see, the following Sunday. Wade's inarticulate attempts to characterise the stranger had struck his friend. The human revelation had for Bernald a poignant and ever-renewed interest, which his trade, as the dramatic critic of a daily paper, had hitherto failed to diminish. And he knew that Bob Wade, simple and undefiled by literature—Bernald's specific affliction—had a free and personal way of judging men, and the diviner's knack of reaching their hidden springs. During the days that followed, the young doctor gave Bernald further details about John Winterman: details not of fact—for in that respect the stranger's reticence was baffling—but of impression. It appeared that Winterman, while lying insensible in the Park, had been robbed of the few dollars he possessed; and on leaving the hospital, still weak and half-blind, he had quite simply and unprotestingly accepted the Wades' offer to give him shelter till such time as he should be strong enough to work.

"But what's his work?" Bernald interjected. "Hasn't he at least told you that?"

"Well, writing. Some kind of writing." Doctor Bob always became vague when he approached the confines of literature. "He means to take it up again as soon as his eyes get right."

Bernald groaned again. "Oh, Lord—that finishes him; and *me!* He's looking for a publisher, of course—he wants a 'favourable notice.' I won't come!"

"He hasn't written a line for twenty years."

"A line of *what?* What kind of literature can one keep corked up for twenty years?"

Wade surprised him. "The real kind, I should say. But I don't know Winterman's line," the doctor added. "He speaks of the things he used to write merely as 'stuff that wouldn't sell.' He has a wonderfully confidential way of *not* telling one things. But he says he'll have to do something for his living as soon as his eyes are patched up, and that writing is the only trade he knows. The queer thing is that he seems pretty sure of selling *now*. He even talked of buying the bungalow of us, with an acre or two about it."

"The bungalow? What's that?"

"The studio down by the shore that we built for Howland when he thought he meant to paint." (Howland Wade, as Bernald knew, had experienced various "calls.") "Since he's taken to writing nobody's been near the place. I offered it to Winterman, and he camps there—cooks his meals, does his own housekeeping, and never comes up to the house except in the evenings, when he joins us on the verandah, in the dark, and smokes while my mother knits."

"A discreet visitor, eh?"

"More than he need be. My mother actually wanted him to stay on in the house—in her pink chintz room. Think of it! But he says houses smother him. I take it he's lived for years in the open."

"In the open where?"

"I can't make out, except that it was somewhere in the East. 'East of everything—beyond the day-spring. In places not on the map.' That's the way he put it; and when I said: 'You've been an explorer, then?' he smiled in his beard, and answered: 'Yes; that's it—an explorer.' Yet he doesn't strike me as a man of action: hasn't the hands or the eyes."

"What sort of hands and eyes has he?"

Wade reflected. His range of observation was not large, but within its limits it was exact and could give an account of itself.

"He's worked a lot with his hands, but that's not what they were made for. I should say they were extraordinarily delicate conductors of sensation. And his eye—his eye too. He hasn't used it to dominate people: he didn't care to. He simply looks through 'em all like windows. Makes me feel like the fellows who think they're made of glass. The mitigating circumstance is that he seems to see such a glorious landscape through me." Wade grinned at the thought of serving such a purpose.

"I see. I'll come on Sunday and be looked through!" Bernald cried.

II.

Bernald came on two successive Sundays; and the second time he lingered till the Tuesday.

"Here he comes!" Wade had said, the first evening, as the two young men, with Wade's mother, sat on the verandah, with the Virginian creeper drawing, between the arches, its black arabesques against a moon-lined sky.

Bernald heard a step on the gravel, and saw the red flit of a cigar through the shrubs. Then a loosely-moving figure obscured the patch of sky between the creepers, and the spark became the centre of a dim bearded face, in which Bernald, through the darkness, discerned only a broad white gleam of forehead.

It was the young man's subsequent impression that Winterman had not spoken much that first evening; at any rate, Bernald himself remembered chiefly what the Wades had said. And this was the more curious because he had come for the purpose of studying their visitor, and because there was nothing to distract his attention in Wade's slow phrases or his mother's artless comments. He reflected afterward that there must have been a mysteriously fertilising quality in the stranger's silence: it had brooded over their talk like a raincloud over a dry country.

Mrs. Wade, apparently fearing that her son might have given Bernald an exaggerated notion of their visitor's importance, had hastened to qualify it before the latter appeared.

"He's not what you or Howland would call intellectual—" (Bernald winced at the coupling of the names)—"not in the least *literary;* though he told Bob he used to write. I don't think, though, it could have been what Howland would call writing." Mrs. Wade always named her younger son with a reverential drop of the voice. She viewed literature much as she did Providence, as an inscrutable mystery; and she spoke of Howland as a dedicated being, set apart to perform secret rites within the veil of the sanctuary.

"I shouldn't say he had a quick mind," she continued, reverting to Winterman. "Sometimes he hardly seems to follow what we're saying. But he's got such sound ideas—when he does speak he's never silly. And clever people sometimes *are,* don't you think so?" Bernald sighed an unqualified assent. "And he's so capable. The other day something went wrong with the kitchen range, just as I was expecting some friends of Bob's for dinner; and do you know, when Mr. Winterman heard we were in trouble, he came and took a look, and knew at once what to do? I told him it was a dreadful pity he wasn't married!"

Close on midnight, when the session on the verandah ended, and the two young men were strolling down to the bungalow at Winterman's side, Bernald's mind reverted to the image of the fertilising cloud. There was something brooding, pregnant, in the silent presence beside him: he had, in place of any circumscribing personal impression, a large hovering sense of manifold latent meanings. And he felt a thrill of relief when, half-way down the lawn, Doctor Bob was checked by a voice that called him back to the telephone.

"Now I'll be with him alone!" thought Bernald, with a throb like a lover's.

Under the low rafters of the bungalow Winterman had to grope for the lamp on his desk, and as its light struck up into his face Bernald's sense of the rareness of the opportunity increased. He couldn't have said why, for the face, with its bossed forehead, its shabby greyish beard and blunt Socratic nose, made no direct appeal to the eye. It seemed rather like a stage on which remarkable things might be enacted, like some shaggy moorland landscape dependent for form and expression on the clouds rolling over it, and the bursts of light between; and one of these flashed out in the smile with which Winterman, as if in answer to his companion's thought, said simply, as he turned to fill his pipe: "Now we'll talk."

So he'd known all along that they hadn't yet—and had guessed that, with Bernald, one might!

The young man's sudden glow of pleasure left him for a moment unable to meet the challenge; and in that moment he felt the sweep of something winged and summoning. His spirit rose to it with a rush, but just as he felt himself poised between the ascending pinions, the door opened and Bob Wade reappeared.

"Too bad! I'm so sorry! It was from Howland, to say he can't come to-morrow after all." The doctor panted out his news with honest grief.

"I tried my best to pull it off for you, Winterman; and my brother *wants* to come—he's keen to talk to you and see what he can do. But you see he's so tremendously in demand. He'll try for another Sunday later on."

Winterman gave an untroubled nod. "Oh, he'll find me here. I shall work my time out slowly." He waved his hand toward the scattered sheets on the kitchen table which formed his desk.

"Not slowly enough to suit us," Wade answered hospitably. "Only, if Howland could have come he might have given you a tip or two—put you on the right track—shown you how to get in touch with the public."

Winterman, his hands in his pockets, lounged against the bare pine walls, twisting his pipe under his beard. "Does your brother enjoy the privilege of that contact?" he questioned gravely.

Wade stared a little. "Oh, of course Howland's not what you'd call a *popular* writer; he despises that kind of thing. But whatever he says goes with—well, with the chaps who count; and every one tells me he's written *the* book on Pellerin. You must read it when you get back your eyes." He paused, as if to let the name sink in, but Winterman drew at his pipe with a blank face. "You must have heard of Pellerin, I suppose?" the doctor continued. "I've never read a word of him myself: he's too big a proposition for *me*. But one can't escape the talk about him. I have him crammed down my throat even in hospital. The internes read him at the clinics. He tumbles out of the nurses' pockets. The patients keep him under their pillows. Oh, with most of them, of course, it's just a craze, like the last new game or puzzle: they don't understand him in the least. Howland says that even now, twenty-five years after his death, and with his books in everybody's hands, there are not twenty people who really understand Pellerin; and Howland ought to know, if anybody does. He's—what's their great word?—*interpreted* him. You must get Howland to put you through a course of Pellerin."

And as the young men, having taken leave of Winterman, retraced their way across the lawn, Wade continued to develop the theme of his brother's accomplishments.

"I wish I *could* get Howland to take an interest in Winterman: this is the third Sunday he's chucked us. Of course he does get bored with people consulting him about their writings—but I believe if he could only talk to Winterman he'd see something in him, as we do. And it would be such a god-send to the poor devil to have some one to advise him about his work. I'm going to make a desperate effort to get Howland here next Sunday."

It was then that Bernald vowed to himself that he would return the next Sunday at all costs. He hardly knew whether he was prompted by the impulse to shield Winterman from Howland Wade's ineptitude, or by the desire to see the latter abandon himself to the full shamelessness of its display; but of one fact he was assured—and that was of the existence in Winterman of some quality which would provoke Howland to the amplest exercise of his fatuity. "How he'll draw him—how he'll draw him!" Bernald chuckled, with a security the more unaccountable that his one glimpse of Winterman had shown the latter only as a passive subject for observation; and he felt himself avenged in advance for the injury of Howland Wade's existence.

III.

THAT THIS HOPE WAS to be frustrated Bernald learned from Howland Wade's own lips, the day before the two young men were to have met at Portchester.

"I can't really, my dear fellow," the Interpreter lisped, passing a polished hand over the faded smoothness of his face. "Oh, an authentic engagement, I assure you: otherwise, to oblige old Bob I'd submit cheerfully to looking over his foundling's literature. But I'm pledged this week to the Pellerin Society of Kenosha: I had a hand in founding it, and for two years now they've been patiently waiting for a word from me—the *Fiat Lux*,* so to speak. You see it's a ministry, Bernald—I assure you, I look upon my calling quite religiously."

As Bernald listened, his disappointment gradually changed to relief. Howland, on trial, always turned out to be too insufferable, and the pleasure of watching his antics was invariably lost in the impulse to put a sanguinary end to them.

"If he'd only kept his beastly pink hands off Pellerin," Bernald sighed, thinking for the hundredth time of the thick manuscript condemned to perpetual incarceration in his own desk by the publication of Howland's "definitive" work on the great man. One couldn't, *after* Howland Wade, expose one's self to the derision of writing about Pellerin: the eagerness with which Wade's book had been devoured proved, not that the public had enough appetite for another, but simply that, for a stomach so undiscriminating, anything better than Wade had given it would be too good. And Bernald, in the confidence that his own work was open to this objection, had stoically locked it up. Yet if he had resigned himself to the fact that Wade's book existed, and was already passing into the immortality

*Let there be light (Latin).

of perpetual republication, he could not, after repeated trials, adjust himself to the author's talk about Pellerin. When Wade wrote of the great dead he was egregious, but in conversation he was familiar and fond. It might have been supposed that one of the beauties of Pellerin's hidden life and mysterious taking off would have been to guard him from the fingering of anecdote; but biographers like Howland Wade are born to rise above such obstacles. He might be vague or inaccurate in dealing with the few recorded events of his subject's life; but when he left fact for conjecture no one had a firmer footing. Whole chapters in his volume were constructed in the conditional mood and made up of hypothetical detail; and in talk, by the very law of the process, hypothesis became affirmation, and he was ready to tell you confidentially the exact circumstances of Pellerin's death, and of the "distressing incident" leading up to it. Bernald himself not only questioned the form under which this incident was shaping itself before posterity, but the very fact of its occurrence: he had never been able to discover any break in the dense cloud enveloping Pellerin's end. He had gone away—that was all that any of them knew: he who had so little, at any time, been with them or of them; and his going had so slightly stirred the public consciousness that the news of his death, laconically imparted from afar, had dropped unheeded into the universal scrap-basket, to be long afterward fished out, with all its details missing, when some enquiring spirit first became aware, by chance encounter with a volume in a London book-stall, not only that such a man as John Pellerin had died, but that he had ever lived, or written.

It need hardly be noted that Howland Wade had not been the pioneer in question: his had been the safer part of swelling the chorus when it rose, and gradually drowning the other voices by his own. He had pitched his note so screamingly, and held it so long, that he was now the accepted authority on Pellerin, not only in the land which had given birth to his genius but in the Europe which had first acclaimed it; and it was the central point of pain in Bernald's sense of the situation that a man who had so yearned for silence should have his grave piped over by such a voice as Wade's.

Bernald's talk with the Interpreter had revived this ache to the momentary exclusion of other sensations; and he was still sore with it when, the next afternoon, he arrived at Portchester for his second Sunday with the Wades.

At the station he had the surprise of seeing Winterman's face on the platform, and of hearing from him that Doctor Bob had been called away to assist at an operation in a distant town.

"Mrs. Wade wanted to put you off, but I believe the message came too late; so she sent me down to break the news to you," said Winterman, holding out his hand.

Perhaps because they were the first conventional words that Bernald had heard him speak, the young man was struck by the quality his intonation gave them.

"She wanted to send a carriage," Winterman added, "but I told her we'd walk back through the woods." He looked at Bernald with a kindliness that flushed the young man with pleasure.

"Are you strong enough? It's not too far?"

"Oh, no. I'm pulling myself together. Getting back to work is the slowest part of the business: not on account of my eyes—I can use them now, though not for reading; but some of the links between things are missing. It's a kind of broken spectrum . . . here, that boy will look after your bag."

The walk through the woods remained in Bernald's memory as an enchanted hour. He used the word literally, as descriptive of the way in which Winterman's contact changed the face of things, or perhaps restored them to their deeper meanings. And the scene they traversed—one of those little untended woods that still, in America, fringe the tawdry skirts of civilisation—acquired, as a background to Winterman, the hush of a spot aware of transcendent visitings. Did he talk, or did he make Bernald talk? The young man never knew. He recalled only a sense of lightness and liberation, as if the hard walls of individuality had melted, and he were merged in the poet's deeper interfusion, yet without losing the least sharp edge of self. This general impression resolved itself afterward into the sense of Winterman's wide elemental range. His thought encircled things like the horizon at sea. He didn't, as it happened, touch on lofty themes—Bernald was gleefully aware that, to Howland Wade, their talk would hardly have been Talk at all—but Winterman's mind, applied to lowly topics, was like a lens that brought out microscopic delicacies and differences.

The lack of Sunday trains kept Doctor Bob for two days on the scene of his surgical duties, and during those two days Bernald seized every moment of communion with his friend's guest. Winterman, as Wade had said, was reticent concerning his personal affairs, or rather concerning the practical and material questions to which the term is generally applied. But it was evident that, in Winterman's case, the usual classification must be reversed, and that the discussion of ideas carried one much farther into his intimacy than familiarity with the incidents of his life.

"That's exactly what Howland Wade and his tribe have never understood about Pellerin: that it's much less important to know how, or even why, he disapp——"

Bernald pulled himself up with a jerk, and turned to look full at his companion. It was late on the Monday evening, and the two men, after an hour's chat on the verandah to the tune of Mrs. Wade's knitting-needles, had bidden their hostess good-night and strolled back to the bungalow together.

"Come and have a pipe before you turn in," Winterman had said; and they had sat on together till midnight, with the door of the bungalow open on the heaving moonlit bay, and summer insects bumping against the chimney of the lamp. Winterman had just bent down to refill his pipe from the jar on the table, and Bernald, jerking about to catch him in the circle of lamplight, sat speechless, staring at a fact that seemed suddenly to have substituted itself for Winterman's face, or rather to have taken on its features.

"No, they never saw that Pellerin's ideas *were* Pellerin . . ." He continued to stare at Winterman. "Just as this man's ideas are—why, *are* Pellerin!"

The thought uttered itself in a kind of inner shout, and Bernald started upright with the violent impact of his conclusion. Again and again in the last forty-eight hours he had exclaimed to himself: "This is as good as Pellerin." Why hadn't he said till now: "This *is* Pellerin"? . . . Surprising as the answer was, he had no choice but to take it. He hadn't said so simply because Winterman was *better than Pellerin*—that there was so much more of him, so to speak. Yes; but—it came to Bernald in a flash—wouldn't there by this time have been any amount more of Pellerin? . . . The young man felt actually dizzy with the thought. That was it—there was the solution of the problem! This man was Pellerin, and more than Pellerin! It was so fantastic and yet so unanswerable that he burst into a sudden laugh.

Winterman, at the same moment, brought his palm down with a crash on the pile of manuscript covering the desk.

"What's the matter?" Bernald cried.

"My match wasn't out. In another minute the destruction of the library of Alexandria would have been a trifle compared to what you'd have seen." Winterman, with his large deep laugh, shook out the smouldering sheets. "And I should have been a pensioner on Doctor Bob the Lord knows how much longer!"

Bernald looked at him intently. "You've really got going again? The thing's actually getting into shape?"

"This particular thing *is* in shape. I drove at it hard all last week, thinking our friend's brother would be down on Sunday, and might look it over."

Bernald had to repress the tendency to another wild laugh.

"Howland—you meant to show *Howland* what you've done?"

Winterman, looming against the moonlight, slowly turned a dusky shaggy head toward him.

"Isn't it a good thing to do?"

Bernald wavered, torn between loyalty to his friends and the grotesqueness of answering in the affirmative. After all, it was none of his business to furnish Winterman with an estimate of Howland Wade.

"Well, you see, you've never told me what your line *is*," he answered, temporising.

"No, because nobody's ever told *me*. It's exactly what I want to find out," said the other genially.

"And you expect Wade——?"

"Why, I gathered from our good Doctor that it's his trade. Doesn't he explain—interpret?"

"In his own domain—which is Pellerinism."

Winterman gazed out musingly upon the moon-touched dusk of waters. "And what *is* Pellerinism?" he asked.

Bernald sprang to his feet with a cry. "Ah, I don't know—but you're Pellerin!"

They stood for a minute facing each other, among the uncertain swaying shadows of the room, with the sea breathing through it as something immense and inarticulate breathed through young Bernald's thoughts; then Winterman threw up his arms with a humorous gesture.

"Don't shoot!" he said.

IV.

Dawn found them there, and the sun laid its beams on the rough floor of the bungalow, before either of the men was conscious of the passage of time. Bernald, vaguely trying to define his own state in retrospect, could only phrase it: "I floated . . . floated . . ."

The gist of fact at the core of the extraordinary experience was simply that John Pellerin, twenty-five years earlier, had voluntarily disappeared, causing the rumour of his death to be reported to an inattentive world; and that now he had come back to see what that world had made of him.

"You'll hardly believe it of me; I hardly believe it of myself; but I went away in a rage of disappointment, of wounded pride—no, vanity! I don't know which cut deepest—the sneers or the silence—but between them, there wasn't an inch of me that wasn't raw. I had just the one thing in me: the message, the cry, the revelation. But nobody saw and nobody listened. Nobody wanted what I had to give. I was like a poor devil of a tramp looking for shelter on a bitter night, in a town with every door bolted and all the windows dark. And suddenly I felt that the easiest thing would be to lie down and go to sleep in the snow. Perhaps I'd a vague notion that if they found me there at day-light, frozen stiff, the pathetic spectacle might produce a reaction, a feeling of remorse . . . So I took care to be found! Well, a good many thousand people die every day on the face of the globe; and I soon discovered that I was simply one of the thousands; and when I made that discovery I really died—and stayed dead a year or two . . . When I came to life again I was off on the under side of the world, in regions unaware of what we know as 'the public.' Have you any notion how it shifts the point of view to wake under new constellations? I advise any who's been in love with a woman under Cassiopeia to go and think about her under the

Southern Cross*. . . It's the only way to tell the pivotal truths from the others . . . I didn't believe in my theory any less—there was my triumph and my vindication! It held out, resisted, measured itself with the stars. But I didn't care a snap of my finger whether anybody else believed in it, or even knew it had been formulated. It escaped out of my books—my poor still-born books—like Psyche† from the chrysalis, and soared away into the blue, and lived there. I knew then how it frees an idea to be ignored; how apprehension circumscribes and deforms it . . . Once I'd learned that, it was easy enough to turn to and shift for myself. I was sure now that my idea would live: the good ones are self-supporting. And meanwhile *I* had to learn to be so; and I tried my hand at a number of things . . . adventurous, menial, commercial . . . It's not a bad thing for a man to have to live his life—and we nearly all manage to dodge it. Our first round with the Sphinx may strike something out of us—a book or a picture or a symphony; and we're amazed at our feat, and go on letting that first work breed others, as some animal forms reproduce each other without renewed fertilisation. So there we are, committed to our first guess at the riddle; and our works look as like as successive impressions of the same plate, each with the lines a little fainter; whereas they ought to be—if we touch earth between times—as different from each other as those other creatures—jelly-fish, aren't they, of a kind?—where successive generations produce new forms, and it takes a zoologist to see the hidden likeness . . .

"Well, I proved my first guess, off there in the wilds, and it lived, and grew, and took care of itself. And I said, 'Some day it will make itself heard; but by that time my atoms will have waltzed into a new pattern.' Then, in Cashmere one day, I met a fellow in a caravan, with a dog-eared book in his pocket. He said he never stirred without it—wanted to know where I'd been, never to have heard of it. It was *my guess*—in its twentieth edition! . . . The globe spun round at

---

*Cassiopeia: northern constellation named for Andromeda's mother in classical mythology; the Southern Cross: constellation whose four brightest stars form the shape of a cross; visible only from the Southern Hemisphere.

†In Greek mythology, Psyche is a princess loved by Cupid; often represented as a butterfly, she is a symbol of the human soul. (In ancient Greece, the word *psyche* meant both "butterfly" and "soul.")

that, and all of a sudden I was under the old stars. That's the way it happens when the ballast of vanity shifts! I'd lived a third of a life out there, unconscious of human opinion—because I supposed it was unconscious of *me*. But now—now! Oh, it was different. I wanted to know what they said . . . Not exactly that, either: I wanted to know *what I'd made them say*. There's a difference . . . And here I am," said John Pellerin, with a pull at his pipe.

So much Bernald retained of his companion's actual narrative; the rest was swept away under the tide of wonder that rose and submerged him as Pellerin—at some indefinitely later stage of their talk—picked up his manuscript and began to read. Bernald sat opposite, his elbows propped on the table, his eyes fixed on the swaying waters outside, from which the moon gradually faded, leaving them to make a denser blackness in the night. As Pellerin read, this density of blackness—which never for a moment seemed inert or unalive—was attenuated by imperceptible degrees, till a greyish pallor replaced it; then the pallor breathed and brightened, and suddenly dawn was on the sea.

Something of the same nature went on in the young man's mind while he watched and listened. He was conscious of a gradually withdrawing light, of an interval of obscurity full of the stir of invisible forces, and then of the victorious flush of day. And as the light rose, he saw how far he had travelled and what wonders the night had prepared. Pellerin had been right in saying that his first idea had survived, had borne the test of time; but he had given his hearer no hint of the extent to which it had been enlarged and modified, of the fresh implications it now unfolded. In a brief flash of retrospection Bernald saw the earlier books dwindle and fall into their place as mere precursors of this fuller revelation; then, with a leap of rage, he pictured Howland Wade's pink hands on the new treasure, and his prophetic feet upon the lecture platform.

V.

"It won't do—oh, he let him down as gently as possible; but it appears it simply won't do."

Doctor Bob imparted the ineluctable fact to Bernald while the two men, accidentally meeting at their club a few nights later, sat together over the dinner they had immediately agreed to share.

Bernald had left Portchester the morning after his strange discovery, and he and Bob Wade had not seen each other since. And now Bernald, moved by an irresistible instinct of postponement, had waited for his companion to bring up Winterman's name, and had even executed several conversational diversions in the hope of delaying its mention. For how could one talk of Winterman with the thought of Pellerin swelling one's breast?

"Yes; the very day Howland got back from Kenosha I brought the manuscript to town, and got him to read it. And yesterday evening I nailed him, and dragged an answer out of him."

"Then Howland hasn't seen Winterman yet?"

"No. He said: 'Before you let him loose on me I'll go over the stuff, and see if it's at all worth while.'"

Bernald drew a freer breath. "And he found it wasn't?"

"Between ourselves, he found it was of no account at all. Queer, isn't it, when the *man* . . . but of course literature's another proposition. Howland says it's one of the cases where an idea might seem original and striking if one didn't happen to be able to trace its descent. And this is straight out of bosh—by Pellerin . . . Yes: Pellerin. It seems that everything in the article that isn't pure nonsense is just Pellerinism. Howland thinks Winterman must have been tremendously struck by Pellerin's writings, and have lived too much out of the world to know that they've become the textbooks of modern thought. Otherwise, of course, he'd have taken more trouble to disguise his plagiarisms."

"I see," Bernald mused. "Yet you say there *is* an original element?"

"Yes; but unluckily it's no good."

"It's not—conceivably—in any sense a development of Pellerin's idea: a logical step farther?"

"*Logical?* Howland says it's twaddle at white heat."

Bernald sat silent, divided between the satisfaction of seeing the Interpreter rush upon his fate, and the despair of knowing that the state of mind he represented was indestructible. Then both emotions were swept away on a wave of pure joy, as he reflected that now, at last, Howland Wade had given him back John Pellerin.

The possession was one he did not mean to part with lightly; and the dread of its being torn from him constrained him to extraordinary precautions.

"You've told Winterman, I suppose? How did he take it?"

"Why, unexpectedly, as he does most things. You can never tell which way he'll jump. I thought he'd take a high tone, or else laugh it off; but he did neither. He seemed awfully cast down. I wished myself well out of the job when I saw how cut up he was."

Bernald thrilled at the words. Pellerin had shared his own pang, then—the "old woe of the world" at the perpetuity of human dulness!

"But what did he say to the charge of plagiarism—if you made it?"

"Oh, I told him straight out what Howland said. I thought it fairer. And his answer to that was the rummest part of all."

"What was it?" Bernald questioned, with a tremor.

"He said: 'That's queer, for I've never read Pellerin.'"

Bernald drew a deep breath. "Well—and I suppose you believed him?"

"I believed him, because I know him. But the public won't—the critics won't. And if the plagiarism is a pure coincidence it's just as bad for him as if it were a straight steal—isn't it?"

Bernald sighed his acquiescence.

"It bothers me awfully," Wade continued, knitting his kindly brows, "because I could see what a blow it was to him. He's got to earn his living, and I don't suppose he knows how to do anything but write. At his age it's hard to start fresh. I put that to Howland—asked him if there wasn't a chance he might do better if he only had a little encouragement. I can't help feeling he's got the essential thing in him. But of course I'm no judge when it comes to books. And Howland says it would be cruel to give him any hope." Wade paused, turned his wineglass about under a meditative stare, and then leaned across the table toward Bernald. "Look here—do you know what I've proposed to Winterman? That he should come to town with me to-morrow and go in the evening to hear Howland lecture to the Uplift Club. They're to meet at Mrs. Beecher Bain's, and Howland is to repeat the lecture that he gave the other day before the Pellerin Society at Kenosha. It will give Winterman a chance to get some notion of what Pellerin *was:* he'll get it much straighter from Howland than if he tried to plough through Pellerin's books. And then afterward—as if accidentally—I thought I might bring him and Howland together. If Howland could only see him and hear him talk, there's no knowing what might come of it. He couldn't help feeling the man's force, as we do; and he might give him a pointer—tell him what line to take. Anyhow, it would please Winterman, and take the edge off his disappointment. I saw that as soon as I proposed it."

"Some one who's never heard of Pellerin?"

Mrs. Beecher Bain, large, smiling, diffuse, reached out through the incoming throng on her threshold to detain Bernald with the question as he was about to move past her in the wake of his companion.

"Oh, keep straight on, Mr. Winterman!" she interrupted herself to call after the latter. "Into the back drawing-room, please! And remember, you're to sit next to me—in the corner on the left, close under the platform."

She renewed her interrogative clutch on Bernald's sleeve. "Most curious! Doctor Wade has been telling me all about your friend—how remarkable you all think him. And it's actually true that he's never heard of Pellerin? Of course as soon as Doctor Wade told me *that,* I said 'Bring him!' It will be so extraordinarily interesting to watch the first impression.—Yes, do follow him, dear Mr. Bernald, and be sure that you and he secure the seats next to me. Of course Alice Fosdick insists on being with us. She was wild with excitement when I told her she was to meet some one who'd never heard of Pellerin!"

On the indulgent lips of Mrs. Beecher Bain conjecture speedily passed into affirmation; and as Bernald's companion, broad and shaggy in his visible new evening clothes, moved down the length of the crowded rooms, he was already, to the ladies drawing aside their skirts to let him pass, the interesting Huron of the fable.

How far he was aware of the character ascribed to him it was impossible for Bernald to discover. He was as unconscious as a tree or a cloud, and his observer had never known any one so alive to human contacts and yet so secure from them. But the scene was playing such a lively tune on Bernald's own sensibilities that for the moment he could not adjust himself to the probable effect it produced on his companion. The young man, of late, had made but rare appearances in the group of which Mrs. Beecher Bain was one of the most indefatigable hostesses, and the Uplift Club the chief medium of expression. To a critic, obliged by his trade to cultivate convictions, it was the essence of luxury to leave them at home in his hours of ease; and Bernald gave his preference to circles in which less finality of judgment prevailed, and it was consequently less embarrassing to be caught without an opinion.

But in his fresher days he had known the spell of the Uplift Club and the thrill of moving among the Emancipated; and he felt an odd sense of rejuvenation as he looked at the rows of faces packed about the embowered platform from which Howland Wade was presently to hand down the eternal verities. Many of these countenances belonged to the old days, when the gospel of Pellerin was unknown, and had required considerable intellectual courage to avow one's acceptance of the very doctrines he had since demolished. The latter moral revolution seemed to have been accepted as submissively as a change in hair-dressing; and it even struck Bernald that, in the case of many of the assembled ladies, their convictions were rather newer than their clothes.

One of the most interesting examples of this readiness of adaptation was actually, in the person of Miss Alice Fosdick, brushing his elbow with exotic amulets, and enveloping him in Arabian odours, as she leaned forward to murmur her sympathetic sense of the situation. Miss Fosdick, who was one of the most advanced exponents of Pellerinism, had large eyes and a plaintive mouth, and Bernald had always fancied that she might have been pretty if she had not been perpetually explaining things.

"Yes, I know—Isabella Bain told me all about him. (He can't hear us, can he?) And I wonder if you realise how remarkably interesting it is that we should have such an opportunity *now*—I mean the opportunity to see the impression of Pellerinism on a perfectly fresh mind. (You must introduce him as soon as the lecture's over.) I explained that to Isabella as soon as she showed me Doctor Wade's note. Of course you see why, don't you?" Bernald made a faint motion of acquiescence, which she instantly swept aside. "At least I think I can *make you see why*. (If you're sure he can't hear?) Why, it's just this—Pellerinism is in danger of becoming a truism. Oh, it's an awful thing to say! But then I'm not afraid of saying awful things! I rather believe it's my mission. What I mean is, that we're getting into the way of taking Pellerin for granted—as we do the air we breathe. We don't sufficiently lead our *conscious life* in him—we're gradually letting him become subliminal." She swayed closer to the young man, and he saw that she was making a graceful attempt to throw her explanatory net over his companion, who, evading Mrs. Bain's hospitable signal, had cautiously wedged himself into a seat between Bernald and the wall.

"*Did* you hear what I was saying, Mr. Winterman? (Yes, I know who you are, of course!) Oh, well, I don't really mind if you did. I was talking about you—about you and Pellerin. I was explaining to Mr. Bernald that what we need at this very minute is a Pellerin revival; and we need some one like you—to whom his message comes as a wonderful new interpretation of life—to lead the revival, and rouse us out of our apathy . . .

"You see," she went on winningly, "it's not only the big public that needs it (of course *their* Pellerin isn't ours!) It's we, his disciples, his interpreters, we who discovered him and gave him to the world—we, the Chosen People, the Custodians of the Sacred Books, as Howland Wade calls us—it's *we* who are in perpetual danger of sinking back into the old stagnant ideals, and practising the Seven Deadly Virtues; it's *we* who need to count our mercies, and realise anew what he's done for us, and what we ought to do for him! And it's for that reason that I urged Mr. Wade to speak here, in the very inner sanctuary of Pellerinism, exactly as he would speak to the uninitiated—to repeat, simply, his Kenosha lecture, 'What Pellerinism Means'; and we ought all, I think, to listen to him with the hearts of little children—just as *you* will, Mr. Winterman—as if he were telling us new things, and we——"

"Alice, *dear*——" Mrs. Bain murmured with a warning gesture; and Howland Wade, emerging between the palms, took the centre of the platform.

A pang of commiseration shot through Bernald as he saw him there, so innocent and so exposed. His plump pulpy body, which made his evening dress fall into intimate and wrapper-like folds, was like a wide surface spread to the shafts of irony; and the ripples of his voice seemed to enlarge the vulnerable area as he leaned forward, poised on confidential finger-tips, to say persuasively: "Let me try to tell you what Pellerinism means."

Bernald moved restlessly in his seat. He had the sense of being a party to something not wholly honourable. He ought not to have come; he ought not to have let his companion come. Yet how could he have done otherwise? John Pellerin's secret was his own. As long as he chose to remain John Winterman it was no one's business to gainsay him; and Bernald's scruples were really justifiable only in respect of his own presence on the scene. But even in this respect he ceased to feel them as soon as Howland Wade began to speak.

VI.

It had been arranged that Pellerin, after the meeting of the Uplift Club, should join Bernald at his rooms and spend the night there, instead of returning to Portchester. The plan had been eagerly elaborated by the young man, but he had been unprepared for the alacrity with which his wonderful friend accepted it. He was beginning to see that it was a part of Pellerin's wonderfulness to fall in, quite simply and naturally, with any arrangements made for his convenience, or tending to promote the convenience of others. Bernald perceived that his docility in such matters was proportioned to the force of resistance which, for nearly half a lifetime, had kept him, with his back to the wall, fighting alone against the powers of darkness. In such a scale of values how little the small daily alternatives must weigh!

At the close of Howland Wade's discourse, Bernald, charged with his prodigious secret, had felt the need to escape for an instant from the liberated rush of talk. The interest of watching Pellerin was so perilously great that the watcher felt it might, at any moment, betray him. He lingered in the drawing-room long enough to see his friend enclosed in a mounting tide, above which Mrs. Beecher Bain and Miss Fosdick actively waved their conversational tridents; then he took refuge, at the back of the house, in a small dim library where, in his younger days, he had discussed personal immortality and the problem of consciousness with beautiful girls whose names he could not remember.

In this retreat he surprised Mr. Beecher Bain, a quiet man with a mild brow, who was smoking a surreptitious cigar over the last number of the *Strand.*[2] Mr. Bain, at Bernald's approach, dissembled the *Strand* under a copy of the *Hibbert Journal,* but tendered his cigar-case with the remark that stocks were heavy again; and Bernald blissfully abandoned himself to this unexpected contact with reality.

On his return to the drawing-rooms he found that the tide had set toward the supper-table, and when it finally carried him thither it was to land him in the welcoming arms of Bob Wade.

"Hullo, old man! Where have you been all this time?—Winterman? Oh, *he's* talking to Howland: yes, I managed it finally. I believe Mrs. Bain has steered them into the library, so that they shan't be disturbed. I gave her an idea of the situation, and she was awfully kind. We'd better leave them alone, don't you think? I'm trying to get a croquette for Miss Fosdick."

Bernald's secret leapt in his bosom, and he devoted himself to the task of distributing sandwiches and champagne while his pulses danced to the tune of the cosmic laughter. The vision of Pellerin and his Interpreter, face to face at last, had a Titanic grandeur that dwarfed all other comedy. "And I shall hear of it presently; in an hour or two he'll be telling me about it. And that hour will be all mine—mine and his!" The dizziness of the thought made it difficult for Bernald to preserve the balance of the supper-plates he was distributing. Life had for him at that moment the completeness which seems to defy disintegration.

The throng in the dining-room was thickening, and Bernald's efforts as purveyor were interrupted by frequent appeals, from ladies who had reached repleteness, that he should sit down and tell them all about his interesting friend. Winterman's fame, trumpeted abroad by Miss Fosdick, had reached the four corners of the Uplift Club, and Bernald found himself fabricating *de toutes pièces** a Winterman legend which should in some degree respond to the Club's demand for the human document. When at length he had acquitted himself of this obligation, and was free to work his way back through the lessening groups into the drawing-room, he was at last rewarded by a glimpse of his friend, who, still densely encompassed, towered in the centre of the room in all his sovereign ugliness.

Their eyes met across the crowd; but Bernald gathered only perplexity from the encounter. What were Pellerin's eyes saying to him? What orders, what confidences, what indefinable apprehension did

---

*Out of whole cloth (French).

their long look impart? The young man was still trying to decipher their message when he felt a tap on the arm, and turned to meet the rueful gaze of Bob Wade, whose meaning lay clearly enough on the surface of his good blue stare.

"Well, it won't work—it won't work," the doctor groaned.

"What won't?"

"I mean with Howland. Winterman won't. Howland doesn't take to him. Says he's crude—frightfully crude. And you know Howland hates crudeness."

"Oh, I know," Bernald exulted. It was the word he had waited for—he saw it now! Once more he was lost in wonder at Howland's miraculous faculty for always, as the naturalists said, being true to type.

"So I'm afraid it's all up with his chance of writing. At least *I* can do no more," said Wade, discouraged.

Bernald pressed him for further details. "Does Winterman seem to mind much? Did you hear his version?"

"His version?"

"I mean what he said to Howland."

"Why, no. What the deuce was there for him to say?"

"What indeed? I think I'll take him home," said Bernald gaily.

He turned away to join the circle from which, a few minutes before, Pellerin's eyes had vainly and enigmatically signalled to him; but the circle had dispersed, and Pellerin himself was not in sight.

Bernald, looking about him, saw that during his brief aside with Wade the party had passed into the final phase of dissolution. People still delayed, in diminishing groups, but the current had set toward the doors, and every moment or two it bore away a few more lingerers. Bernald, from his post, commanded the clearing perspective of the two drawing-rooms, and a rapid survey of their length sufficed to assure him that Pellerin was not in either. Taking leave of Wade, the young man made his way back to the drawing-room, where only a few hardened feasters remained, and then passed on to the library which had been the scene of the late momentous colloquy. But the library too was empty, and drifting back to the inner drawing-room Bernald found Mrs. Beecher Bain domestically putting out the candles on the mantel-piece.

"Dear Mr. Bernald! Do sit down and have a little chat. What a wonderful privilege it has been! I don't know when I've had such an intense impression."

She made way for him, in a corner of the sofa to which she had sunk; and he echoed her vaguely: "You *were* impressed, then?"

"I can't express to you how it affected me! As Alice said, it was a resurrection—it was as if John Pellerin were actually here in the room with us!"

Bernald turned on her with a half-audible gasp. "You felt that, dear Mrs. Bain?"

"We all felt it—every one of us! I don't wonder the Greeks—it *was* the Greeks?—regarded eloquence as a supernatural power. As Alice says, when one looked at Howland Wade one understood what they meant by the Afflatus."

Bernald rose and held out his hand. "Oh, I see—it was Howland who made you feel as if Pellerin were in the room? And he made Miss Fosdick feel so too?"

"Why, of course. But why are you rushing off?"

"Because I must hunt up my friend, who's not used to such late hours."

"Your friend?" Mrs. Bain had to collect her thoughts. "Oh, Mr. Winterman, you mean? But he's gone already."

"Gone?" Bernald exclaimed, with an odd twinge of foreboding. Remembering Pellerin's signal across the crowd, he reproached himself for not having answered it more promptly. There had been a summons in the look—and it was certainly strange that his friend should have left the house without him.

"Are you quite sure?" he asked, with a startled glance at the clock.

"Oh, perfectly. He went half an hour ago. But you needn't hurry away on his account, for Alice Fosdick carried him off with her. I saw them leave together."

"Carried him off? She took him home with her, you mean?"

"Yes. You know what strange hours she keeps. She told me she was going to give him a Welsh rabbit, and explain Pellerinism to him."

"Oh, if she's going to explain——" Bernald murmured. But his amazement at the news struggled with a confused impatience to reach his rooms in time to be there for his friend's arrival. There could be no stranger spectacle beneath the stars than that of John Pellerin carried off by Miss Fosdick, and listening, in the small hours, to her elucidation of his doctrines; but Bernald knew enough of his sex to be aware that such an experiment may appear less humorous to its subject than to the detached observer. Even the Uplift Club and its connotations might benefit by the attraction of the unknown; and it was conceivable that to a traveller from Mesopotamia Miss Fosdick might present elements of interest which she had lost for the frequenters of Fifth Avenue. There was, at any rate, no denying that the affair had become unexpectedly complex, and that its farther development promised to be rich in comedy.

In the contemplation of these possibilities Bernald sat over his fire, listening for Pellerin's ring. He had arranged his modest quarters with the reverent care of a celebrant awaiting the descent of his deity. He guessed Pellerin to be careless of visual detail, but sensitive to the happy blending of sensuous impressions: to the spell of lamplight on books, and of a deep chair placed where one could watch the fire. The chair was there, and Bernald, facing it across the hearth, already saw it filled by Pellerin's lounging figure. The autumn dawn came late, and even now they had before them the promise of some untroubled hours. Bernald, sitting there alone in the warm stillness of his room, and in the profounder hush of his expectancy, was conscious of gathering up all his sensibilities and perceptions into one exquisitely-adjusted instrument of notation. Until now he had tasted Pellerin's society only in unpremeditated snatches and had always left him with a sense, on his own part, of waste and shortcoming. Now, in the lull of this dedicated hour, he felt that he should miss nothing, and forget nothing, of the initiation that awaited him. And catching sight of Pellerin's pipe, he rose and laid it carefully on a table by the arm-chair . . .

"No. I've never had any news of him," Bernald heard himself repeating. He spoke in a low tone, and with the automatic utterance that alone made it possible to say the words.

They were addressed to Miss Fosdick, into whose neighbourhood chance had thrown him at a dinner, a year or so later than their encounter at the Uplift Club. Hitherto he had successfully, and intentionally, avoided Miss Fosdick, not from any animosity toward that unconscious instrument of fate, but from an intense reluctance to pronounce the words which he knew he should have to speak if they met.

Now, as it turned out, his chief surprise was that she should wait so long to make him speak them. All through the dinner she had swept him along on a rapid current of talk which showed no tendency to linger or turn back upon the past. At first he ascribed her reserve to a sense of delicacy with which he reproached himself for not having credited her; then he saw that she had been carried so far beyond the point at which they had last faced each other, that she was finally borne back to it only by the merest hazard of associated ideas. For it appeared that the very next evening, at Mrs. Beecher Bain's, a Hindu Mahatma was to lecture to the Uplift Club on the Limits of the Subliminal; and it was owing to no less a person than Howland Wade that this exceptional privilege had been obtained.

"Of course Howland's known all over the world as the interpreter of Pellerinism, and the Aga Gautch, who had absolutely declined to speak anywhere in public, wrote to Isabella that he could not refuse anything that Mr. Wade asked. Did you know that Howland's lecture, 'What Pellerinism Means,' has been translated into twenty-two languages, and gone into a fifth edition in Icelandic? Why, that reminds me," Miss Fosdick broke off—"I've never heard what became of your queer friend—what was his name?—whom you and Bob Wade accused me of spiriting away the night that Howland gave that very lecture at Hatty Bain's. And I've never seen *you* since you rushed into the house the next morning, and dragged me out of bed to know what I'd done with him!"

With a sharp effort Bernald gathered himself together to have it out. "Well, what *did* you do with him?" he retorted.

She laughed her appreciation of his humour. "Just what I told you, of course. I said good-bye to him on Isabella's door-step."

Bernald looked at her. "It's really true, then, that he didn't go home with you?"

She bantered back: "Have you suspected me, all this time, of hiding his remains in the cellar?" And with a droop of her fine lids she added: "I wish he *had* come home with me, for he was rather interesting, and there were things about Pellerinism that I think I could have explained to him."

Bernald helped himself to a nectarine, and Miss Fosdick continued on a note of amused curiosity: "So you've really never had any news of him since that night?"

"No—I've never had any news of him."

"Not the least little message?"

"Not the least little message."

"Or a rumour or report of any kind?"

"Or a rumour or report of any kind."

Miss Fosdick's interest seemed to be revived by the undeniable strangeness of the case. "It's rather creepy, isn't it? What *could* have happened? You don't suppose he could have been waylaid and murdered?" she asked with brightening eyes.

Bernald shook his head serenely. "No. I'm sure he's safe—quite safe."

"But if you're sure, you must know something."

"No. I know nothing," he repeated.

She scanned him incredulously. "But what's your theory—for you must have a theory? What in the world can have become of him?"

Bernald returned her look and hesitated. "Do you happen to remember the last thing he said to you—the very last, on the doorstep, when he left you?"

"The last thing?" She poised her fork above the peach on her plate. "I don't think he said anything. Oh, yes—when I reminded him that he'd solemnly promised to come back with me and have a little talk he said he couldn't because he was going home."

"Well, then, I suppose," said Bernald, "he went home."

She glanced at him as if suspecting a trap. "Dear me, how flat! I always inclined to a mysterious murder. But of course you know more of him than you say."

She began to cut her peach, but paused above a lifted bit to ask, with a renewal of animation in her expressive eyes: "By the way, had you heard that Howland Wade has been gradually getting farther and farther away from Pellerinism? It seems he's begun to feel that there's a Positivist element in it which is narrowing to any one who has gone at all deeply into the Wisdom of the East. He was intensely interesting about it the other day, and of course I *do* see what he feels . . . Oh, it's too long to tell you now; but if you could manage to come in to tea some afternoon soon—any day but Wednesday—I should so like to explain——"

XINGU[1]

I.

Mrs. Ballinger is one of the ladies who pursue Culture in bands, as though it were dangerous to meet alone. To this end she had founded the Lunch Club, an association composed of herself and several other indomitable huntresses of erudition. The Lunch Club, after three or four winters of lunching and debate, had acquired such local distinction that the entertainment of distinguished strangers became one of its accepted functions; in recognition of which it duly extended to the celebrated "Osric Dane," on the day of her arrival in Hillbridge,[2] an invitation to be present at the next meeting.

The club was to meet at Mrs. Ballinger's. The other members, behind her back, were of one voice in deploring her unwillingness to cede her rights in favor of Mrs. Plinth, whose house made a more impressive setting for the entertainment of celebrities; while, as Mrs. Leveret observed, there was always the picture-gallery to fall back on.

Mrs. Plinth made no secret of sharing this view. She had always regarded it as one of her obligations to entertain the Lunch Club's distinguished guests. Mrs. Plinth was almost as proud of her obligations as she was of her picture-gallery; she was in fact fond of implying that the one possession implied the other, and that only a woman of her wealth could afford to live up to a standard as high as that which she had set herself. An all-round sense of duty, roughly adaptable to various ends, was, in her opinion, all that Providence exacted of the more humbly stationed; but the power which had predestined Mrs. Plinth to keep a footman clearly intended her to maintain an equally specialized staff of responsibilities. It was the more to be regretted that Mrs. Ballinger, whose obligations to society were bounded by the narrow scope of two parlour-maids, should have been so tenacious of the right to entertain Osric Dane.

The question of that lady's reception had for a month past profoundly moved the members of the Lunch Club. It was not that they felt themselves unequal to the task, but that their sense of the opportunity plunged them into the agreeable uncertainty of the lady who weighs the alternatives of a well-stocked wardrobe. If such subsidiary members as Mrs. Leveret were fluttered by the thought of exchanging ideas with the author of "The Wings of Death," no forebodings disturbed the conscious adequacy of Mrs. Plinth, Mrs. Ballinger and Miss Van Vluyck. "The Wings of Death" had, in fact, at Miss Van Vluyck's suggestion, been chosen as the subject of discussion at the last club meeting, and each member had thus been enabled to express her own opinion or to appropriate whatever sounded well in the comments of the others.

Mrs. Roby alone had abstained from profiting by the opportunity; but it was now openly recognised that, as a member of the Lunch Club, Mrs. Roby was a failure. "It all comes," as Miss Van Vluyck put it, "of accepting a woman on a man's estimation." Mrs. Roby, returning to Hillbridge from a prolonged sojourn in exotic lands—the other ladies no longer took the trouble to remember where—had been heralded by the distinguished biologist, Professor Foreland, as the most agreeable woman he had ever met; and the members of the Lunch Club, impressed by an encomium that carried the weight of a diploma, and rashly assuming that the Professor's social sympathies would follow the line of his professional bent, had seized the chance of annexing a biological member. Their disillusionment was complete. At Miss Van Vluyck's first off-hand mention of the pterodactyl Mrs. Roby had confusedly murmured: "I know so little about metres—" and after that painful betrayal of incompetence she had prudently withdrawn from farther participation in the mental gymnastics of the club.

"I suppose she flattered him," Miss Van Vluyck summed up—"or else it's the way she does her hair."

The dimensions of Miss Van Vluyck's dining-room having restricted the membership of the club to six, the non-conductiveness of one member was a serious obstacle to the exchange of ideas, and some wonder had already been expressed that Mrs. Roby should care to live, as it were, on the intellectual bounty of the others. This feeling was increased by the discovery that she had not yet read "The

Wings of Death." She owned to having heard the name of Osric Dane; but that—incredible as it appeared—was the extent of her acquaintance with the celebrated novelist. The ladies could not conceal their surprise; but Mrs. Ballinger, whose pride in the club made her wish to put even Mrs. Roby in the best possible light, gently insinuated that, though she had not had time to acquaint herself with "The Wings of Death," she must at least be familiar with its equally remarkable predecessor, "The Supreme Instant."

Mrs. Roby wrinkled her sunny brows in a conscientious effort of memory, as a result of which she recalled that, oh, yes, she *had* seen the book at her brother's, when she was staying with him in Brazil,[3] and had even carried it off to read one day on a boating party; but they had all got to shying things at each other in the boat, and the book had gone overboard, so she had never had the chance—

The picture evoked by this anecdote did not increase Mrs. Roby's credit with the club, and there was a painful pause, which was broken by Mrs. Plinth's remarking: "I can understand that, with all your other pursuits, you should not find much time for reading; but I should have thought you might at least have *got up* 'The Wings of Death' before Osric Dane's arrival."

Mrs. Roby took this rebuke good-humouredly. She had meant, she owned, to glance through the book; but she had been so absorbed in a novel of Trollope's[4] that—

"No one reads Trollope now," Mrs. Ballinger interrupted.

Mrs. Roby looked pained. "I'm only just beginning," she confessed.

"And does he interest you?" Mrs. Plinth enquired.

"He amuses me."

"Amusement," said Mrs. Plinth, "is hardly what I look for in my choice of books."

"Oh, certainly, 'The Wings of Death' is not amusing," ventured Mrs. Leveret, whose manner of putting forth an opinion was like that of an obliging salesman with a variety of other styles to submit if his first selection does not suit.

"Was it *meant* to be?" enquired Mrs. Plinth, who was fond of asking questions that she permitted no one but herself to answer. "Assuredly not."

"Assuredly not—that is what I was going to say," assented

Mrs. Leveret, hastily rolling up her opinion and reaching for another. "It was meant to—to elevate."

Miss Van Vluyck adjusted her spectacles as though they were the black cap of condemnation. "I hardly see," she interposed, "how a book steeped in the bitterest pessimism can be said to elevate, however much it may instruct."

"I meant, of course, to instruct," said Mrs. Leveret, flurried by the unexpected distinction between two terms which she had supposed to be synonymous. Mrs. Leveret's enjoyment of the Lunch Club was frequently marred by such surprises; and not knowing her own value to the other ladies as a mirror for their mental complacency she was sometimes troubled by a doubt of her worthiness to join in their debates. It was only the fact of having a dull sister who thought her clever that saved her from a sense of hopeless inferiority.

"Do they get married in the end?" Mrs. Roby interposed.

"They—who?" the Lunch Club collectively exclaimed.

"Why, the girl and man. It's a novel, isn't it? I always think that's the one thing that matters. If they're parted it spoils my dinner."

Mrs. Plinth and Mrs. Ballinger exchanged scandalised glances, and the latter said: "I should hardly advise you to read 'The Wings of Death' in that spirit. For my part, when there are so many books one *has* to read, I wonder how any one can find time for those that are merely amusing."

"The beautiful part of it," Laura Glyde murmured, "is surely just this—that no one can tell *how* 'The Wings of Death' ends. Osric Dane, overcome by the awful significance of her own meaning, has mercifully veiled it—perhaps even from herself—as Apelles, in representing the sacrifice of Iphigenia, veiled the face of Agamemnon."[5]

"What's that? Is it poetry?" whispered Mrs. Leveret to Mrs. Plinth, who, disdaining a definite reply, said coldly: "You should look it up. I always make it a point to look things up." Her tone added—"though I might easily have it done for me by the footman."

"I was about to say," Miss Van Vluyck resumed, "that it must always be a question whether a book *can* instruct unless it elevates."

"Oh—" murmured Mrs. Leveret, now feeling herself hopelessly astray.

"I don't know," said Mrs. Ballinger, scenting in Miss Van Vluyck's tone a tendency to depreciate the coveted distinction of entertaining

Osric Dane; "I don't know that such a question can seriously be raised as to a book which has attracted more attention among thoughtful people than any novel since 'Robert Elsmere.'"[6]

"Oh, but don't you see," exclaimed Laura Glyde, "that it's just the dark hopelessness of it all—the wonderful tone-scheme of black on black—that makes it such an artistic achievement? It reminded me when I read it of Prince Rupert's *manière noire*[7] . . . the book is etched, not painted, yet one feels the colour-values so intensely. . . ."

"Who is *he?*" Mrs. Leveret whispered to her neighbour. "Some one she's met abroad?"

"The wonderful part of the book," Mrs. Ballinger conceded, "is that it may be looked at from so many points of view. I hear that as a study of determinism Professor Lupton ranks it with 'The Data of Ethics.'"*

"I'm told that Osric Dane spent ten years in preparatory studies before beginning to write it," said Mrs. Plinth. "She looks up everything—verifies everything. It has always been my principle, as you know. Nothing would induce me, now, to put aside a book before I'd finished it, just because I can buy as many more as I want."

"And what do *you* think of 'The Wings of Death'?" Mrs. Roby abruptly asked her.

It was the kind of question that might be termed out of order, and the ladies glanced at each other as though disclaiming any share in such a breach of discipline. They all knew there was nothing Mrs. Plinth so much disliked as being asked her opinion of a book. Books were written to read; if one read them what more could be expected? To be questioned in detail regarding the contents of a volume seemed to her as great an outrage as being searched for smuggled laces at the Custom House. The club had always respected this idiosyncrasy of Mrs. Plinth's. Such opinions as she had were imposing and substantial: her mind, like her house, was furnished with monumental "pieces" that were not meant to be disarranged; and it was one of the unwritten rules of the Lunch Club that, within her own province, each member's habits of thought should be respected. The meeting therefore closed with an increased sense, on the part of the other ladies, of Mrs. Roby's hopeless unfitness to be one of them.

---

*Work by English philosopher Herbert Spencer (1820–1903).

II.

Mrs. Leveret, on the eventful day, arrived early at Mrs. Ballinger's, her volume of Appropriate Allusions in her pocket.

It always flustered Mrs. Leveret to be late at the Lunch Club: she liked to collect her thoughts and gather a hint, as the others assembled, of the turn the conversation was likely to take. To-day, however, she felt herself completely at a loss; and even the familiar contact of Appropriate Allusions, which stuck into her as she sat down, failed to give her any reassurance. It was an admirable little volume, compiled to meet all the social emergencies; so that, whether on the occasion of Anniversaries, joyful or melancholy (as the classification ran), of Banquets, social or municipal, or of Baptisms, Church of England or sectarian, its student need never be at a loss for a pertinent reference. Mrs. Leveret, though she had for years devoutly conned its pages, valued it, however, rather for its moral support than for its practical services; for though in the privacy of her own room she commanded an army of quotations, these invariably deserted her at the critical moment, and the only phrase she retained—*Canst thou draw out leviathan with a hook?*[8]—was one she had never yet found occasion to apply.

To-day she felt that even the complete mastery of the volume would hardly have insured her self-possession; for she thought it probable that, even if she *did*, in some miraculous way, remember an Allusion, it would be only to find that Osric Dane used a different volume (Mrs. Leveret was convinced that literary people always carried them), and would consequently not recognise her quotations.

Mrs. Leveret's sense of being adrift was intensified by the appearance of Mrs. Ballinger's drawing-room. To a careless eye its aspect was unchanged; but those acquainted with Mrs. Ballinger's way of arranging her books would instantly have detected the marks of recent perturbation. Mrs. Ballinger's province, as a member of the Lunch Club, was the Book of the Day. On that, whatever it was, from a novel to a treatise on experimental psychology, she was confidently, authoritatively "up." What became of last year's books, or last week's even; what she did with the "subjects" she had previously professed with equal authority; no one had ever yet discovered. Her mind was an hotel where facts came and went like transient lodgers, without leaving their address behind, and frequently without paying for their board. It was Mrs. Ballinger's boast that she was "abreast with the Thought of the Day," and her pride that this advanced position should be expressed by the books on her table. These volumes, frequently renewed, and almost always damp from the press, bore names generally unfamiliar to Mrs. Leveret, and giving her, as she furtively scanned them, a disheartening glimpse of new fields of knowledge to be breathlessly traversed in Mrs. Ballinger's wake. But to-day a number of maturer-looking volumes were adroitly mingled with the *primeurs* of the press—Karl Marx jostled Professor Bergson, and the "Confessions of St. Augustine" lay beside the last work on "Mendelism";* so that even to Mrs. Leveret's fluttered perceptions it was clear that Mrs. Ballinger didn't in the least know what Osric Dane was likely to talk about, and had taken measures to be prepared for anything. Mrs. Leveret felt like a passenger on an ocean steamer who is told that there is no immediate danger, but that she had better put on her life-belt.

It was a relief to be roused from these forebodings by Miss Van Vluyck's arrival.

"Well, my dear," the new-comer briskly asked her hostess, "what subjects are we to discuss to-day?"

Mrs. Ballinger was furtively replacing a volume of Wordsworth by a copy of Verlaine.† "I hardly know," she said, somewhat nervously. "Perhaps we had better leave that to circumstances."

---

*Karl Marx (1818–1883): German socialist philosopher; Henri-Louis Bergson (1859–1941): French humanistic philosopher; "Confessions of St. Augustine": spiritual record of the fifth-century Church Father; Mendelism: theory of heredity developed by Austrian scientist Gregor Mendel (1822–1884).

†William Wordsworth (1770–1850): English Romantic poet; Paul Verlaine (1844–1896): French Symbolist poet.

"Circumstances?" said Miss Van Vluyck drily. "That means, I suppose, that Laura Glyde will take the floor as usual, and we shall be deluged with literature."

Philanthropy and statistics were Miss Van Vluyck's province, and she resented any tendency to divert their guest's attention from these topics.

Mrs. Plinth at this moment appeared.

"Literature?" she protested in a tone of remonstrance. "But this is perfectly unexpected. I understood we were to talk of Osric Dane's novel."

Mrs. Ballinger winced at the discrimination, but let it pass. "We can hardly make that our chief subject—at least not *too* intentionally," she suggested. "Of course we can let our talk *drift* in that direction; but we ought to have some other topic as an introduction, and that is what I wanted to consult you about. The fact is, we know so little of Osric Dane's tastes and interests that it is difficult to make any special preparation."

"It may be difficult," said Mrs. Plinth with decision, "but it is necessary. I know what that happy-go-lucky principle leads to. As I told one of my nieces the other day, there are certain emergencies for which a lady should always be prepared. It's in shocking taste to wear colours when one pays a visit of condolence, or a last year's dress when there are reports that one's husband is on the wrong side of the market; and so it is with conversation. All I ask is that I should know beforehand what is to be talked about; then I feel sure of being able to say the proper thing."

"I quite agree with you," Mrs. Ballinger assented; "but—"

And at that instant, heralded by the fluttered parlour-maid, Osric Dane appeared upon the threshold.

Mrs. Leveret told her sister afterward that she had known at a glance what was coming. She saw that Osric Dane was not going to meet them half way. That distinguished personage had indeed entered with an air of compulsion not calculated to promote the easy exercise of hospitality. She looked as though she were about to be photographed for a new edition of her books.

The desire to propitiate a divinity is generally in inverse ratio to its responsiveness, and the sense of discouragement produced by Osric Dane's entrance visibly increased the Lunch Club's eagerness to please her. Any lingering idea that she might consider herself under an obligation to her entertainers was at once dispelled by her manner: as Mrs. Leveret said afterward to her sister, she had a way of looking at you that made you feel as if there was something wrong with your hat. This evidence of greatness produced such an immediate impression on the ladies that a shudder of awe ran through them when Mrs. Roby, as their hostess led the great personage into the dining-room, turned back to whisper to the others: "What a brute she is!"

The hour about the table did not tend to revise this verdict. It was passed by Osric Dane in the silent deglutition of Mrs. Ballinger's menu, and by the members of the club in the emission of tentative platitudes which their guest seemed to swallow as perfunctorily as the successive courses of the luncheon.

Mrs. Ballinger's reluctance to fix a topic had thrown the club into a mental disarray which increased with the return to the drawing-room, where the actual business of discussion was to open. Each lady waited for the other to speak; and there was a general shock of disappointment when their hostess opened the conversation by the painfully commonplace enquiry: "Is this your first visit to Hillbridge?"

Even Mrs. Leveret was conscious that this was a bad beginning; and a vague impulse of deprecation made Miss Glyde interject: "It is a very small place indeed."

Mrs. Plinth bristled. "We have a great many representative people," she said, in the tone of one who speaks for her order.

Osric Dane turned to her. "What do they represent?" she asked.

Mrs. Plinth's constitutional dislike to being questioned was intensified by her sense of unpreparedness; and her reproachful glance passed the question on to Mrs. Ballinger.

"Why," said that lady, glancing in turn at the other members, "as a community I hope it is not too much to say that we stand for culture."

"For art—" Miss Glyde interjected.

"For art and literature," Mrs. Ballinger emended.

"And for sociology, I trust," snapped Miss Van Vluyck.

"We have a standard," said Mrs. Plinth, feeling herself suddenly secure on the vast expanse of a generalisation; and Mrs. Leveret, thinking there must be room for more than one on so broad a statement, took courage to murmur: "Oh, certainly; we have a standard."

"The object of our little club," Mrs. Ballinger continued, "is to concentrate the highest tendencies of Hillbridge—to centralise and focus its intellectual effort."

This was felt to be so happy that the ladies drew an almost audible breath of relief.

"We aspire," the President went on, "to be in touch with whatever is highest in art, literature and ethics."

Osric Dane again turned to her. "What ethics?" she asked.

A tremor of apprehension encircled the room. None of the ladies required any preparation to pronounce on a question of morals; but when they were called ethics it was different. The club, when fresh from the "Encyclopædia Britannica," the "Reader's Handbook" or Smith's "Classical Dictionary," could deal confidently with any subject; but when taken unawares it had been known to define agnosticism as a heresy of the Early Church and Professor Froude* as a distinguished histologist; and such minor members as Mrs. Leveret still secretly regarded ethics as something vaguely pagan.

Even to Mrs. Ballinger, Osric Dane's question was unsettling, and there was a general sense of gratitude when Laura Glyde leaned forward to say, with her most sympathetic accent: "You must excuse us, Mrs. Dane, for not being able, just at present, to talk of anything but 'The Wings of Death.'"

"Yes," said Miss Van Vluyck, with a sudden resolve to carry the war into the enemy's camp. "We are so anxious to know the exact purpose you had in mind in writing your wonderful book."

"You will find," Mrs. Plinth interposed, "that we are not superficial readers."

"We are eager to hear from you," Miss Van Vluyck continued, "if the pessimistic tendency of the book is an expression of your own convictions or—"

"Or merely," Miss Glyde thrust in, "a sombre background brushed in to throw your figures into more vivid relief. *Are* you not primarily plastic?"

---

*James A. Froude (1818–1894): writer and historian at Oxford University.

"*I* have always maintained," Mrs. Ballinger interposed, "that you represent the purely objective method—"

Osric Dane helped herself critically to coffee. "How do you define objective?" she then enquired.

There was a flurried pause before Laura Glyde intensely murmured: "In reading *you* we don't define, we feel."

Osric Dane smiled. "The cerebellum," she remarked, "is not infrequently the seat of the literary emotions." And she took a second lump of sugar.

The sting that this remark was vaguely felt to conceal was almost neutralised by the satisfaction of being addressed in such technical language.

"Ah, the cerebellum," said Miss Van Vluyck complacently. "The club took a course in psychology last winter."

"Which psychology?" asked Osric Dane.

There was an agonising pause, during which each member of the club secretly deplored the distressing inefficiency of the others. Only Mrs. Roby went on placidly sipping her chartreuse. At last Mrs. Ballinger said, with an attempt at a high tone: "Well, really, you know, it was last year that we took psychology, and this winter we have been so absorbed in—"

She broke off, nervously trying to recall some of the club's discussions; but her faculties seemed to be paralysed by the petrifying stare of Osric Dane. What *had* the club been absorbed in? Mrs. Ballinger, with a vague purpose of gaining time, repeated slowly: "We've been so intensely absorbed in—"

Mrs. Roby put down her liqueur glass and drew near the group with a smile.

"In Xingu?" she gently prompted.

A thrill ran through the other members. They exchanged confused glances, and then, with one accord, turned a gaze of mingled relief and interrogation on their rescuer. The expression of each denoted a different phase of the same emotion. Mrs. Plinth was the first to compose her features to an air of reassurance: after a moment's hasty adjustment her look almost implied that it was she who had given the word to Mrs. Ballinger.

"Xingu, of course!" exclaimed the latter with her accustomed promptness, while Miss Van Vluyck and Laura Glyde seemed to be plumbing the depths of memory, and Mrs. Leveret, feeling apprehensively for Appropriate Allusions, was somehow reassured by the uncomfortable pressure of its bulk against her person.

Osric Dane's change of countenance was no less striking than that of her entertainers. She too put down her coffee-cup, but with a look of distinct annoyance; she too wore, for a brief moment, what Mrs. Roby afterward described as the look of feeling for something in the back of her head; and before she could dissemble these momentary signs of weakness, Mrs. Roby, turning to her with a deferential smile, had said: "And we've been so hoping that to-day you would tell us just what you think of it."

Osric Dane received the homage of the smile as a matter of course; but the accompanying question obviously embarrassed her, and it became clear to her observers that she was not quick at shifting her facial scenery. It was as though her countenance had so long been set in an expression of unchallenged superiority that the muscles had stiffened, and refused to obey her orders.

"Xingu—" she said, as if seeking in her turn to gain time.

Mrs. Roby continued to press her. "Knowing how engrossing the subject is, you will understand how it happens that the club has let everything else go to the wall for the moment. Since we took up Xingu I might almost say—were it not for your books—that nothing else seems to us worth remembering."

Osric Dane's stern features were darkened rather than lit up by an uneasy smile. "I am glad to hear that you make one exception," she gave out between narrowed lips.

"Oh, of course," Mrs. Roby said prettily; "but as you have shown us that—so very naturally!—you don't care to talk of your own things, we really can't let you off from telling us exactly what you think about Xingu; especially," she added, with a still more persuasive smile, "as some people say that one of your last books was saturated with it."

It was an *it*, then—the assurance sped like fire through the parched minds of the other members. In their eagerness to gain the least little clue to Xingu they almost forgot the joy of assisting at the discomfiture of Mrs. Dane.

The latter reddened nervously under her antagonist's challenge. "May I ask," she faltered out, "to which of my books you refer?"

Mrs. Roby did not falter. "That's just what I want you to tell us; because, though I was present, I didn't actually take part."

"Present at what?" Mrs. Dane took her up; and for an instant the trembling members of the Lunch Club thought that the champion Providence had raised up for them had lost a point. But Mrs. Roby explained herself gaily: "At the discussion, of course. And so we're dreadfully anxious to know just how it was that you went into the Xingu."

There was a portentous pause, a silence so big with incalculable dangers that the members with one accord checked the words on their lips, like soldiers dropping their arms to watch a single combat between their leaders. Then Mrs. Dane gave expression to their inmost dread by saying sharply: "Ah—you say *the* Xingu, do you?"

Mrs. Roby smiled undauntedly. "It *is* a shade pedantic, isn't it? Personally, I always drop the article; but I don't know how the other members feel about it."

The other members looked as though they would willingly have dispensed with this appeal to their opinion, and Mrs. Roby, after a bright glance about the group, went on: "They probably think, as I do, that nothing really matters except the thing itself—except Xingu."

No immediate reply seemed to occur to Mrs. Dane, and Mrs. Ballinger gathered courage to say: "Surely every one must feel that about Xingu."

Mrs. Plinth came to her support with a heavy murmur of assent, and Laura Glyde sighed out emotionally: "I have known cases where it has changed a whole life."

"It has done me worlds of good," Mrs. Leveret interjected, seeming to herself to remember that she had either taken it or read it the winter before.

"Of course," Mrs. Roby admitted, "the difficulty is that one must give up so much time to it. It's very long."[9]

"I can't imagine," said Miss Van Vluyck, "grudging the time given to such a subject."

"And deep in places," Mrs. Roby pursued; (so then it was a book!) "And it isn't easy to skip."

"I never skip," said Mrs. Plinth dogmatically.

"Ah, it's dangerous to, in Xingu. Even at the start there are places where one can't. One must just wade through."

"I should hardly call it *wading,*" said Mrs. Ballinger sarcastically.

Mrs. Roby sent her a look of interest. "Ah—you always found it went swimmingly?"

Mrs. Ballinger hesitated. "Of course there are difficult passages," she conceded.

"Yes; some are not at all clear—even," Mrs. Roby added, "if one is familiar with the original."

"As I suppose you are?" Osric Dane interposed, suddenly fixing her with a look of challenge.

Mrs. Roby met it by a deprecating gesture. "Oh, it's really not difficult up to a certain point; though some of the branches are very little known, and it's almost impossible to get at the source."

"Have you ever tried?" Mrs. Plinth enquired, still distrustful of Mrs. Roby's thoroughness.

Mrs. Roby was silent for a moment; then she replied with lowered lids: "No—but a friend of mine did; a very brilliant man; and he told me it was best for women—not to. . . ."

A shudder ran around the room. Mrs. Leveret coughed so that the parlour-maid, who was handing the cigarettes, should not hear; Miss Van Vluyck's face took on a nauseated expression, and Mrs. Plinth looked as if she were passing some one she did not care to bow to. But the most remarkable result of Mrs. Roby's words was the effect they produced on the Lunch Club's distinguished guest. Osric Dane's impassive features suddenly softened to an expression of the warmest human sympathy, and edging her chair toward Mrs. Roby's she asked: "Did he really? And—did you find he was right?"

Mrs. Ballinger, in whom annoyance at Mrs. Roby's unwonted assumption of prominence was beginning to displace gratitude for the aid she had rendered, could not consent to her being allowed, by such dubious means, to monopolise the attention of their guest. If Osric Dane had not enough self-respect to resent Mrs. Roby's flippancy, at least the Lunch Club would do so in the person of its President.

Mrs. Ballinger laid her hand on Mrs. Roby's arm. "We must not forget," she said with a frigid amiability, "that absorbing as Xingu is to *us,* it may be less interesting to—"

"Oh, no, on the contrary, I assure you," Osric Dane intervened.

"—to others," Mrs. Ballinger finished firmly; "and we must not allow our little meeting to end without persuading Mrs. Dane to say a few words to us on a subject which, to-day, is much more present in all our thoughts. I refer, of course, to 'The Wings of Death.'"

The other members, animated by various degrees of the same sentiment, and encouraged by the humanised mien of their redoubtable guest, repeated after Mrs. Ballinger: "Oh, yes, you really *must* talk to us a little about your book."

Osric Dane's expression became as bored, though not as haughty, as when her work had been previously mentioned. But before she could respond to Mrs. Ballinger's request, Mrs. Roby had risen from her seat, and was pulling down her veil over her frivolous nose.

"I'm so sorry," she said, advancing toward her hostess with outstretched hand, "but before Mrs. Dane begins I think I'd better run away. Unluckily, as you know, I haven't read her books, so I should be at a terrible disadvantage among you all, and besides, I've an engagement to play bridge."

If Mrs. Roby had simply pleaded her ignorance of Osric Dane's works as a reason for withdrawing, the Lunch Club, in view of her recent prowess, might have approved such evidence of discretion; but to couple this excuse with the brazen announcement that she was foregoing the privilege for the purpose of joining a bridge-party was only one more instance of her deplorable lack of discrimination.

The ladies were disposed, however, to feel that her departure—now that she had performed the sole service she was ever likely to render them—would probably make for greater order and dignity in the impending discussion, besides relieving them of the sense of self-distrust which her presence always mysteriously produced. Mrs. Ballinger therefore restricted herself to a formal murmur of regret, and the other members were just grouping themselves comfortably about Osric Dane when the latter, to their dismay, started up from the sofa on which she had been seated.

"Oh wait—do wait, and I'll go with you!" she called out to Mrs. Roby; and, seizing the hands of the disconcerted members, she administered a series of farewell pressures with the mechanical haste of a railway-conductor punching tickets.

"I'm so sorry—I'd quite forgotten—" she flung back at them from the threshold; and as she joined Mrs. Roby, who had turned in surprise at her appeal, the other ladies had the mortification of hearing her say, in a voice which she did not take the pains to lower: "If you'll let me walk a little way with you, I should so like to ask you a few more questions about Xingu . . ."

III.

The incident had been so rapid that the door closed on the departing pair before the other members had time to understand what was happening. Then a sense of the indignity put upon them by Osric Dane's unceremonious desertion began to contend with the confused feeling that they had been cheated out of their due without exactly knowing how or why.

There was a silence, during which Mrs. Ballinger, with a perfunctory hand, rearranged the skilfully grouped literature at which her distinguished guest had not so much as glanced; then Miss Van Vluyck tartly pronounced: "Well, I can't say that I consider Osric Dane's departure a great loss."

This confession crystallised the resentment of the other members, and Mrs. Leveret exclaimed: "I do believe she came on purpose to be nasty!"

It was Mrs. Plinth's private opinion that Osric Dane's attitude toward the Lunch Club might have been very different had it welcomed her in the majestic setting of the Plinth drawing-rooms; but not liking to reflect on the inadequacy of Mrs. Ballinger's establishment she sought a roundabout satisfaction in depreciating her lack of foresight.

"I said from the first that we ought to have had a subject ready. It's what always happens when you're unprepared. Now if we'd only got up Xingu—"

The slowness of Mrs. Plinth's mental processes was always allowed for by the club; but this instance of it was too much for Mrs. Ballinger's equanimity.

"Xingu!" she scoffed. "Why, it was the fact of our knowing so much more about it than she did—unprepared though we were—that made Osric Dane so furious. I should have thought that was plain enough to everybody!"

This retort impressed even Mrs. Plinth, and Laura Glyde, moved by an impulse of generosity, said: "Yes, we really ought to be grateful to Mrs. Roby for introducing the topic. It may have made Osric Dane furious, but at least it made her civil."

"I am glad we were able to show her," added Miss Van Vluyck, "that a broad and up-to-date culture is not confined to the great intellectual centres."

This increased the satisfaction of the other members, and they began to forget their wrath against Osric Dane in the pleasure of having contributed to her discomfiture.

Miss Van Vluyck thoughtfully rubbed her spectacles. "What surprised me most," she continued, "was that Fanny Roby should be so up on Xingu."

This remark threw a slight chill on the company, but Mrs. Ballinger said with an air of indulgent irony: "Mrs. Roby always has the knack of making a little go a long way; still, we certainly owe her a debt for happening to remember that she'd heard of Xingu." And this was felt by the other members to be a graceful way of cancelling once for all the club's obligation to Mrs. Roby.

Even Mrs. Leveret took courage to speed a timid shaft of irony. "I fancy Osric Dane hardly expected to take a lesson in Xingu at Hillbridge!"

Mrs. Ballinger smiled. "When she asked me what we represented—do you remember?—I wish I'd simply said we represented Xingu!"

All the ladies laughed appreciatively at this sally, except Mrs. Plinth, who said, after a moment's deliberation: "I'm not sure it would have been wise to do so."

Mrs. Ballinger, who was already beginning to feel as if she had launched at Osric Dane the retort which had just occurred to her, turned ironically on Mrs. Plinth. "May I ask why?" she enquired.

Mrs. Plinth looked grave. "Surely," she said, "I understood from Mrs. Roby herself that the subject was one it was as well not to go into too deeply?"

Miss Van Vluyck rejoined with precision: "I think that applied only to an investigation of the origin of the—of the—"; and suddenly she found that her usually accurate memory had failed her. "It's a part of the subject I never studied myself," she concluded.

"Nor I," said Mrs. Ballinger.

Laura Glyde bent toward them with widened eyes. "And yet it seems—doesn't it?—the part that is fullest of an esoteric fascination?"

"I don't know on what you base that," said Miss Van Vluyck argumentatively.

"Well, didn't you notice how intensely interested Osric Dane became as soon as she heard what the brilliant foreigner—he *was* a foreigner, wasn't he?—had told Mrs. Roby about the origin—the origin of the rite—or whatever you call it?"

Mrs. Plinth looked disapproving, and Mrs. Ballinger visibly wavered. Then she said: "It may not be desirable to touch on the—on that part of the subject in general conversation; but, from the importance it evidently has to a woman of Osric Dane's distinction, I feel as if we ought not to be afraid to discuss it among ourselves—without gloves—though with closed doors, if necessary."

"I'm quite of your opinion," Miss Van Vluyck came briskly to her support; "on condition, that is, that all grossness of language is avoided."

"Oh, I'm sure we shall understand without that," Mrs. Leveret tittered; and Laura Glyde added significantly: "I fancy we can read between the lines," while Mrs. Ballinger rose to assure herself that the doors were really closed.

Mrs. Plinth had not yet given her adhesion. "I hardly see," she began, "what benefit is to be derived from investigating such peculiar customs—"

But Mrs. Ballinger's patience had reached the extreme limit of tension. "This at least," she returned; "that we shall not be placed again in the humiliating position of finding ourselves less up on our own subjects than Fanny Roby!"

Even to Mrs. Plinth this argument was conclusive. She peered furtively about the room and lowered her commanding tones to ask: "Have you got a copy?"

"A—a copy?" stammered Mrs. Ballinger. She was aware that the other members were looking at her expectantly, and that this answer was inadequate, so she supported it by asking another question. "A copy of what?"

Her companions bent their expectant gaze on Mrs. Plinth, who, in turn, appeared less sure of herself than usual. "Why, of—of—the book," she explained.

"What book?" snapped Miss Van Vluyck, almost as sharply as Osric Dane.

Mrs. Ballinger looked at Laura Glyde, whose eyes were interrogatively fixed on Mrs. Leveret. The fact of being deferred to was so new to the latter that it filled her with an insane temerity. "Why, Xingu, of course!" she exclaimed.

A profound silence followed this challenge to the resources of Mrs. Ballinger's library, and the latter, after glancing nervously toward the Books of the Day, returned with dignity: "It's not a thing one cares to leave about."

"I should think *not!*" exclaimed Mrs. Plinth.

"It *is* a book, then?" said Miss Van Vluyck.

This again threw the company into disarray, and Mrs. Ballinger, with an impatient sigh, rejoined: "Why—there *is* a book—naturally. . . ."

"Then why did Miss Glyde call it a religion?"

Laura Glyde started up. "A religion? I never—"

"Yes, you did," Miss Van Vluyck insisted; "you spoke of rites; and Mrs. Plinth said it was a custom."

Miss Glyde was evidently making a desperate effort to recall her statement; but accuracy of detail was not her strongest point. At length she began in a deep murmur: "Surely they used to do something of the kind at the Eleusinian mysteries—"

"Oh—" said Miss Van Vluyck, on the verge of disapproval; and Mrs. Plinth protested: "I understood there was to be no indelicacy!"

Mrs. Ballinger could not control her irritation. "Really, it is too bad that we should not be able to talk the matter over quietly among ourselves. Personally, I think that if one goes into Xingu at all—"

"Oh, so do I!" cried Miss Glyde.

"And I don't see how one can avoid doing so, if one wishes to keep up with the Thought of the Day—"

Mrs. Leveret uttered an exclamation of relief. "There—that's it!" she interposed.

"What's it?" the President took her up.

"Why—it's a—a Thought: I mean a philosophy."

This seemed to bring a certain relief to Mrs. Ballinger and Laura Glyde, but Miss Van Vluyck said: "Excuse me if I tell you that you're all mistaken. Xingu happens to be a language."

"A language!" the Lunch Club cried.

"Certainly. Don't you remember Fanny Roby's saying that there were several branches, and that some were hard to trace? What could that apply to but dialects?"

Mrs. Ballinger could no longer restrain a contemptuous laugh. "Really, if the Lunch Club has reached such a pass that it has to go to Fanny Roby for instruction on a subject like Xingu, it had almost better cease to exist!"

"It's really her fault for not being clearer," Laura Glyde put in.

"Oh, clearness and Fanny Roby!" Mrs. Ballinger shrugged. "I daresay we shall find she was mistaken on almost every point."

"Why not look it up?" said Mrs. Plinth.

As a rule this recurrent suggestion of Mrs. Plinth's was ignored in the heat of discussion, and only resorted to afterward in the privacy of each member's home. But on the present occasion the desire to ascribe their own confusion of thought to the vague and contradictory nature of Mrs. Roby's statements caused the members of the Lunch Club to utter a collective demand for a book of reference.

At this point the production of her treasured volume gave Mrs. Leveret, for a moment, the unusual experience of occupying the centre front; but she was not able to hold it long, for Appropriate Allusions contained no mention of Xingu.

"Oh, that's not the kind of thing we want!" exclaimed Miss Van Vluyck. She cast a disparaging glance over Mrs. Ballinger's assortment of literature, and added impatiently: "Haven't you any useful books?"

"Of course I have," replied Mrs. Ballinger indignantly; "I keep them in my husband's dressing-room."

From this region, after some difficulty and delay, the parlour-maid produced the W–Z volume of an Encyclopædia and, in deference to the fact that the demand for it had come from Miss Van Vluyck, laid the ponderous tome before her.

There was a moment of painful suspense while Miss Van Vluyck rubbed her spectacles, adjusted them, and turned to Z; and a murmur of surprise when she said: "It isn't here."

"I suppose," said Mrs. Plinth, "it's not fit to be put in a book of reference."

"Oh, nonsense!" exclaimed Mrs. Ballinger. "Try X."

Miss Van Vluyck turned back through the volume, peering short-sightedly up and down the pages, till she came to a stop and remained motionless, like a dog on a point.

"Well, have you found it?" Mrs. Ballinger enquired after a considerable delay.

"Yes. I've found it," said Miss Van Vluyck in a queer voice.

Mrs. Plinth hastily interposed: "I beg you won't read it aloud if there's anything offensive."

Miss Van Vluyck, without answering, continued her silent scrutiny.

"Well, what *is* it?" exclaimed Laura Glyde excitedly.

"*Do* tell us!" urged Mrs. Leveret, feeling that she would have something awful to tell her sister.

Miss Van Vluyck pushed the volume aside and turned slowly toward the expectant group.

"It's a river."

"A *river?*"

"Yes: in Brazil. Isn't that where she's been living?"

"Who? Fanny Roby? Oh, but you must be mistaken. You've been reading the wrong thing," Mrs. Ballinger exclaimed, leaning over her to seize the volume.

"It's the only *Xingu* in the Encyclopædia; and she *has* been living in Brazil," Miss Van Vluyck persisted.

"Yes: her brother has a consulship there," Mrs. Leveret interposed.

"But it's too ridiculous! I—we—why we *all* remember studying Xingu last year—or the year before last," Mrs. Ballinger stammered.

"I thought I did when *you* said so," Laura Glyde avowed.

"*I* said so?" cried Mrs. Ballinger.

"Yes. You said it had crowded everything else out of your mind."

"Well *you* said it had changed your whole life!"

"For that matter, Miss Van Vluyck said she had never grudged the time she'd given it."

Mrs. Plinth interposed: "I made it clear that I knew nothing whatever of the original."

Mrs. Ballinger broke off the dispute with a groan. "Oh, what does it all matter if she's been making fools of us? I believe Miss Van Vluyck's right—she was talking of the river all the while!"

"How could she? It's too preposterous," Miss Glyde exclaimed.

"Listen." Miss Van Vluyck had repossessed herself of the Encyclopædia, and restored her spectacles to a nose reddened by excitement. " 'The Xingu, one of the principal rivers of Brazil, rises on the plateau of Mato Grosso, and flows in a northerly direction for a length of no less than one thousand one hundred and eighteen miles, entering the Amazon near the mouth of the latter river. The upper course of the Xingu is auriferous and fed by numerous branches. Its source was first discovered in 1884 by the German explorer von den Steinen, after a difficult and dangerous expedition through a region inhabited by tribes still in the Stone Age of culture.' "

The ladies received this communication in a state of stupefied silence from which Mrs. Leveret was the first to rally. "She certainly *did* speak of its having branches."

The word seemed to snap the last thread of their incredulity. "And of its great length," gasped Mrs. Ballinger.

"She said it was awfully deep, and you couldn't skip—you just had to wade through," Miss Glyde added.

The idea worked its way more slowly through Mrs. Plinth's compact resistances. "How could there be anything improper about a river?" she enquired.

"Improper?"

"Why, what she said about the source—that it was corrupt?"

"Not corrupt, but hard to get at," Laura Glyde corrected. "Some one who'd been there had told her so. I daresay it was the explorer himself—doesn't it say the expedition was dangerous?"

" 'Difficult and dangerous,' " read Miss Van Vluyck.

Mrs. Ballinger pressed her hands to her throbbing temples. "There's nothing she said that wouldn't apply to a river—to this river!" She swung about excitedly to the other members. "Why, do you remember her telling us that she hadn't read 'The Supreme Instant' because she'd taken it on a boating party while she was staying with her brother, and some one had 'shied' it overboard—'shied' of course was her own expression."

The ladies breathlessly signified that the expression had not escaped them.

"Well—and then didn't she tell Osric Dane that one of her books was simply saturated with Xingu? Of course it was, if one of Mrs. Roby's rowdy friends had thrown it into the river!"

This surprising reconstruction of the scene in which they had just participated left the members of the Lunch Club inarticulate. At length, Mrs. Plinth, after visibly labouring with the problem, said in a heavy tone: "Osric Dane was taken in too."

Mrs. Leveret took courage at this. "Perhaps that's what Mrs. Roby did it for. She said Osric Dane was a brute, and she may have wanted to give her a lesson."

Miss Van Vluyck frowned. "It was hardly worth while to do it at our expense."

"At least," said Miss Glyde with a touch of bitterness, "she succeeded in interesting her, which was more than we did."

"What chance had we?" rejoined Mrs. Ballinger. "Mrs. Roby monopolised her from the first. And *that,* I've no doubt, was her purpose—to give Osric Dane a false impression of her own standing in the club. She would hesitate at nothing to attract attention: we all know how she took in poor Professor Foreland."

"She actually makes him give bridge-teas every Thursday," Mrs. Leveret piped up.

Laura Glyde struck her hands together. "Why, this is Thursday, and it's *there* she's gone, of course; and taken Osric with her!"

"And they're shrieking over us at this moment," said Mrs. Ballinger between her teeth.

This possibility seemed too preposterous to be admitted. "She would hardly dare," said Miss Van Vluyck, "confess the imposture to Osric Dane."

"I'm not so sure: I thought I saw her make a sign as she left. If she hadn't made a sign, why should Osric Dane have rushed out after her?"

"Well, you know, we'd all been telling her how wonderful Xingu was, and she said she wanted to find out more about it," Mrs. Leveret said, with a tardy impulse of justice to the absent.

This reminder, far from mitigating the wrath of the other members, gave it a stronger impetus.

"Yes—and that's exactly what they're both laughing over now," said Laura Glyde ironically.

Mrs. Plinth stood up and gathered her expensive furs about her monumental form. "I have no wish to criticise," she said; "but unless the Lunch Club can protect its members against the recurrence of such—such unbecoming scenes, I for one—"

"Oh, so do I!" agreed Miss Glyde, rising also.

Miss Van Vluyck closed the Encyclopædia and proceeded to button herself into her jacket. "My time is really too valuable—" she began.

"I fancy we are all of one mind," said Mrs. Ballinger, looking searchingly at Mrs. Leveret, who looked at the others.

"I always deprecate anything like a scandal—" Mrs. Plinth continued.

"She has been the cause of one to-day!" exclaimed Miss Glyde.

Mrs. Leveret moaned: "I don't see how she *could!*" and Miss Van Vluyck said, picking up her note-book: "Some women stop at nothing."

"—but if," Mrs. Plinth took up her argument impressively, "anything of the kind had happened in *my* house" (it never would have, her tone implied), "I should have felt that I owed it to myself either to ask for Mrs. Roby's resignation—or to offer mine."

"Oh, Mrs. Plinth—" gasped the Lunch Club.

"Fortunately for me," Mrs. Plinth continued with an awful magnanimity, "the matter was taken out of my hands by our President's decision that the right to entertain distinguished guests was a privilege vested in her office; and I think the other members will agree that, as she was alone in this opinion, she ought to be alone in deciding on the best way of effacing its—its really deplorable consequences."

A deep silence followed this outbreak of Mrs. Plinth's long-stored resentment.

"I don't see why *I* should be expected to ask her to resign—" Mrs. Ballinger at length began; but Laura Glyde turned back to remind her: "You know she made you say that you'd got on swimmingly in Xingu."

An ill-timed giggle escaped from Mrs. Leveret, and Mrs. Ballinger energetically continued "—but you needn't think for a moment that I'm afraid to!"

The door of the drawing-room closed on the retreating backs of the Lunch Club, and the President of that distinguished association, seating herself at her writing-table, and pushing away a copy of "The Wings of Death" to make room for her elbow, drew forth a sheet of the club's note-paper, on which she began to write: "My dear Mrs. Roby—"

ENDNOTES

Ethan Frome

1. (p. 8) *Ethan Frome:* Wharton began this novel in 1907 as an exercise in writing in the French language. She took up the work again in the summer of 1910, when she wrote to a friend that she was "hard at work on a short novel" (*The Letters of Edith Wharton,* p. 217; see "For Further Reading"). The work first appeared serially in *Scribner's Magazine* (August–October 1911). After receiving advice from her friend Walter Berry, Wharton made additional revisions for the book version, also published in 1911; she added an author's introduction for a 1922 edition.
2. (p. 8) *Starkfield, Massachusetts:* Wharton wrote to American art critic Bernard Berenson (1865–1959) from Paris in January 1911, informing him of her progress on the novel. Using the language of "mise-en-scène," she commented: "The scene is laid at Starkfield, Mass., and the nearest cosmopolis is called Shadd's Falls. It amuses me to do that décor in the rue de Varenne" (*Letters,* p. 232). The village is a "stark field" on which the action of the novel takes place.
3. (p. 9) *Mrs. Zenobia—or Mrs. Zeena—Frome:* Zeena Frome is named after the third-century queen of Palmyra, who expanded her reign into the Roman empire in the East until she was defeated in 272; her name has become associated with ruthlessness and ambition. The name Zenobia appears in several other works of fiction: William Ware's popular novel *Letters of Lucius Piso, from Palmyra* (1837), later titled *Zenobia,* contrasted Roman values and those of the East; the passionate Zenobia in Hawthorne's *The Blithedale Romance* (1852) dies by drowning herself.
4. (p. 19) *"It's like being in an exhausted receiver":* An exhausted receiver is a type of vessel, as that used with an air pump, from which the air has been withdrawn. In other words, Frome is thinking of a vessel of which the interior is a vacuum. Drawn from the world of science, this simile, like others in the novel, suggests drained energy or expended resources.
5. (p. 19) *a technological college at Worcester:* The name of this technical school is perhaps imprecise: The Worcester County Free Institute of Industrial Science, founded by John Boynton in 1865, was sometimes known as the Scientific School, the School of Industrial Science, the Technical School, the Worcester Free Institute, and, locally, "the Tech"; in July 1887 the school's name was

changed to Worcester Polytechnic Institute. (See Mildred McClary Tymeson, *Two Towers: The Story of Worcester Tech 1865-1965*, Worcester Polytechnic Institute, 1965.)

6. (p. 21) *The musicians hurried to their instruments, the dancers . . . fell into line:* Some critics have suggested that a dance would be an unlikely event in a New England Congregationalist meetinghouse during the early twentieth century; but this activity is what Wharton refers to as Mattie's opportunity for "some chance of amusement" (p. 22) amidst the drudgery of her household work.

7. (p. 36) *She could . . . recite "Curfew shall not ring to-night," and play "The Lost Chord":* "Curfew Must Not Ring Tonight," a ballad by American poet Rose Hartwick Thorpe (1850–1939), was published in a Detroit newspaper in 1867 and subsequently was copied in various publications around the country; an illustrated edition was published in 1882. The melodramatic poem tells how a woman tries to save her lover at his execution by clinging to the clapper of a bell. "The Lost Chord" is another sentimental poem, written by Adelaide Anne Procter (1825–1864) and set to music by English composer Sir Arthur Sullivan (1842–1900). Wharton also refers to "The Lost Chord" in her earlier short story "A Cup of Cold Water," which appeared in *The Greater Inclination* (1899).

8. (p. 37) *Jotham Powell:* Jotham is an Old Testament name; it reflects the legacy of Puritanism in New England.

9. (p. 37) *He had scrambled up on the logs:* Because Frome operates a saw-mill, one critic has suggested that here Wharton should have used "boards" rather than "logs." At other points in the novel she refers to a shipment of lumber.

10. (p. 42) *his period of study at Worcester:* Frome associates Worcester with "fellows doing things," with a wider world of "lectures and big libraries" (p. 42). As a midsize town in central Massachusetts that lacked a navigable body of water, waterpower, and raw materials, Worcester may seem an unlikely candidate as an industrial center. After the Civil War, however, the city's extensive railroad connections made its products—paper, wire, textiles, boots, shoes, and leather belting—accessible to new markets. Between 1820 and 1850 the town's population multiplied nearly five times, and by 1870 it had doubled again. As the spread of the railroad transformed the area's economy, the most striking feature of the social landscape was a sharper division between city and country towns—with the smaller outlying towns losing numbers as well as vitality. Wharton seems sensitive to these changes in noting that the railroad made the Frome farm seem even more remote and isolated. As Ethan notes, "We're kinder side-tracked here now, . . . but there was considerable passing before the railroad was carried through to the Flats. . . . But after the trains begun running nobody ever come by here to speak of" (p. 17). Wharton also mentions Worcester in her 1917 novel *Summer*.

11. (p. 46) *ETHAN FROME AND ENDURANCE HIS WIFE:* It is interesting to note here that the Hebrew word *'eythan*, or *ethan*, means permanent, or enduring; there are several Old Testament Ethans.

12. (p. 87–93) *They had reached the top of School House Hill. . . . There was a last instant when the air shot past him like millions of fiery wires; and then the elm:* In the novel, the name of the sledding hill—School House Hill—is symbolic. The sledding accident described here may be traced to a real-life event: In March 1904, five teenagers from Lenox High School had been involved in a disastrous sledding accident in which their sled crashed into a lamppost at the bottom of the hill. One of the teenagers died; three suffered serious injuries and, in one case, permanent lameness.

"The Pretext"

1. (p. 101) *The Pretext:* "The Pretext" appeared in *Scribner's Magazine* (August 1908) before being collected in *The Hermit and the Wild Woman and Other Stories* (1908). Note 10 below gives more about the genesis of the story (the information is provided later to avoid giving away key elements of the plot).

2. (p. 103) *every old-fashioned house in Wentworth:* The old-fashioned houses, the area's venerable and inward-turning traditions, and self-conscious "tone" of this college setting seem to suggest a town like Amherst or Williamstown, Massachusetts.

3. (p. 107) *to be accused of looking "New Yorky!":* Wharton here has some good fun by contrasting conservative New England tastes in demeanor and dress with those of the New Yorker, Miss Brant. The contrasting values of the two areas are suggested by the title of a chapter in Wharton's autobiography, *A Backward Glance,* "New York and the Mount," in which she noted: "It was not until I went to Boston on my marriage that I found myself in a community of wealthy and sedentary people seemingly too lacking in intellectual curiosity to have any desire to see the world. I have always been perplexed by the incuriosity of New England with regard to the rest of the world" (pp. 61–62).

4. (p. 108) *In a world without traditions . . . such little expiring centres of prejudice and precedent make an irresistible appeal to those instincts for which a democracy has neglected to provide:* Although Wharton pokes gentle fun at tradition-bound Wentworth, she notes in *A Backward Glance* that the values and precedents of her parents' generation—education, good manners, integrity in private and business affairs—faced challenges in the more open, democratic society that her generation confronted. In parts of "The Pretext," Mrs. Ransom seems to reflect Wharton's views.

5. (p. 111) *Some one in the family had "asked for the Chiltern Hundreds":* "Hundred" was a term used to describe a division of an English county, in this case of the Chiltern Hills, a large chalk escarpment in southern England, most prominent in the county of Buckinghamshire. Because members of Parliament were not allowed to resign their seat, those wishing to resign applied for one of several paid positions under the British Crown that would disqualify them from serving. Two such positions were Steward and Bailiff of the three Chiltern Hundreds of Stoke, Desborough, and Burnham and of the Manor of Northstead.

6. (p. 111) *Elder Brother of the Trinity House:* Trinity House (formed as the Trinity House Corporation in 1514) performs several functions: It is the general lighthouse authority for England, Wales, the Channel Islands, and Gibraltar; a deep-sea pilotage authority; and a charitable organization for the safety, welfare, and training of mariners. The Corporation is led by a Court of Elder Brethren under the Master (the duke of Edinburgh).

7. (p. 111) *some one was in command at Devonport:* Devonport, in southwestern England, was the dockyard for the Royal Navy; its origins date back to 1691. In outlining the political, military, naval, and educational connections of the Dawnish family, Wharton emphasizes the young man's social pedigree, carrying a host of associations that contrast with "the Ransom situation at Wentworth," which was as "featureless as the top-shelf of a dark closet" (pp. 110–111).

8. (p. 114) *the Library cupola assumed a Bramantesque grace:* Donato Bramante (1444–1514) was an influential Italian architect and painter whose buildings in Rome are considered the most characteristic examples of High Renaissance architectural style. His early work was picturesque and decorative; his later work had Gothic touches.

9. (p. 126) *"The longitudinal arches of Lincoln have an approximately elliptical form":* The Lincoln Cathedral, in Lincolnshire, England, was built in 1092 and, after a damaging fire and then an earthquake, reconstructed beginning in 1192. Rebuilt in the Gothic style, the cathedral, with its pointed arches and ribbed vaults, is one of the most imposing Gothic structures in England.

10. (p. 132) *"a convex curve to the surface of the vaulting conoid":* In January 1908 Henry James wrote to Wharton about a *petite donnée* (small gift): The incident of a young Englishman attending Harvard, who had defied family wishes and fallen in love with the wife of a professor. In his letter, James turned the idea of the story over to Wharton to use as she saw fit. According to their imagined resolution, an English relative would confront the professor's wife, a middle-aged woman, with the news that the young man had used her as a "pretext" for breaking an engagement with a woman back in England (*Henry James and Edith Wharton: Letters: 1900–1915,* pp. 87–88). In *Edith Wharton and Henry James: The Story of Their Friendship* (George Braziller, 1965), author Millicent Bell identifies the character Guy Dawnish as John Pollock, who attended Harvard Law School from 1903 to 1904. According to Bell, Wharton brings English values and cultural traits into the story via her characterization of Dawnish, but makes the story uniquely her own rather than a facile imitation of James's idea.

"Afterward"

1. (p. 133) *Afterward:* "Afterward" was published in *Century Magazine* (January 1910) before being collected in *Tales of Men and Ghosts* (1910).

2. (p. 135) *Dorsetshire:* Dorsetshire, known today as Dorset, is a county in the south of England; it was part of the "Old West Saxons," known as Wessex, the setting for novels by Thomas Hardy (1840–1928).

3. (p. 137) *Mary Boyne, abruptly exiled from New York by her husband's business, had endured for nearly fourteen years the soul-deadening ugliness of a Middle Western town:* Just as in *Ethan Frome* Wharton notes the cultural deprivation of parts of New England, in this story Mary Boyne notes the "soul-deadening" fourteen years she endured in the Midwest, cut off from America's cultural centers.

4. (p. 138) *waiting in the library for the lamps to come, she rose from her seat and stood among the shadows of the hearth:* Several key scenes in Wharton's supernatural fiction occur in a library. A library, for example, is the setting for the telling of ghostly tales in her short story "The Eyes" (1910). Some critics have suggested that this setting intrigued Wharton because of the importance of her father's library during her formative years. As she noted in *A Backward Glance,* "The old New York to which I came back as a little girl meant to me chiefly my father's library." The library "had a leading share in my growth," and "the library calls me back" (p. 64).

5. (p. 163) "*I guess it's what the scientists call the survival of the fittest*": The phrase "survival of the fittest" derives from English naturalist Charles Darwin's theory of natural selection; it was presumably coined by English philosopher Herbert Spencer (1820–1903). Some social Darwinists applied Darwin's scientific ideas to the social and business world, attempting to account for the advantages the strong appear to have over the weak. Wharton credited her friend Egerton Winthrop with introducing her to "the wonder-world of nineteenth-century science," as she called it in *A Backward Glance* (p. 94). In addition to Darwin's *On the Origin of Species by Means of Natural Selection* (1859), Wharton read the works of Spencer, English naturalist Alfred Russel Wallace (1823–1913), and English biologist Thomas Henry Huxley (1825–1895).

"The Legend"

1. (p. 169) *The Legend:* "The Legend" was published in *Scribner's Magazine* (March 1910) before it was collected in *Tales of Men and Ghosts* (1910).

2. (p. 193) *the* Strand: This British periodical was perhaps best known as the publisher of the detective fiction of Sir Arthur Conan Doyle (1859–1930), most notably his Sherlock Holmes stories, the first of which appeared in July 1891. The periodical was founded in 1891 by Sir George Newnes (1851–1910).

"Xingu"

1. (p. 201) *Xingu:* "Xingu" was first published in *Scribner's Magazine* (December 1911) before being collected in *Xingu, and Other Stories* (1916). Wharton noted that most of the stories in that collection were composed before the outbreak of World War I.

2. (p. 203) *Hillbridge:* Hillbridge is a fictional university town Wharton used in an earlier story, "The Recovery" (1901), as well as in other works.
3. (p. 205) *Brazil:* Xingu is in fact a river in Brazil. Wharton may have gotten information about this tributary of the Amazon from Henry James, whose brother William once participated in a scientific expedition to Brazil.
4. (p. 205) *she had been so absorbed in a novel of Trollope's:* Wharton enjoyed the fiction of English novelist Anthony Trollope (1815–1882), especially in her later years. Mrs. Roby is amused by Trollope, while the self-conscious and pretentious members of the Lunch Club believe literature has other aims: to elevate and to instruct.
5. (p. 206) *"as Apelles, in representing the sacrifice of Iphigenia, veiled the face of Agamemnon":* The celebrated Greek painter Apelles (c.330 B.C.) rendered mythological stories in his paintings; but it was another painter of ancient Greece, Timanthes (c.400 B.C.), whose *Sacrifice of Iphigenia* portrayed the legend of Agamemnon's sacrifice of his daughter Iphigenia. In the painting Timanthes veiled Agamemnon's face, choosing not to portray his emotions; the "veil of Timanthes" has become synonymous with emotional restraint.
6. (p. 207) *"which has attracted more attention among thoughtful people than any novel since 'Robert Elsmere'":* *Robert Elsmere* (1888) was a popular spiritual romance by English novelist Mrs. Humphry Ward. Wharton visited Ward's English estate in the summer of 1909.
7. (p. 207) *"It reminded me when I read it of Prince Rupert's* manière noire*":* *Manière noire* is French for "dark manner." Ruprecht of Pfalz (1619–1682), known as Prince Rupert, Count Palatine of the Rhine, was a general and an artist; he was instrumental in bringing the art of mezzotint portraiture to England. His *The Executioner's Head,* better known as "The Little Executioner," is perhaps his most celebrated work.
8. (p. 208) Canst thou draw out leviathan with a hook?: The quotation comes from the Bible, Job 41:1–2 (King James Version). The full passage reads: "Canst thou draw out leviathan with an hook? Or his tongue with a cord which thou lettest down? Canst thou put an hook into his nose? Or bore his jaw through with a thorn?"
9. (p. 215) *"It's very long":* Wharton here begins a series of puns on Xingu, which the club members, with the exception of the playful Mrs. Roby, interpret as some kind of profound and perhaps even dangerous philosophy.

COMMENTS & QUESTIONS

In this section, we aim to provide the reader with an array of perspectives on the text, as well as questions that challenge those perspectives. The commentary has been culled from sources as diverse as reviews contemporaneous with the works, letters written by the author, literary criticism of later generations, and appreciations written throughout the works' history. Following the commentary, a series of questions seeks to filter Edith Wharton's Ethan Frome and Selected Stories *through a variety of points of view and bring about a richer understanding of these enduring works.*

Comments

THE *NEW YORK TIMES SATURDAY REVIEW OF BOOKS*

In "The Pretext" . . . we have a bit of pattern weaving of considerable intricacy and of balanced and harmonious design. There are half a dozen possible answers to the suggested question, but the construction of the story is consistent and firm. The characters are clearly seen and produce upon us the effect they would produce in life. There is, perhaps, too obvious a denigration of the narrow setting—there have been pictures of narrower and colder aspects of our American scene that have managed to retain their local charm without the application on the part of their historian of a flattering coat of rose color; but the painter of human character is only rarely as competent a portraitist of places, and Mrs. Wharton is above all a delineator of character.

—October 3, 1908

LOUISE COLLIER WILLCOX

There is a certain inexorableness about Mrs. Wharton, as if she herself were constitutionally opposed to happiness, as if she were somewhat compelled to interpret life in terms of pain. Hence her beautifully told but somber tales are so unrelieved, fate in them is so persistently adverse, that they are sometimes not quite convincing. For after all, what men account as Fate does sometimes smile, and pain is pain by contrast with joy. But this particular story of three people, Ethan Frome, his wife Zeena, and Mattie Silver, is so swift, direct, and inevitable that it commands belief. The man, Ethan Frome, an undeveloped idealist, marrying, not for love, but because of feminine proximity and an instinctive recoil from loneliness, then finding beside him his fitting counterpart; the mutual happiness so wan and brief, the swift end, and then the long twilight of that truest heroism—the heroism of endurance—this finely self-consistent story takes firm hold of mind and imagination. And it is told, of course, with all Mrs. Wharton's rare skill. The forcible right words, like apples of gold in frames of silver, are all here. The seeing and perceiving eye and the divining mind, with all their complexities of observation and penetration, have opened up for their fortunate possessor another field in which her hand seems as sure and certain as in the more urban life she usually portrays, and in the more sophisticated people she usually sets before us.

—from the *North American Review* (January 1912)

FRANCES HACKETT

"Xingu" is perhaps the cleverest of these stories. It is also the least valuably perceptive. A satire on the excessive seriousness, the pretentiousness, the false zealotry of a small American "culture" club, it goes rather too far in an acrimonious caricature of the women as human beings. Mrs. Wharton's acid bites fairly into their idiocy as the pursuers of culture, it scarifies them too deeply in their social character. The Laura Glyde and Mrs. Plinth and Mrs. Leveret of real life would be equally insufferable about books, but Mrs. Wharton's cold dislike for their natures is quite unjustified. It is in dealing with such women as these, women who if anything would err on the side of amiability and whose main mistake is to take too seriously the obligations imposed on them by a culture not native, that Mrs. Wharton becomes frigidly conventional. Her Mrs. Plinths and Mrs. Leverets are misjudged from the vantage point of Lenox or Tuxedo, or wherever it is that women do not allow even their illiteracy to detract from their self-confidence.

—from the *New Republic* (February 10, 1917)

BLANCHE COLTON WILLIAMS

Ethan Frome has indisputable claim to rank as the greatest short story in America. Its close unity, its three main characters, its Greek exaltation of Fate as supreme ruler of man and his affairs, its circumscription of place, and more, lend to it the salient marks of the brief fictive form, though its length places it in the novelette class.

—from *Our Short Story Writers* (1920)

EDITH WHARTON

It was not until I wrote "Ethan Frome" that I suddenly felt the artisan's full control of his implements. When "Ethan Frome" first appeared I was severely criticized by the reviewers for what was considered the clumsy structure of the tale. I had pondered long on this structure, had felt its peculiar difficulties, and possible awkwardness, but could think of no alternative which would serve as well in the given case; and though I am far from thinking "Ethan Frome" my best novel, and am bored and even exasperated when I am told that it is, I am still sure that its structure is not its weak point.

—from *A Backward Glance* (1934)

CARL VAN DOREN

From the first [Edith Wharton] had had a satirical flair which at times gave her—as in her short story *Xingu*—the flash and glitter, and the agreeable artificiality, of polite comedy. The many futile women whom she enjoyed ridiculing belong nearly as much to the menagerie of the satirist as to the novelist's gallery. In these moments of satire she indicated her own disposition: her impatience with stupidity and affectation and muddy confusion of mind and purpose; her dislike of dinginess; her toleration of arrogance when well-bred; her little concern with the sturdy or burly or homely, or with broad laughter. She was lucid and detached. Her self-possession held critics, and readers, at arm's length, somewhat as her chosen circles hold the barbarians. No doubt she assigned to decorum a larger power than it often exercises, even in such societies as she wrote about. Decorum is binding upon those who accept it, but not upon passionate or logical natures, who treat it with violence or neglect; neither does it bind those who stand too surely to be shaken. The coils of circumstance and the pitfalls of inevitability with which Mrs. Wharton beset the careers of her characters were in part an illusion deftly employed for their effect. She multiplied them as romancers multiply adventures.

She notably did this in *Ethan Frome,* a short novel often singled out as her best work though she herself did not consider it that. She had begun it as a book to be written in French, some years before she wrote it over and completed it in English. The scene was laid not in her own world but in rural New England, near Lenox in the Berkshires where she had lived in summer. While she knew little at first-hand about people like Ethan Frome, his nagging wife Zenobia, and Mattie Silver whom he loves, Edith Wharton had felt some resemblance between their community and hers. If a metropolis had its hard decorum, so had a village. And in a village there was the further compulsion of a helpless poverty which could bind feet and wings, and dull life to an appalling dinginess.

—from *The American Novel* (1940)

Questions about Ethan Frome

1. What would you say is the underlying cause of the tragedy in *Ethan Frome*? Is it poverty? The New England frame of mind? Zeena's personality? Sexual desire? The cultural and social and material vacuum in which the principal characters live?

2. Does Mattie's decision that she and Ethan should commit suicide seem plausible? Is it foreshadowed by anything earlier in the novel?

3. What is a just view of Ethan? Is he weak? Repressed? Should he simply have run off with Mattie? Should he have been less indulgent of Zeena's self-pity and asserted himself?

4. Is this novel too grim to be enjoyed? Or is there a way in which distressing material can be made to give aesthetic pleasure?

FOR FURTHER READING

Biographies and Related Materials

Benstock, Shari. *No Gifts from Chance: A Biography of Edith Wharton.* New York: Scribner's, 1994.

Dwight, Eleanor. *Edith Wharton: An Extraordinary Life.* New York: Harry N. Abrams, 1994.

Henry James and Edith Wharton: Letters: 1900–1915. Edited by Lyall H. Powers. New York: Scribner's, 1990.

Lewis, R. W. B. *Edith Wharton: A Biography.* New York: Harper and Row, 1975.

Lubbock, Percy. *Portrait of Edith Wharton.* New York: Appleton-Century, 1947.

Wharton, Edith. *A Backward Glance.* New York: Appleton-Century, 1934.

———. *The Letters of Edith Wharton.* Edited by R. W. B. Lewis and Nancy Lewis. New York: Scribner's, 1988.

Other Resources

Davis, Owen, and Donald Davis. *Ethan Frome: A Dramatization of Edith Wharton's Novel.* Foreword by Edith Wharton. New York: Scribner's, 1936.

Wharton, Edith. "Life and I." In *Edith Wharton: Novellas and Other Writings.* Edited by Cynthia Griffin Wolff. New York: Library of America, 1990, pp. 1,069–1,096.

Selected Critical Studies

Ammons, Elizabeth. *Edith Wharton's Argument with America.* Athens: University of Georgia Press, 1980.

Nevius, Blake. *Edith Wharton: A Study of Her Fiction.* Berkeley: University of California Press, 1953.

———, ed. *Edith Wharton's Ethan Frome: The Story, with Sources and Commentary.* New York: Scribner's, 1968.

Singley, Carol J. *Edith Wharton: Matters of Mind and Spirit.* New York and Cambridge: Cambridge University Press, 1995.

———, ed. *A Historical Guide to Edith Wharton.* New York and Oxford: Oxford University Press, 2003.

White, Barbara A. *Edith Wharton: A Study of the Short Fiction.* New York: Twayne Publishers, 1991.

———, ed. *Wharton's New England: Seven Stories and Ethan Frome.* Hanover, NH: University Press of New England, 1995.

Wolff, Cynthia Griffin. *A Feast of Words: The Triumph of Edith Wharton.* New York: Oxford University Press, 1977. Revised edition: Reading, MA: Addison-Wesley, 1995.